FROM THE LAND ALL THE GOOD THINGS COME

S. B. Saunders

S. B. Saunders

From the Land All the Good Things Come
© 2019 S. B. Saunders. All rights reserved.

Please note that this is a work of fiction. Any resemblance of characters to actual persons, living or dead, is purely coincidental.

From the Land All the Good Things Come

For Theresa.

Because your communal laundry room gives the lie to the lies.

S. B. Saunders

Acknowledgments

For their invaluable ideas, suggestions, observations, corrections, and moral support, I would like to thank the following people:

>CM of Paris
>DC of Bucharest
>GF of Oxford
>NG of Nipstone Rock
>TS of Minnesota

From the Land All the Good Things Come

'But TRUTH is immortal; and, though she may be silenced for a while, there always, at last, comes something to cause her to claim her due and to triumph over falsehood.'

William Cobbett, *A History of the Protestant Reformation, in England and Ireland; Showing How That Event Has Impoverished and Degraded the Main Body of the People in Those Countries. In A Series of Letters, Addressed to All Sensible and Just Englishmen.*

'Be wary of a government which stops you from knowing the truth of your people's past and from imagining your people's future. Because where there is no vision, the people perish. O England, where camest thou, and whither wilt thou go?'

Charles Swanson, *The English, God's Chosen*

CONTENTS

Chapter 1	1
Chapter 2	6
Chapter 3	14
Chapter 4	21
Chapter 5	26
Chapter 6	31
Chapter 7	41
Chapter 8	49
Chapter 9	54
Chapter 10	63
Chapter 11	73
Chapter 12	82
Chapter 13	86
Chapter 14	93
Chapter 15	100
Chapter 16	111
Chapter 17	121

Chapter 18	127
Chapter 19	129
Chapter 20	135
Chapter 21	151
Chapter 22	159
Chapter 23	169
Chapter 24	180
Chapter 25	193
Chapter 26	198
Chapter 27	200
Chapter 28	206
Chapter 29	215
Chapter 30	228
Chapter 31	248
Chapter 32	258
Chapter 33	268
Chapter 34	289
Chapter 35	297
Chapter 36	305
Chapter 37	325
Chapter 38	333
Chapter 39	345
Chapter 40	353
Chapter 41	359

Chapter 42	373
Chapter 43	391
Chapter 44	398
Chapter 45	407
Chapter 46	425
Chapter 47	436
Chapter 48	447
Chapter 49	470
Chapter 50	483
Chapter 51	496
Chapter 52	510
Chapter 53	529

CHAPTER 1

The Heads fascinated the children.

'Remember, don't go up to the Heads. Ever. It's dangerous.'

Each time a child was given a warning about the limitations of the city, or someone mentioned the Heads in passing, it only made the idea of the borderlands all the more exciting. The adult response was always the same: *Never you mind the Heads. You shouldn't even be going as far as the checkpoints. And never ever think about sneaking past them. There are mines in the ground. It's not a place for little boys to play.*

Among themselves, the children speculated what happened at the Heads. Andrew said that the spirits of the dead SAU soldiers were on the look-out for little English boys to snatch and take to Hell. Ambrose said that that was a load of rubbish, that the only danger in going there was from the checkpoint soldiers who might shoot you by mistake. But nobody knew for sure, and everyone wanted to find out.

'I saw a head once.' Sam Ashton beamed proudly, his blond hair shining like gold in the last solar rays of the spring equinox. Of course, Sam was always full of boasts to impress the other boys. It was his way. But in this instance, it might be true. Sam's father was part of the Northwest Division's Reconnaissance Unit, and he was close to his eldest son. It was clear that he wanted the ten-year-old to know as much as it was possible for a ten-year-old to understand. And Sam's father made regular trips up to Cumbria in an armed convoy to pick up supplies from Scotland. Sam said that he had been on one of these trips. Everyone was a bit wary of Sam, because he was tall and confident, and because of his father. He sometimes joined the group, but he wasn't really *of* the group.

'So what was it like then?' Thomas decided to speak for everyone. Six faces looked expectantly at Sam.

The tallest of the boys by an inch and a quarter, Sam drew himself up to his full height of five feet six inches and paused to maximise the suspense and his own sense of self-importance. 'It was disgusting. The eyes were all picked out by crows and his lips had rotted away. He still had his SAU helmet on though. There were like, *bits* that still dangled from the neck. His face was all shrivelled and a sort of purply-black.'

The boys surrounded him in the March twilight, agog and eager for more details. The allure of finding a way to visit the Heads had just got ten times stronger.

'How many heads were there?'

'I don't know. I think there were at least twenty that I saw from the back. They are spaced out in rows across the land. I got pulled away from the window as soon as they realised I could see them.'

The boys stood around in silence as they absorbed this new information. They were still seen as children by the English Front, but within a couple of years some of them would begin their military training and would soon afterwards be patrolling those very borderlands. Some might even be *making scarecrows*, as it was known. Their Life Duty, their role in the city, would be decided by the city's elders, people like Sam's dad, based on the people's need, and the temperament and aptitude of the boys themselves. Some would become mechanics, some builders, some engineers and some would become 'general jacks'. The coders and Intelligence tended to be spotted earlier in school, and began their training a few years before. These were the quieter, nerdy boys. Everyone had a role to play in the defence of the city. A boy could choose not to do an apprenticeship, but then he was sent to fight in the Wolf Division, and he knew that this meant that would be sent on the most dangerous missions, which were often suicidal. No man got a free ride in English Front territory. The English could not afford to have passengers.

Twelve was the age when a boy started to be treated like a man. Every one of these ten-year-olds dreamt about their *twelving*. After their twelving they could join the English Front Youth, which was much more grown-up than the Young Pups. Right now, without having taken the Oath, they were just seen as little children in the domain of their mothers, and it was frustrating.

'Don't worry, your time will come,' Andrew's big brother had once said laughingly, as he mussed the younger boy's hair on returning home from a night patrol. Matthew was eighteen and was engaged to be married to Perpetua, who was two years younger. She smelt of strong perfume and had blonde hair and wore make-up. She was very glamorous. Andrew was jealous of his older brother, who was a proper grown-up. Still, he was bigger than his three younger brothers and sisters, and that made him feel better.

Most of the boys came from big families, and

most had big brothers and uncles. They passed the time with each other on the wasteland behind bombed-out houses on Helston Avenue, practicing the fighting moves they had been taught by Mr. Downes at school, playing war games among the tree stumps, trying to catch rabbits and occasionally starting fires. But the curfew bell would not be long in tolling the knell of the parting day, and one by one the boys all received messages on their lerters to get home for supper.

CHAPTER 2

William Ashton worked hard to impose onto his men the importance of physiognomy and instinct.

'You need to make a split-second judgment if a man is friend or foe. Don't rely on colour. That's a rookie's mistake, and it could get you killed. It might also get your city killed. The converts would blend into this room. Remember who is behind the SAU.'

There had been multiple incursions into the city by night over the past two months, and last night, a twelve-year-old girl called Ursula Lambton had been taken from her bed from a house in Moss Bank Road, her parents shot in the head as they slept. Those SAU soldiers had risked their lives to sneak past the checkpoints, but they also knew that posting the torture and rape of this English girl on the Internet would be counted as a huge victory for local SAU forces, as it would demoralise the English. Although it would also serve to rile the English population to anger, *and sometimes that was needed*, thought William. As hard as it might be to believe, people had got used to the sixteen-year stalemate between the EF and the SAU, and had almost got comfortable. *People will get used to anything if they are subjected to it long enough*, William mused to himself.

It was pointless doing a raid on SAU territory to find young Ursula; she would be dead by now. But security would need to be beefed up, and reprisals taken. Some of the heads on the borderlands were starting to look a bit tatty and a lot of the lower jaws were falling off. Most of the *scarecrows* had been made in the 2030s, when the early English Front had its self-styled Berserkers, with the distinctive boars on the crests of their helmets. Clearly, some fresh heads would be needed to remind the SAU who England belonged to. Ashton was certainly in the mood for head-hunting tonight.

He would take with him his favourite eighteen-year-old Wolves, who relished the danger and wanted to get their fingers wet again. Shooting down drones was fun, but it didn't get the blood pumping. Burnham had cleared the mission. They weren't going to attack the Urmston flank, which was closest and where the SAU were probably expecting them. No, they were going to drive for a couple of hours and attack Blackburn. They wouldn't be expected so far north. He could also do a bit of recco while he was there.

William wondered how long this territorial deadlock could go on for. In terms of overall numbers, the English Front still had the upper hand, but the Shuhada al-Ummah were catching up fast, and would soon win the demographic war, crucial in a conflict in which the side most prepared to sacrifice lives would emerge victorious. The SAU were also backed by the Old Families, and the descendants of those who had stayed faithful to the Agenda, including the remnants of that section of the British Army who had not joined the insurgents. All of these people understood that if the English Front forces were to triumph over the so-called *Martyrs of the Community*, their fate, and the fate of all generations after them, was sealed. The government operating out of London had no effective jurisdiction over EF territory, but it was not something that they wanted to admit internationally. It was a tense situation. The SAU, led currently, as far as it was known, by Saifullah Mahmud, was hungry to get its paws on the entirety of the government's arsenal, but the elites in charge knew that both America and Russia were watching the situation closely, ready to strike. A genocide of the English people could give America the *casus belli* it needed to annex the island

and form the transatlantic ethnic state that had been talked about since the establishment of the North American Confederation in 2042. Meanwhile, across the North Sea the Russian double-headed eagle watched from its new eyrie in the Scandinavian Mountains, waiting for the right moment to swoop in with its aerial bombardments and mobilised troops. There was also a strong possibility that one of the superpowers might conquer England via the north, as an independent Scotland, having miraculously managed to keep the conflict out of its own borders with Irish back-up so far, was very vulnerable to attack. It was a dead man walking. No-one knew how this situation would play out, but this fragile impasse was unsustainable.

William knew was that it was a powder keg, and yet it had been a powder keg for so long that the English people had somehow got used to it. Meanwhile, his own objectives were to help keep supply lines open to the smugglers in Scotland, and to push back against the SAU occupation of the M62 corridor. It was imperative that the SAU be driven back into the heart of Manchester – if the SAU took Liverpool that would effectively cut EF territory in half, a disaster for the English. It would also mean the enemy gaining control of Liverpool's port, a crucial point of entry for weapons, equipment and basic supplies. If it hadn't been for Liverpool's port and the EF's connections with Belfast and Boston, the Northwest EF might have been wiped out twenty years ago by SAU forces. With the SAU and their Old Family financiers controlling London and most of the Home Counties, Liverpool was an essential asset, and it was overshadowed by the huge Islamic conurbation of Greater Manchester. Small wonder then that, even taking into account the Southeast Division's unenviable proximity to London, the Northwest of England was the most dangerous of the five EF-controlled regions for an Englishman to live in 2060.

Still, just as the Palestinians had adapted to their conditions after the ill-fated Israel project decided to mark them for genocide, so the English people had rediscovered a stoicism unknown for over a century. Perspectives had changed. Material accumulation for its own sake no longer meant anything in a land where possession of the land itself was not secure, and the only status that counted among men was glory in battle. Women competed with each other to produce the most sons. Death held no fear. Every year the EF gave awards to civilians to recognise those who sacrificed the most to support the community and assist the military. In this way the whole of England, the English people, was part of the same cause. They thought as one. Traitors and spies were shot, where they were found, but after three generations, they were much less numerous. Communities were tight, and EF members became experts in scrutinising a man's skin tone, his bone structure, his mannerisms, and the slightest difference in accent. Strangers were not welcome without paperwork and the strongest personal guarantees of character.

No-one wanted a return of the killing years of the 30s, when the major rivers foamed red with the blood of corpses, guilty and innocent floating side by side. Many guilty of nothing more than being in a land in which they could not be accepted by either side, and were therefore a danger to both. Those who were lucky managed to return to their ancestral homelands, others had no ancestral homelands to go to. The last of the little Jews, whose numbers had bled towards Israel since the middle of the 2020s, left definitively for Jerusalem in 2028. There were still some mixed-race people in EF territory, living at the discretion of the EF leaders, but they knew that they were there at the sufferance of the people, and that this could change at any time. Many were accepted because their loyalty was not in doubt, and more importantly because they had skills which were essential to the EF. But they understood their place, and how precarious it was. Tribalism had been forced on the Englishman through treachery and barbarism. And there was no going back.

William sent a group lert to the Haresfinch Wolves squad. They had been expecting it. All were eager for the revenge mission. He arranged to pick them up in three hours, and they would be on the road by sundown. That gave him time to go home and get something to eat.

When he got home, Sam could sense that something was going to happen. His mum had gone quiet as she worked in the kitchen and there was a tension in the air. He sat close to his father in an expectant silence, knowing better than to try to ask his father directly. William sensed the boy's curiosity, but had to let him down with 'I can't tell you son, you'll find out these things when you're older'.

Sam watched his father go upstairs, and he knew where his father would be going. Sam was not allowed into his father's cupboard, but he knew what was in there. It was part of the EF Covenant that all households behind EF lines had to have at least one adult male residing, and the majority possessed at least one gun for general self-defence. Sam's father, being a corporal in the EF Army, had a small arsenal in his possession, as well as other assorted equipment for night raids. Sam realised that his father must be going out on a raid. He felt suddenly anxious when he realised that this meant his father might end up dead, but he said nothing.

The boy loitered in the hallway, while his father came back downstairs and went into the kitchen to speak to his mother. He didn't hear what they were saying; they kept their voices low. When his father made his way to the front door Sam wordlessly went to hug him. William laughed as he caught his breath with the surprise of the gesture.

'Don't worry, son, I'll be back tomorrow morning. I'll see you before school.'

Then he disappeared into a waiting van.

CHAPTER 3

'I've got an amazing surprise for you!'

Morgenna's eyes gleamed at CeeCee as she stepped over the threshold of the paint-chipped doorway with a large paper parcel. *What did she have this time?* CeeCee wondered.

But Morgenna wasn't going to reveal her secret any time soon. In a decade where supplies of virtually every commodity were hard to come by, the pleasure of a new luxury had to be eked out to its final moment. And Morgenna was determined to tease out the suspense a little bit longer. 'Do you have any black tea?' She smiled.

This surprise must be a big one, thought CeeCee, *if she is asking for a black tea.*

Luckily for Morgenna, CeeCee had managed to sell a few of her jumpers for some basic supplies and she had a bag of loose tea in the house. She glanced at the clock. It was still an hour before six o'clock which meant she'd need to fire up the gas stove. 'Give me five minutes.'

From the Land All the Good Things Come

Morgenna sat back on CeeCee's battered old couch and surveyed the room. The obligatory Agnus Dei on the wall was partially obscured by boxes piled against it, and bags with all kinds of fabrics and craft supplies sat near the armchair. Like many people of 2060, CeeCee and her brother had a tendency towards hoarding, an understandable habit for anyone in such straightened times, but especially when one of the hoarders was a Crafter, a highly-respected profession in a city which struggled to import finished goods. Many women came to Crafter Clare for advice, instruction, and to buy or barter for her finished work. CeeCee's designs were known throughout the Northwest Territory, and had inspired many imitations. Far from being irritated at others copying her designs, CeeCee was flattered by people paying homage to her work.

It was because of sentiments like these that CeeCee was not just held in high esteem for her talent, which stretched across disciplines, but for her generosity of spirit. A lifelong spinster, she devoted her time to others, and had taught several generations of the community how to knit, sew, mend, dye, salvage fabric and wool, make soap and candles, grow vegetables, make jam and even make perfume, though CeeCee was the first to admit that her rose-petal perfume wasn't very good. No matter where she was, her hands were never still, as she took to heart the biblical injunction to *sow your seed in the morning, and at evening let your hands not be idle.* There were always two or three unfinished jobs on the go at any given moment: a half-sewn christening gown, a crocheted jacket for a child, an embroidered panel for a wedding dress.

CeeCee's mother Eileen had also been what was known as 'a good pair of hands', and it appeared that, as with Eileen, God had decided to concentrate all of his blessings into CeeCee's hands. With her ruddy, plain face, her greying hair scraped back carelessly and a homely figure encased in an old jumper which had seen its best days before the Rebellion, CeeCee McAllister was a woman singularly lacking in vanity. Nor did she give much thought to the old house that she shared with her brother, which hadn't seen a change in wallpaper in fifty years. From first appearances then, one would be forgiven for not believing that she produced articles of exquisite delicacy and beauty, all the more remarkable when one considered the battles she had to undertake to acquire raw materials and the ingenuity needed to transform them.

One thing that people called on CeeCee to make, and for which they would pay well, were her elaborately textured greetings cards for major events, which she would tailor to the individual family, with a meaningful poem rendered in copperplate calligraphy. In a time ravaged by war, suffering and deprivation, families held together by making ceremonies around the milestones of life: the christenings, the birthdays, the engagements, the weddings, the twelvings, and the all-too-frequent funerals. Cards could be stored and transported easily, important at a time when a family might have to move house at short notice. Her calligraphy for mezzie scrolls was also highly sought after, and she designed templates for metal mezzie cases which her brother Colin then engraved.

CeeCee came back into the dark living room with the two mugs of tea. She put down the mugs on the side table and lit a large lard lamp on the mantelpiece, which suddenly threw a flickering light on a charcoal portrait of David Caldwell, sketched, as always, from his right side. The light drew Morgenna's attention to the picture. *It was likely to be a portrait of a portrait*, she thought. The EF leader was reluctant to have his image reproduced, fearing the dangers that came with a cult of personality. But despite his wishes, those who loved him would have their image of him. Even if they had to draw it themselves, using an unreliable source.

CeeCee drew Morgenna out of her reverie.

'OK, I've waited long enough. So what have you got to show me?'

Morgenna beamed and passed the paper parcel forward.

CeeCee cut apart the parcel with her customary great care to save the paper. Inside were six large balls of gold and silver metallic wool. And the skeins still had their labels on. *This was brand new yarn!* She gasped.

'Where did you get this from?'

Morgenna touched the side of her nose conspiratorially. 'It's been planned for a while,' she said. Vivien and I wanted to thank you properly for Wilfrid's twelving shirt. And I knew that this is what you would like.

Tears sprang into CeeCee's eyes. She looked down at the masses of this new yarn. *New yarn!* Her mind ran crazily with ideas of how she could use it. As the English slipped further and further into the direst poverty, luxuries had been the first things to be sacrificed. And living in poverty ground down the soul, especially the souls of women, even as they tried to take comfort in Saint Peter and Saint Paul's ascetic ideas on female beauty. Crafter Clare began to realise that the more a people falls into penury, the more gold and silver objects come to be cherished. So she began the fashion of knitting with gold and silver wool, and embroidering with gold and silver thread. Her designs had become hugely popular, and would have shocked the more restrained English of a century before, who would have considered her designs to be gaudy, more befitting of gypsies or Jews. Perhaps it was because the English people had been robbed of all of their physical gold and silver, but they could still wear it symbolically in their dresses, their jumpers, the hems of their skirts and cuffs of their shirts. Perhaps, in these dangerous times, when one naturally became more superstitious, it was an atavistic return to sympathetic magic, which decreed that by wearing golden designs one would attract wealth and good fortune into one's life. Perhaps it was simply that in a crumbling civilisation in which all but the most essential of civic repairs were left neglected and power rationed, and official days of fasting were decreed to hide food shortages, the glint of gold would reflect something of the sun during the day and of the firelight at night, and remind the group that better times would eventually return, that not all was lost. That there was still beauty in the world.

Morgenna's lerter sounded. She peered down at

it in the gloom.

A few seconds later, her smile faded.

It's from Seb. He said that Edwin still hasn't come back from last night and he hasn't answered his lerter. I need to get home.

CeeCee got up, and gave her friend a hug. As her arms tightened around Morgenna's body she felt the tears that had welled up over her friend's thoughtfulness fall onto her cheeks.

'Let me know when he gets back. I'm sure he'll be fine. He'll just be out with his friends. You know what teenagers are like.'

Morgenna nodded, unconvinced. 'I'll lert you later and let you know.' Suddenly mindful of how this change of mood had taken the shine off the surprise for her friend, she forced a smile. 'Enjoy your wool. Let me know what you make of it.'

'Oh I will, don't you worry' said CeeCee, as Morgenna walked into the driveway. CeeCee watched the figure of her friend get smaller as it made its way up the hill. Suddenly a horrible feeling came over her. A horrible feeling that something had happened to Edwin.

CHAPTER 4

Unbeknown to Morgenna as she sat sipping black tea in the shabby house on Newlands Road, an emergency meeting had been summoned for St Helens' top brass to discuss the disaster of the night before. What should have been a routine raid on enemy territory had gone badly wrong. The van had gone out of range for secure lerts to be picked up, and when global lerts were issued, nothing had come back. Without the GPS technology of forty years ago, the EF had to rely on camera drones to look for the van. So far there had been nothing.

'I can't believe I fucking let him go.' Kai Burnham sat slumped against a table, and rubbed his temples. 'It was a stupid idea from the start. It hadn't been planned properly. I think we just got used to so many wins that we... we got cocky.' He considered for a moment that the EF's decentralised military structure, with its dependence on strategic corporals and its indulgence towards the Wolves justified by the biblical *let the young men now arise and play before us*, could sometimes be a weakness.

Every man in the room wondered to himself if the soldiers were still alive, but no one said anything.

The instinct of every soldier present was to go directly into SAU territory and rip out the hearts of every man, woman and child until their comrades, or the bodies of their comrades, were found. But they had to think this through. Ill-prepared, kneejerk reactions led to disasters like the one last night. And if the party was still alive, reprisals might seal their fate.

'What are SAU saying on the Internet?' The voice came from Ryan Rigby, a commander of around fifty.

The response came from a young man behind a laptop screen.

'Nothing so far'.

The EF Intelligence guys needed to have fluency in Arabic, Punjabi and Arabo-Swedish to understand the Shuhada al-Ummah in the UK. Other languages were spoken, such as Urdu and Pashto, but Arabic, Punjabi and Arabo-Swedish were the main ones. Still, the SAU were always finding new ways to communicate, with new amalgams of their heritage languages and English appearing all the time. It made gathering intel very difficult, and put the EF on the back foot with the enemy. For this reason, the SAU were much more active on the open Internet than the EF, because they knew that the EF was incapable of monitoring all of their communications. Monolingual outside of Wales, the EF ordered its people to avoid the Internet under pain of sanction and to use the EF's own lerter system which, aside from not violating the religious injunction against audiovisual reproduction, was more secure and did not work outside of EF-controlled ranges. Internet usage was limited to certain monitored locations, and people could get messages to others elsewhere in England by going through official EF channels. News for relatives abroad had to be signed off by high command due to the carefully controlled relationships maintained with other nations. It was imperative that the enemy, not just the SAU but the legacy government in London, knew as little as possible of what was happening in the Five Divisions.

The men sat around in silence. They knew that if they were to retrace Ashton's journey the SAU forces would have the route staked out, in wait for them. Usually the policy was to treat these missions as suicide missions, but William Ashton was a valuable soldier. What the hell was he doing outside Blackburn in the small hours of the morning? Kai held his head in his hands. If the EF was to go on a big offensive, this could spark off a major conflict that could lead to the loss of a lot of English lives, both military and civilian. And there was no guarantee that the EF would win.

Kai knew that if he asked the rank and file if they wanted to join a rescue mission there would be no shortage of hands looking to find their brothers. But he was wary of throwing away good men for nothing. If the team hadn't come back, they were dead, and the SAU would certainly never give them up alive. But not to suggest a rescue mission would look heartless and would alienate the men on the ground. Kai rubbed his temples again.

Suddenly, the young man behind the laptop spoke up. 'A lert has just come in from Preston. Two of the eight are alive.'

* * *

The raid had been a disaster. It was as if the SAU had read William's mind to visit Blackburn that night, and had ambushed the van as it drove into Nab's Head, on the outskirts of SAU territory. The driver and one of the front passengers escaped by throwing themselves out of the driver's door before a rocket launcher blew the vehicle to pieces. There were no other survivors. The two remaining soldiers managed to stay alive by hiding in the bushes for a few hours and then slowly making their way towards Preston, a journey greatly slowed up by the fact that the driver, William, had broken his ankle and they had to wait until daylight before making a move. Even then, they had got lost a few times.

Six men dead. Six young men whose families would be devastated. Burnham drew up the list of the presumed dead and between them the leaders decided who would visit each family that night.

CHAPTER 5

It was the hardest job that Kevin had to do. Not least because, as the EF asked local men to deliver the news, he knew most of the parents personally. Morgenna was an active member of the community and a pillar of the church. Her shock of curly auburn hair at the front of church services was a reassuring constant for attendees. His son Andrew was the same age as her boy Sebastian.

And his son Matthew was the same age as Edwin.

He crossed himself.

Like a broken cathedral roof that occasional allowed bright shards of sunlight to penetrate the gloom, leaden clouds imperfectly covered the sky over Hawes Avenue. Kevin knocked on the Weston family's door and stood back and looked up at the sky. The heavens seemed to be conspiring to oppress the inhabitants of the dilapidated little house. The red cross painted on the front door had not been enough to shield the family from the angel of death taking their first-born son.

The door was answered within seconds. Morgenna had probably been watching the driveway. Kevin didn't need to speak. They both knew each other too well, and both had talked to each other in the past about their children.

He nodded silently at the question asked by her imploring eyes.

'It's Edwin.'

Morgenna collapsed onto the hallway stairs. She had known of course. But still, the confirmation of what she knew inside hit her like a rock. She lay against the staircase, stunned. Edwin's young girlfriend Felicity came in from the back garden. She saw Morgenna's grey face and she started screaming uncontrollably. Kevin went to grab the girl, to keep her arms by her sides, to keep her still and try to calm her. He straddled her legs awkwardly as she kept screaming, not seeming to know where she was, as he struggled to shuffle her towards the armchair nearest the living-room door. Morgenna started crying uncontrollably. It suddenly hit her why Felicity was screaming so hard.

Morgenna realised then that she had to take control of herself. She got up and went to the girl, and put her arms around her. Felicity screams turned into sobs.

Morgenna started stroking her head. 'It's ok, it's ok, we'll look after you. This will be ok.' Something inside told Morgenna that Felicity was one or two months pregnant, and that if they didn't get Felicity calmed down immediately, she could lose the baby. A tiny piece of Edwin was still on the earth, and Morgenna had to fight to protect it. Tears came back to her eyes as she thought of her son, and the tiny seed of her grandson inside this frightened young girl's belly. She moved the girl into the living room and sat her down on the sofa.

'It will be ok,' she said.

Seb arrived home from the shop with the small bottle of whisky his mother had asked him to buy. He came into the living room and knew immediately what had happened. Kevin spoke on behalf of the women. 'It's your brother Edwin, Seb. He's dead.' The EF did not talk in euphemisms when it came to death. It was better to face it head-on. Boys needed to be men, and people respected the truth.

He drew the boy to him. 'It's ok to cry, son.'

But Seb pulled away from him and sat down, trying to take in the news. His father was currently in America, part of a contingent who had been sent over to further EF foreign policy goals with America's new leader. He would not get the news until he returned. Seb sat there, numb, and thought of the EF slogan. *To every house, its man to lead.* At ten years old, if only until his father returned, Sebastian Weston was now the *man to lead* in this house.

His mother's voice broke his inner monologue. 'Let's have some of that whisky, son. Go on, get some glasses.'

He went into the kitchen with the bottle and after a few minutes came back with three glasses of half-filled whisky. He hadn't been sure how much to put in, but he knew that whisky was only supposed to be drunk in small amounts on occasions like this. It wasn't like juice.

Kevin was about to refuse his glass, but he felt it vaguely disrespectful to the memory of the dead. Morgenna passed a glass to Felicity, telling her 'don't worry, a little bit won't hurt.' She stopped herself from saying 'the baby' because she didn't want Felicity to know that she knew, and saying it aloud might drive Felicity back into hysterics.

A calm settled on the living room as the figures sat hunched under the gaze of the lamb in the Agnus Dei print above the fireplace. Kevin spoke. 'Morgenna. As you probably realise,

Edwin wasn't the only soldier to be lost in the mission. We are organising a special memorial service tonight. It won't be an official military funeral service, that won't be for another week. But we know that a lot of people will want to come together tonight and...'

Morgenna nodded. She didn't need to hear the rest. She was an active member of the Church and she knew exactly why these events were necessary. If she hadn't been one of the grieving parents she would have suggested it herself.

She had to pull herself together. Edwin was a Wolf. She had been worrying about this day arriving since he was 15. And now this day, so many times dreamt of and imagined, had finally come. In her mind, she had always imagined John would be with her, somewhere around. And she had never imagined that Felicity would be pregnant. She felt unprepared for this particular scenario.

'Yes, of course I'll be there', she said, clearing the last of her whisky in her glass. She shot a glance at Seb, who sat forlornly in the armchair in the corner. 'We'll all be there.'

CHAPTER 6

The Church of Christ in Albion, or Albionic Church, was the curious fruit of the English people's discovery that the spiritual vacuum of the 20th century was unsustainable in the reality of 21st century bloodshed. Despite rumours of it being a conscious invention for social control, it had in fact risen organically from popular and intellectual currents, but no-one could deny that while it met the spiritual needs of a balkanised English people, something that no organised religion had been able to do for the last hundred years, it also fulfilled expedient political ends, its dogma in lockstep with the EF Covenant.

Far from the Christianity of modernity, once famously described by one Albionic priest as *wholehearted Bolshevism under a tinsel of metaphysics*, the worldview of the Albionic Church was merciless in its truth, and adhered largely to natural law and the vaguely brutal, pragmatic and tribal Anglo-Saxon soul. The Christ of Albion himself was the Christ who came bearing a sword, the Christ of Righteousness, the Christ who understood the nature of evil. The religion was underpinned by the love of the English people, which meant that what mattered most in religious law was physical and moral health of the individual and of society as a whole. Weakness and deviance from the path were not tolerated, let alone celebrated. Behaviours born of individual ambition and hedonism were mortal sins, while eugenic behaviour was promoted, even if it meant that the sexual puritanism of traditional Christianity was overlooked for expedience. The bravest, most ruthless fighters often did not make good husbands or fathers, but they made the kind of babies that the EF needed. So blind eyes were turned when young Wolves returned jubilant from gory missions, the enemy's blood still caking their boots, their triumph over death wishing to cement itself in the creation of new life. The energies of bloodlust to protect the tribe were transformed into sexual lust with the Church's tacit blessing.

Understanding how to channel the subtle energies of nature was just one of the ways in which the Church of Christ in Albion incorporated pagan elements which resonated with the folkways of the people. As a reaction to the horrors of the killing years, all kinds of animistic practices had sprung up among the English, quite inconsonant with the technology of the time. People had begun lighting candles for their ancestors, and this evolved into a form of ancestor worship, with prayers not just to those family members and EF soldiers who had been killed in recent battles, but prayers to those fallen English soldiers of both previous world wars, who were seen as part of a greater historical chain of national sacrifice. From these ideas, necromantic practices developed logically, with the besieged English striving to awaken the dead souls of the land, to make their forebears' spirits arise from the grave in ghostly battalions to exact vengeance upon the invaders and the traitors. Others believed that these ancestors lived within them through the blood, and by honouring them with acts of bravery and sacrifice, they would be further empowered by these 'guardians of the bloodline'. Many were tempted to say that the myriad uncanny events which befell England at this time were due to successful necromantic practices, but it was impossible to know for certain.

In the thick of this hopeful witchery, a man called Charles Swanson authored a book reputed to be divinely revealed. In *The English, God's Chosen*, biblical hermeneutics made the case that the battle for the English land and soul was part of a greater spiritual and racial battle which had been raging since the births of Cain and Abel. According to Swanson, the English were the Elect Nation, singled out by God for a divine purpose and destiny. The book was published in 2038 to great acclaim and revived the idea that Christianity could again be the religion on which the fulcrum of English identity could rest, but a robust Christianity founded on the racial identity and continuance of the English people throughout the millennia. Christ became the Lamb of Albion, an avatar for the English spirit, and woe betide the enemy who dared to wage war against the Lamb. Combined with an ancestor worship and an honour system based around blood, the Albionic Church was a powerful tribal alternative to SAU Islam and a spiritual bulwark against the communism of the legacy culture, which even after so much of its bitter fruit had been eaten, still had the power to seduce and disintegrate the minds, bodies and souls of Western Europe's unguarded flock.

Chastised by the lessons of history, the English Front ensured that the Albionic Church was the only religion and ideology permissible within its territory. The most celebrated warriors gave it visible support, which washed the Church with a masculine, militaristic energy, important at a time when people sought physical security as well as spiritual certainty. Even other sects of Christianity were banned under pain of banishment or death, as the EF understood all too well how dangerous ideas could be slipped to the people via subversive methods. Culture creep was watched for with the vigilance of a new mother watching over a sickly infant.

The EF was wise enough however to understand that certain supernatural practices which had become popular during the 30s, particularly divination and callings, would only be driven underground if they were banned, so the Church chose strength in flexibility, and regulated the charismatics who practiced ancillary spiritual rituals. Unlicensed practitioners of prophesy and necromancy were subject to the same penalties as heretics, not least to ensure the maximum possible exclusion of dark forces from EF territory and to protect the legions of the bereaved.

Unknown to the vast majority of worshippers, there was also an esoteric side to the church, which practiced powerful rituals at astrologically preordained times and geomantically predestined places, known only by a very few initiates. Certainly Morgenna, who was sitting in the front row of the church, with a subdued Felicity and Seb on either side of her, had little idea, if any, of the Church's esoteric heart, or the political discussions that took place between EF generals and Church elders. She only knew the teachings of the Bible as mediated by Swanson, and took strength from praying to the Great Mother and the Albionic Saints.

She looked up at the crucifix behind the alter. The blue-eyed Jesus staring down glassily from the cross looked so young, like a youngster of 18 or 19. *He had been a martyr for his people just like Edwin*, Morgenna thought. She knew that Edwin had died a hero's death, the way he would have wanted to die, serving his people through the martyr's baptism of blood, but it was still torture to her. She felt numb, like she was halfway into death herself, like she should be dead already. Her beautiful boy, at the peak of life. She sat staring at the crucifix, not listening to the priest, trying to remember to keep breathing and not start screaming as she wanted to. *If thou canst not behold high and heavenly things, rest thou in the passion of Christ and dwell willingly in His sacred wounds.* Clinging to that advice which now surfaced to the top of her mind, she focussed on blood dripping around the Lamb's crown of thorns, and tried to drown her own pain in His own.

She made a conscious effort to focus on the spark of life inside Felicity's belly. *This* would be her hope for the future. She imagined the tiny baby inside the young girl, stirring and growing. Edwin's child. Maybe Edwin's son? Something told her that it would be a little boy. Maybe one of the charismatics could tell her. Or maybe she shouldn't tempt fate by trying to find out. She leaned rightwards and gave Felicity's left hand a squeeze, then looked towards her son and leant into him so that her shoulder touched his. He was still a little boy really, but she didn't want to be too motherly with him in public. He wouldn't like that. He was starting to see himself as a man, and she needed to encourage that. Men bore the ultimate responsibility before God, which was why, although God punished the snake, Eve and Adam for the original sin, he punished Adam the hardest. Mothers who were too soft with their sons tended to ruin them for the future. She thought of Annika Coogan's boy. Annika was never the same after what happened. Yes, you had to be careful about being too open with your feelings when it came to sons, even if it pained you inside. You had to treat them differently to girls, because they had a different role. Males had to be tough, so you had to be tough. You had to treat them like little soldiers from an early age, so that they learned emotional resilience. A man who hesitated, a man who worried, or cared, was a man who ended up dead. *And I don't want another dead son*, thought Morgenna.

The choir had stopped singing. The priest was now talking about the nature of sacrifice and how the blood of the fallen would nourish the land for the next generation. That their sacrifice would not be forgotten. Morgenna wondered if Edwin's spirit was here, listening to this. She imagined it was. She feared a calling ceremony because she didn't want to keep him in this plane. He needed to move on because the sooner he ascended the sooner he could return. Maybe by the time he returned she would be dead. But she couldn't imagine a livewire like Edwin would not want to return to help finish this battle for his people's homeland.

> *The silver cord is severed,*
> *and the golden bowl is broken;*
> *the pitcher is shattered at the spring,*
> *and the wheel broken at the well,*
> *the dust returns to the ground it came from,*
> *and the spirit returns to God who gave it.*
>
> *Blessed are the mothers who offer up their firstfruits of their womb to the Lord for this our sacred struggle.*

The holy man's eye fell on Morgenna as he said this, and Morgenna comforted herself with the thought that Edwin would be watching this service and would be already planning when to return to continue the fight. *We will all be back,* she thought, *this is our land. How dare they take it from us? We will all come back to help fulfil the destiny of the English people.* She imagined herself as one of a legion of spirits spread across the moorlands, anchored into the ground by their sense of belonging, bathed by the light of a bright yellow sun rising up on the horizon behind them. This combination of mystical reflection and righteous indignation immediately made Morgenna feel better. It took her out of herself and her own pain. This just wasn't about her, in this time and in this place. This was everyone's struggle, and it was timeless.

She stole a glance at the other grieving families. She knew them all. All the other mothers had their husbands with them, except for Joanna, who was widowed. Poor Joanna, with her six kids and no man behind her, keeping everything together with the meagre EF pension for her fallen husband. Wistan had been her second eldest son, and now he was gone. She made a mental note that if she couldn't get a chance to see Joanna after the service, she would visit her tomorrow.

She looked down at Seb, and noticed that he was staring straight ahead, looking miserable and numb, his eyes glazed with unspilled tears. She put her left arm around his back and gave him a big reassuring squeeze.

S. B. Saunders

'It won't be long, son.'

CHAPTER 7

Alexander 'Trey' Hansen was a born leader for the North American Confederation. At 6'4", broad shoulders and a shock of ash blonde hair, a rare throwback to an America of an earlier century, he stood now on the podium as he addressed the English delegation, flanked by the generals who had given him their confidence. An intensely hard and practical man, his origins in America could be traced back to pious Norwegian immigrants who came to farm the plains of Pennsylvania bringing no more culture from their homeland than a worn leather-bound Bible in Danish blackletter, the family's genealogy scrawled on the back flyleaf, and an already threadbare edition of Dorothe Englebretsdotter's *Siælens Sang-Offer*, a work of Christian devotion. Hansen had been born a few years after the dawn of the 21st century, and came of age just as the civil conflict began. He had enlisted in the US Marines, and from there ascended to Lieutenant General before getting into the more difficult world of politics, when he was selected with virtual unanimity by his peers and superiors for the difficult job of President of the North American Confederation.

Hansen was the first President to be elected by *secure democracy*, after his predecessor, Arnold Balderson, was the final president to be elected by mass suffrage, in an election marred by violence and accusations of fraud. When the Balderson administration struggled to maintain control due to mass civil unrest in America's major cities, an unrest fomented over seventy years by communist agitators and banking elites, Balderson declared martial law, and the army began a serious clean-up operation of the country, as the European stock which founded America now found itself at war with every other ethnic group, including their fellow European descendants who had fallen for communism's siren song. The technologies of mass killing were useless for situations in which friend and foe were living in close proximity, and as a result the Balderson government encouraged the Patriots, or Jacksonites as they called themselves, those who still lived in the big cities across America, to make the difficult journey to the designated North and Midwest states. Some provisionally named Safe Zones had been created in these states, and checkpoints and quarantine camps had been set up for the newcomers who had made the journey. Entry was far from assured. For towns and cities which had been cleansed of its communists, invaders, parasites and criminals, it was not about to risk recontamination from unauthorised newcomers. Despite such an idea never being explicitly stated, non-Whites presumed that getting past the quarantine zones would be well-nigh impossible. There were also rumours that refugees who failed the quarantine were shot, and their bodies fed to the guarding pitbulls or incinerated. These rumours were disregarded by those who took them as communist propaganda, designed to dissuade people from trying to escape the violence, looting, disease and imminent starvation.

Eventually the Safe Zones of these Northern and Midwest states pushed downwards and outwards and stabilised into a unified territory defined by its ethnicity and political ideology. By 2042, though it became clear that a fight would be needed to reclaim the American territory still occupied by the enemy, Balderson's government could at last breathe easier with a stable if diminished American territory, and work on rebuilding defence, infrastructure and civic institutions.

It was also a perfect opportunity to forge transnational alliances. Freedom for Canada was a nativist revolutionary movement which had begun life as a military-trade syndicate. The syndicate itself had arisen in order to stabilize and guarantee supply networks in the face of government sanctions against rebel farmers unwilling to continue falling into poverty to feed Canada's urban conurbations. A joint operation with the Jacksonites resulted in the FCC painlessly requisitioning the self-styled Global Sanctuaries and Safe Spaces of Toronto, Ottawa and Montreal. Supply lines were cut to the cities, leaving the enemy population of urbanites to fall into famine, violence and disease, their LGBT-themed fiat currency useless for international exchange, the country's reserves of the *barbarous relic* having long ago been sold off at firesale prices. Mothers watched in horror as their children starved and began reverting back to their original sexual characteristics, as genderising hormone shots were subject to the same embargo as wheat and milk. Canadian boys began to lose their breasts and the girls began to lose their beards, while rival ethnic groups of newcomers, no longer fed by government initiative, began to prey upon the weak. The utopian vision of Canada as the global flagship for Radical Humanity had collapsed, and in the wake of this success, Freedom for Canada decided to consolidate their victory by allying with the Jacksonites to create the North American Confederation, or NAC.

Now with the threat from the north averted, and internal enemies no longer able to escape back and forward across sovereign borders, the state could employ government weapons of mass killing that would previously have been unviable. Balderson then had to decide if and how he wanted to use these weapons. There were no longer any supranational organisations to condemn these actions, but this was about how the North American Confederation was to define itself as a people for the future. How a nation was founded mattered. Karma mattered. The cataclysmic fate of Israel was proof of that. There were voices who suggested that the North American Confederation should not waste needless resources, time and lives on recapturing territory that would implode with the forces of entropy within a few decades, but Balderson understood that the enemies of the NAC remained a danger while they existed. There were many conversations conducted over drinks in dark corners, as Balderson's high command contemplated acts of warfare which might not be against any international law, for now there was none, but which might haunt them as human beings and bring damnation down on the heads of their descendants.

Decisions were finally taken to unleash a weapon which caused so much suffering to their enemies on the North American continent that they were effectively neutralised as a risk to the new state, which had given the NAC almost two decades to rebuild, reorganise, and consolidate its global position. By the time of the EF delegation's visit in 2060, the NAC was the strongest Western nation in the world after Russia, and had dealt conclusively with its ideological and ethnic enemies. Only the communist stronghold of New York remained any kind of threat, but that would be dealt with in due course. *One acts more shrewdly when one bides one's time, and New York requires a shrewd solution*, Balderson had once famously been quoted as saying. Now the new leader Hansen had been waiting for this momentous face-to-face meeting with the English Front, a meeting that the Albionic astro-theologians had planned to coincide with the momentous Great Conjunction, seeing a powerful correspondence in the alignment of the great filial planets, Saturn and Jupiter, with the summit meeting between the old land of England and the New America, England's child by blood.

After Hansen's speech, John learned exactly what had been done for the Jacksonites to take back their country. He sat with his comrades in the specially built amphitheatre, watching the Hologram playbacks of *The Purging of the Dross*, specially filmed on Holomakers for posterity. Later generations of schoolchildren were able to live the experiences of their forefathers and understand what they had gone through to take back their nation, and how it must never be endangered again. As he watched the scenes in front of him, recreated through time, John recognised the names of some of those executed from his lessons at school, while with others he recognised their faces. His friend Tony nudged him when a famous actor of the 2020s came into view, begging for his life, but most of the people - politicians, journalists, judges, academics, celebrities - John had never heard of. But he was polite enough to try to keep interested throughout the spectacle, which went on for almost four hours. He glanced around the room. Most of the British delegation were utterly transfixed, perhaps imagining what some of England's own executions must have been like. *Not as orderly as this*, John thought. The attempted coup had been a bit shambolic, and resulted in the beast being wounded but its back unbroken. It was why England had been in a stalemate of opposing forces for sixteen years.

After what felt like an eternity, the Holograms ended, and the ceiling lights came back up. The audience blinked in a blood-blinded stupor. A few of the men looked thoughtful, while others looked quite queasy under the glare of the lights.

While the show had been going on, Hansen and Caldwell, the head of the EF, had slipped into the room next door, seemingly unnoticed by the rest of the English, who were watching Hologram technology for the first time in their lives. The talks of the past several days had coalesced in this private discussion, where they both agreed on the final details of what had been mooted. Such privacy was necessary as even with decades of purges and careful vetting, spies did still exist for the other side, and the communists still held global power bases in the great Western capitals, albeit ceding ground every year.

Perhaps it was because John had started to get bored by the banality of the killing, despite its perfect simulation in seven dimensions, that he had noticed Caldwell slip back into the darkened room before the end of the show. He knew then that the purpose of this trip had concluded. The important decisions had been made, and now John could only hope that Caldwell had been wise in what he had agreed to.

CHAPTER 8

Morgenna was waiting at the port for the ship coming in, and although on dry land, she felt as unsteady on her feet as if she were at sea. She was nervous, and buffeted by conflicting waves of emotion. She longed to see her husband's face again and she needed him by her side, but at the same time she dreaded the moment she would have to tell him the news.

But when she finally saw John's face look towards her as he cleared the security area, she knew that he had already been briefed. His face was ashen and his eyes looked vacant in a way she had never seen before. And Morgenna had seen John through a lot of incidents involving the deaths of his men.

But never the death of his own son.

He came up to her and mechanically touched her arm. She could tell that he didn't want any more physical contact than that. He was in shock. He looked down at Seb. It was at this point that his face broke with emotion. Sebastian buried his face into his father's chest and put his arms around him, suddenly becoming the ten-year-old boy he could be again now that his father was home. Morgenna struggled to contain her emotions. She knew that John wouldn't appreciate her crying in public.

Collins, John's commanding officer, approached John discreetly. 'We've got a car waiting for you, John. We assumed you'd want to go straight home.'

Startled at Collins' use of his first name, John realised that Collins knew what had happened, and had arranged this. He felt a wave of gratitude to his superior. Collins had also lost his oldest son, Stephen. Three years ago it must be now. John nodded wordlessly, looking towards the ground. He knew that if he looked at Collins in the eye he would see his own pain reflected back at him and it would be too much to bear. He needed to get out from under this vast open air whose skies threatened to crush him. And away from all the strangers.

❊ ❊ ❊

A silence reigned over the house. Morgenna held John as he lay on the bed, trying to take in the hugeness of the news. Unlike Morgenna, he had not gone through the scenarios of his boy not coming home, he had dealt with the uncertainty by simply not thinking about it. Now he was forced to, for the first time. Morgenna wondered when she should break the silence. She inhaled, and heard the sound of her own voice echo above the bed.

'I think that Felly is pregnant.'

She felt John's body go rigid momentarily under her arms. He lifted his head and looked at her.

'Are you sure?'

'As sure as a woman can be. I'm going to talk to her about it today.'

This news seemed to stir John from his listlessness and after a few minutes he sat up. It was as if the news was Edwin calling to him from the other side. There was a new life to look after. *A grandson.*

John tried to lighten the atmosphere by an attempt at a laugh. 'Fucking hell, he didn't hang around, did he?' He rubbed the bristles on his chin. 'That's my boy. Where *is* Felicity, by the way?'

'She's gone to visit her father. He's on leave. He's bringing her back tomorrow.'

John took a deep breath. 'We have to keep

things together for Felly and Seb. It's what Edwin would have wanted.' He remembered his son, a seething mass of energy, testosterone and baritone laughter who would bound around the house leaving broken ornaments and that pungent smell peculiar to teenage boys in his wake. Even at eighteen, he was already two inches taller than his father, and the two would play-wrestle each other in the living room, as Edwin tested the results of his weight-training in his attempts to get his father into headlocks, or to floor him completely. John felt the air leave his body as he realised he would never feel his son's arms grapple with him again.

After a minute, he reached for the lerter on his belt.

'I think that I should go and see William, and find out exactly what happened.'

His fingers tapped a feverish message into the lerter. Half sitting up now, John leant back against the headboard, awaiting a response.

Morgenna continued to lie flat on the bed, and cuddled into her husband's waist in a bid to will him to stay with her. 'Before you go, tell me about America. You haven't told me what America was like.'

John looked down at his wife and smiled.

'It was incredible. They declared their ethnic state eighteen years ago. Eighteen years of peace and order. It's amazing what they have been able to do in that time. When we arrived on their shores we were like a war-torn bunch of ragamuffins. Hansen and his men did not have a hair out of place. But seeing them has given us inspiration regarding what can be done. And they are going to help us get there.'

He kissed his wife on the head. 'This nightmare is soon going to be over.'

Gently extricating himself from his wife's arms, he got up off the bed and called for Seb, which made it clear to Morgenna that this was the most he would say about the trip to America.

CHAPTER 9

The Haresfinch boys still met up in the wasteland behind Helston Avenue, but nothing had been the same since that fateful night a month ago. Sam was very quiet. Andrew noticed that he didn't boast about his dad in the same way anymore. He seemed keener to be a member of the gang, to be just like everyone else. Seb had turned quite sullen and now only wanted to talk about his twelving and what he was going to do when he left school. He had wanted to go into the Wolves like his brother, but his parents, backed by the EF, did not support that choice due to his brother's death. Irritated by this decision, he regularly put down the other boys when they acted childishly, like he was sick of being in their company. He was particularly irritated by Sam. Aware of Sam's previous dominant status among the boys, Seb regularly shot him aggressive looks and jibes, as if challenging him to fight.

But Sam made a big effort to avoid any conflict with Seb. He knew that getting into a fight with him would be a lose-lose situation. If he won a fight with Seb, Sam would be made to look like he was bullying a boy who had just lost his brother, and Sam knew this would upset his father, who was still on crutches. William still did things for the EF, but it was like something was missing from him now. He would snap at Sam and his mother, and go off into the bedroom to be on his own, and asked not to be disturbed. Sam knew that his dad blamed himself for what had happened, and that since that night, he didn't trust his own decisions. He hesitated now. His emotions were constantly close to the surface, and Sam had to be careful in everything he said and did. Fighting with Seb, Edwin's brother, would not help his dad. Sam was broken away from his chain of thought by the sound of Seb's voice:

'Have you got a problem, you fucking cock-muncher?'

Seb was looking straight at Sam, his eyes boring into the taller boy with hatred. If Seb had been asked to explain why he was trying to break Sam, the ten-year-old probably couldn't have given any kind of clear answer. It was a visceral thing. Maybe it had to do with Sam being the son of the man who had led his big brother to an early death. Maybe it had to do with Seb proving himself as a man by defeating the de facto leader of the group. Whatever it was, Sam knew that he had to respond in some way. Being accused of homosexuality was a severe challenge to his honour. There were only three crimes that the English Front automatically punished with death: treachery, sodomy and… he forgot the other one. But calling someone a homosexual was to challenge a man to fight.

'You want to fight me, is that it?'

Sam didn't have the stomach for a fight, but he knew that he had to end this quickly. Before Seb had a chance to answer, Sam had swung around and caught Seb in the face. Seb fell to the ground and Sam quickly put his foot on Seb's throat.

'Seb, come on, stop it. We don't need to fight like this. You're like a brother to me.'

Immediately Sam realised that he had said the wrong thing. Seb twisted from under Sam's foot and bit Sam's ankle. Sam yelped in pain and jumped back. Seb jumped to his feet and lunged at Sam. The two boys proceeded to trade punches, pull at each other's hair and try to scratch each other's eyes out in a flurry of half-blinded panic. Suddenly both boys were yanked apart by a big pair of arms.

'Fucking ENOUGH!'

It was John, Sebastian's father. In shock, both

boys immediately dropped their animosity towards each other. *What was HE doing here?*

'You two, come with me. NOW!' Seb's dad had the natural kind of authority that made grown men cede to his will, so two ten-year-old boys, with their T-shirt collars still gripped by his fist, could put up no resistance. 'The rest of you, get your arses home if you know what's good for you.'

The other boys looked around sheepishly and, unwilling to make eye contact with Seb's dad, started to disperse.

As John marched both of the boys onto the beginnings of the broken tarmac that formed the deserted road of Helston Avenue and away from the others, he started to ask questions.

'Do you mind telling me what that was about?'

Seb looked sullen. He wasn't about to start explaining himself. He didn't see why he had to.

John wondered for a moment if this had something to do with Edwin's death, so he didn't push Seb for a response, and instead decided to quiz Sam.

'Sam, what have you got to say for yourself? What is your dad going to say about this?'

'He… he called me a cockmuncher.' Sam was almost on the verge of tears.

John let go of the boys, and started to laugh. A big throaty laugh, like he couldn't contain himself. The two boys looked on, stunned. *Why was he acting like this?*

When John saw the dismay on the two boys faces, he launched into another round of laughter, this time having to hold his knees to stop himself completely doubling up.

'You mean... you mean, all of this started because one of you accused the other of being a... cockmuncher?' Tears were starting to come out of his eyes now, and his laughter started to make the boys smile out of sheer contagion. 'A fucking *cockmuncher*!' He set off into another round of laughter again. Seb couldn't really see what was so funny, but he was just glad that his dad wasn't angry with him. He saw the relief in Sam's face as well, and realised that he wasn't really angry with Sam.

'Oh fuck... oh lads, I needed that. Come on.' He put a hand onto each boy's back and led them onto the inhabited streets of the town. 'Yeah, you really don't want to be a cockmuncher. I can see why Sam fought back. For fuck's sake, lads.' He shook his head as he brought it to his mind. 'The things you boys come up with. Yeah, nothing ever changes.'

Ten minutes later, they had reached Sam's front door. William father answered and looked immediately concerned when he saw his son, whose swollen and bloody face and dirty T-shirt suggested he had been the victim of a violent attack. 'Don't worry, Bill, these two have just been scrapping. Over nothing. They have agreed to be friends. Haven't you, lads?' There was a new edge in John's voice that told Seb and Sam that this wasn't a question. 'It was a fair fight, and it was a draw. Now I want you to shake on it.'

Both boys reluctantly put out their hands, but shook as John instructed.

There was a silence of around a second, and in that silence both fathers immediately sensed that this fight was the result of William's actions that night a month ago which had led to Edwin's death. In a way, the sons were acting out the fight on behalf of the fathers. John wanted to make clear that there was no fight to be had. He looked at both the boys with his sternest face.

'In the English Front, you don't fight your brothers. There is only one war out there, and that is with our enemy. Do you hear me?'

Both boys nodded. He looked at William. William knew that that statement was really for him, to say that John forgave him, that he didn't resent him for Edwin's death. He felt emotions rising to the surface that he had been struggling with for the past four weeks.

'Thanks, John. We'll deal with this.' William ushered Sam inside, and Moira immediately pulled Sam into the kitchen for his wounds to be cleaned.

John nodded. 'I'll see you around, Bill. Take it easy on that foot.'

William watched the figures as they walked up the garden path and towards the north side of town into the fading twilight. From the west, the curfew bell began to ring through the streets.

Back home, Sam immediately wanted to control the topic of conversation before his father came into the kitchen to berate him, so he asked his mother about capital crimes in the English Front in the hope that his father would be distracted. 'The three crimes that the EF automatically punishes with death. Treachery, sodomy and what's the other one?'

'Coining.' Sam's mother did not take her eyes off his forehead as she continued to dab at his face with a cotton wool ball soaked in rubbing alcohol.

Sam's face crinkled into puzzlement, making

his mother's job more difficult. 'Why is that a capital crime? It's not that serious, is it?'

'It is.' The voice came from William, who had just walked into the kitchen. 'It's very serious. A coin minted by the EF is the perfect and just measure of labour, and to tamper with it, or to counterfeit it, is an abomination in God's sight.'

Seeing that further explanation was unforthcoming, Sam asked why.

'Because it's an abuse of trust. Without trust, you don't have a society that works. We, the English people, had the trust in our society destroyed by people who wanted to destroy our spirit, so that they could then destroy our flesh and blood. They began that destruction by breaking the integrity of our weights and measures. It cost many English lives to put our weights and measures right again and to get back the trust in our society. And we will protect that trust with death if we have to.'

Sam fell silent as he sat on the stool in the middle of the kitchen floor, letting his mother now fuss over the cuts on his hands. He wondered how many other ways there were to break the trust in a society. He had another question.

'Is breaking someone's trust the same as lying

to them?' He looked straight up at this father with the one blue eye which had not swollen shut.

William went up to his son and ruffled his hair. 'Yes, son, it is.'

He paused as he thought of England's history of the last hundred years. 'It certainly is.'

CHAPTER 10

One thing that the children learned early at school and at church was the importance of keeping secrets. A person who broke a confidence was the lowest of the low. The only exception to that was if the secret was going hurt the lives of English people if it were kept. At school, Mrs. Venables used to go through different scenarios of what the children should do if they found out various types of information, so that they would always know that they were doing the right thing.

Alban thought of Mrs. Venables now when he was told that at the tender age of twelve that he was going to be subject to a big secret of the Northwest Division.

'If you tell anyone about what I am going to show you, well, you know what will happen. This is Category B information.' The voice belonged to Dr. Wansbrough, a big hairy man of around sixty whose rough demeanour belied a first-class intellect. He was one of the intelligence trainers for the EF, and Alban had been under his tutelage for the past three years, learning Arabic and Arabo-Swedish. Now Dr. Wansbrough was going to show his young pupil something very special.

They went into the back garden of what appeared to be a bunch of semi-derelict tenement houses a few streets from the Intelligence Training Centre. Alban followed Dr. Wansbrough's stiff gait down the stone steps to a cellar with a crimson-painted door. *Was this a weapons cache?* Weapons were hidden all over the city in diverse locations and the heavy padlock and chain on the door, which Alban noticed was steel under the chipped paint, would suggest that guns were hidden here. Dr. Wansbrough opened the padlock, pulled the chain out from the metal handles and hauled open the heavy door. He stepped into the darkness. A light was flicked on. Alban waited until he was invited to follow his master.

'Come in, son, quick. And shut the door behind you.'

Alban went to shut the door and noticed that there was a metal bar to bolt it from the inside. He pulled the bar downwards. Now they were safe. No-one could open the door without breaking it down.

He turned and looked into the cellar. Dr. Wansbrough was walking forward into the gloom, switching on more lights. Alban realised that he was in a secret library.

The shelving units were metal, like it had been appropriated from an old workshop, and shelving lined the room from floor to ceiling. Books were stacked on every shelf. There was a table with three chairs and an angle-poise lamp in the centre of the room, and behind this, three freestanding units of shelves in the middle of the floor, also full of books.

'Wow, there must be thousands of books here,' said Alban. He had never seen so many books in his life.

'Yes, there are over three thousand,' said Dr. Wansbrough. 'Three thousand three hundred and eighty-eight, if my memory serves. They are all catalogued, although I might have to revise the classification system.' A half-smile danced across his lips. 'I'm an imperfect librarian.'

Alban had seen libraries before. There were libraries of dilapidated old books from before the war that a few old women still used for a bit of escapism or entertainment. Murder mysteries, romances, things like that. But those libraries were out in the open, run by volunteers. They weren't in a dark cellar, behind a steel door.

Dr. Wansbrough understood what the boy was thinking. 'These are special books. Books of truth. Books that the government tried to hunt down and destroy as the battle for ideas intensified in the 2020s and 2030s. They would still destroy them now, if they could. Because these books give you the real story of why England is in the position it's in today, in this, the year of our Lord, 2060. It is the material record of the crimes that have been committed against the English people, and the record of who we are. **As the monk Orderic lamented a thousand years ago, when the books perish, the deeds of the men of old fall into oblivion. Therefore it is vital that the books do not perish.**'

Alban wandered around the shelves. There was a musty smell about the place, and a few desiccant bags hung from the walls to catch the moisture in the air. The books were old, very old, with canvas peeling from the board covers which were themselves becoming unstitched at the spines. He wondered when the last time was that some of these books were opened. No-one really read books in England anymore. Not big serious books. There wasn't time, and it was hard to get peace in small, crowded houses. Information was passed around via lerters or via the chappies that rarely went beyond a dozen pages and were passed across

switching on more lights. Alban realised that he was in a secret library.

The shelving units were metal, like it had been appropriated from an old workshop, and shelving lined the room from floor to ceiling. Books were stacked on every shelf. There was a table with three chairs and an angle-poise lamp in the centre of the room, and behind this, three freestanding units of shelves in the middle of the floor, also full of books.

'Wow, there must be thousands of books here,' said Alban. He had never seen so many books in his life.

'Yes, there are over three thousand,' said Dr. Wansbrough. 'Three thousand three hundred and eighty-eight, if my memory serves. They are all catalogued, although I might have to revise the classification system.' A half-smile danced across his lips. 'I'm an imperfect librarian.'

Alban had seen libraries before. There were libraries of dilapidated old books from before the war that a few old women still used for a bit of escapism or entertainment. Murder mysteries, romances, things like that. But those libraries were out in the open, run by volunteers. They weren't in a dark cellar, behind a steel door.

Dr. Wansbrough understood what the boy was thinking. 'These are special books. Books of truth. Books that the government tried to hunt down and destroy as the battle for ideas intensified in the 2020s and 2030s. They would still destroy them now, if they could. Because these books give you the real story of why England is in the position it's in today, in this, the year of our Lord, 2060. It is the material record of the crimes that have been committed against the English people, and the record of who we are. **As the monk Orderic lamented a thousand years ago, when the books perish, the deeds of the men of old fall into oblivion. Therefore it is vital that the books do not perish.**'

Alban wandered around the shelves. There was a musty smell about the place, and a few desiccant bags hung from the walls to catch the moisture in the air. The books were old, very old, with canvas peeling from the board covers which were themselves becoming unstitched at the spines. He wondered when the last time was that some of these books were opened. No-one really read books in England anymore. Not big serious books. There wasn't time, and it was hard to get peace in small, crowded houses. Information was passed around via lerters or via the chappies that rarely went beyond a dozen pages and were passed across garden fences. Sometimes people got together and someone with a good voice like Hamish Crozier would read aloud and make a performance out of the ballads, which typically recounted recent military victories and the lives of English heroes and martyrs. Other chappies had more of a religious than a nationalist focus, to the extent that it was possible to tell the difference. Alban doubted that a proper book had been printed on English Front soil since he had been born. He remembered that old book they had been taught in school, the book about the importance of knowing about history. He decided to ask Dr. Wansbrough.

'What was that thing about whoever controls the past, controls the future? Or something like that.'

The man who had been given the honorary appellation of doctor for his vast auto-didactic knowledge beamed at the boy. 'That was George Orwell. *Nineteen Eighty-Four*. When he wrote it, the year 1984 was decades into the future. Now it feels like ancient history, but it isn't really. He was a prophet of the English people and is now an Albionic Saint. There is a statue of him in the church in Southwold. What he said was, "who controls the past controls the future: who controls the present controls the past". Right now, we control the present, at least in EF territories. So we need to make sure that we also control the past. This library is our control of that past. It's why knowledge of the library's location, even its existence, is strictly limited. Very few people know about this library, and it needs to stay that way.'

Alban nodded. He wandered around the books. Most of them were in English, but he saw that there were a few shelves of books in foreign languages. He recognised French, German and Russian titles. He was frightened to touch the books in case he got shouted at, so he just wandered around. He wondered what truths these books held between their covers, and if one day he would ever know these truths.

'To give you an idea of how precious these books are, some of the books on these shelves may be the very last copies in existence. At least in Western Europe. The great libraries began to be purged of their *problematic material* in the 2020s. Not all purges were successful. In 2031, a principled librarian at the National Library of the Netherlands managed to smuggle out some books which were destined for the furnace, and he got them into safe hands. He was shot for his trouble, and that shot rang out around the civilised world. As the communists started to lose more and more of the culture war, they started to bomb national libraries, out of spite more than anything else. They just wanted to destroy the history and order of the West. God alone knows what we will be able to salvage when this is all over...' Dr. Wansbrough's voice trailed off as he imagined himself picking through the wreckage of the great libraries of Europe.

'Will it ever be over, sir?'

Dr. Wansbrough smiled at the seemingly astute question from the twelve-year-old. 'Yes, at some point it will end. That is to say, the wars in Western Europe and North America will end. But the dark forces that caused the war will never be completely eradicated. They grow on the social body like a fungus, a ferment of decomposition if you will, and they seek to enact the triumph of weakness over strength, of bestiality over intelligence, and of quantity over quality. And they will not stop until they achieve a complete Satanic inversion of Western civilization's Christian values. It will therefore fall to the victors to ensure that the society they create is irradiated from the forces of subversion as completely as is possible. The people must remain forever vigilant and stamp out would-be revolutionaries without mercy. We must become the ultimate barbarians if we want to keep Western civilization from being extinguished.'

Alban nodded. He loved it when Dr. Wansbrough talked in visionary terms like this. He wished that his dad was more like Dr. Wansbrough, instead of being just a mechanic for the EF. Alban often imagined being Dr. Wansbrough's son, being able to ask him questions like this all the time, even outside of lessons. He would love to knew everything that Dr. Wansbrough knew. Dr. Wansbrough understood everything that was going on.

There was a silence. Alban wondered briefly why he had been brought there. Dr. Wansbrough seemed to read the boy's mind when he answered the unspoken question.

'I know that you have your hands full with the language work, but I really want to teach you something of history and, eventually, historiosophy. I want you to be familiar with all of the books in this library. Obviously, you will be unable to read the foreign language books, though who knows with time perhaps you'll be able to attempt some of them. You're twelve. You have decades of learning ahead of you. I want you to understand the authors, the titles, the *value* of these books.' He sighed. 'Alban, I'm sixty-two years old, and my health isn't great. Heart disease runs in my family, and I don't know how much longer I have, realistically. I need someone who can carry on my work, who can carry the flame of erudition through this, the darkest time in England's history. Books are not enough if no-one ever opens them. Books allow knowledge to be held in cold storage across the centuries, but this knowledge only truly lives if it is given expression in a breathing human body. You are young enough to be able to carry the knowledge I can give you for another fifty or sixty years, a half century in which to teach others. Eventually you would have the keys to this library. Do you think that you would be up to the task?'

Alban felt his heart bursting out of his chest with pride. *Dr. Wansbrough had picked him to be his protégé!*

Dr. Wansbrough continued. 'It would mean a lot of work. Very intensive. You would have to come and live with me. And you would not have a normal teenager's life. It would be a life of strict discipline.

Alban didn't care. What did the doctor mean by a *normal teenager's life* anyway? He wasn't sure what a teenager was, but nor did he care. Didn't it say in the Bible that no discipline was pleasant, but produced a harvest of righteousness and peace? Here he was being offered the chance to take hold of the tree of life from the most revered historian of the Northwest territory, if not the whole of England. He looked at the canvas-covered spines of the books in the gloom of the cellar, the sea of burgundy, olive green and blue with their secrets of the centuries, and imagined himself in forty years being as respected and listened to as Dr. Wansbrough was now. 'It would be an honour,' he said quietly, and hoped that he didn't sound too sycophantic. But it was how he felt.

Dr. Wansbrough pulled himself up gruffly. 'Good, good. That's what I like to hear. Well, I've spoken to your parents, and they are happy for you to come under my tutelage full-time. You'll still see them, of course, but your studies will come first.' He took a dusty old ring-binder full of plastic folders off the shelf nearest the door. 'The most important book in every library is its catalogue, so we'll start there.'

He gestured for Alban to take a seat at the table.

CHAPTER 11

The Russians had finally declared sovereignty over Danish territory. This came as no surprise to anyone, least of all the Danish, who had been controlled by Russia in fact if not in deed since Russia's annexation of Sweden over twenty years before, when they memorably entered the country one rainy Monday afternoon in January 2038 and defeated all Islamic and communist resistance within the week. All sorts of jokes went around at the time about the Russians being even more committed to the creation of order than God himself, when rather than resting on the seventh day the returning Rus saw fit to use the Sunday to swear in a satellite government loyal to the Orlov dynasty. As could be predicted, this so-called *vosstanovlenie poryadka*, loosely translated into English as 'restoration of order', set off the chain reaction of waves of Muslim fighters and refugees fleeing Sweden for England, hundreds of thousands of battle-hardened men who were welcomed by SAU forces.

The control of Sweden, from which the 'friendly' agreement with Norway soon followed, gave the Russians complete control of the Sound and the Baltic Sea. This meant that Denmark found herself at the mercy of Russia for basic food supplies and munitions. The Russians effectively called the shots in Denmark, and the only mystery was why the Russians themselves had not declared their hegemony at any point over the past twenty years. In all likelihood, they wanted to play down the fact that they were camped out on Germany's border, on both her north and the east flanks, waiting for the perfect moment to put the land of loyalty out of her Islamocommunist misery at the point that her bloody war of attrition had reached maximum tactical advantage for the Eagle, whose greatest fear was the emergence of takfiri caliphates on two fronts, but whose precious troops were spread ever more thinly over her vast landmass. The Russians did not want German men wiped out, far from it, nobody built or engineered or organised like the Germans, but nor they did not want them at a level of strength which could ever form a barrier to continued Russian hegemony. With sufficient patience, time would deliver the Orlovs a German people who would be grateful for a Russian *restoration of order*, and enemy forces mopped up with minimal troop deployment. From there, the Russians could sweep easily into the lands that had once been Holland, Belgium and France.

The fact that Russia had declared Denmark to be Russian territory now suggested that a Russian move further westward into the continent was imminent. For the North American Confederation, it meant that its own plans to secure the British Isles needed to be brought forward. Time was of the essence. Caldwell had already discussed the finalised Hansen Plan with the five divisional EF leaders and they had agreed that secrecy and the element of surprise was their best weapon for the key part of the offensive, which had been codenamed Operation Azrael. Offensives needed to be coordinated on both sides of the Atlantic to ensure that enemies on either side could not prepare a defence. Now that the plans were laid, it was felt that both sides needed to move fast, before spies discovered the agenda. Everything was set to move. All they were waiting on was the word from Omaha.

Felicity, of course, knew nothing of her country being poised on a knife-edge of mass slaughter. She had a tiny baby growing in her belly, an effervescent bundle of cells that pulsed with Edwin's energy which would soon emerge into the world with a spirit all of its own. She would shape its destiny. All of her waking thoughts were poured into this wisp of new life that stood between dimensions of existence, and whose future she strained to glimpse between waking fantasy and dreams. Dark storm clouds were gathering in the vast open sky above the deserted industrial estate through which she needed to walk to get to Mayfield Street, but as her flimsy shoes pounded the broken tarmac, Felicity with her skinny little legs was indifferent to the possibility of being caught in the May rain. If anything, she welcomed it. She loved being out in the fresh air, under the heavens. It helped her connect to Edwin.

She was on her way to meet Perpetua, a friend with whom she wanted to discuss the possibility of getting advice from Perpetua's fiancé's grandmother Aoife, a known charismatic but someone who had publicly renounced using her gift after an unforeseen event a few years ago. Felicity knew that she herself had very little chance of getting Aoife to change her mind about using her spirit of prophesy; others who knew her had tried without success. Perhaps, Felicity reasoned, if she spent time with Perpetua and Matt together at Matt's house, Aoife might come to see her as one of the family, and might be more predisposed towards helping. The Osborne house was always very crowded and lively; they didn't mind visitors, or people coming and going. It was a nice place to be.

Felicity knocked on Perpetua's door, and stood back off the step, waiting for her friend to answer. Perpetua was never on time. She was always fixing her hair. She had been the most glamorous girl in the school, at a time when it was difficult to be glamorous. Make-up was frowned upon by the Church, being seen as the first step towards demonic possession, whoredom, and the eventual fate of being eaten by dogs in the street. But even without artificial help, Perpetua's classical, delicately balanced features lit up a room, and all eyes were drawn to her. Even in times of religious asceticism and material deprivation, the beautiful still claimed their right to primacy in the world. Luckily for Perpetua's character, the taboos on photography and female self-expression meant that she did not have the overweening narcissism which would have destroyed her in previous generations.

'Right, I'm ready.'

Perpetua stepped out of the front door. She had put her much-envied blonde hair in a top knot, and was wearing white plastic drop earrings which easily dated to before the war. Perhaps they were her great grandmother's.

Perpetua and Felicity talked less effusively

these days. Prior to Edwin's death, all of their talk had been about Perpetua's upcoming wedding and how Felicity should break the news to Edwin about her pregnancy, if she should wait until the third month. Perpetua was still excited about her wedding, but she spoke about it in more muted tones now whenever Felicity was around. She realised that all the talk of her dress and the celebration was like a knife in the heart of her friend, whose burgeoning womb, a sad little bump in her dress, was the only trace left of a tragic romance. Felicity however, was desperate not to be the ghost at Perpetua's feast, and encouraged Perpetua to talk about her wedding plans. 'Don't worry about me,' Felicity would say. 'I might not have my wedding, but I've got my baby. God moves in mysterious ways. We cannot know why he planned it this way.' Talk would then turn to Felicity's baby and if it was a boy or a girl.

'I had another dream about the baby last night.'

Perpetua said nothing. Felicity had been getting increasingly mystical in her outlook over the past two weeks, and Perpetua wasn't sure if it was a good thing. It was probably her way of coping with the grief and the uncertainty, but it couldn't be healthy. Mysticism could easily tip over into delusion. Perpetua still had a vague memory of when people used to visit Aoife knowing that she had the gift, and some of those visitors were delusional. She didn't want to see Felicity become like one of those people. Felicity had been reporting lots of dreams about her unborn baby, which was a natural topic for her to dream about of course, but the young girl's dreams had started becoming ever more messianic. She was convinced that her baby was a boy, and recently she had been having dreams of **a bright sun shining forth from her belly, casting its golden beams onto the faces of the people around her. From this came Felicity's growing conviction** that her son was destined to be some kind of sacred leader of the English people. Perpetua wasn't sure about what to do. The dreams might actually be real signs from the heavens about Felicity's child, but Perpetua suspected that they were just the fantasies of a pregnant teenage girl, terrified of the prospect of single motherhood.

Perpetua became aware that her friend was waiting on her to respond. She obliged.

'So what was it about?' She tried to sound genuinely curious. In a way, she was, but she also dreaded having to deal with an answer which was grandiose or bizarre, as Felicity's dreams had come to be lately. She worried about her friend.

'It was actually a really weird dream, not like the others. I had dreamt that you and me were on a refugee ship bound for America. It was too dangerous for us to be here as pregnant women because things had got much worse. The SAU were managing to get into EF territory, so we were sent to America for our own safety.'

Perpetua shuddered. There had been English refugee ships in the early 2040s, but America had only allowed in one or two due to the inherent danger of subversives, and had instead sent help in the form of weaponry. Many English died in that decade, as the EF structure was still finding its final form.

Felicity continued 'but when we got to America, we were put in quarantine camps. We were told it was to monitor us for The Infection.' She looked at her friend's face and realised it probably wasn't a good idea to continue with her dream, which would just frighten her. 'I won't say what happened, but it's the kind of thing that makes me wonder if the spirits are trying to tell me something. I've only started getting these dreams since Edwin died. Maybe it's Edwin trying to communicate with me.'

Perpetua wondered if her friend was starting to lose her mind. Morgenna was keeping Felicity busy with the allotment and getting Edwin's room ready for her and the baby, but maybe it wasn't enough. Perpetua wondered if she should try to talk to Aoife on her own, to ask for advice about what was going on. Maybe Aoife wouldn't do a reading for Felicity, but she might be able to help in some other way. Perpetua resolved to chat to Aoife about Felicity when she was next at Matthew's house.

Felicity seemed to read Perpetua's mind. 'I was wondering if Matt's gran would be able to help me interpret my dreams. Or just help me to understand what's going on. Do you think she would?'

Perpetua's baby-smooth skin folded into an uncharacteristic crease between her perfectly groomed brows. 'I don't know. I remember that when she said she was through with opening the door, she really meant it. She was adamant. I'll try to talk to her about your situation but I can't promise anything. And I don't think you should mention this to anyone else. If she thinks I've plotted with you to get her to open again I know for a fact that she'll definitely say no.' Perpetua paused, and looked at the blackening sky. 'Come on, let's get to the church. It's the League meeting at six, and it's definitely going to rain.'

CHAPTER 12

Caldwell was standing in *The Cross Keys* with several of the EF regulars. He had never been a drinker, but since his return from America he had found himself wishing to hide away in one of the public houses frequented by many Northwest officers, where he would sit for hours saying nothing, just thinking. Other patrons knew well enough not to disturb him when he sat with a pint of ale, uncharacteristically taciturn. Sometimes he would stand at the bar, sipping a pint in silence, with a face that made it clear that he just wanted to listen to others' conversations, to simply be among his men. Those who were not party to the knowledge of Operation Azrael assumed that he had been given some bad news that he was trying to digest in his own time. The few who did have access to the details of Azrael knew why Caldwell's character had changed. It was a lot for one man to bear on his shoulders. Others did not have the same ethical qualms as he did, but they would not be the ones on whose shoulders rested the ultimate responsibility for this act. They were not the one who gave the final order, and nor would their names go down through history as having done so.

Caldwell was a bull of a man with such a strong presence that his seriousness could change the entire mood of whatever room he was in. Here, in the public house, jokes died on the lips of the teller, and fiddles found themselves put back in their cases when Caldwell's large head with its dead left eye stooped under the oak lintel, followed by those oxen shoulders that filled the width of the doorway, and all hope for a chance of merriment or even just consolation from the starkness of life leached from the drinkers' bones. It was as if there were a dark aura that hung over the place which needed to be expelled, and Harry, the pub landlord, was looking for an exorcism. Not of Caldwell himself, for whom Harry had the greatest of respect, but of the demon that had haunted Caldwell since that fateful visit to Omaha which had led him to seek out alcohol and solitude in company. Harry shot a look at Busby and Kerrigan as Caldwell's portentous footfall marked the beginning of another silent session in the bar. It was a desperate look that said that its bearer didn't know what was going on, but that it was up to Busby and Kerrigan to fix this situation.

James Busby waited until Caldwell had

ordered his second pint before he turned to his lifelong friend Michael Kerrigan, with whom he had cooked up so many subterfuges since childhood that both made mischief with one mind, and he threw out a stage whisper over their whisky chasers.

'Yeah, well, I've been thinking about what you were saying about the limits of warfare, and I've only got two words to say to you. South Africa.'

There was a shift in the room. The words 'South Africa' had the power to chill the blood of even the toughest Englishman. All adults over the age of 15 knew what had happened there, and it lay in deep subconscious of every grown man with a family, every so often springing into life at 3 a.m. and weighing heavily on his body, a black demon of bulbous-eyed glares and flaring nostrils. The victim would wake up bathed in sweat with a silent scream on his lips after seeing visions of macheted children, baby heads being kicked around the farmhouse floor, and women with their eyes gouged out, their lower abdomens spilling out their life's blood. The horrors of the genocide - the three-year-old girl crucified on her parents' kitchen table and raped as her parents bled out yards away, the four-year-old girl being bundled up in newspaper and set alight after surviving rape by three adult men, the children

bility for this act. They were not the one who gave the final order, and nor would their names go down through history as having done so.

Caldwell was a bull of a man with such a strong presence that his seriousness could change the entire mood of whatever room he was in. Here, in the public house, jokes died on the lips of the teller, and fiddles found themselves put back in their cases when Caldwell's large head with its dead left eye stooped under the oak lintel, followed by those oxen shoulders that filled the width of the doorway, and all hope for a chance of merriment or even just consolation from the starkness of life leached from the drinkers' bones. It was as if there were a dark aura that hung over the place which needed to be expelled, and Harry, the pub landlord, was looking for an exorcism. Not of Caldwell himself, for whom Harry had the greatest of respect, but of the demon that had haunted Caldwell since that fateful visit to Omaha which had led him to seek out alcohol and solitude in company. Harry shot a look at Busby and Kerrigan as Caldwell's portentous footfall marked the beginning of another silent session in the bar. It was a desperate look that said that its bearer didn't know what was going on, but that it was up to Busby and Kerrigan to fix this situation.

James Busby waited until Caldwell had

ordered his second pint before he turned to his lifelong friend Michael Kerrigan, with whom he had cooked up so many subterfuges since childhood that both made mischief with one mind, and he threw out a stage whisper over their whisky chasers.

'Yeah, well, I've been thinking about what you were saying about the limits of warfare, and I've only got two words to say to you. South Africa.'

There was a shift in the room. The words 'South Africa' had the power to chill the blood of even the toughest Englishman. All adults over the age of 15 knew what had happened there, and it lay in deep subconscious of every grown man with a family, every so often springing into life at 3 a.m. and weighing heavily on his body, a black demon of bulbous-eyed glares and flaring nostrils. The victim would wake up bathed in sweat with a silent scream on his lips after seeing visions of macheted children, baby heads being kicked around the farmhouse floor, and women with their eyes gouged out, their lower abdomens spilling out their life's blood. The horrors of the genocide - the three-year-old girl crucified on her parents' kitchen table and raped as her parents bled out yards away, the four-year-old girl being bundled up in newspaper and set alight after surviving rape by three adult men, the children boiled alive and the elderly farmers necklaced - weren't permitted to be told to children. No fear of a putative 'bogeyman' could come close to the night terrors that the true story of South Africa would bring.

The mere sound of the words 'South Africa' in the air seemed to have a powerful effect over all of those within earshot. A silence fell over the bar for a few minutes. Busby shot a glance at Caldwell finishing his pint, noting that leader's face looked grim, but decided. The object of their concern then straightened up briskly and slid Harry a ten coin.

'Keep the change.'

The leader walked towards the door, nodding in the direction of Busby and Kerrigan as he passed them. Something about his demeanour said that he wouldn't be back.

The front door of the pub closed with a thud. Busby smiled and took another sip of his whisky. A bag of pork scratchings slid noiselessly across the bar towards him as Harry, turning his back, poured out two more whiskies.

CHAPTER 13

Four or five of Aoife's youngest grandchildren were running around the living room in a chaos of pale skinny limbs and loud shrieking, their undernourishment appearing to have little impact on their energy for play. **The climate of want in which they lived seemed to leave little mark on the children of the English Front, who lived in palaces of the imagination filled with fairies and princesses, heroes and dragons.** It was too much for old Aoife who, after 61 winters of often extreme deprivation, with bones that weighed like lead and arthritic joints restricting her into stillness, felt herself to be the personification of Saturn in her armchair by the fire. Though her dark hair had thinned it still retained most of its colour, and her green eyes, while lacking precision in focus, still shone brightly in her withered face. Her poor vision meant that she observed life through a glass darkly, but her sixth sense took the measure of a man in an instant, and she could penetrate into the heart of any person or situation that was placed before her, even if this were only in her mind's eye. It was for this reason that many people avoided her company, as her habit of bringing to the surface the most recondite secrets was too much for those who were just trying to survive the day-to-day grind. Others sought her out, knowing that in her presence she would put her finger into long closed-up wounds and help them to feel again, at a time when most people struggled to feel anything.

With her elf-shot joints Aoife struggled to be much use to the household beyond feeding the chickens, which even then was done with great difficulty. Most of the time she was left to oversee the younger children, with the understanding that her duties would not need to extend beyond occasionally shouting in their direction. The house, as with most of the English houses, was in the direst poverty, and everyone had to work. When Aoife was a practicing seer, money and goods flowed into the house from those seeking visions of the location of treasures hidden during the war, the identity of an unknown nemesis, a message from beyond the grave or, most crucially for those so afflicted, an insight into the mystery of a lover's heart. When the old woman, citing failing health, had announced the withdrawal of her services, people had clamoured from far and wide to access her famed vision before the door closed forever. But it was an experience in 2058 had finally persuaded her that she had pushed her luck with the spirit world. She refused to do another summoning or scrying, fearing the consequences for her family if she did so. Something had terrified her that Saint George's Eve, and she refused to be drawn on it.

Eventually she withdrew from the world, reluctant to receive visitors, as it became ever more clear that those who visited with an ostensible concern for her health always had an ulterior motive in mind. Her world was a lonely one, as her farsightedness made reading her Bible or her books on Albionic theology impossible, and young children were no company.

It was in this way that Perpetua saw a way to get closer to Matt's grandmother.

'Grandma Aoife, is there anything I can do for you?'

The old woman turned towards the beautiful blonde girl who had just walked into the living room. Aoife understood that the girl before her was no longer a virgin, though affected otherwise to her parents. She sensed the girl's loyalty to her grandson, however. Perpetua was an affectionate girl, but no whore.

The teenage girl looked down at the floor, sud-

if this were only in her mind's eye. It was for this reason that many people avoided her company, as her habit of bringing to the surface the most recondite secrets was too much for those who were just trying to survive the day-to-day grind. Others sought her out, knowing that in her presence she would put her finger into long closed-up wounds and help them to feel again, at a time when most people struggled to feel anything.

With her elf-shot joints Aoife struggled to be much use to the household beyond feeding the chickens, which even then was done with great difficulty. Most of the time she was left to oversee the younger children, with the understanding that her duties would not need to extend beyond occasionally shouting in their direction. The house, as with most of the English houses, was in the direst poverty, and everyone had to work. When Aoife was a practicing seer, money and goods flowed into the house from those seeking visions of the location of treasures hidden during the war, the identity of an unknown nemesis, a message from beyond the grave or, most crucially for those so afflicted, an insight into the mystery of a lover's heart. When the old woman, citing failing health, had announced the withdrawal of her services, people had clamoured from far and wide to access her famed vision before the door closed forever. But it was an experience in 2058 had finally persuaded her that she had pushed her luck with the spirit world. She refused to do another summoning or scrying, fearing the consequences for her family if she did so. Something had terrified her that Saint George's Eve, and she refused to be drawn on it.

Eventually she withdrew from the world, reluctant to receive visitors, as it became ever more clear that those who visited with an ostensible concern for her health always had an ulterior motive in mind. Her world was a lonely one, as her farsightedness made reading her Bible or her books on Albionic theology impossible, and young children were no company.

It was in this way that Perpetua saw a way to get closer to Matt's grandmother.

'Grandma Aoife, is there anything I can do for you?'

The old woman turned towards the beautiful blonde girl who had just walked into the living room. Aoife understood that the girl before her was no longer a virgin, though affected otherwise to her parents. She sensed the girl's loyalty to her grandson, however. Perpetua was an affectionate girl, but no whore.

The teenage girl looked down at the floor, suddenly embarrassed by the intensity of the old woman's stare. She tried to empty her mind of all thought, lest the old woman read her mind as she was known to do. She sat down on the couch as two of Matthew's younger brothers ran past her.

'No, there is nothing. I'm fine.'

Aoife again scrutinised the girl. She saw the two children that Perpetua would eventually bear, how she would gain weight around the hips in that classic English pear shape and how her face would coarsen, with crow's feet around the eyes and a slightly downturn to her plump lips as life's hardships rode a streak of cynicism into her countenance. She would still be very attractive, and her childish love of sensual beauty would ripen into the overt sexuality of a grown woman, but nothing would rival this first bloom of adolescence. Now was a time of fulgence whose days had to be savoured, and Aoife could see from the touches Perpetua made to her body that Perpetua herself was conscious of this evanescence. *He has made everything beautiful in its time.*

The sudden intrusion of the Bible verse into the old woman's mind made her turn back towards the fire. According to scripture, even hatred and killing and destruction were beautiful when they took place at their providential time. The time that they were living in now.

Seeing that Aoife had become engrossed in her own thoughts, as the elderly English tended to do, Perpetua tried again.

'I was wondering, I know that you don't like the hassle of going to church, with all the people there. But would you like me to read to you sometime? I know that it is difficult for you to read, and the books are small print.'

Aoife's eyes narrowed and she smiled at the girl. Yes, something was afoot. A young girl whose mind is on nothing but her own beauty and her own romantic future has no interest in reading to an old woman. She understood that at some point there would be a quid pro quo expected for these good deeds. But she struggled to see what it would be. And she could always flatly refuse. A part of her wanted to say no, to scupper this young girl's scheme. But another part of her wanted to hear Swanson's soaring rhetoric and Pritchard's occult philosophy just one more time. She was also quite curious as to what the young girl would want from her. It certainly wouldn't be an interest in occult matters – this child, as ethereally beautiful as she was, had no spiritual capacity whatsoever. Aoife was intrigued. She liked the idea of being useful to people again.

Even so, she wanted to make sure. 'You know that I no longer scry or summon the fathers.'

'Oh yes, yes, of course,' Perpetua was in a hurry to reassure her. 'I just thought that I could help to make your life more pleasant.' Perpetua found it hard to maintain eye contact with the old woman, so she pretended to be interested the Agnus Dei print above the fireplace.

Aoife almost laughed at the teenager's poor attempt at dissimulation. Practically every home in the English Front territories had a copy of *that lamb print* and had done since before the girl was born. No, the reason that Perpetua was suddenly pretending to be captivated by the cheap monochrome image that everyone saw but no longer looked at, was because no sexually active sixteen-year-old girl at the height of her beauty had ever thought to volunteer her time to read religious texts to an elderly widow out of charity. Something was going on. But Aoife liked a good mystery. It brought her back into the warmth and bustle of the world, and further from the cocoon of her own thoughts, which were increasingly orientated towards joining the spirits with whom she had had so much contact over her lifetime.

'Whenever you want to start,' said Aoife, 'but

you will have to get the children to go and play out in the garden.'

CHAPTER 14

Ten-year-old Andrew had mixed feelings about becoming a pig farmer. He knew, of course, how essential it was to be producing food – that had been drummed into him since the age of seven with the maps at school, which showed the principal EF farming lands and the supply routes from the farmlands and the fishing ports to the people in the towns. Producing food and protecting the means of food production and transport was the single biggest priority for the EF. If anything, this war on English soil was all about access to food – the side which did not have adequate food starved, and couldn't grow their population. The SAU had most of the major cities in the Midlands and the Southeast, but their access to rural arable land was limited. Even when they did have access to this land, they lacked the knowledge of how to farm English soil properly, and the number of enslaved English farming families whose lands fell under SAU control were withering away. As a result, the Islamocommunist food supply was much more precarious than that of the English Front, and the Old Families could only meet the needs of their ectopic populations via the continued importation of container shipments from Asia that were channeled through their controlled southern ports. Even so, the enemy lived on a knife-edge. When the SAU weren't trying to rustle the EF livestock that wasn't porcine, they were eating food that had been unloaded in the London docks. Andrew knew exactly how important his job as pig farmer would be.

Still, he felt that his destiny was being imposed upon him. He saw the other jobs that were being done, jobs that were more social, more glamorous, that earned more admiration from the men due to their complexity or their bravery, and he felt wistful. Not that pig farming wasn't respected. It was. It was vital to the people. But perhaps it was its very necessity for the wheels of English society to turn that made it so nondescript. A boy who yearned for adventure or recognition did not go into pig farming.

In the English society of the mid-21st century, pigs were everywhere. As a symbol of the only Abrahamic faith which allowed the eating of pork, pigs were the food source that both affirmed English identity and which was relatively safe from being stolen for food. If the

SAU ever did manage to raid one of the EF's extensive pig farms, they took their revenge by setting fire to the pig carcasses, but they didn't benefit from the pigs as food. Pigs, in theory at least, never provided a benefit to the enemy. Although there were rumours that during the Siege of Swansea, not only pigs but *people* were eaten. Andrew wasn't sure about that last bit though. That might just have been his big brother Matt trying to scare him.

But the fact remained that for the SAU, eating pork was as taboo as eating human flesh, which is why pigmeat in all its forms was so ubiquitous in English territory. No part of the pig was wasted, just as no food generally was wasted. And pigs were notorious for eating anything. *Anything*. As part of the psychological campaign against the enemy, EF forces were known to feed the beheaded bodies of SAU soldiers to the pigs, and Andrew knew this to be true, because he had once seen a human finger stick out of the pig swill at his great-uncle's farm when he was seven. He had run away screaming to the old man, who had laughed and told him not to be silly, that the piggies love the taste of SAU meat the best. 'It's the saltiest' said Uncle Bob, 'and piggies fed on commies make the juiciest bacon.' Uncle Bob's eyes gleamed, and Andrew didn't know to what extent his uncle was being serious. Andrew knew from Bob that the corpses of traitors were also fed to the pigs without compunction, although the corpses of sodomites were burnt to ashes.

'Even in death they are a fucking liability,' was all Uncle Bob had to say about the sodomites.

Andrew asked what the difference was between the corpses of sodomites and traitors, but Uncle Bob just ruffled the child's hair and told him that all this would be told to him after his twelving, the age when it was deemed that **the child knew how to *refuse the evil and choose the good*. Then** his Life Duty of swineherd would be made official, and he would come to live with his Uncle Bob on his farm twenty miles north of the city. 'In the meantime,' said Uncle Bob, 'you get on with bringing the sacks from the barn. You'll find out all you need to know soon enough.'

Andrew trudged reluctantly to the cold barn. He was burning with questions. When he was younger he had asked about the feeding-people-to-pigs thing. Something deep inside himself told him it was wrong, and it disgusted him on a visceral level. He even stopped eating pork for a few weeks afterwards. When he asked his mother about it she just said 'Matthew fifteen eleven' in an abrupt tone which told him that she wouldn't be expanding on her answer. When he asked his brother Matt about it he was told that it was the ultimate humiliation for the SAU – 'first they are eaten by pigs, which are in turn eaten by us, their mortal enemies. Imagine knowing that when you die you are just going to give strength and vitality to the men that killed you.'

'But isn't it...' - Andrew struggled to find the right word - '...uncivilised?' He wasn't sure where that word had come from all of a sudden, but it seemed to be the one he needed.

Andrew's comment had caused his big brother to laugh so hard that he had to bend double to catch his breath, much to the younger boy's consternation. Seeing his little brother's face, his confused and hurt expression intensified by the pathos of facial features that still bore traces of infancy, Matt suddenly felt bad for laughing at him, and did his best to explain. 'Look little matey, by that stage, it's all just protein. And the group with the most access to the best-quality protein wins. It's as simple as that. Protein is the vital building-block of the body. It makes muscle. It doesn't matter where the protein comes from. All that matters is that we win.' He paused. '*Winning* is civilization.'

Andrew remembered this conversation as he struggled to bring the sacks out of the barn. *Winning is civilization.* He had remembered that phrase because he knew that he would need to ponder it later, as he didn't really understand it. His knees were starting to buckle under the weight and his spine felt like it was going to break. Maybe Matt was right, maybe it *was* all about the protein. Andrew knew that Uncle Bob was giving him these jobs to make him strong, but it was painful. However, to complain would make him seem like a child, so he didn't dare to say anything.

When he had finished and Uncle Bob had praised him for the detail of taking the empty sacks back to the barn without being told, he plucked up the courage to ask about the Siege of Swansea. 'Is it true that the SAU ended up eating people, Uncle?'

Andrew watched the old man's face darken and go very serious, not the reaction he was expecting.

'Yes, it's true. And it's not something to make light of. When human beings are dying of hunger, they will do terrible things. Things that you cannot imagine. Which is why we must ensure that nothing of that sort happens here. There must always be food for the people.'

He looked at Andrew straight in the eyes, and nodded, as if passing on the baton of a venerable wisdom down to the selected member of the youngest generation who was soon to take

From the Land All the Good Things Come

it up. 'Back when I was a child, people used to take food for granted. They didn't think about it, it was just there. Believe it or not, they didn't give thanks to God before meals, and they wasted food, like it was nothing. And yet, when the food runs out, you get chaos. Society crumbles. Nothing functions. Barbarity returns with the first rumbling stomach.' He put a protective arm around Andrew's slender back.

'Come on, son, let's go in. You've worked hard today. You'll make an excellent provider of the people.'

Andrew realised that being a pig farmer wasn't going to be so bad. In fact, he should probably consider himself lucky to have been chosen for the job.

CHAPTER 15

Despite the strangeness of how they had come about, Perpetua had actually started to look forward to her sessions with Aoife. It wasn't at all like she imagined it would be. Far from the idea of her reading to a silent old woman while keeping a discreet eye on the clock, Perpetua found that Aoife would often motion for her to stop after a certain phrase or paragraph in order to talk about the text, or about something that had happened in her past. The old woman seemed to come to life during these sessions in a very entertaining way, leading Perpetua to come to learn a lot about what the world was like at **the turn of the** century. And what she learned was much more interesting than anything she had ever learned in school. Aoife also made comments during the readings of her Bible, although these comments were usually quite cryptic, and she appeared to be commenting for herself more than Perpetua given that she tended to wave away Perpetua's attempts at questioning.

Perpetua was very surprised at Aoife's candidness. Most of the elderly generation, at least the ones she knew, did not want to talk about what life was like before what became known as the Rivers of Blood decade. The pain of betrayal and of watching one's country being destroyed to an official celebratory fanfare was impossible to get the young to understand, those who had been born into an already balkanised England and who had been breastfed with the warring spirit. Many old people felt that the young could never understand the psychological warfare that had been exacted upon the people before the Rebellion, and the shock that came to many of them when their world fell apart. When all of what they thought they understood about the world was shown to be a lie, a lie told to them by the people they trusted most. Some people went insane during this period. They could not cope with the curtain being pulled back, to find that they had been dispossessed of everything that mattered. But most were angry. Once the shock had worn off the rage could not be contained. Perhaps it was for this reason that the old rarely talked of this time. Many people did not want to be reminded of the horrors that took place, or of the acts that they themselves committed.

It had not happened overnight, of course.

It had been brewing for decades, and tensions finally boiled over with the M62 Rebellion in the summer of 2027, so-called because the conflicts began in the towns along the M62 corridor, particularly the Lancashire mill towns north of Manchester. Regardless of how the government tried to cover it up from the eyes of the rest of the country, towns like Oldham and Rochdale were in a state of low-level civil war, and this reality could no longer be denied when the police station bombings began. But so many people, absorbed in the fantasy blue-light world of their simulated moving images, did not look up to see the skies darkening. Or perhaps they sensed the skies darkening and buried themselves in the traditional cultural products that served them the same old reassuring message that none of their unvoiced fears would come to pass. That everything was going to be just fine, as it always had been. But they were sleeping on the edge of Vesuvius, and it had to blow sometime. That sometime was June 7, 2028, when a co-ordinated attack against two major television stations and a national newspaper left 96 people dead and hundreds injured.

'Of course, at that time,' said Aoife, 'it wasn't as much of a surprise as you might think. Things were happening on virtually a daily basis around Europe and North America. Most people assumed that it would be Islamists, and they just rolled their eyes. A lot of people had stopped watching these TV stations anyway, because they had become so associated with propaganda. Certainly, the newspaper office that their gunmen targeted had been losing millions every year – it was only in existence to prop up the communist message. But these attacks were much more important than the Heathrow attack the year before, or the slaughter of the 300 schoolchildren who had been held hostage at Ampleforth, even though fewer people died overall. Much, much more important.' She paused for emphatic effect. 'Because this attack had been carried out by the English themselves. This was something new, very new. Perpetua, can you get me my whisky from the shelf over there? There should be a glass there too.' Aoife nodded in the direction of the display cabinet behind the couch.

Perpetua hurried to get the crystal decanter of whisky with a glass from the top shelf, which had miraculously managed to stay in one piece despite the constant presence of boisterous children. When Aoife asked for a nip of whisky it was a sign that her comments were going to be particularly interesting, and Perpetua, eager to hear more, didn't want her to lose her pace.

Aoife's gnarled fingers struggled to grip the glass stopper against the force of air-tight seal and wordlessly passed it to Perpetua as she continued her commentary.

'Yes, this was something completely new. It was traumatizing, of course, but it was also a powerful symbol that the people had had enough of the lies. The authorities tried to patch things together afterwards, and more people watched TV than usual out of curiosity, but it was clear that journalists and presenters were now afraid to put their faces out there. Television had lost its veneer of neutrality decades before, but now it was open for everyone to see. Television and the gutter press pretty much died that day.'

She took a sip of her whisky and sat back, letting the pendulum of the clock swung backwards and forwards like a metronome, giving a soothing massage to the flow of time. 'Of course, you won't know what television is like. It shaped the people's consciousness and manufactured consent for the England our enemies wanted to impose on us. And this destruction of European peoples ran internationally. It's why Europe and North America went up in flames around the same time, with the cities of the nations falling simultaneously. The nationalists knew right away that television and the mobile network had to go. Transmitters all over England were bombed, and there were surgical strikes against the power grid, leaving millions in darkness, and just as importantly, without the reassurance of the 24-hour news cycle. The EF wanted to ensure that there was no longer a centralised narrative direct from the government to the people. The message became fractured and local, and was mediated through EF forces. Government surveillance systems were destroyed, cameras and recording equipment banned in territory the EF controlled, control which they consolidated as the government was forced to deal with the rioting and looting in the biggest cities.' Aoife took a deep breath, and another sip of her whisky.

'But you wouldn't believe the upheaval that the disruption to television caused. Even though we'd had a decade of bombings, filth and savagery, it seemed that people could keep it all together in their minds and as long as the TV keep pumping out its familiar programming. Television was the main prop shoring up this fake universal conscience and when it went down, the reality of the situation could be avoided no longer.'

Aoife swirled the whisky and watched the golden liquid climb the sides of the glass. 'It was a very bad time for me. I had two young sons at that point, and I was getting visions, lots of visions. It was very hard for me to know what was real, what I was dreaming, and what was actually a vision of future reality. I found myself sleeping all the time. Impossibly vivid dreams that I couldn't wake up from. At its worst it seemed like I was only awake for an hour a day. And when I was awake there was a constant tension in my ears, like there was an intense high-pitched screech that was in the air but which others didn't hear. My mother-in-law had to take the kids.'

Perpetua nodded. She wondered if she should mention Felicity and her dreams at this point, but lost her nerve and the moment slipped away.

Aoife continued. 'It was terrible to be snared in such an evil time. It wasn't just the violence. It was the suspicion of others that was the worst thing. People who had grown up together as friends suddenly turned on each other, as skin colour and facial features defined a person more than years of shared history. Because people were frightened. And when you're frightened, you're too scared to take a risk. The worst part though was the fact that it wasn't just an ethnic thing. There is this idea that we went tribal along racial lines, but that's not true. The most shocking violence took place between the English themselves – those who supported the nationalist cause and those who supported the government and the existing culture. It was bitter... sick.' Aoife took another sip from the glass as she remembered the fighting. 'The real hate was between the English themselves, because this was a hatred that had been festering long before any immigrants arrived to this island. Long before. The resentment went back centuries and just needed an excuse to bubble to the surface.' She stared at Perpetua with those lively green eyes, and Perpetua imagined how much energy Aoife must have had as a young woman. 'The greatest hatred was for the traitors. Why do you think that the communists and the Old Families are so terrified in their London stronghold, surrounding themselves with their Islamic ring of steel?' She wagged an arthritic finger in Perpetua's direction. 'Because they know what will happen to them when the English Front eventually get their hands on them. And mark my words, that time is coming.' She finished the last of the whisky, and held out her glass to Perpetua in expectation of it being refilled.

'But what worries me is that the *polity of unjust stewards* have a trick up their sleeves. We can't continue in this standoff, but the danger in trying to crush the head of the snake is immense. They would not think twice about using the Samson Option against us if they were facing their own destruction.'

Perpetua frowned. She knew the story of Samson, about how he had been betrayed by Delilah who had cut his hair, but she didn't see what that had to do with the situation here.

Aoife sensed the girl's lack of understanding. 'Samson destroyed the temple with himself in it, because his main concern was killing his enemies. This is what worries me – that their desire to see their enemies dead far outstrips their own will to survive. They are really counting on winning the war in Europe.'

Perpetua said nothing, because she could think of nothing intelligent to say. Aoife suddenly seemed to realise that she was talking to a sixteen-year-old girl because she pulled herself up with an unconvincing attempt at chatty feminine jollity.

'So, when are you getting married?' Aoife knew the answer of course, but she wanted to change the subject – thinking about such dark topics was very unhealthy for a young girl, a girl who she knew would soon be carrying the first of her great-grandchildren.

'Six weeks' said Perpetua, in a daze. Thoughts of her upcoming wedding seemed a bit surreal given what they had been talking about.

'Good, good!' said Aoife. 'You mustn't let me

get you down when I ramble on. It's exactly because our lives are so difficult that we have to cherish these occasions. That love and hope survive through this is all the more reason to celebrate. That's the thing, Perpetua, these people tried to take away our humanity, and weddings and baptisms are reminders that even through all of this, people are falling in love and making a commitment to each other, and striving to create families, to survive through time. You won't remember this of course, but they tried to take all that away before the war. Because *they...*' Aoife almost spat the word in disgust '...know that love, real unconditional love, and the bonds of family that it leads to, are the most important thing for the soul of a people.'

Perpetua found something to say. 'Have you seen my dress?'

Aoife smiled. 'No, no, I haven't. Tell me about it.'

Aoife sat back and prepared to escape into a world of sequins, lace and the design alterations that CeeCee had made to a used wedding dress to create something new and special for the girl that everyone knew would be a stunning young bride. She tried to remember what it was like being sixteen years old, when everything was exciting and new, and life, even at its darkest moments, was still full of promise and hope because she had time on her side. She imagined what stories Perpetua would tell when she herself was 61, in an England at the beginning of the 22nd century. Would there even be an England? She could, of course, find out if she really wanted to, but she had closed the doors to the knowledge of eternity for a very good reason.

As Aoife watched the animated girl talk about her arrangements for the wedding party, something inexplicable itched in the old woman about the decision she had taken two years ago.

CHAPTER 16

William was on one of his regular journeys down to Wales as part of a large trading convoy. While these convoys took place every week, this particular expedition would be different, as it would require a detour to Aberystwyth. There were hopes that the Keeper of the National Library could be persuaded to part with at least some of his medieval vernacular manuscripts for export to America, where a collector was willing to pay a very high price for any, ideally all, of the collection. The Welsh were desperately poor, and the EF needed the injection of vital supplies that such an exchange would bring, but at the same time West Wales was one of the safest parts of EF territory, and the Welsh were fiercely proud of their heritage. Discussions about the matter had been held with Cardiff, who had finally told the Northwest EF that any decision would finally rest with Hywel, the Keeper of the Collection. Clearly, the Welsh EF understood that, by passing the decision over to him, there would be no risk of any manuscript leaving the country.

Relations with the Welsh EF were fraught with tension, as the oxymoron of their name itself would imply. During the 2020s, anti-English feeling had been particularly strong in Wales, as the rich liberal urbanites who had been steadily leaving the multicultural cities of England for a 'better quality of life' in rural Wales found themselves among a hostile population who blamed them for the state of Britain, and who did not want them doing to rural Wales what they had done to England. As the flow of *Saxons seeking hospitality* increased, the anti-English killings began, with one former marketing executive from Hoxton being impaled on a stake in the front garden of his Manordeilo cottage in 2032. News of this killing had the intended effect of frightening many English refugees back over the Danube (as the Severn was jokingly called), but the local militias knew that they had to put an end to such ethnic conflicts. Strength lay in numbers, and the men of Wales knew that they would need both English cooperation and knowhow if they were to retake the South from SAU-communist control and keep it. Even if it meant Wales effectively falling under the English Front's protection.

On the understanding that the newcomers would have to earn their place, grateful Eng-

From the Land All the Good Things Come

lish refugees began pouring into Wales in large numbers. But despite the Welsh leadership's message to the people that petty nationalisms had to be set aside for the greater good, that the fate of England would seal the fate of Wales, it stood to reason that many of the Welsh population felt resentful of being pushed yet further west by the Anglo-Saxons. Understanding where such resentments could lead, the English worked to mitigate the rising popular notion of a *new English annexation* by adopting the tactics of Fourth Generation warfare, running supplies to isolated local people, letting the Welsh deal with their own troublemakers, and helping to organise *eisteddfodau*. But with the situation deteriorating, it soon became clear to everyone that greater goals had to be achieved, and it was not long before the Welsh and English formed a singular fighting force as they laid siege to Cardiff and Swansea, eventually clearing the land of their enemies and closing the chapter on the long 20th century.

The trade in national treasures was nothing new. It had begun before the war had even started, with the venal Conservative government of the day raising eyebrows when it sold Thomas Becket's relic casket to the Chinese as part of a debt restructuring deal, thus paving the way for a flow of antiquities out of the UK to China that wags dubbed *the pewter road*. The Conservatives argued that the sale of art and antiquities was a practical solution to the plummeting pound, weak bond markets, and a crisis in council funding. Given that many museums and galleries struggled to keep the lights on, to say nothing of the extra staffing and security costs that these buildings now required, the government argued that it made sense to leverage English heritage for the greater national interest. Crucially, polls showed that only the older members of the legacy population held any real objection to the practice.

Unsurprisingly, it was not long before nationalists, with the collusion of concerned curators, began removing key pieces from museums and art galleries. After an asylum seeker's paring knife sliced through the milky white flesh of two of the bathing beauties in *Hylas and the Nymphs* in April 2022, many paintings and sculptures were permitted to be put into storage due to the risk of malicious damage, a risk deemed to be particularly high when the work of art in question could be interpreted as celebrating female beauty, British history or the Christian religion. After the *Hylas incident*, as it came to be known, curators understood that it was imperative to get the exhibits to safety, and many of the items in storage appeared in the inventory but not in fact, with a well-wrapped replica standing in its place. At this point, with insurance costs soaring, it made sense to replace even many of the items on public show with reproductions. It was not only the public that the curators had to fear – legislation passed in 2023 allowed the government to requisition any item deemed 'English heritage' from a public institution whenever it wished, and such an item could, and often did, mysteriously reappear in a Saudi palace or Qatari hotel a few weeks later.

Not only were the more beautiful items at risk. Rumours had been circulating that the Swedish Minister for Culture had ordered that newly discovered Viking artefacts be melted down and recycled, with her reported to have said of the policy 'we don't need more nails and torque bangles for blond Nazis to masturbate over – we need money to pay for heating and school meals'. It may have only been fake news invented in the wake of the increasingly regular power blackouts in Sweden around the same time, but it spurred a great deal of curators and historians to start quietly removing the smaller and more nondescript exhibits that would not be so greatly missed.

As the civil war went hot and public order broke down, opposing forces raced to loot the galleries and museums for the black market. The EF made several arrangements with American dealers, crucial at a time when funds were needed to buy weaponry from abroad. Over the course of years, crates and crates of centuries of English art, antiques and antiquities made their way to the New World, with little argument from the English of the big cities who knew that although it pained them to see the material legacy of their ancestors leave their native soil, *where it belonged*, the land itself was not secure enough to ensure that these treasures would not be stolen or destroyed.

But this request for the Welsh medieval manuscripts, with particular interest in the White Book of Rhydderch and the Red Book of Hergest, was highly unusual. Given that the ninety-year-old Welsh-speaking Keeper now slept in the Collections room, it was highly unlikely that he would agree to part with any of the artefacts, which he considered under his protection. It was he who had painstakingly catalogued and researched the manuscripts at the turn of the century and then published his findings in a three-volume catalogue twenty years later, never realizing that one day, this catalogue would be the means by which a foreign collector would covet these treasures and seek to remove them from the country. The collection spanned over a thousand years of Welsh scribes, who first wrote in Latin and then in Middle Welsh as the centuries progressed, and was substantially augmented during the 2020s when concerned Oxbridge scholars arranged for manuscripts housed within their institutions to be sent indefinitely to Aberystwyth for 'exhibitions'. William knew that the collection was priceless and should never be removed from Wales.

And yet. After Hywel's spirit passed in turn into the history of the land, would there be a single scholar in Wales with such intellect and training who could decipher these texts, often written in impossible handwriting, and in scripts which haven't been used in a millennium? Was it so important that the texts remain on the land, if there were no-one who could read them? Wouldn't it be more meaningful for the texts to be with those who were able to understand them, rather than those who could appreciate them only as totems of history? And if this collector were of Welsh ancestry, would this strengthen his case for purchase?

William knew that such arguments would hold little sway with the Welsh. The Albionic Church understood more than most how a celebrated ancient object could become sacred in the minds of the people, possessing to all intents and purposes magical powers which made it crucial to the fate of the nation. When this occurred, all rational notions such as material benefit, even for survival itself, meant nothing. If there were any risk to the library's integrity then of course the objects could be taken by force, but Aberystwyth, on the west coast of Wales, was at the safest edge of the most secure zone of EF territory, barring the Cornish Peninsula. If Aberystwyth fell it was because the entire EF had been defeated, and at that stage the Welsh would not be concerned with the fate of their manuscripts. The Albionic Church, which adapted its teachings within Welsh territory to include the mythos of the *original Britons* lest a millennium-old wound become reopened at the most inopportune time in British history, would say that the manuscripts should remain in Wales as long as the blood of the scribes' descendants still pumped through their hearts, even it meant the eventual oblivion of the manuscripts. Such romantic dogmatism was generally helpful for steeling national resolve, but it could occasionally be obstructive when more pragmatic aims needed to be achieved.

But opening discussions with Hywel could still bear fruit in the long term. He might be persuaded that after his death the manuscripts would be better on American soil for their long-term preservation, because no-one had devoted his life to the collection as he had. If he wrote a testament giving his blessing for their sale after his death, that would go a long way to striking up an agreement with the buyer, who was talking in terms of millions of NAC dollars. A man who was prepared to pay such money even for a few of these manuscripts was a man who would work to preserve them for eternity. *After all,* as William reasoned to himself, *refugees had been sent to America in the 2040s for their own safety, so why not our chronicles?* He was glad not to be leading the negotiations. That was being left to Wansbrough, who had asked to join the convoy for this trip to be able to meet the renowned Hywel Huws. Wansbrough had brought his protégé along with him as well, no doubt so that the boy could see a bit of the Welsh countryside and the now-dilapidated National Library.

The green rolling hills and hedgerows flew past the van window. It was easy to forget that a civil war had torn the country apart as one travelled through the countryside of what one commentator had dubbed 'the breadbasket of England'. But it was a region which was still very insecure on the borderlands and which required much defence. It would only about be another hour now until they reached the coast. William was anxious for that moment when he could get out of the van and walk around the quiet pristine town of the coast, but at the same time he knew that the journey's end would bring him closer to the time that he would no longer get to experience that vague sense of respite and peace from the pressures of England.

CHAPTER 17

Morgenna had woken again with her heart pounding. Another dream of Edwin, this time of his spirit wandering around the road where he died, trying to find the cold grey parts of his body that had been scattered in the bomb blast over the fields around Blackburn. His ghost had been pleading for a proper burial. Since that night, Morgenna had actively tried to suppress all thought of the moment that her eldest son had been killed, and the pain he must have felt, but as John had reassured her, he would have known nothing about it.

'It would have been over in seconds,' John had told her on the night he got back from America, after he came into the room to find her sitting in silence on the edge of their bed, her head bowed in a wordless prayer to God.

But the thoughts that Morgenna actively worked to suppress during the day came to avenge themselves in her dreams, and over the past week these dreams had been especially vivid. An enemy drone had managed to fly into the area around St Helens, but rather than drop a bomb, it had decided to drop flyers with photographs of the mutilated corpses of the dead. EF soldiers had been quick to gather up and destroy these flyers, but not before a few had been picked up by children and taken home, and word spread about the identity of the corpses featured. Morgenna had overheard the rumour that Edwin's mutilated corpse was among the photographs. There was no way of finding out for sure: talking about the matter was an arrestable offence and the few remaining flyers that had escaped the first requisition had been tracked down and destroyed. The SAU might not have dropped a physical bomb that night, but it had dropped an emotional one, and it was one that devastated Morgenna. She struggled in the mornings now, as the terrors of the night left her more exhausted than the endless chores of the day.

The SAU had taken to dropping flyers onto EF territory, or *nickelling* as it was known, when they came to realise that the Internet videos they made of the humiliation, torture and rape of English girls and captured soldiers did not reach the eyes of the target population. The sophisticated Internet propaganda put out by London was almost as unsuccessful. This led to dirty, rain-soaked flyers beginning to appear in random streets, apparently having dropped from the sky. Flyers which spread plausible allegations about named EF commanders and which accused specific Albionic priests of sodomy and Satanism. Even when flyers were quickly confiscated, and their possession made a floggable offence, they were effective in spreading fear and suspicion. It led the EF high command to wonder how London could be gathering such intelligence, which in turn led to the suspicion of spies within the camp. Morgenna knew that it was the reason why John, like most husbands, said so little about EF business.

The flyers also gave mothers a new fear to add to those that they already had; that their children might come across a frightening flyer while they were out playing. Morgenna shuddered at the thought of Seb having picked up a flyer with an image of his dead brother's face on it.

'Take this to protect you.'

Morgenna pressed a tiny vial into Seb's hand as he was getting ready to leave the house. These water amulets, which by their nature contained a drop of blood, were unauthorised by the Church, but a mother's lust for miracles would always be more compelling than religious scruple. Seb said nothing. He had no particular belief in the validity of these charms but he knew that it was important to his mother and he could tell from the dark circles under her eyes that she had not slept well. He would do whatever it took to make her feel better.

'Don't dawdle on the way there. You know that drone-strikes can happen during the day too.'

Seb could tell from his mother's pinched, pale face that it would not be productive to point out that he was more at risk of being killed in the school building than in the street. He knew that deep down she knew this herself. It was why, after the Merton Bank kindergarten bombing in 2056 in which 29 babies and infants were killed and 53 others viciously maimed, many of these injured children dying long, drawn-out deaths from infection months later, that parents started to find more decentralised solutions for their childcare. It was also the reasons why school numbers were kept small, and why locations for teaching were changed every year. The SAU knew that when English children were killed the community was most heavily affected.

He put his arms around his mother to say goodbye and then opened the door to leave. The English now lived with much more immediacy. Priorities were different. The smallest blessings that God bestowed were appreciated and the adversities of life were born with stoicism, if only because there was no-one to complain to. Everyone was in the same boat. Everyone had suffered. Many had lost children – if not to the fighting or the drone strikes, then to the epidemics which periodically swept through the land. Morgenna remembered how back in 2048 a few of Edwin's classmates died during the measles outbreak and Edwin himself was so ill that they thought they were going to lose him too.

Death had returned to sitting on the shoulder of every English family, and giving life its true perspective.

Morgenna wondered for a minute what it was like for the SAU mothers. Death took their children too. They too suffered during the epidemics. But any sympathy she may have had soon evaporated when she remembered that they had no place in these lands, and that their very presence was causing the suffering and death of her own people. As for the ambitious middle- and upper-class English who vied for office in the occupied territories, who sent their children to Arabic tutors and madrassas for that all important cultural edge when competing for the civil service jobs which still needed English blood to function with any form of competence, well, she had no words for them. She loathed them more than anyone else. They had swapped their dignity as human beings for the preservation of their wealth and influence, in a country in which markers of class and social status **was** *everything* to people like them. But the new regime had had the last laugh at these pathetic attempts to maintain the old English caste system. SAU courts, where a native Englishman would never be allowed to preside as judge, would always rule that the *diya*, or blood-price, for a dead white man was half that of anyone in the *communities*. And native women and children were worth even less. Despite their best efforts at assimilation and religious conversion, the social realities for the native English were the same. *They may as well still be wearing those yellow crosses sewn onto their coats and shirts*, thought Morgenna. But she had no sympathy for them. They were the lowest of the low.

She watched her beautiful young boy make his way up the garden path. Through her tiredness she could feel a strange feeling in her belly that she hadn't felt in years. Her thoughts were cut short by the sound of her lerter going off in the living room.

It was John.

The Russians had finally invaded German territory.

CHAPTER 18

They had decided to wait the four days until the new moon, so that the drones would neither form a dark silhouette against the moonlit sky nor cast a shadow against the ground. The black machines stirred into life like monsters of Frankenstein and hovered silently in the air as if waiting for the bidding of their masters. They rose up high into the sky and shot away without conscience or emotion, blindly obedient to their role as the agents of death on the orders of their creator. Like legions of minor demons unleashed from the portals of Hell opened up in several corners of England, the drones crossed moorland, field, fen and river, until soil ceded to tarmac and concrete, and the mechanised vampire bats floated silently over rooftops and cathedral spires.

At the designated co-ordinates, hundreds of millions of tiny spores, packaged into millions of tiny seeds, blew out onto the wind. Seeds which would eventually fall to earth, and settle imperceptibly on every surface.

The angels of death had passed over the people and began the return to their origins in the darkness. Now only time would reveal the sentence on the people that the angels had delivered.

CHAPTER 19

Nothing had changed qualitatively for the people of Merseyside since the news of the Russian invasion of Germany. There was simply a nervousness. The endgame, which the English had been waiting on for over fifteen years, could not be long in coming. The Russians were intent on restoring order to Germany, and bringing it into the fold of Orlov Empire as the final Baltic satellite state. Germany was tired, very tired, and vassalage to a militantly Christian Russia could not be worse than the degradation that its good people had been forced to suffer over many generations for having once dared to defend themselves. It was impossible to know how long it would take to subdue the Germanic territories, however. Islamic Germany had strong ties to Turkey and, psychologically, the Turks saw themselves as the rightful inheritors of the land. Turkey, which sat in opposition to the Russian-backed Iranian-Syrian alliance which dominated the Middle East, needed the Islamocommunist alliance of Western Europe to prevail or it would find itself isolated on all sides and extremely vulnerable. To achieve this end, Turkey was sending northwards its most vicious and dedicated fighters.

Certainly, Perpetua, as she read Pritchard's *Dimensions* to Aoife, who was lying back in her armchair, had little idea of what was happening on the continent. It was all so complicated and boring. A bit like this book. The words were very long and weird, and she kept stumbling because she didn't know how to pronounce them.

> *Is our very flesh annulled with the certainty that everything has already been written and history is at its end, and we are left to create our own meanings in the soul-crushing void? A young woman who sacrifices her sexual essence by cutting off her own breasts and excising the life-giving womb from her body, in a futile bid to imitate the Platonic ideal that exists only outside of time and space, renders herself phantasmal in this plane, but is told that she realises herself in another. Is this drive to turn our people into figless trees less the work of a racial enemy than a jealous demiurge?*

She looked up after yet another guess at saying a word, wondering what Aoife would say, but the old woman had her eyes closed.

Aoife sensed the girl's silence, and listened to the pendulum of the clock clicking backwards and forwards, marking off each passing second. Finally, she spoke. 'The old Satanic order was about destroying the polarities. Especially the sexual polarity of masculine and feminine, which is a very powerful force of nature. But they did not succeed, of course. Under this new order, or should I say *old order*, the natural order, we have restored the polarities to our society.' Still with her eyes closed, she continued. 'So are you going to tell me about your pregnant friend's dreams?'

Perpetua gasped. *How did she know?*

Aoife, still with her eyes closed, smiled. 'Did nobody tell you that the longer you sit in my presence the more I will tune with your energy and merge with your soul?' She laughed while still feigning sleep. 'Why do you think I sit without company most of the time?' Her eyes sprang open and looked straight at Perpetua.

Perpetua knew that honesty could be the only option in this instance.

'It's my friend Felicity. She's three months pregnant, but her boyfriend was a Wolf who was killed about six weeks ago. Since then she has been having all sorts of dreams about her baby. I'm worried that she is losing touch with reality because she doesn't want to deal with her situation. But it might also be that her dreams are real, and they are giving us messages about the future that we need to heed. I don't know whether to try to get her help, or to listen to her. I'm worried about her.'

'You are right to be worried,' said Aoife. 'There are strange things happening in England right now, all kinds of prodigies and monstrous births. Jael Adcock's young son is very sick, and the doctors don't know what it is. This morning a crow sat on the window ledge and tapped on the window with its beak three times. Three times, Perpetua. It is clear that the spirits want to get a message through. I have felt them tingling at my flesh these past few weeks as they try to merge with me but I have deliberately kept myself closed to them. But with the crow this morning I feel that if I do not yield to their request then something terrible will happen. For them to intercede in the physical world like this means that it is very important. Very important indeed.'

Perpetua wanted to make sure that she got her best friend to the house before Aoife changed her mind. 'When would you like to see Felicity? I can bring her here today if you like.' Perpetua reached for her lerter as she waited for Aoife to answer.

'Yes, yes, if you can bring her here before the children come home.' Aoife suddenly looked distracted.

Perpetua did not need to be told twice. She lerted Felicity, telling her get to Matt's house as soon as possible. *Aoife had agreed to see her!*

The young girl looked back at the old woman, as the gnarled fingers passed feverishly over the hematite beads of her Albionic rosary. Perpetua wasn't sure if the muttering to herself wasn't a prayer.

'The spirits of our ancestors are incredibly close at the moment,' said Aoife. 'They are so close as to be stalking the land. They are longing to materialise on this plane. I can tell that this is because the final battle is soon to come.'

Perpetua looked anxious. 'Will it be before my wedding?' Her wedding was a month away, and it would be just her luck that it would be called off because of the war. If the world was to burn, could it at least burn after her special day, so that she could die as a married woman?

Aoife's eyes looked towards Perpetua, but seemed to be looking through her, as if at the future itself. 'You will get your wedding. It will not be as you expect, but you will be married.' She changed her focus of attention to the lerter in Perpetua's hands. 'What has your friend said? Is she coming today?'

'Oh yes,' said Perpetua. 'She's on her way now.'

CHAPTER 20

A brisk evening breeze tugged at the tussock grass and sent a million lightly-singing grains of sand in rippling waves across the Aberystwyth sands. Dr. Wansbrough lifted his hand from the old tartan blanket spread out underneath the two of them, and brushed distractedly at the tiny grains that had settled into the hair on the back of his hand. His mind had briefly wandered, as it was its wont, to darker concerns. He returned his attention to Alban and broke his moment of introspection with a broad smile. 'The stars are showing already.'

Alban looked towards the dying light of the horizon but couldn't see what his master was referring to. He looked back at his teacher who smiled and pointed upwards. Following the vertical direction of his master's finger, the boy realised that he could see the stars if he bent his head right back against the nape of his neck so that the skin touched, and looked straight upwards, where the sky was darkest.

Dr. Wansbrough watched the boy throwing his

head back with the ease and insouciance of youth. It had been a good idea to bring him here, with all of this space and the waves of the sea just a few yards away.

Alban heard the old man's voice over the crashing of the waves. 'Look at how the floor of heaven is thick inlaid with patins of bright gold!' Alban brought his blond head back down to the terrestrial plane and looked at Dr. Wansbrough quizzically.

'Shakespeare,' Dr. Wansbrough explained. The boy seemed quite happy with that explanation, and turned his face back up to the skies.

Dr. Wansbrough ran his fingers through the silky sand, and looked up at the same constellations that were absorbing the boy. After a minute, the doctor spoke. 'I have a question for you, young Alban. It's a bit of a puzzle. I want you to think about it.

'Okay', said Alban. Alban liked the doctor's puzzles. They were always very interesting.

'You know how Judas was given thirty pieces of silver to betray Jesus?'

Alban nodded.

'Well, imagine that instead of buying his field of blood, he decided to lend out one of his pieces of silver, call it a silver pound, at six percent interest. And then imagine that the debt was never repaid, and it kept growing. And growing. Until now. How many silver pounds do you think that Judas would be owed?'

Alban smiled. *That was over two thousand years ago! How was he supposed to work that one out, sitting on a beach?* He thought hard. *This must be a trick question, or Dr. Wansbrough would not be asking it.* He decided to be ridiculous, because he really had no idea.

'I think,' said Alban, 'that after two thousand years Judas would be owed a million pounds.'

Dr. Wansbrough smiled and raised an eyebrow. 'So little?'

Alban screwed up his face. *What was the guy talking about? Six percent wasn't that much interest, that was just, like, sixpence on the pound. And a million pounds was a lot of money! This must be another of his trick scenarios.*

Dr. Wansbrough seemed to read Alban's mind. 'No, it really is just six percent interest. The answer is, that if you borrowed a silver pound from Judas at the time of Jesus's crucifixion you would be due 409 million pounds...' Dr. Wansbrough paused, enjoying seeing Alban's reaction, '... that is, 409 million pounds, followed by forty-two zeros. Or 4.09 pounds times ten to the power of fifty.' Dr. Wansbrough paused again, to give the boy time to try to understand what he was saying. 'That's four hundred quindecillion pounds, more or less. Give or take the odd quindecillion.' The old man smiled again at the boy's consternation.

After a moment of doubt Alban looked again at Dr. Wansbrough, who nodded in confirmation. The young boy shook his head in disbelief. He didn't even know what a quindecillion was.

'Four hundred quindecillion. Is that more than the number of grains of sand on this beach?'

Dr. Wansbrough grinned broadly and picked up a handful of sand in his left hand. Holding this hand up high, he let the sand run through his fingers dramatically. 'It's more than the total number of grains of sand in all the beaches and all the deserts... of the world!' The doctor laughed loudly when he saw the boy shake his head again trying to understand it.

There was a silence as Alban thought for a moment. 'Is that more than all the stars in the sky?'

Dr. Wansbrough kept smiling, but pursed his lips at the boy's canny question. 'It's more than all the stars in the Milky Way, which is our galaxy, but not in the entire universe. You would need a slightly higher interest rate for *that*.' He chuckled softly at his own joke.

Alban starting playing with the sand on the beach, letting the fine grains slip through his fingers as the breeze from the tide blew towards them both and the last light from the hidden sun glowed above the horizon. He liked being with Dr. Wansbrough like this, being told all of these wonderful things, but he was confused by all of the large numbers that his teacher was throwing at him. It didn't seem possible. He knew though that it must be true because Dr. Wansbrough never lied. Ever. Even if it made him seem rude to some people.

'The point of my puzzle is, young Alban, that compound interest, which is the basis of money-lending, is evil, because it destroys everything it touches. No amount of wealth production in the world can keep up with it. Because of that, it wrecks families, governments and nations without fail. All that is needed to complete the destruction is the dimension of time. It takes everything the debtor has. Forget Doctor Faustus, it's usury that is the original pact with the devil.' Dr. Wansbrough sighed. 'The English elites made that pact with the devil hundreds of years ago, and it led us to where we are today. By the grace of God we are still here, just, having narrowly avoided our own genocide, a genocide which was factored into the loan payments.

It's why state-backed usury always leads to war. Because the money-lenders need more and more. The world is not enough for them.'

There was a lull in the conversation as Alban tried to take in what he was being told. Dr. Wansbrough continued. 'The King of Spain, Philip the Second, owned every single silver and gold mine in the New World. Imagine that. All of the precious metals of the Americas. And this was when gold and silver was the only valid money. But still he went bankrupt because of money he owed to his usurer. A government in debt requires the conquest and plunder of entire continents just to keep up with repayments, but even then the debt gets too much. It's why the Habsburg Empire went bankrupt, and why the United States of America crumbled into war. Compound interest.'

Alban was confused. 'Isn't... money-lending a sin in the Bible?'

'Yes, it is. The ancient philosophers, both Testaments, the Fathers of the Church, they all declared that to take money for the use of money is sinful. Officially. But just as usury makes a select few very rich and powerful, so they pay the best sophists to distort the faith of the nation in order to rationalise the practice and justify the theft. They forget, however, that God sees all.' Dr. Wansbrough closed his eyes and recited the verse:

> *Your silver has become dross,*
> *your choice wine is diluted with water.*
> *Your rulers are rebels,*
> *partners with thieves;*
> *they all love bribes*
> *and chase after gifts.*

'It's why Philip the Second's banker put money aside for the poor to pray for his soul in perpetuity. Twice a day, even now, over a hundred Germans are duty-bound to pray for the soul of Jakob Fugger, usurer. But there will be no love in their prayers, and as such, the prayers will go unheeded by God. Even after death, the bankers think that they can use their loot to buy their way out of the reckoning for their crimes.' Dr. Wansbrough shook his head. 'But they are very much mistaken. They are stuck for eternity in the seventh circle of Hell, along with the sodomites. Because both turn fertile young bodies into nothing but a weight of carrion flesh.'

He stood up, vaguely irritated, and threw a pebble towards the foaming tide, which was edging closer. There was clearly no purpose to throwing the stone, other than to expend the restless energy which had built up as he spoke.

'Confucius, an ancient Chinese philosopher,

once said: "the beginning of wisdom is to call things by their proper name". Which is the key to how the English were kept stupid for so long. They didn't know the proper names for the things that were happening to them. As such, they could not properly understand their own world. To solve a problem, you first need to understand the nature of the problem.' He looked towards Alban for confirmation that he understood, and the boy nodded. 'The capitalism of the West was nothing but state-backed usury, a usuriocracy, if you like. It was borrowing from the future the fruits of the labour of the as-yet-unborn.' Dr. Wansbrough looked seriously at Alban's inquisitive young face, as one of those who had not yet been born when past governments had thought nothing of loading down his generation with an unpayable debt in order to keep themselves in favour. 'But then the future came. The unborn were born. And they did not have the means to pay the quadrillions of the national debt.'

'Once the usurers take control of the money supply, they control everything, EVERYTHING, until the imbalances within the system grow so strong that society itself eventually disintegrates. Before the Rebellion, we had a debt-based economy and debt-based currency, which meant that, with every transaction, money flowed upward towards a few private hands, leaving less and less for the people, which drove them to ever more desperate measures. Normally, in these situations, when there is a total collapse, the usurers move on to feast on the flesh of new victims, to loot new civilisations, but for the first time in history the collapse was global, meaning that *the cankerworm that spoileth* for once could not fly away.'

Alban reckoned that he was understanding about half of what Dr. Wansbrough was talking about, but he hoped that if his teacher kept talking, it would make more and more sense.

'Couldn't they have run to China?' Alban knew that China had been the only major country to have avoided civil war. If anything, it has capitalised on the conflicts in Europe and North America to make bold moves into Africa to plunder its mineral riches.

'No. The Chinese barred all immigration of non-Chinese into China and Australia. Not that the Western elites would want to run to Australia anyway. It's not called *China's Afghanistan* for nothing.'

Alban nodded, though he didn't understand the Afghanistan reference. He didn't want to ask and get Dr. Wansbrough off-topic, as Dr. Wansbrough could go off on tangents for a long time. Sometimes even his tangents went off into tangents. And this subject was interesting.

'They are trapped in London, aren't they?'

'Yes, mainly. But they've also got most of the Home Counties. Paris is another major stronghold. New York, though the New York enclave has already split into three parts. Soon that will be gone. They are dotted around, protected by their mercenary armies in a very fragile alliance. They think that they can ride the Islamic tiger as it destroys their enemies, but they risk becoming cat food themselves. The so-called great men of the earth thought that they could stand far off and watch the torment from their tax-havens in the Caribbean, but life became very difficult for them once the British military withdrew from the Overseas Territories.'

As the old man talked, Tommy Spencer, one of the soldiers of the convoy who had been riding with them in the same lorry on the journey down, shouted across the sand and came to join them. He was carrying a knapsack in one hand.

'How are you two getting on? I bet the good doctor has been filling your brain with lots of good stuff, eh?' He slapped the young lad's back affectionately. Alban's rare presence as a child in the convoy had made the soldiers feel very paternal towards him.

Dr. Wansbrough smiled. 'We've just been talking about economics.'

Tommy made a wincing noise. 'Ooh, rather you than me, Alban me lad. Economics is beyond me!'

Alban felt the need to defend his mentor, even though in truth he knew that he didn't understanding half of it. 'Oh no, not at all. It's really interesting.' As if to prove his enthusiasm for the older man's talks, he decided to ask a question that had been nagging at him for a while, but for which he had hoped to find the answer on his own. He turned to his beloved mentor.

'Sir, why are our enemies called communists, if the bankers were capitalists, and everybody's chasing money? I really don't get that. Isn't communism the opposite of capitalism?'

Dr. Wansbrough nodded thoughtfully at the question, like he was pleased that Alban had thought of it. Tommy crouched down near the edge of the rug, but stayed silent and busied himself with looking in his bag, as if he wanted to hear the answer but was frightened of being called upon to participate a response, being a fellow adult.

'That is a *very* good question, Alban. And a question that a lot of people won't even have thought about. On the surface, communism is very good at diagnosing the problems of capitalism, which is why people assume that they are antithetical to each other. But in fact, the so-called solution that communism offers leads to exactly the same dead-eyed bondage as the problem it claims to solve. Because, like capitalism, it is atheistic and internationalist. Like capitalism it is purely based in the material, and people are nothing but units of production and consumption. Like capitalism it strips the individual from the meaning of family, seeing only his or her importance as worker. As Jesus said in Matthew seven, *you shall know them by their fruits*. And what are the fruits of communism? An enforced equality that ensures a dysgenic and dispiriting effect on the individual, and which gives him nothing, *nothing,* to call his own. Not even a family. Not when the state takes the place of father and mother. But strangely, communism still ends up with the same class of oligarchs as in capitalism, who own, sorry, *manage*, all of the community's assets. Communism is, in fact, the logical endgame of global capitalist democracy, even though superficially, they seem like oppositional systems.' Dr. Wansbrough paused to think for a moment. 'But far from seeing them as opponents, it is better to see capitalism and communism as evil Siamese twins – contending heads attached to the same body.'

Alban nodded, not quite understanding that last bit. Dr. Wansbrough often gave a lot of information at once. There would be a lot to think about when he was on his own.

Even Tommy sat there silently in thought. Finally, he spoke. 'That's the best explanation I've ever heard for it. I've always thought of the communism bit from the cultural angle, you know, as in helping the capitalists create the ultimate consumer. It would still be capitalism in name, but like communism in that the masses would still own nothing – because it would all be on rolling finance. I wasn't alive when all that stuff peaked – I only remember the war, but my dad told me about it and it blew my mind. Especially about the promotion of men in dresses who called themselves women, and everyone had to go along with it or risk getting thrown into prison. That's insane.' He reached into his knapsack and took a swig from a bottle. 'Does anybody want some? It's local cider. I got a couple of bottles to take back.'

Dr. Wansbrough shook his head, and Alban followed his teacher's lead even though he would have liked to have tasted it. It was starting to get difficult to see each other in the gloom. When Dr. Wansbrough replied to Tommy, Alban realised that his teacher hadn't been distracted by the offer of cider as he had.

'You're right, in that we call them communists as a shorthand, but they'll use any ideology interchangeably if it serves their final purpose for us. Why else would they have formed an alliance with the SAU?' Seeing that no-one answered what was in essence a rhetorical question, Dr. Wansbrough decided that it was probably best to call it a day, or night, as it now was. 'Look at how dark it is! We'd better get back. Come on.'

He motioned Alban and Tommy to stand so that he could gather up the tartan rug. Alban didn't want to go. He had wanted to enjoy the quiet beach in the dark, with just the stars above and the waxing gibbous moon making occasional appearances behind the clouds, reflecting its cool light on the waves, which were now just the length of three men from the edge of the rug. He didn't want the night to end.

'But you haven't talked about the system we have now. I was looking forward to that.'

Tommy laughed. 'Yes, I'd like to hear about that one as well. I'm almost thirty-five and I don't understand it myself.'

Dr. Wansbrough smiled. 'It's getting late, and that's a whole other topic. We'd be here all night and the sea is almost on top of us. But be-

From the Land All the Good Things Come

fore we go, Alban, a final test. Where is Polaris in the sky? Tommy?' The older man gestured to Tommy to volunteer an answer.

Tommy shook his head. 'I don't have a clue. I'll have to leave that one to the young prodigy here.'

The two older men stood in silence as the boy scanned the sky. Finally, he pulled at Dr. Wansbrough's sleeve and pointed. 'That's it there. Above the Plough.'

Dr. Wansbrough squinted towards where the boy was pointing and then beamed. 'Well done! Come on, let's get back. It's an early start tomorrow.'

The three walked back towards the few lights that indicated that they were getting close to the promenade. All three were deep in their own personal thoughts. It was Alban who broke the silence.

'I'm wondering. What if Judas betrayed Jesus for the thirty pieces of silver because he needed to pay a debt? You said yourself that people do desperate things when they are in debt.'

Dr. Wansbrough smiled broadly, to the boy's delight. 'I think it's fair to say that the scriptures don't bear out that hypothesis, but I like your thinking. It's because of thinking like that

that I picked you to be my protégé.'

CHAPTER 21

Morgenna sat in CeeCee's chaotic but homely living room, and waited for her friend to return from the kitchen with the tea.

As soon as she had seen her friend's face on opening the door, Clare knew that something big had happened and that her plans for rest of the day would need to be abandoned. When her doorbell had rung unannounced, CeeCee was in the kitchen with two of the teenage girls from the League of English Maidens, showing them how to put the finishing glaze on the mezzies that the children had made, which had been fired in the kiln that Colin had rigged up in the shed. But when CeeCee saw the distress on Morgenna's face she knew that she would have to cut the glazing session short and, asking her friend to wait outside a minute while she got the house straight, darted back to the kitchen where, full of rushed apologies, she ushered the two girls out of the back door, promising to lert them when things had returned to normal.

Morgenna could have wandered through to the kitchen to help CeeCee with the tea-making, as she often did, but on this particular day she wanted to remain sitting. This wasn't a day for idle chit-chat. She needed CeeCee's calm wisdom to help get her head around this new situation.

CeeCee sat Morgenna's cup of tea down on the coaster, and told her it was only dandelion because she had run out of proper tea. But Morgenna seemed not to hear her.

'I'm pregnant.'

CeeCee's managed to convert her open-mouthed surprise into a smile at the news but then found her smile stopping short. She understood Morgenna's consternation. Edwin's spirit was still earthbound. The forty days had not yet passed. But she knew she had to say something.

'How do you feel?'

'I just can't believe it. Why now? I'm 42 for God's sake!'

Both women knew that in a community which prized large families, Morgenna's small brood of two boys had raised eyebrows among the Albionic Church community who didn't know that Morgenna and John had been trying ever since Edwin's birth to conceive again without success. The fact that Seb had come along after eight years was seen as nothing short of miraculous, so it had been no surprise to either of them that *the mysterious tickle* had never been felt in the ten years since his birth. It had not altered John's great love and respect for his wife, and they came to accept it as God's plan for them, with Morgenna throwing herself into church and community work, becoming a practical and emotional keystone for mothers with a much greater domestic burden to bear.

'It's just such a shock… I don't feel ready for this. And I don't know if I'll ever be ready. I should feel overjoyed. But it feels… strange.'

The two women sat in silence for a few moments, drinking their dandelion tea. Then CeeCee spoke.

'I'm not surprised you feel conflicted about what should be joyous news. Your heart is still wounded for the loss of Edwin. Maybe you are frightened that with your heart so sore, it won't be strong enough for the burden of a new child. Maybe you are reluctant to open your heart again to make the room for a new child, because, well…'

She didn't want to know how to finish her thought. She could understand why Morgenna would be frightened to open her heart for her new child, because who wanted to open herself up to the possibility of more pain, of going through another child's death? There was also the horror of daring to feel the joy of preparing for a new life, and the pregnancy not going to term. She was 42, after all.

Morgenna thought back to what must have been the night of conception. It had been John's first night home from America. Holding each other silently in bed, their bodies had united in grief, wordlessly, their gentle but intense coming together a reminder to each other that, despite everything, their lifelong love for each other still shone undimmed through the dark events of the earth, and they were still one flesh.

Morgenna looked into the kind eyes of her older friend, and knew that she too was thinking about Edwin's death.

'It's not just fear of the future, CeeCee, it's guilt as well. I mean I know it's stupid but I feel that this pregnancy is bad timing. That right now I should be mourning Edwin, that this is *his time*, you know? I'm scared that if I start thinking about this new baby Edwin will think I'm putting him the past, that I've replaced him.' Morgenna stopped and looked flustered. Does any of that make any sense?'

'Oh yes, yes it does,' CeeCee hurried to reassure

her friend.

'...and then maybe I'm worrying about nothing. I'm barely a month gone. I mean, I could lose this child at any time. Especially at my age.' She fixed her blue eyes on CeeCee. 'But it's weird. When I first found out I felt a surge of excitement, even though I felt guilty about feeling that excitement.'

'Wait a minute...' Crafter Clare got up suddenly and went into the kitchen. Morgenna heard a cupboard being opened and then the sound of metal clanging together.

CeeCee came back into the living room with a biscuit tin. 'I decided to use up the last of my sugar yesterday. It looks like it was a wise move.'

Morgenna's started to laugh, as CeeCee stood beside her with the open tin.

'Biscuits! Wow, CeeCee, you really *do* have everything! It's been so long since I've tasted something properly sweet.'

She took one of the giant home-made biscuits and bit into it. The door to the kitchen had been left open, and bright sunshine was beginning to break through a cloud and now streamed into the living room where Morgenna was sitting, bathing her face and temporarily dazzling her. Suddenly aware that she had been sitting the whole time as CeeCee was moving around, Morgenna got up and followed CeeCee back into the kitchen, still eating her biscuit. Her attention fell on the half-glazed mezzies on the kitchen table.

'Oooh... mezzies!' Morgenna peered over them, looking at the various shapes and designs.

'Yes, the children have been making them in church. They just need the final glaze then they're ready to go...'

There was a pause '...*upon the door posts of thine house, and upon thy gates*,' Morgenna couldn't help smiling at her own wit. She felt pleased with herself for remembering the verse and for being quick enough to finish her friend's sentence with scripture. That was not like her at all. CeeCee looked up at her in surprise.

In a bid to pretend that she hadn't noticed her friend's surprise, Morgenna picked up one of the mezzies and examined it in the sunlight. 'The green glitter on them is really gorgeous.' She wasn't lying. The glitter refracted the sunlight into a thousand tiny coloured lights. To Morgenna's unsophisticated eyes, it looked like something from heaven. 'Where did you manage to get the glitter from?'

CeeCee tapped the side of her nose and smiled

mischievously. 'God's providence is a marvellous thing.'

The women and children of the EF loved glitter, and it was a hard commodity to come by. It could not be denied that when one went to a neighbour's door, the momentary sparkle of a glittery mezzie brightened one's day. A few years before, a rumour had been put around, no doubt by the more puritan elements of the Church, that glitter should not be used on religious objects because they attracted demons. CeeCee knew that this was a reaction to the seductive cult of beauty and sensuality which had taken root before the war, but still it had annoyed her and she had stood her ground against the *bloody gnostics* and won. 'Beautiful' did not necessarily mean 'demonic'. The English did not have to feel suspicious of the beautiful or the elegantly designed. It was not a sin to appreciate aesthetics, at least not when the object also had a practical use. So much of EF territory was poverty-stricken, broken and ugly, that it was important to create beauty where one could. God of all people would understand this.

The two women stood in silence for a few moments looking at the mezzies on the table and cooing over the childrens' efforts. Morgenna put her arm round CeeCee's large motherly body and laid her head against her friend's shoulder. She breathed in CeeCee's familiar smell of earth and soap and felt the mohair wool against her cheek.

The sound of CeeCee's voice resonated through her body and vibrated into Morgenna's head, which reassured her. 'It's ok to feel happy, you know. As the church says, new life is new hope.'

Morgenna's eyes turned to look up at her friend, as she leant into her shoulder. She nodded slowly in agreement though her voice wavered. 'Yes, it's going to be ok.'

CHAPTER 22

There were more people in *The Cross Keys* than usual. Harry sometimes wondered if the lunar cycle didn't have something to do with his normally quiet pub filling with people, as a few of the times that the pub got most unexpectedly busy, Harry had noticed the moon to be full or almost full. It was a theory, certainly, but the fluctuations in his pub's trade might also be connected to the returns of the convoys from Wales and Cumbria, successes in skirmishes with the enemy, and the occasional visits from outsiders. On this particular night, the self-described bard, comedian and goods-negotiator Hamish Crozier was on a visit from his trading post in Carlisle, accompanied by musicians, so it would be safe to say that the full moon soon to rise had little to do with the energetic atmosphere around the bar.

Spirits were high generally among the EF command. Harry wasn't sure to what this change of mood owed itself, but he was happy that it meant a greater sociability and greater footfall for his pub.

Hamish was sitting in far-left corner deep in conversation with two of the musicians. Harry counted a bodhran, two fiddles, a guitar, and a guy with a tin whistle. Warm bucolic rays of a rose-gold sunset filtered through the high window panes facing west, casting an ethereal glow onto the drinkers below, and giving the sense that this evening somehow stood outside of time, that this tableau of the English public house was eternal. Something told Harry that this would be one of those nights that would remain alive in local folk memory for a long time to come.

Slowly rising up above the chatter, the music became heard throughout the bar. Harry recognised the song as *The Lonesome Boatsman*, an Irish song but one of particular resonance in this, a port region with a strong Irish heritage. As the tin whistle soared and trilled delicately in its minor key the people fell silent, and its sweet woman's voice of anguish and loss caused the bar to fall into such a torpid wistfulness that even as the guitar and bodhran rolled rousingly at the end the patrons struggled to stir.

Old Hamish got to his feet and clapped his hands.

'Come on, we'll *hae nae mair* o' this maudlin

From the Land All the Good Things Come

mood – I do believe it's time for one of my famous ballads. Music, maestros!' He motioned to the musicians, who began a rousing reel and Hamish feigned a stiff Highland jig around imagined swords to the sound of the music.

The people laughed. The spell had been broken. Hamish leaned forward and clapped his hands again. The music stopped but for the guitar marking time gently in the background.

'What will it be? *Dr Kelly in the Forest? Charlie, Defender of the Faiths?*'

An old man beside the bar shouted 'What about the one about the guy with the yacht?'. Hamish looked puzzled for a moment, then a middle-aged woman near the door shouted 'Yeah, the one about the Green guy'.

'Ah, the ballad of Philip Green! Our very own lonesome boatsman!' Hamish exclaimed, making reference to the previous song. The few people who got the joke laughed. Most people didn't know the story behind this 'ancient' ballad, but they enjoyed it all the same. The bodhran rolled a Celtic drumbeat to announce the beginning, and Hamish cleared his throat, delivering the ballad strongly and confidently in his strong Scots accent.

> *Philip Green, Philip Green, he's always so chipper*

> *As one would expect from our top asset-stripper*
>
> *It's all that he knows, Mammon is his measure,*
>
> *his only true love, his only real treasure.*
>
> *He knows nothing at all of the value of life*
>
> *Which is why to dodge tax laws that he took a wife*
>
> *He has no real roots, as a gypsy he moves*
>
> *From haven to haven as profit behooves*

A few people made groaning noises. Hamish responded to these groans with a stage whisper to an imagined critic 'Aye, behooves. Ye got a problem wi' that, like?' People laughed. Hamish continued in his previous declamatory tone:

> *He goes robbing the folk o' their labour and health*
>
> *To build for himself tawdry trappings of wealth.*
>
> *But for of all his billions this tick without roots*
>
> *Is laughed at by people for his rotten fruits*
>
> *Rancid fruit of his loins, the cheap harlot*

and whore

Embarrassed the custom-made dresses she wore

A sea of thrilled and amused faces looked back at Hamish as he said those last lines. This ballad never failed to delight in its scandal. He went on.

Opening her legs for a gangster's caress

As the gangster saw gold in this little heiress

And gold he achieved, his bad seed finding home

In the thief-daughter's womb, and a baby was born

At this point a few people groaned at the bad rhyme. Hamish made a face of nonchalant indifference, and shrugged visibly, causing a ripple of laughter.

Now the billions of ill-gotten gains they will flow

To this mongrelised bastard of villain and ho'.

At this point a lot of people laughed loudly, and Hamish waited a few seconds to resume.

So then like goes to like and the lesson is cited:

That shite canna' flow upward, even if it is knighted.

A cheer went up, and the room erupted into laughter. The few that were anxious for the last part tried to hush the laughter so that Hamish could continue.

We all find our level, the mirror is true

So Green is condemned to sail the ocean blue

In his floating gin palace that never does anchor

He circles forever, the greasy fat wanker.

At the last word, old Hamish's voice was drowned out by the audience, who out of tradition prepared joyously for the end to shout the word 'wanker'. The whole pub erupted into the laughter, and the musicians caught this energy, counting themselves into a lively, up-tempo version of *She Moves Through the Fair*. Hamish moved from the centre of the floor and up to the bar, through a gauntlet of congratulation and pats on the back. The bar itself was thronged, and Harry, stuck behind the bar, lerted his stepdaughter Wenna to come and lend a hand. Chloe was worth her weight in gold, but there were those rare times when even two people were not enough.

Two EF soldiers Harry didn't recognise came up to the bar. He stole a longer glance at the men's faces via their reflection in a side mirror and decided that he had never seen them before, especially the darker one, whose features were quite distinctive. But Harry was smart enough not to ask questions. Soldiers from the other EF divisions were not unknown in these parts, and discretion was everything in EF territory. These men would not be here if Armstrong, sitting in the corner, had not approved their presence.

'What will it be lads?'

The swarthy soldier spoke. Harry thought he caught a twang of the West Country accent, maybe Bristol.

'Two pints of that pale ale and a bag of scratchings, mate'

Harry turned and bent down to get the pint glasses from the low shelf. Over the noises of the fiddle, he overheard the dark soldier talk to his friend. He decided to look busy sorting the glasses for a few seconds longer in order to eavesdrop more subtly. '*So yeah, they reckon it's going to be another two months. Things are looking good so far. But they don't want to rush it. A few weeks more, and we'll be good to go.*'

Harry turned back towards the bar and the

pump, in time to see the second man nod. He looked around and above the heads of the men, and noticed that the bar was filling up with more EF soldiers, who looked like they had come to the bar in groups. Some of the faces were new to Harry, and he caught the odd words of couple of regional accents which he didn't recognise. Some were definitely from the Southwest Division, like these two men, but others he was less certain of. Harry though he heard some East Anglian vowels, but it was hard to be sure, as so many of the southern accents were all mixed up after the mass migrations from the Home Counties and the Midlands. He wondered what was going on to bring these men here. Officially, the EF high command did not encourage drinking, so to see so many EF people in the pub at one time was very unusual. The musicians were good, but the laughter and jubilance in the air told Harry that there was something going on beyond the desire to see Hamish and the musicians.

The publican turned back towards the pints, which he had left for a few minutes to settle, and put a foamy head on them.

'Here you go, lads.' Harry placed the pints and the packet of dried bacon bits in front of the men and took the money that was passed over the bar. He noticed that the last of the sunset was turning to a few blindingly bright yellow fingers of light that skimmed the top of the tallest men's heads and bounced off picture frames, but the bar overall was falling into a deeper gloom. Wenna made her way to the front of the bar, and Harry asked her to light the lard lamps.

The noise level rose along with the music, but Harry knew that with the calibre of EF figures present, nothing would get out of hand. It was nights like this that kept his business afloat, and Harry would keep the bar open as long as Armstrong wanted it to be. He looked along the length of the bar, checking that everyone had drinks and removed a couple of empty glasses. His eyes settled on the two soldiers that he decided were definitely from Bristol. They had been joined by another two men about half an hour ago, and the four had been standing in a small circle, alternately telling and laughing at funny stories. But something made Harry suddenly fix his attention on the group. The postures of the men were no longer loose-limbed and relaxed, their demeanours no longer happy and expansive. The faces had fallen into seriousness, and Harry noticed that they were leaning in towards the dark soldier from Bristol who looked vaguely confused at their concern. Harry saw the dark soldier touch his face.

His nose was bleeding.

Quite profusely. Quickly, Harry grabbed some paper napkins from the bar and passed them to the blond stocky man who was nearest him. Harry thought he saw a look of vague irritation cross the man's features at the publican's intervention, but he reasoned that it was probably just caused by worry for his friend.

Harry wanted to keep watching the men, but Wenna came back up to the bar clutching empty glasses and told him that Armstrong wanted a word. As he made his way to the snug in which Armstrong was holding court, Harry had to turn his back on the four men of the Southwest Division, and he missed them slip out of the main door and into the cold light of the newly risen full moon.

CHAPTER 23

Aoife sat in her armchair. Her feet were numb with cold and it felt like unseen hands with sharp nails, or it could be claws, were squeezing tightly around her kneecaps to cause a constricting pain. But this was no demonic attack. This was her rheumatoid arthritis announcing a change in the air pressure, and she took from this that a storm was on the way. A big one. Probably in the next few hours.

She thought back to the visit of the young pregnant girl who was having the dreams. When Felicity first walked through the door of the living room she struck Aoife as being like one of those skinny stray cats that used to be common during the 2030s, when people were too concerned about feeding themselves to be feeding animals. There had been one particular pregnant black cat, barely out of kittenhood and on the brink of starvation, that Aoife used to lay food out for in the autumn of 2031. She had tried to coax it into the house, not because she particularly liked cats but because she was frightened that it would die outside in the cold. It had trusted her enough to approach the plates of food that Aoife laid on the garden path as long as the woman stepped back into the doorway, but there was no hope of this shy but semi-feral little animal trusting her enough to step over the threshold. Aoife had fed the little cat for just over two weeks before it never returned, although by that point events in Aoife's own life had prevented her from caring about the animal's fate too deeply.

Felicity, with her straggly thin dark hair, small unassuming features, underfed limbs, growing belly and lack of confidence to meet a stranger's gaze, reminded Aoife of that poor little stray. The sense of tragedy that around the silent girl, whose name had proven to be a careless or bitter tempting of fate, announced to Aoife that the girl was motherless, and that her family line had been much marked with neglect, tragedy and abuse, even if she had seen little of it herself. Aoife sensed that the curse on young Felicity, for a curse it was, stemmed from a maternal great-grandmother, a vicious alcoholic who had greatly abused Felicity's grandmother. Emotional trauma and self-hatred had echoed down through the generations, albeit less pronounced as each emotionally crippled woman took her turn in guessing at the role of motherhood. As a result of this emotionally barren beginning, Felicity didn't hate herself, but she didn't love herself either. She was a sad little cipher buffeted on the winds of life, who had little in terms of ego or personality, and who sought only to please others. When Edwin came into her life at the age of 13, at one of the Albionic church dances organised by the community to bring young people together, her desire to absorb her own unsure sense of self into a stronger personality made her the perfect match for Edwin, who wanted an uncomplicated girlfriend. Felicity offered Edwin a simple, unconditional devotion, a love whose stabilizing constancy in Edwin's life was greatly underestimated by Edwin's friends, who sneered at her servility, her plainness and her shyness around strangers.

It was to be expected therefore, that for Felicity, who had been without a mother since the age of nine and whose distant military father had opted for barracks life, the loss of Edwin would be particularly devastating. Although Morgenna had done what she could to be a surrogate mother when she took Felicity in as a fourteen-year-old, it was clear that Felicity already only existed in the reflection of Edwin's eyes, and his loss left her utterly bereft. It had only been the pregnancy which had kept her anchored to the earth and given her the will to keep going. If she had not been pregnant she would probably have followed her mother and grandmother to an early grave, after a short, unremarkable and unfulfilled life, another quiet victim of the brutalised and brutalizing remnants of the pre-war English underclass.

But she *was* pregnant. Aoife remembered Felicity again in her mind's eye. This young girl, already burdened by a widow's grief without ever having known the joy of a wedding, was now with a tiny baby in her belly, in a world in which suffering and despair stalked the land, despite the best efforts of the church and the military to instill a sense of defiance and hope in the people. In these circumstances, it was not remotely surprising that Felicity had been experiencing prophetic dreams.

As Aoife had listened to the girl, her gaze had drifted from the living room and settled on the view outside the window. She remembered that it had been a sunny day, with a brisk breeze blowing through the last of the blossom on the rowan tree. Nothing to augur the storm to come. Aoife had predicted that the dreams she was about to be told would be nothing but the overactive imagination of a lonely teenage girl, whose intergenerational life traumas manifested themselves in cryptic underwater symbols. But there would be nothing of the future in them.

Then something Felicity said had jolted Aoife to attention.

'I've been having dreams about being a refugee. And last night I dreamt that all the pregnant women were being put on a ship bound for America, but for some reason I got held up and I couldn't get on board in time.'

Aoife had asked her to tell her more about the dream, but Felicity had responded that she couldn't remember much, only the desperation to get on board, and that the panic at seeing the ship leave the dock caused her to wake up. Aoife didn't know why this had drawn her attention, and she knew that she would have to spend more time with this imagery in her mind for it to become clear to her. But she also knew that this girl, with a weakened psychic aura emanating from the curse of generations, was being besieged by evil spirits, and that it was vital to protect her. Aoife seriously doubted that the girl carried inside her the beginnings of a sleeping king who would save the land, but she also felt that in this case an intervention was needed to stop the natural entropic processes of a cursed bloodline from playing out.

It was quite unlike Aoife to wish to intervene in such matters, but there was a goodness about this otherwise insipid girl which she couldn't put her finger on, and it had occurred to Aoife for some unknown reason it might be worth seeing her again in another few months.

She had instructed Felicity to go into the front garden and bring her back a small twig from the rowan tree outside. This done, she then asked the girl to fetch the big sewing box from the cupboard under the stairs. Felicity had watched as the old woman, greatly hampered by an unsteady hand and arthritic fingers, cut the twig into two pieces around three inches long, then took some red thread and bound the two twigs into a cross shape, mumbling strange sounds under her breath as she did so. Aoife used so much red thread, that by the end of her binding a small ball of red was present in the centre of the cross.

She then passed the cross to Felicity and asked her to tie a knot in the thread as her stiff joints could not manage such a delicate operation. When Felicity asked what kind of knot, Aoife had replied 'A knot so fiendish that the devil himself could not untie it. But pass it back to me before you pull the knot tight.'

Felicity did her best. She passed the cross to the old woman to inspect her handiwork, and watched as the old woman blew on the half-finished knot.

Aoife had told the girl to keep the amulet in

her pocket or by her bedside at all times. 'It will ward off the evil eye,' Aoife had said. 'You were born in such circumstances that you do not have a strong energetic presence on the earth, and you are being called from the other world. It seeks to take you back there, and the spirits, being lazy and viceful, will always be drawn to the easiest targets. They sniff out the spiritually wounded, those afflicted by negative emotions, the way a shark smells blood. The spirits also sometimes work through the human beings who have a natural disdain for the weakest in the tribe. It is nature's way to favour the strong and to cull the weak. Call it eugenics, call it Darwinism. It might even be a divine process. Several times in the gospels, Jesus himself said, "To he that has, more shall be given, and from he that has not, even what he has will be taken away."'

Aoife remembered that the girl had said nothing, but just looked towards her shyly.

'I fear that unless we reverse the tragic course of your life, Felicity, what is left to you will be taken away. We need to thwart the processes that began before you were born. Being pregnant is a particularly vulnerable time for a girl whom the spirits have their eye on, so we need you to be strong and grounded.'

Aoife knew that she had made Felicity feel uncomfortable with her penetrating gaze, as over the years many people had reported the sensation of the seer's eyes drilling into their very marrow, but Felicity later told Aoife that her visit had also made her feel reassured and safe for the first time since Edwin's death.

'There is a powerful ceremony to dispel the spirits that I would perform with you, but you are pregnant and it may lead to miscarriage. Never mind, we will do it when the baby is born. In the meantime, to ensure that the baby *is* born, I want you to do the following things...'

'Anything,' Felicity had said.

'I want you to go out and find red clothes. Ideally, these would be new clothes that will not have the energy of another person attached to them. But if these *are* second-hand clothes, ensure that they come from a strong personality. You do not need to wear red from top to toe, but at least one main item of clothing should always be bright red. Red is an aggressive colour, it announces your presence in the world, and it repels demonic attack and the evil eye. It is the colour of blood, and blood is life.'

Felicity had looked doubtful. 'I don't like wearing bright colours.'

Aoife had smiled. 'I know you don't. That's

exactly why you need to do it.'

Felicity had nodded her consent, but made a wry face. 'That's funny. When I think of Satan, I always think of red and fire.'

Aoife had waved away the girl's comment. 'That's just a hangover from the Middle Ages. Trust me, hell is a frozen tundra.' The expansive gesture of dismissal had caused pain to shoot down Aoife's arm, making her wince. 'The devil, as a negative entity and an angel devoid of love, is very much a creature of the ice.'

Felicity had nodded and said that she had never really thought about it before, but that Aoife's explanation made sense to her.

'This is another thing I want you to do,' Aoife had said, 'and that is to understand your place in the world. You must seek to avoid all behaviours, places and people that bring you closer towards death than life, and bring yourself into ways that strengthen your life force.'

Felicity had frowned in confusion, as Aoife had half-expected she would, and the old woman made a further comment which she knew would make the girl understand.

'I know that you constantly tell yourself that you are worthless.'

Felicity's cheeks went red with embarrassment, but she said nothing.

Aoife explained. 'Death and life are not binary, because they are not absolutes, but polarities. A person can die in increments, a thousand times a day. Think of each death as one of a series of tiny cuts to your self-esteem and to your health. You need to understand that every thought, every interaction, every exchange that takes place in time either strengthens or diminishes your life force. **The air is as full of demons and evil spirits as a sunbeam is of tiny specks, and they all seek to take from your vital energy.** So you must make sure that every element of your life strengthens your will to be here and your link to the earth. I want to see you eating more meat, especially black pudding. Black pudding will be excellent for your pregnancy. Recite the Albionic prayer every day; read the Gospel of John. Concentrate your will. And stay out of shadows.'

'Shadows?'

'Yes. The spirit world loves the shadow. Don't put yourself in the path of malevolent attack by putting yourself in a shadow cast by the Lights, especially the Moon. And make sure not to be in the shadow of another person. It is very symbolic in ways that you cannot imagine, and our physical universe adheres to the laws of the moral and symbolic order more than anything Newton could ever have understood.' Aoife sighed. 'Or anyone else for that matter.' She leaned back in her chair and closed her eyes for a few minutes as the pain racked her body, oblivious to the young girl in her presence.

Now Aoife recalled the scene, recreating the young pregnant girl sitting on the couch opposite in her mind's eye. Sometimes the fundamental truths about a person's nature were more obvious in their absence, and it was only in solitude, with her eyes focused elsewhere, that Aoife could began to make sense of this young girl's most recent dreams. The sky was starting to darken with storm clouds and the dampness in the air pervaded the cold living room. Aoife felt the damp snaking its way into every joint in her body, forming a toxic mould that coated the ends of her ancient bones like the weeds that grew in the crevices of abandoned Roman masonry, which displaced the stonework to such an extent that eventually the monument crumbled. Her body was a ruined fortress that both the spirit and the natural world could enter at will. And every new breath became difficult as Aoife realised the significance of this young girl's visit.

CHAPTER 24

'Mind your head against the hatch! Be careful!'

Alban looked up and saw the faces of Jack Little and Dr. Wansbrough peering down at him through the darkness. He was slightly annoyed that they didn't think he was capable of climbing a ladder by himself. He was *twelve*, for God's sake!

Jack and the doctor pulled him up into the attic, and it took a minute for Alban's eyes to become accustomed to the gloom. The attic was filled with all kinds of bric-a-brac from the past hundred years. Furniture, ornaments and toys were the most obvious items that Alban recognised, but there were other things that he had no idea what they were. He would love to spend hours in here, exploring on his own.

'It has been very kind of Jack to invite us to his salvage mission,' said Dr. Wansbrough. 'This will be a great opportunity for you to see a salvager at work, and hopefully the books that he has discovered will be of interest to us. It was very smart-thinking of him to remember us when he saw the books.' Dr. Wansbrough nodded in Jack's direction. 'I'm very grateful to you, sir.' Alban decided that the *sir* was said light-heartedly, as both men were the same age and appeared to see each other as equals.

Jack laughed heartily. 'Not at all. To be honest, there is no demand for books. Mrs. Ellacombe asked me to clear out the attic and in exchange has allowed me to keep anything of value. I saw those books in the corner and they looked pretty old. I thought it was best that you take a look at them in case there is something worthwhile there. Otherwise, let's be frank, they would probably just end up as fuel on the church fire.'

Alban saw Dr. Wansbrough wince when Jack made that last statement, although Jack was cheerfully oblivious to the doctor's reaction. So much destruction had taken place since the Rivers that Dr. Wansbrough didn't want to think about it. Obviously, some books were barely even fit for the fire. Such *furnace fodder*, as these books were disparagingly called, proliferated in the 20th and 21st centuries, and while Dr. Wansbrough understood the argument that some of these books should be kept for future generations to show them the madness of their forefathers, he also understood the argument that their falsehoods be condemned to the flames, lest another generation be seduced by the siren call of *equality* and *liberal democracy*. Dr. Wansbrough shuddered as he thought how the term *furnace fodder* had eventually extended beyond its original designation for communist media, to cover the people who had internalised these ideas.

Such was the extent of false doctrine over the previous century that by 2060 it was very unlikely that they would find any books that were not furnace fodder, but Jack, with his twenty years of salvage experience, had good instincts about a place. And in this instance, he may have struck gold. Mr. Ellacombe had died a very old man at the age of 82, and much of the contents of this attic had belonged not only to him but to his father, from whom he inherited his *collecting* tendencies.

Jack seemed to read the mind of Dr. Wansbrough as he saw him looking around. 'There might be stuff here which is genuinely **antique**, and has an export value. But even the salvage stuff here will be valuable once the crafters have worked their magic.'

Dr. Wansbrough nodded. 'So where are the books?'

Jack pointed to a corner. 'They're in that big trunk over there. There might be some more books in the boxes and suitcases I haven't yet opened, but while you are looking through that truck I can let you know.'

Dr. Wansbrough nodded, and eased his way over to the corner. Alban followed him, though he was sorry to leave Jack, who had just started to unpack a large cardboard box of objects wrapped in soft plastic and printed paper. His eyes stayed on the salvageman, and he watched as Jack unwrapped a large vase and whistled through his teeth.

'I reckon Mrs. Ellacombe doesn't really know what's up here. Come and take a look at this.'

Dr. Wansbrough made his way back to where Jack was sitting. Wansbrough was no expert, but even he could tell that great workmanship had gone into the vase, of an iridescent cameo glass, gradated from blue to orange to imitate the colours of a sunset. The sensuous curves of the vase were swathed in the silhouettes of ferns and dragonflies, with silver engraving picking out the tiny details of the dragonflies' eyes and the veins in their wings. Alban moved towards the pair to get a closer look.

'If I'm not mistaken...' said Jack, holding the vase up close to the lamp hanging from the main beam as he peered down his spectacles, '...this is... yes, this is an original Gallé'. He ran his finger along the small signature in a space in the design and showed it to Dr. Wansbrough. 'There is an inscription on it too, in French. Can you read what it says?' He held the vase under the light for Dr. Wansbrough to squint at.

Dr. Wansbrough read out the inscription etched around the bottom of the vase. '*Nos racines sont au fond des bois, parmi les mousses, autour des sources.*' He paused. 'Our roots are deep in the woods, among the mosses, around the river springs.'

There was a silence as the men took in the exquisiteness of this *verrerie parlante* from a time in which France formed the pinnacle of Western cultural expression, its art and literature emulated and envied by the rest of the world, and yet which only a few years later would suffer the cataclysm that triggered a century of civilisational collapse. Jack whistled quietly in appreciation at the precious object he had in his hands. 'I will need to go carefully in this attic, and let Mrs. Ellacombe know that this is more than just standard pre-war salvage. It would not be fair for the church to take all of the profits of this mission.'

Alban had picked up a crumpled-up ball of the printed paper lying on the attic floor that had served as packing in one of the boxes, and he was now flattening it out. It was covered in pictures and big letters. 'What is this paper?'

Jack laughed at the question and turned to Dr. Wansbrough. 'I've just unearthed an authentic Émile Gallé, and your boy is more interested in a page of *The Sun*!'

Dr. Wansbrough smiled, because it was quite a funny situation, but he also understood the boy's question, because he knew that Alban would never have seen a newspaper before. 'It's a newspaper. They were very popular before the Rivers of Blood decade. They were printed every day, to inform people of news and current affairs...'

Jack started laughing so hard that he had to tighten his grip on the vase to stop himself from dropping it. When his laughter subsided he could see, through the tears in his eyes, the man and boy looking back at him, and knew he would have to explain himself. 'Oh no, your teacher is right, lad. I'm just laughing because, well, what newspapers were supposed to be and what they actually *were*, were two different things. I'm sure that the doctor himself can explain it.'

Dr. Wansbrough smiled. 'Yes, Jack's right. As time went on it became clear to the people that newspapers were simply propaganda, to control how and what people thought. Most of what was found in newspapers was absolute junk, at least in our century. As it became obvious to people that newspapers were peddling controlled and even fake narratives, they stopped buying them. Eventually newspapers had to be given away for free.'

Alban thanked the doctor for his explanation, and watched as the men turned back to the vase and the contents of the suitcase. He peered down at the smoothed-out printed sheet in front of him and made out the date: *October 25, 2018. This piece of paper was over forty years old!* But the men had turned away from him towards the suitcase so clearly it wasn't of interest to them, Alban reasoned. He scanned the sheet of paper in his hands. He could tell that it came from a bigger book of pages because it had a big fold in it and the page numbering made no sense.

His eyes made out the images and writing of the newsprint. One entire page was about giving the prices of food. He recognised the symbol beside the number as being a pound sign, but he didn't know really how it translated into EF money. But that wasn't the most interesting bit. There was an article about a man giving birth to twins, and how wonderful it all was. He screwed up his face. *That wasn't possible.* He read the article. No, they definitely said it was a man. They talked about *him* giving birth, and how happy *he* was. It showed a picture of the man with his two babies. He looked like a man. He had a beard.

Alban looked up from the newspaper and checked to see how busy Dr. Wansbrough was. He looked very busy, and he knew better than to interrupt the doctor when he was in conversation with another adult. He waited until he thought he saw a lull between the two men as Jack went to open another box. He called out.

'How can a man give birth to a baby?'

The doctor and Jack looked at each other and Alban tried to work out what they were both thinking. Dr. Wansbrough came up to Alban and took the piece of newspaper off him, and looked at the headline. 'That's not a man, Alban, that's a woman with a mental illness.'

Alban was confused. 'But if it's a woman, why does she have a beard? I don't understand.'

'It's a woman who has taken male hormones, and the newspaper is pretending it is a man, to go along with her delusion.' The doctor sighed. 'It was part of the reason we ended up having a war. To end the insanity.' He turned back towards the box, by way of saying that he wasn't prepared to go into another of his long talks right at that moment.

Alban caught the hint and said nothing. *THAT was a WOMAN?* It made no sense. He stared at the picture again. *Where were the breasts?* The man... woman... was bare-chested, and it looked like he... she... had a man's chest from what he could see between the babies he or she was holding. *But didn't a woman need breasts to breastfeed her children?* He had so many questions he would have to try to memorise for later, when he and Dr. Wansbrough were back at the house on their own. He felt that there was something very important here that he wasn't being told.

He then saw a photograph of two soldiers in uniform coming out of a church under a canopy of swords being held up by other soldiers. *The two soldiers were kissing!* He looked at the headline: *Navy SEALed With a Kiss*. Alban frowned. Now he really didn't understand anything. He read the story. It was celebrating the gay marriage of two US Navy SEALs, the first in the history of the American military. He didn't know what 'gay marriage' meant, but it didn't make sense. *Two men couldn't marry each other!* But then Alban remembered something that he had once heard from his older cousin Jeffrey about men being able to marry other men before the war. Even priests got married to other men, Jeffrey had told him, and they put their willies into their husband's bottoms as part of the holy marriage sacrament. At the time, Alban had laughed at him, and told him to stop making stuff up.

Now Alban flushed with embarrassment as he realised that Jeffrey had been telling him the truth and that it was he who had been the innocent child. This newspaper proved it. He looked at the picture again and cringed.

He turned the page over. He was startled when he saw a woman in a bikini (or at least he thought it was a woman) showing off her huge distended breasts and a gigantic bum. She had weird fish lips and she looked like a monster. The words in big letters read: *Porn-Star OFSTED Chief Defies Critics.* Smaller-lettered words in quote marks underneath said: 'I will not resign at attempts to slut-shame'. Alban at this point did not understand anything. It felt like he was reading something from a thousand years ago, in a different language. There had to be something that he could understand.

His eyes were drawn to a small paragraph in a corner of one of the pages. 'France: Paramedic Murdered'. In the smallest of print, it briefly described how an ambulance crew in Toulouse had been ambushed and their bullet-proof vests, which were standard uniform, had not been enough to save one of them. As Alban read the details, he heard Dr. Wansbrough's loud voice interrupting his thoughts.

'Alban, you've been quiet a long time. What

are you reading?' Dr. Wansbrough made a side-comment to Jack under his breath: 'I'm always suspicious when a boy of that age is quiet'.

Alban decided to say he was reading about the murder. 'An ambulance driver in France was stabbed to death despite his wearing a bullet-proof vest, when an ambulance was called to a vulnerable area of the city, as part of a deliberate ambush.'

Dr. Wansbrough frowned. 'An ambulance crew having to wear bullet-proof vests? Where was this?'

Alban peered back at the newspaper as he couldn't remember the name of the town. 'Towl-owce'.

Dr. Wansbrough smiled. 'Spoken like a true Anglo-Saxon. But the French themselves called it *Toulouse*. God knows what it's called now.' He then turned to Jack. 'Toulouse. The heart of Cathar country. Looks like that distaste for bodily existence never left them.' He shook his head, as if to shake off the horror of what he had heard. 'Come on, let's get to the book trunk. Let's see what unknown treasures lie hidden in its depths.'

'Can I take this piece of newspaper with me?'

Dr. Wansbrough thought for a moment. 'No. It really would be best going on the fire.'

Alban was disappointed, but he knew that it was useless to argue with Dr. Wansbrough when he had made up his mind.

They opened the trunk. Dr. Wansbrough started to take out the books. He asked Alban to help, even though he knew that the boy would be unlikely to spot any of the books that would be of interest to a scholar of history. Alban didn't recognise any of the authors of the books that he was taking out of the trunk.

Finally, Alban came across a book that he had heard of. He was sure it was the one that was written by that famous German with the serious face. He tugged at Dr. Wansbrough's sleeve to draw his attention to it.

The doctor pursed his lips into a mischievous smile.

'Is this a rare book?' Alban asked.

'No, not really,' said Dr. Wansbrough. 'But it does indicate that we might find some interesting things in here.'

Dr. Wansbrough continued to dig through the pile. His eyes lit up and Alban watched him frantically uncovering more books. 'Ah ha ha ha! Who needs *Mein Kampf* when you've got the real *samizdat*!'

He thrust a book with a colourful cover in front of Alban's face. Alban read the title. Now he was really confused.

'*Five Go to Smuggler's Top* by Enid Blyton?'

'Yep, and look,' Dr. Wansbrough found the correct page and held it open up to Alban's gaze. 'First edition. Before the later revisions, when they realised that it was more effective to 'correct' books than to ban them outright from libraries and schools. There must be at least a dozen Blytons here, maybe more. This is an important find, Alban.'

Alban decided that he didn't understand anything at all. It just looked like a load of old children's books.

Jack called over to Dr. Wansbrough in a jokey manner. 'So it has been worth your time coming here then?'

Dr. Wansbrough looked up from a copy of *The Land of Topsy Turvy* that he had been flicking through. Another first edition. 'Jack, your instincts never fail you. Alban and I are going to be here for a while.'

CHAPTER 25

'Die, you traitor to the people!'

Sebastian was jabbing at Thomas with a short piece of branch that he was pretending was a dagger. As a reward for doing so well on their maths test, Mr. Downes had made good on his promise to show the boys some key close-combat moves with a knife, and he had passed out some knife-shaped blocks of wood for the boys to practice, with him marking them for technique. Mr. Downes was the best teacher ever. Now the boys were trying to recreate the moves he had shown them using lengths of a beech-tree branch that Sam had cut with great difficulty using his penknife. It had taken Sam so long to cut the thick branch into sections that he had lost all enthusiasm for the mock fights, an enthusiasm further diminished by the beginnings of a callus on his right index finger and a cut on his left hand. He sat on a concrete pipe with Ambrose and Andrew, the three of them alternating their attention between the two mock knife fights playing out in front of their eyes. He watched in despair as the parrying between Jimmy and Chad descended into Jimmy smacking his opponent around the head with the 'knife'.

'Well, *that* was a waste of time,' said Sam. His attention went from scanning the wasteland on which his friends were fighting to his left hand, which he checked for splinters. He squeezed the skin around the cut so that it bled. Sam's dad had told him to squeeze the skin as soon as he ever got a skin cut in order to make sure that the blood would wash out any dirt or poisons. It was always important to worry about cuts to the skin when the few antibiotics that might be available so often proved to be useless, but now there was this new mysterious illness to worry about. Even if the adults weren't saying much about it.

'Have you heard anything new about the illness?'

Sam called it the illness, because he wasn't sure what to call it. There was a silence as Ambrose and Andrew racked their brains to remember the conversations they had overheard over the past week.

Andrew spoke first. 'My Uncle Bob called it "the dreaded lurgy". He said that pig farmers wouldn't get it.'

Sam nodded, and assimilated this new information into what he had gathered so far. *The dreaded lurgy*. This sounded to Sam like something that was known to the British people and came around every so often like measles or monkeypox. There was also that famous cholera epidemic in 2033 that had begun in Sparkhill but which ended up devastating large parts of Birmingham, by that point a greatly overcrowded city. It made the English people in other parts of Britain extremely careful about their water supply. Clean water could no longer be taken for granted. He was sure though that if this was cholera his mum would have mentioned it. She was paranoid about what Sam drank and made sure that he washed his hands before eating.

'Do people die from the dreaded lurgy?'

This was the question that Sam, and everyone else, really wanted to know.

Ambrose chose to reply. 'Nobody is talking about it. I've heard that as soon as someone gets sick they are taken to a special hospital run by the EF.' He paused. 'My mum told me that Hereward Adcock is dead. They took him to hospital. But he might not have had the lurgy though. I don't think he had any nosebleeds.'

The boys ruminated on this new information. Seb came over with Thomas.

'What are you talking about?'

'We're talking about the dreaded lurgy. The new illness that's going about.'

Seb nodded. 'I've got a theory about that. Have you noticed that the people who have been getting it are, well, a bit mixed?'

'Mixed?' Sam looked at Seb quizzically.

'Well, I don't want to say mixed blood, because I'm not sure if all of these people *are* mixed blood. But they are certainly dark. Or, at least, you're not sure. They could be. I do know that there are black soldiers who have definitely been taken to hospital. And Esther Davidson has got an Indian grandfather, and she was taken away last night.'

Thomas nodded in agreement. 'I heard my dad say to my mum that it's only the tar-brush people who will be affected. He said that we are being told it's a new flu bug, but he doesn't believe it.'

Now Sam was really confused. *What did tar-brush people mean?* Esther Davidson's father was part of the Intelligence Unit. He was friends with Sam's dad. And Hereward Adcock had blonde hair. He wasn't dark. *This made no sense.*

Sam decided not to ask any more questions and make himself look ignorant in front of his peers. He was seen in the group as an authority and asking questions would diminish his standing. He would wait until he got home and would ask his dad about it.

The boys had lost interest in trying out their knife-fight moves. It wasn't the same without Mr. Downes giving advice on what to do and being the judge of the fight. It just descended into chaos. The boys realise that they were bored and were starting to get hungry. They threw down the bits of stick and went home.

CHAPTER 26

'Dad, what is a tar-brush person?'

'Wh... what?' William looked up distracted, vaguely annoyed. His lerter had just announced that the Norwegians had retaken the Shetland Islands. Everyone knew what this meant. He would need to get to HQ pronto. The EF might need to bring the final assault forward, but all sorts of issues would get in the way. Men were dropping like flies, and there was mistrust in the ranks about what was going on. People were talking amongst themselves and there was a bad atmosphere.

'A tar-brush person,' Sam clarified, clearly oblivious to his father's expression. 'We were talking about this new illness, and Thomas said that only tar-brush people were getting it. What does that mean?'

William went pale. If schoolboys were talking about this then it meant that everyone knew what was happening.

'Who the fuck told you that?'

'T-Thomas.' Sam stammered on hearing his father swear and sensing the aggression in his angry tone. 'He... he said it was just a theory.'

William's eyes bore down on his son with an intensity that was completely new to the ten-year-old. He had never seen his father like this. He didn't know what he had said to cause this anger, but tears started to well up in his eyes and his throat felt tight. He wished he could turn back the clock two minutes.

There was the sound of a vehicle pulling up outside and a noisy handbrake.

His father spoke in a low hiss which Sam had never heard before. It frightened Sam more than if his father had shouted at him. '*Never* repeat what you have just said to me again. To anyone. Do you hear me? *Never*. This is not a joke. What you have heard are rumours... lies. They could do a lot of damage. You must never repeat them. Never. On pain of death.' He gave Sam a look which told him that he was serious about the death bit.

William strode past his chastened son towards the front door.

'Tell your mother that I won't be back for a while.'

CHAPTER 27

Morgenna stood back from the trestle table and surveyed her work. She had finished cutting the tissue paper into the shapes set out by CeeCee for the final pattern. It was sad that it had come to this, but there was no way that they could get proper stained glass for the windows. Brother Dunstan had told her that this church once did have stained-glass windows, but that was before they were blown out in 2042 by the blast of a SAU bomb. Decorative windows in these times were an unthinkable luxury, a particularly painful admission for a town once famous for its plate glass.

While the windows on the left-side had shattered, God in his grace and wisdom had seen fit to deliver the church of greater structural damage, but a crater left in the tarmac of the car park served to show the next generation of children the nature of the enemy that they were up against. Shortly afterwards the EF implemented their draconian Dark Sky policy, which went hand-in-hand with the official curfew for civilians. It meant that travelling after dark, even short distances, was an extremely dangerous undertaking, but it did mean that for the first time in two hundred years the people of St Helens saw the night sky in its full constellatory brilliance. The fear of mundane darkness was tempered by the wonderment and awe that came with the vast array of heavenly lights, which in turn gave the English a much-needed reminder of their deserved place in the cosmic order.

But right at that moment Morgenna's concern was not to showcase God's magnificence in the night sky, but to refract the light of His sun into all the colours of the rainbow, so that the congregation would feel their hearts stir as the rays fell upon them on a sunny day. She didn't quite have all the colours she needed. She only had the tissue paper for six colours, if she included white. Even so, CeeCee had crafted a beautiful design that deftly disguised their limited palette. Morgenna was just concerned that she would not have the talent to translate CeeCee's vision into reality.

CeeCee had done her best with the materials available, even deciding on a Noah's Ark design which would work around the fact that there was a preponderance of blue over every other colour of tissue paper. Still, it was a reminder of how far the English had fallen. Morgenna remembered being dazzled by the stained-glass windows of a church in nearby village of Ashton-in-Makerfield when it was still under English control. The windows above the apse and the main door of St Oswald and St Edmund had been designed by the famous Irish artist Harry Clarke, and when she was a child Morgenna's grandmother would take her to this church and tell her stories about the saints the windows depicted. The windows became notorious when an American collector offered a vast sum of money to have the panes relocated to North America, and the EF, tired of losing lives for a village that was getting harder and harder to defend, decided to agree to the sale. Just as the EF was about to make their agreement official, Morgenna remembered the emergence of the accusation that the EF were taking communion with gold coins instead of sacramental bread, a powerful libel which was weaponised still further by the dissemination of a cartoon which depicted a fat, cigar-smoking American in a priest's cassock placing gold coins into the open mouths of piously kneeling EF soldiers. To heighten the sense of outrage, the anonymous cartoonist had given the American buyer anachronistic Semitic features, a cynical move which betrayed the artist's mastery of nationalist propaganda. But it was enough to stop the sale of the windows.

In the face of such popular resistance, the EF could only relent to the people's indignation. But they could not hold the village. On the 26th of April 2044, the SAU took what was left of Ashton-in-Makerfield. Almost all of the English had fled by that stage. Out of nothing but what would have been the frustration at finding no female war booty to rape and sell at the slave market in Leeds, the SAU smashed every window of St Oswald and St Edmund church. Morgenna hung her head for a moment when she thought of the brave EF soldiers who had stayed behind to defend the church despite knowing that their loyalty would most certainly lead to torture and death. She wondered if the spirit of Saint Tarcisius, evoked through his glass portrait, had inspired the young men to stay to sacrifice their own lives to protect the sacred.

Her head still bowed, Morgenna sighed. There had been so much suffering. Sometimes she struggled to get through all the tasks of the day, so many memories assailed her and weighed on her body. But she had to go on. So many other people depended on her that she had to stay strong and look to the future. She had no choice.

'Is everything ok?'

It was CeeCee's voice. Seeing CeeCee's matronly form clad in a pink shapeless woollen jumper was like a balm to Morgenna.

'Yes, yes, everything's fine. I'm just wondering how we are going to manage gluing the pieces on the top half of the window. It's higher than I realised.'

'Well, you are not going anywhere near that stepladder being pregnant.' CeeCee smiled, but with a face that told Morgenna that in this case it would be pointless trying to protest. 'Forget it.'

CeeCee came up to the trestle table and surveyed the coloured pieces that Morgenna had cut out.

'What you have done is great. It aligns perfectly with the template. I think that perhaps now the best thing would be for me to sketch out the design on the window itself. This will make the placement of the pieces easier for someone balancing on a stepladder. Because you can't step back and judge the position from up-close, and a few wrongly placed elements could throw off the whole design. And we don't have enough leftover tissue paper to allow for mistakes.'

Morgenna looked doubtful. 'Will you be ok up there? You're not as young and supple as you used to be. Maybe we should wait for the League girls to come and help.'

CeeCee laughed. 'Ha! Wait two hours for the League girls to arrive? You know what the Bible says about procrastination. *Whoever watches the wind will not plant; whoever looks at the clouds will not reap.* **Don't worry,** I'm lighter on my feet than I look. I'll be ok if I go slow. And anyway, you're here to catch me if I fall.'

CeeCee smiled to herself at her friend's apprehensive face, as it was obvious to CeeCee that Morgenna did not realise that she was joking.

CHAPTER 28

He was having that dream again.

He was back to being twelve years old, and walking with his mum in the Arndale Centre. They had decided to go into the centre of Manchester because the GAME store had an exclusive version of *Call of Duty: Black Ops*, and he had birthday money to spend. The game was 18-rated, but his dad had cleared it, saying that a war game wouldn't do a twelve-year-old boy any harm. David had waited outside while his mother went in to get the game. It was while he was standing on his own in the arcade that a gang of Pakistani men spied him as they walked past. He had made the mistake of making eye contact with one of the men, who led the group towards him.

'Fucking...' The next word David didn't understand. It was in their language. But he was very sure from their tone and their aggression that it was to do with him being English.

They pushed him. He fell back against the window. They laughed.

As they stood around, David's mum came out of the shop, and immediately got between the men when she saw what was happening. She was clearly frightened. They laughed at her and called her a whore. One of the men, a short, squat man with dark circles under the eyes in his pug-like face, spat on her and said something in his language. The others laughed, and they all started to move on, turning their backs on David and his mother. The vile globule of spit was still glistening on Helena's jacket.

They had spat on his mother!

There was a silence between David and his mother as groups of shoppers filed by with their bags, oblivious to what had happened. David didn't want to look at his mother because he was scared that he would start crying out of frustration. He kept his eyes down, focused on the shoppers' legs.

Then he heard his mother's voice, tremulous despite her best attempts to transform her shock into indignation, in a desperate bid to play down the situation and save face in front of her son. 'Don't worry, I'll be calling the police about this. There's CCTV everywhere in here. The evidence will be easy to find. Don't worry, Davey. We'll get this sorted.'

It was at this point that 54-year-old David Caldwell always woke up. And then, as he came to consciousness, he would remember the letter that his mother received from Greater Manchester Police, saying that they empathised with her complaint, but they did not have enough evidence to proceed with the investigation. To add insult to injury, they then said that David and his mother were welcome to avail themselves of the services of their victim counselling unit, whose counsellors was specially trained to deal with the emotions arising from these types of incident, *blah blah blah*.

Even after 42 years, the rage inside David was just as keen as the day he had read that letter as a 12-year-old. The Arndale Centre had confirmed to David's father that they had received no request from the police to review their CCTV footage.

David's dream was of course now part of English Front legend, and was a story he himself had told many times over the twenty years that he had stood on podiums in the border towns of the EF's fluctuating territory. All of the English knew the story of the moment their beloved leader David Caldwell swore, as a twelve-year-old, that one day he would liberate his people from this foreign occupation, but they never tired of hearing it, no matter how many times it was told. With time, the tale became festooned with embellishments. In some versions David's father took a more prominent role, as a prophet of what was to come, telling his wife that far from harming the boy, an adult war game 'would probably do him good'. Other variants told of David and his mother going into the shop for protection until the gang had moved away. But regardless of the particulars of the story that was told, the story itself became deeply symbolic of a people who were no longer respected or represented in their own country, and who had been put in danger by successive treacherous governments. It was an event like countless others taking place in England every day around that time, yet that particular event, on that particular day, October 20th 2018, would indirectly end up changing the course of British history. Since that day as a young boy, Caldwell the soldier had been involved in many dangerous firefights with the enemy, even some moments of brutal hand-to-hand combat. But even his left eye being gouged out by an enemy combatant in Rochdale could not traumatise him as much as the day that those Arndale Centre 'British' spat on his mother.

He got up from the floor and arched his back. His neck was stiff. In the last few years he had found it easier to sleep directly on the floor face down, his right arm folded underneath his head as a pillow. It meant that he kept his ascetic focus by never getting too comfortable. Every sinew stayed taut. He kept his uniform on, even his boots, in the event that he would be required to respond suddenly. As a result he slept very lightly, and found himself dozing during the day. Sometimes the daytime took on a dream-like quality. He knew that subordinates found it strange, but they were not the ones who had the ultimate responsibility for the English people. And as traitors made a point of striking at the most unexpected moment, he was happy for people to know that their leader slept with his boots on. Since Operation Azrael, he had been particularly paranoid. The EF hospitals were filling up with the sick, and answers were being demanded.

He called for his aide-de-camp Marsden, who was in the next room. Marsden briefed him on the latest *millstonings*.

'The six we were holding in Walton are being taken out today. Gardner says that the five that they are holding in Newcastle will be taken out tomorrow if the weather permits. Norwich has two that are left to deal with, but they are keeping them in prison for the meantime. The other two regions are up-to-date.'

'Good, good.' Caldwell sighed and nodded. He was still tired. Like most leaders, he was starting to age badly. He had always been a self-contained, self-generating man, but lately he was feeling less impervious to the strains of leadership. He rolled his neck from side to side. The millstonings would be good for morale. They reminded people that monsters would be slain, and the EF meant business about keeping the people safe, from internal as well as external threats.

All of the men to be millstoned had been convicted in an EF court, in a process which sought to find the truth rather than award the adversary with the best skills in sophistry or knowledge of legal technicalities. English Front jurisprudence was very much about the spirit of the law rather than the letter, which had led to so many injustices before the Rebellion. Sentencing was also brought back into line with Anglo-Saxon tradition, although in some cases the victim of the crime had the option to request a more merciful punishment if he felt so inclined. But the child victims of sexual predators were never consulted in the sentencing. The sentence for such men was final, and took as its inspiration the words of Jesus Christ himself:

But whoso shall offend one of these little

> *ones which believe in me, it were better for him that a millstone were hanged around his neck, and that he were drowned in the depth of the sea.*

In the early years of the English Front working with the fledgling Church of Christ in Albion to create the new moral-legal code for England, a time in which there was a great killing of The Irredeemable, a sealed missive arrived from Pope Eugenius V in Coimbra addressed to *The Leader of the English People.* It had come on one of the Iberian trading vessels which made regular commercial trips to Plymouth, as part of a valuable trading arrangement between merchants in Great Iberia and the Southwest EF. The letter had given the seal of papal approval to the EF's theologically-based decision on how to deal with pedophiles and pederasts, and was thus a priceless document for legitimizing the regime, both internationally and with the newly converted Catholic contingent of the population. The letter was a calculated move on the part of the Iberians, who had also suffered a great deal of unpleasantness when purging the national and ecclesiastical Peninsular body of its parasites and pathogens, and who sought their own legitimation for revived Holy Inquisitional practices. They stopped short at millstoning, however, stating that they believed that their *máquina de jus-*

ticia nacional, the garrote vil, which had only fifty years' worth of dust to brush off, was more 'compassionate', although undoubtedly the appeal to historical continuity was also a compelling reason for its return to service. It was reported that some of the original machines barely needed oil.

Caldwell was very grateful for Great Iberia's allyship, which implied that they could also count on an at least tepid recognition from the various rival *condottieri* of the Italian regions, for whatever such recognition was worth geopolitically.

But right now, Caldwell had a much bigger headache. He was going to have to address the matter of so many people falling ill, and the fact that the ethnic component of the people who had been quarantined could no longer reasonably be denied. Normally, when a matter troubled him, he took the advice of Macbeth's doctor and ministered to himself, reasoning that the vulnerability that came from sharing his innermost thoughts outweighed any benefit to be gained from insights which rarely matched his own. Yet in this case, he reasoned that it would be worth seeking a second opinion. There was only one person in the world who would truly understand his actions, and whom he was certain would never betray him, under any circumstance. The only person in the world that he could lean on.

Leaving instructions with Ward regarding the day's business so that he wouldn't be disturbed, the Commander-in-Chief of the Five Divisions went to visit his mother.

CHAPTER 29

Perpetua opened the door before Felicity had a chance to knock. She was impatient to show her friend the latest addition to her marriage box and she had some news of her own.

'It's so good to see you!' Felicity smiled brightly as Perpetua showed her into the living room.

Felicity sat down on the couch in her flurry of red shades. Perpetua marvelled at the change in her friend in only a few weeks. There seemed to be more blood in her veins and she was more sure of herself. She was not someone who could be pushed around as easily. Perpetua didn't think it likely that this change was due to her wearing red. The more probably explanation was that, as her pregnancy advanced, Felicity was starting to feel more womanly and 'in the world'. It also looked like Felicity had put on some weight.

'Before I tell you my news, come and see what my auntie has sent me.'

Perpetua took her friend up the stairs to the bedroom that she still shared with her little sister. The Ottoman-sized box sat in the corner of the room. After years of learning the basics of knitting and sewing at junior school, English Front schoolgirls began preparing their marriage boxes at the age of twelve. They also learned how to make and mend clothes. It was a point of pride among EF women that their men's uniforms were skillfully made and repaired, and a superstition ran among the people that a man who wore a garment that had been mended lovingly would not catch a bullet. It was nonsense, of course, but at the same time, the women did not like to take any chances. The idea that a demon might see a ripped pair of trousers or a hole in a vest as a sign that a man was not loved enough, and therefore vulnerable to dark forces, *just might be true*. When men were killed by chance events on a day-to-day basis, every woman became superstitious despite herself.

'Take a look at THIS!'

Perpetua pulled a multi-coloured blanket out of the wooden box. It was made of crocheted wool, and the pattern was of an exquisite detail, consisting of a blanket of tiny flowers in a myriad of colours.

'Wow! This is amazing. Who made it?' Felicity knew that whoever made it, it was an expert Crafter. Most women could crochet – it was something girls were taught at school. But nothing like *this*.

'It's from my Auntie Lisa in Cornwall. She's a Crafter, and she specialises in making natural dyes. All of the colours in this blanket come from plants that she grew herself.'

Felicity took the blanket in her hands and looked closely at all the tiny flowers. She knew that blue came from woad, and yellow came from weld. There was another one, the madder plant, that gave red and pinks. She only knew all of this because Morgenna had helped CeeCee a couple of years ago with her dyeing project, and she had tried to get the dye plants to grow on a patch of wasteland behind the church. The dye plants preferred wasteland, and it was too dangerous to let such invasive species loose in a small domestic garden or allotment which grew vegetables. In all, the project had not been a great success, and CeeCee was still looking for a skilled gardener to collaborate with. So when Felicity looked at the array of pinks, purples, orange and turquoises, she could only imagine the level of skill that Perpetua's Auntie Lisa had.

'Your auntie must be a professional.'

'Oh, she's famous throughout Cornwall. Her

wools and fabrics are very sought after. She normally doesn't have time to make big finished pieces, but of course, this is a special occasion. I'm the oldest daughter of her baby sister.'

Felicity looked back at the blanket, which she imagined from its size was for a new baby. It was such a work of art however, that one would be worried about the baby getting sick or worse onto it. It really was too special to be just *used*.

'I don't know what to say. It's beautiful.'

'Isn't it? It's easily the best piece in the marriage box. All the other items look plain by comparison. My auntie got it sent up early, to make sure it got here in time for the wedding. It arrived yesterday, but Mum couldn't resist showing me it when she opened the parcel. I'm glad she did. I've been taking it out again and again just to look at it, because it fills my heart with joy every time I see it.'

Felicity suddenly remembered a lesson from school, entitled 'Why We Esteem Our Crafters'. Mrs. Calfhill spent the whole lesson teaching how the Crafters took the fruits of the land and made them even more valuable. *The Crafters root us into this English soil, and continue our ancestors' traditions,* she had told the class, or at least that was how Felicity remembered it.

Felicity recreated her old teacher's voice in her mind. *The genius of the crafters make our culture what it is. We understand that we must respect the world around us, and that the objects that we use must be made with love for our objects to be infused with our spirit. For almost a century, our people had a throwaway attitude to the objects that served them. Because all they cared about was money. As if money could buy roots or culture! Now we create a world to last, with workmanship that delights each new generation in turn, whether it be the smooth rocking of a baby's crib or wood that is made to sing. It is the ability to create the beautiful object and to practice the art that is the true wealth. Pride in the mastery of one's own craft is the essence of the English soul, and that is the true permanence. You should all strive to be Crafters in everything that you do.*

'You've got quiet all of a sudden.'

Felicity heard Perpetua's voice break through her reverie, which may have lasted a few seconds or a few minutes, it was impossible to tell. The vision of Mrs. Calfhill standing at the front of the darkened classroom, her face partially obscured by the swirls of dust that had transformed into glitter in the afternoon sunlight, vanished from Felicity's mind.

'I was just wondering,' Felicity said, 'if your auntie had got the blanket officially blessed before she sent it. I couldn't imagine her sending it to you without that, but if she hasn't there is a consecration ceremony next Saturday we could go to.'

Felicity enjoyed the consecration ceremonies held by the Albionic Church, and found any excuse to go to them. People brought all kinds of objects to be baptised with holy water – tools, weapons, even kitchen utensils. It was hoped that by showing their gratitude for these essential and often irreplaceable objects, the spirit of God would protect them.

'Oh, she definitely had it blessed. She wouldn't have let it travel such a long distance without that. Anything could have happened to it otherwise.'

Perpetua was about to say something else when the voice of her mother was heard shouting from the kitchen. The girls went downstairs.

'Hi Felicity! I take it Perpie has been showing you her new blanket. Isn't it amazing? I wish I had inherited my sister's talents.'

Candice Houghton bustled about the kitchen in a worn but well-fitted tea-dress. She was a very attractive woman in her mid-thirties who still retained much of her youthful sexual allure. It was plain to see where Perpetua got her beauty.

'Yes, it is lovely, Mrs. Houghton.' Felicity didn't know what else to add, and wished that she was better at thinking of new things to say when talking to people.

Candice Houghton knew that Felicity was shy and would be embarrassed talking about herself so she beckoned the girl to her side to help her feel more at ease.

'Come and taste this soup. Tell me what you think.'

The older woman held out a large spoon to Felicity's mouth, cupping her left hand under the spoon to catch the drips. Felicity dutifully opened her mouth and took the spoonful of chunky liquid. Mrs. Houghton spoke as Felicity tasted the soup. 'I don't know what it is, but it lacks a certain *something*. My mother always used to say that a woman who hasn't gone through the change always makes bland soup. I don't know why that would be, but I seem to be proving her right.'

'It's delicious, Mrs. Houghton.'

'Candice, call me Candice.' Candice said this every time that she met Felicity, without her request ever meeting success. Felicity clearly found it hard to be familiar with older people. 'Do you think it needs more herbs? Come on, you did herb-lore at school.'

Felicity looked embarrassed. 'Yes, but I wasn't very good at it. You'd be better asking Perpetua. She got much better marks.'

'I would…' said Candice slowly. 'But this soup has got parsley in it.' She drew out the words purposefully, so that Felicity would pick up on the meaning of the sentence. She kept her gleaming eyes on Felicity to confirm the young girl's suspicions. Felicity then looked to Perpetua, who was standing by the kitchen table, half beaming, half blushing.

'We just found out today. I'm pregnant!'

Felicity let out a little scream of excitement. She rushed to her friend and hugged her, jumping up and down as she did so.

Candice called out jokingly, 'Be careful, Felicity, you're pregnant yourself.' But she was laughing too.

Felicity was still holding her friend when she felt something tugging on her sleeve. She looked down. It was Perpetua's little sister Modesta who had come in from the garden on hearing the commotion.

'Auntie Felicity! I didn't know you were here! Come in to the garden and see what I am doing with Mummy!' Felicity felt Modesta's little hand take hers and lead her towards the back door.

Felicity laughed and let herself be led out to the garden, with Perpetua following them. The little girl pointed to some furrows dug in neat parallel lines in the soil.

'Mummy and me have made some furrows. We are going to plant beetroot and turnips.'

Felicity smiled and nodded at the little girl. She didn't know what to say.

Perpetua picked up on Felicity's consternation, and explained. 'Moddie is so excited because she helped Mum work out the north-south direction for the furrows.' She turned to her sister. 'Didn't you, Moddie?'

'Yes, said Modesta proudly. 'We did it at night when Mr. Ramage was here.'

Felicity imagined the old dowser hunched sternly over his rods, oblivious to the silhouette of a little girl skipping joyfully around him in the moonlight. To amuse herself she decided to test Modesta's memory of that night. 'So what end is north, Moddie?'

The little girl hesitated, and looked at both ends of the furrow. Then she looked up at the sky in both directions.

'This one!' She pointed at one of the ends, trying to give an air of authority to her answer, but it was clear that she didn't really know. Felicity smiled and looked at Perpetua.

'So when is the sowing?'

'Not for another two nights. Mum wants to wait until the moon is almost full, to maximise the moisture in the soil.'

The little girl skipped in circles around Felicity on hearing her big sister's answer. 'Isn't it exciting? Mum says I can come out with her to help sow the seeds and do the sowing ceremony with her. She is going to let me stay up til midnight!'

Felicity laughed. 'Yes, that *is* exciting. You're very lucky. Have you memorised the planting prayer?'

Modesta nodded and gave an unconvincing *uh-huh* as she skipped.

Felicity smiled and addressed her best friend. 'Well it's certainly a good way to get children interested in gardening.' She was vaguely envious of this little girl sharing these magical moments with her mother, something that she herself never had. The community itself was divided on the matter of Mrs. Houghton's telluric and chronomantic beliefs being the cause of such abundant vegetable harvests, the roots of the carrots and potatoes pushing with such vigour into the depths of the dark soil, but whatever the explanation, the woman's green fingers could not be denied.

The older girls watched as Modesta skipped towards the hollow behind the trees and the overgrown shrubbery at the back of the garden, to play in what the Houghtons rather optimistically called the fairy copse. Felicity turned to her friend. 'I'm so excited that you're pregnant. Our babies are going to grow up together. Does Matt know yet?'

'No, I was thinking about telling him at the Wedding Eve Meal. That way, if my cooking isn't up to scratch, the good news will more than make up for it. Because everyone knows that a bride's fertility is the most important thing for a good marriage. More important than how doughy her bread is.'

Even as she was trying to be persuade herself that her subterfuge for distraction would be successful, Perpetua sighed after she spoke. The Wedding Eve Meal had become the bane of every young bride-to-be, bar the gifted cooks, and Perpetua had been famous at school for her bad baking. Hers was always the heaviest pastry or the lopsided loaf. It was now an Albionic tradition that the bride-to-be cooked a meal for her in-laws the night before the wedding, including the baking of what came to be known as the Eve Loaf. The bread was particularly important. It was a symbol to the family that the bride would be able to feed her husband and future family. While officially the Wedding Eve Meal was a symbolic gesture – no wedding was ever called off on account of a mediocre roast or watery soup – it became a great source of stress for every bride-to-be, as the success of the meal became a talking-point at the wedding itself, and a poorly organised evening augured bad luck for the marriage. Some old wives had even worked out a system of telling the future of the marriage based on every element of the meal, from a pudding late out of the oven to the choice of side vegetables. As might be expected in such circumstances, it had become laden with a significance that had grown out of all sensible proportion in the teenage bride's mind, and many a young woman found herself paralysed with fear and indecision on the day of the meal itself. No amount of rehearsals at school or in the home seemed to help. In the event, the mother of the bride usually lent a hidden hand. Sometimes even the mother-in-law herself when she and the bride were close. Still, even with help, Perpetua was glad to have her good news to tell, which would the most delicious morsel of all.

'Yes, who cares about the consistency of the meat sauces when a new grandchild is being announced,' Felicity said. 'Truly, this is a blessing.' She leant into her friend's arm. 'Come on, let's go back in to the warm. I want to tell you about the dream I had last night.'

CHAPTER 30

Alban gasped when the huge stone structure loomed into view from the van passenger window. It took him a second to realise that it wasn't the fossilised skeleton of a dinosaur or a giant whale rising up out of the lush greenery, but some kind of ancient magical building of curves and triangles pointing towards the sky. Dr. Wansbrough looked at Alban's enraptured face.

'Hasn't this been worth the trip?' Dr. Wansbrough smiled, shooting a glance at the two EF soldiers who grinned despite themselves at the boy's enraptured face. For a few wonderful moments, the burden of being at war lifted from their shoulders. They were just three men in a van, remembering the joy of what it was like to be twelve, when life was exciting and every day a new discovery. Ogden, the driver, had agreed to take Dr. Wansbrough and Alban with them on their mission to Cardiff so that they could make a small surprise detour to Tintern Abbey on the way back. Sergeant

Ogden had a great respect for Dr. Wansbrough and he had cleared it with HQ. The other guy, Gallagher, hadn't shown much of an opinion either way, although Wansbrough suspected that he had started to get a bit irritated when the van continued on the M4, away from the normal route home. But Dr. Wansbrough stole a look at Gallagher's face now and he could see that he, like Alban, had never seen a ruined monastery before. Plenty of ruined buildings, of course. It was 2060, after all. But never the tragic beauty of a ruined monastery.

Ogden parked up on some weed-broken tarmac close to the abbey and they all got out of the van. Alban wanted to run towards the building to go and explore but he knew that in the company of adult men he had to behave like an adult and walk slowly beside them. And he didn't want to miss what Dr. Wansbrough had to say about what he was looking at.

'Take a good look at this building, lads,' Dr. Wansbrough said. 'You have heard the Bible saying that *one sinner destroyeth much good*? Well, this is what happens when a sinner has power over the land. Henry the Eighth, the biggest psychopath England and Wales has ever known, committed the biggest act of larceny in British history, and destroyed in four years what it had taken the people 900 years to build up. We would not see another megalomaniac of his calibre until Churchill, his spiritual son, exactly 500 years later.'

They walked towards the abbey building. Alban tried to work out how big the archway was as he walked underneath it. He calculated that it must be twenty times his height. Or maybe forty times. It was impossible to work out from directly below.

'Henry the Eighth was a monster ruled by his appetites. For food, drink, women and money. And the thing about lust is that it is never satisfied. So when he wanted more money, he saw the abbeys of England and Wales as nothing but gigantic money pots to be broken and looted.'

'Are abbeys the same as big churches?' It was Alban asking, but the soldiers were paying close attention. They were glad the boy was there.

'No, not in the way that you're thinking. They were religious centres for monks and nuns, which were groups of celibate men and women. Celibate means single – the monks and nuns were unmarried and childless, because they devoted their lives to God and to the welfare of others, having taken a vow of poverty.'

The small group walked through the open archway in front of them into the ruins of the church. No one was saying anything so Dr. Wansbrough decided to continue talking.

'Over time abbeys like this became havens for the wise, the good and the gentle. There were about 800 abbeys in the country, some much bigger than this, and they drew to them all of the most vulnerable in society, those in need of charity, protection, and medical care. Everything the monks did was with an eye on eternity.'

Dr. Wansbrough looked up at the dirty sandstone walls of the abbey interior. Mosses and lichens had found niches for growth around the top of the walls and on the stonework sills of the upper windows. He wondered how long it had been since the stonework had been cleaned. Probably at least a century. 'Whatever they were doing, building, planting, writing, the monks did with all of their heart and soul, because they were providing for the dignity and the wellbeing of generations yet unborn…and it gave the people a great pride in themselves. The wealth was in a perpetual corporation, with the ethos of everyone working for the good of the community, serving others. It was the ideal nation in microcosm.'

Alban piped up. 'Is that where the EF Youth motto, "I serve" comes from?'

'It's the same idea,' said Dr. Wansbrough.

There was another silence, broken only by the birdsong and the faint babbling of the River Wye which flowed behind the abbey complex and which had once supplied the monks with fresh water. The men stood around, looking at mighty columns still holding up the ruined walls. There was a great peacefulness about the place.

'The monasteries not only had hospitals for the old and the sick, but they were the centres of learning for the nation. The monks collected the Greek and Roman authors, they composed and transcribed scholarly books on Music, Logic, Astronomy, Vitruvian Architecture... Wisdom now lost that we cannot even begin to imagine in our degraded age. They chronicled the history of the land. If it hadn't been for the monastic books which survived the Great Looting, we would know nothing about Anglo-Saxon history.'

The small group walked around the vast nave, now carpeted in thick bright grass. Alban looked up at the open sky and felt the wind blow through the wide pointed arches. Some of the window arches still had part of their original traceries.

Dr. Wansbrough spoke again, but this time there was a harder edge in his voice, Alban thought.

'When a government wants to commit an atrocity, it first has to create a pretext. Henry the Eighth did this by getting his henchman fixer, Thomas Cromwell, to compile a dodgy dossier about the monasteries. It was a carefully crafted black legend of the type that England does so well, presented to Parliament so that the killing, looting and destruction could be justified. Sound familiar?'

Alban and Gallagher looked back at his inquiring face blankly. But Sergeant Ogden smiled.

'...not that Parliament had a choice – any dissenters would have lost their heads. But most were in on it, because they were going to get a cut of the spoils. The monasteries had between a quarter and a third of the land in the country, and it represented an unthinkable land grab for around fifty families who amassed vast fortunes overnight. Wealth that had served the social good was now into the hands of thieves, who now had a vested interest in keeping religion in ruins. These magnates grew so powerful that a hundred years from the plundering the sitting monarch of the day was nothing but a salaried puppet in their hands. Revolutions always turn on those who begin them. Cromwell wasn't wise enough to know that... but nor was Henry himself.'

Alban sensed that Dr. Wansbrough was beginning to talk cryptically again, in the way that he did when he sometimes forgot that Alban wasn't an adult like him. He decided to bring the conversation back to a level he could understand.

'So what happened? Did the monks fight back?'

'Oh, they did. But when you've got good and gentle people, steeped in God's word, coming face-to-face with Henry's soldiers, hell-bent on getting rich with pilfered trinkets, there can only be one winner. The monks knew that if they did not sign over everything they would be killed. Even so, some brave men did refuse to surrender. The Abbot of Glastonbury and two of his monks were dragged to the top of Glastonbury Tor, and there they were hung, drawn and quartered, in a demonic parody of Golgotha. At the summit of Avalon itself! The soldiers then hung up the Abbot's severed head, the head of a frail eighty-year-old man of God, on the newly ruined abbey gate, to warn the others what happens when you go against the will of an English tyrant.' Dr. Wansbrough sighed as they ambled in the direction the huge arched space of what was once the great south window, now full of sky, the traceries long destroyed. 'And he was far from the only one. The Abbots of Reading and Colchester met the same fate. A way of life that had lasted almost a millennium, gone in less than five years.'

Dr. Wansbrough, who kept falling behind the others because of the limp that slowed him up, stopped as he passed underneath one of the vast stone arches of the transept, and the others instinctively stopped alongside him. He looked at his audience and turned to cast an arm expansively around in the direction of the abbey's interior, to encouraging the men and the boy to properly look at their surroundings.

'Try to imagine the scene. Cromwell's men enter this monastery, just where we came in –' Dr. Wansbrough pointed to the open archway behind them '– and first they ransack the chests and drawers of the monks. Then they strip the altars to get the gold and silver, and from there burst into the library to tear the ornamented covers off the books. These books were all in manuscript – written laboriously by hand. A single work might take forty years to copy out. *Forty years!* Imagine it. One illuminated manuscript, a life's work, thrown into the mud to be trampled on by boots and horses' hooves after the all-important gold fastener or jewel on the cover had been ripped off. Whole monastic libraries, amassed over centuries of intense labour, sold to grocers for waste paper! I'm being serious. The priceless learning within those texts had no meaning to those barbarians. Nor was religion of any value. They even burned wooden crucifixes that were inlaid with gold or silver in order to get at the metal.'

Gallagher shook his head in anger and kicked at the grass. 'Fucking *cunts*. These people never fucking change, eh? What happened to the monks?'

Dr. Wansbrough looked upwards at the open sky. 'The King's Visitors stole the lead from the abbey roofs, which also had the benefit of making it harder for the evicted monks and nuns to try to reestablish their communities, as it speeded up the destruction of the buildings by the elements. Sometimes the royal agents resorted to gunpowder to try to reduce the buildings to heaps of ruins. But obviously, with buildings like this, built over centuries, even gunpowder can't reduce them completely to rubble.'

The sergeant spoke. 'Thank God for that small mercy. At least we can get an *idea* of what these places must have been like.' He tried to imagine the abbey in the depths of winter, cowled monks gathering together to intone Vespers in the candlelight as the rain battered down on the roof and the wind rattled the stained-glass windows. But it was hard to imagine such a scene, with the noise of the birdsong and the sun directly shining onto them from the open sky above. The abbey, despite the vision of shelter it provided, was now part of the outdoors. It had become as much a part of nature as the trees on the hills behind it, just as they were as subject to the same laws of sacred geometry.

Dr. Wansbrough spoke again. 'Oh, Henry tried to erase English history the best he could. His men even broke apart the tombs of the saints who had brought Christianity to England in the search for the precious metals of their coffins. Even the tomb of Alfred the Great was destroyed in search of booty.'

Alban couldn't believe what he was hearing. He had been taught all about King Alfred in English History at school. *He had done so much for the English people, and his descendants would scatter his bones to the dust looking for things to steal?*

Dr Wansbrough's voice interspersed with Alban's own thoughts '... but of course they needed to erase history if the big wealth transfer was to be successful. They needed people to forget. The land that Alfred was buried in eventually fell into the hands of a big banking family. Barings, I think it was.'

'Fucking hell.' Alban heard the sergeant's deep voice behind him. 'I wonder if Henry thought it was worth it.'

'Well, in the beginning, no doubt it was a very exciting time for him. He pocketed most of the plunder, or *superfluous plate* as he called it. His right-hand man Cromwell sent it to him in bundles. One day he'd be unwrapping a parcel of fifty ounces of gold, the next a parcel of precious stones. But within a few years he had squandered all of the wealth and soon had nothing to show for it. His body was swollen from debauchery and luxury, and stinking from an unhealed wound. Meanwhile his mind was torn by contending passions, which eventually descended into the rages and paranoia which terrified those around him. He had even had his partner-in-crime Thomas Cromwell executed, because there is no honour among thieves. Jesus said, a tree shall be known by its fruits, and after his death the few of Henry's children who survived outside of the womb proved to be unhappy, ill and, most importantly for a man obsessed with dynasty, barren. For despite his best efforts, at the end of a few decades, his house and his name were extinguished forever.' Dr. Wansbrough paused and exchanged glances with those around him, before smiling mischievously. 'No man can ever escape the perfectness of God's justice.'

The sergeant nodded as he took in this information. 'So did it all end when Henry died then?'

Dr. Wansbrough shook his head. 'No. It just made the thieves hungry for more. The looting continued after Henry's death, as his son Edward the Sixth was too young and sickly to stop the noblemen from moving on to the churches and asset-stripping their wealth and properties. As they used to say in England, *easy it is of a cut loaf to steal a shive.* They took the almshouses, the poor hospitals, the candlesticks, the altars... barrels of broken bell-metal were carted off... even the ornately embroidered vestments of the priests were burnt for the gold in the thread. With the loot, they built themselves palaces and awarded themselves dukedoms. They even had the gall to make a virtue of their plunder, as they told the people that the altar of the new state religion, which was created to legitimise the new regime, was better now as a plain wooden table.'

Gallagher muttered something under his breath and rolled his shoulders. 'And did the English people just put up with that?'

Dr. Wansbrough shook his head tiredly. 'No, but the people who stood up to the government were executed by German mercenaries, brought in for that purpose by the foreign-blooded Lord Russell. One priest was hanged by the tower of his own church. This new 'Church of England', became the scorn, not only of the people of England, but of all the nations of Europe. Everyone knew that it was just the new criminal caste of England consolidating its power.

Ogden was thoughtful for a minute. 'It sounds a bit like when the people were told back in the 2020s that England was not a country of the English.'

'Exactly.' Dr. Wansbrough nodded in agreement. 'Never was their contempt for the native people made more evident than earlier this century. But that contempt eventually had to come to an end. The elites of England thought that they could put a boot on the English people's necks, impoverish them and eventually destroy them as an ethnic group, and their economic order would last forever. But in the event their regime only lasted 500 years, which is 400 years less than the monastic one.

The men continued to walk among the ruins. Dr. Wansbrough with his slight limp always a few paces behind the others. Alban, full of boisterous energy, peeled away from the group to walk along a low wall of what was once the monk's refectory and noticed a wild goat watching him warily from a dozen yards away. Ogden spoke again. 'What happened to the peasants who were working the land?' He paused. 'I don't know why I'm asking this – I get a feeling I know the answer.'

Dr. Wansbrough sighed. 'They sank into a poverty from which they never recovered. Within a hundred years of Henry sacking the monasteries, more than half of the population did not have a home or land of their own. They were completely at the mercy of the new private landowners, who raised the rents on the land to gouging levels, and who usually spent the wealth of the land away from their estates, so that it didn't return to the local economy. The land was no longer seen as belonging to the saints, the common pasture where the monks would let the peasants feed their cattle, it was all now 'private property', a term which the ideologues of the new regime were paid to extol and justify at length in cleverly worded books. As a result, a whole class of English farming families were swept off the land, because the new owners found it more profitable to raise sheep.' Dr. Wansbrough stopped. 'Am I boring you?' He was aware that for a lot of people he had a tendency to talk too much.

'No, no,' said Gallagher. 'Though what you're saying is getting me pretty angry.'

'Well you'll probably also be angered, if not remotely surprised, to learn that Henry had also debased the coin of the land, and it was further debased after his death. The rich could afford to hoard or export the good coins, that is, the coins with the proper amount of the gold or silver in them, but the poor were forced to accept bad coins as payment, which meant that they were robbed of part of their wages. And so the poor, robbed of their patrimony by the sacking of the monasteries, were now robbed of their very labour. This debasement of the currency via inflation continued right up until this century.'

Alban spoke as a shard of sunlight broke through the clouds over the hills and hit him squarely in the face. 'Isn't tampering with the currency a capital crime?'

Ogden laughed. 'Yeah, it is now.'

Dr. Wansbrough nodded to the boy. 'Yes, and now you can see why we take these things seriously. There are steps between Heaven and Hell, and the looting of the monasteries was the first step on the path to the creation of the Bank of England. Ever since then the history of England has been the history of looting operations. The last one was the Great Mortgage Scam at the turn of this century, which was engineered, via banking deregulation, to suck the wealth out of bricks and mortar of the land. They had already stripped the assets of the nation's heavy industry a few decades before, so now labour was without value, and property was all that remained. The Great Mortgage Scam was their last act of plunder, the last sucking on the bones of an English nation already bled dry by the financiers and warmongers, before the final act of ethnic genocide. Of course, the Great Mortgage Scam led to a huge financial crash, as they knew it would, but by that point they didn't care. Their ultimate plan was to dissolve the English nation itself, by turning Ariel into Caliban.'

'So what happened to all the monks?' It was Alban who spoke again. He hadn't been listening to the stuff about the banks, and he wanted to get the conversation back to things he could understand.

Dr. Wansbrough thought for a moment before speaking. 'After Henry had his revolution, all of the good and the learned of the land had either been killed, starved to death, or banished from the country. Some clergy were lucky enough to get work as carpenters, blacksmiths or menial servants in gentlemen's houses. Some monks had been promised pensions, but that money stopped being paid after a few years. Others had been reduced to begging, and in a land where the pastures were now enclosed there were plenty of beggars. But the same year that Edward began looting the chantries, and by doing so defrauding past generations of their dying wishes, the government passed a ferocious law against the indigent. Now an Englishmen out of work for more than three days could be branded with a letter V and sold into slavery where they could be chained and beaten. He could even be executed. In England! It was the beginning of England's ragged proletariat and the mammon-centred class system that came to characterise England over other nations. Suddenly, labour was not wanted, and only capital mattered, which led to ordinary Englishmen having to learn ways to ensure that their wives didn't get pregnant, while intellectuals discussed how to rid England of its 'excess population'. Because now the only function of the people was to serve capital.

The men turned back from the stone stumps of the columns of what was once the monks' dayroom and started to make their way back towards the abbey. Dr. Wansbrough spoke again.

'People think that the Reformation was merely a matter of religion. But it wasn't. It was a matter of rights, wealth, happiness, and national greatness. I'm not saying that the monastic system was perfect – no system run by men ever can be. But it gave people dignity.'

Ogden nodded. 'Well, things obviously had to get bad enough before the people said

"Enough." And we've taken the land back.'

Dr. Wansbrough nodded. 'Indeed. Titles and deeds mean nothing when you're fearing for your life. Some of them might actually now see what is important in this life, but it's too late. Five hundred years too late. When the hour of divine vengeance arrives there is nothing on earth can stop it.'

Alban thought about what his teacher had been telling them. Even though all of those bad things had happened here, this place was still somehow very special. He decided to give his opinion. 'I'd really like to come back here again.'

Dr. Wansbrough nodded. 'Well, take your last look around, because I don't think we'll be back any time soon, and I can tell from the way that Sergeant Ogden is shuffling from side to side that we need to get going.' Dr. Wansbrough laughed when he saw Ogden smile guiltily. 'The thing is though, that while the story I've told might sound depressing, the fact that so much of the abbey is still standing after all these centuries is a reminder of the greatness that we were once capable of. And we can create that greatness again. All that is needed is the iron will to do it. And I do believe that the English Front and the Albionic Church possess that will to bring our people back to greatness.'

They made their way back to the van, and Gallagher went for a piss behind a wall.

Alban asked. 'Is this what happened in Ireland as well?'

Dr. Wansbrough laughed. 'I think,' he said, 'we need to keep Ireland for another day. Besides, it's Gallagher's turn to drive, and I don't want to see us ending up in a ditch.'

Sergeant Ogden looked thoughtful and then he turned to the boy. 'I hope that you are taking in everything that Dr. Wansbrough is telling you. More than anything the English Front is going to need good men who can pass on this information to future generations. I can only imagine what my life would have been like if I had had a teacher like Dr. Wansbrough when I was your age.'

Dr. Wansbrough interjected. 'I don't think you'd have liked it, Chris. Alban is on a jolly jaunt right now, but tonight he's got the task of translating a passage of Plato's Republic from English into Arabo-Swedish. Call it an intellectual exercise.'

Sergeant Ogden laughed heartily. 'Yeah, fuck that. Life's too short.'

Gallagher returned to the group and they

opened the vehicle doors.

Alban took one long final look at the abbey, trying to memorise all of its details for future dreams, before he climbed into the van. He wished they could stay here for longer. He wondered what the abbey must be like in the dark. He imagined owls screeching in darkness, bats flying under the arches and hooded ghosts floating around the ruined shell of what was once the library, searching in vain for a precious lost book.

Alban turned towards Dr. Wansbrough and spoke with an earnestness of youth that touched the old man's soul.

'Thank you for bringing me here.'

CHAPTER 31

The incomplete control of the English psyche started to collapse most noticeably around 2014 with the Rotherham scandal, a symbol of the mass countrywide sacrifice of young English girls to a state-backed conquering army. This feeling of anger and discontent crystallised after the betrayal of the 2016 Brexit referendum result, which had revealed the English desire to regain their sovereignty in order to push back against the evil forces seeking to dispossess them of their land, their political voice and their culture. Increasing numbers of English people found themselves unable to look away from this evil, its sickening Canaanite fruits demanding that it be confronted everywhere – in the public square, in the workplace and in their children's nursery.

As this realisation grew in the people, the English egregore began to get stronger. On the physical plane it was borne in the blood, for the energy of a people is in the blood,

> *but as a psychic force it also grew on the astral plane, and infused the land in which the English lived. This force grew ever darker with time, as the thoughts and emotions of the people began to synchronise, and everyone came to understand what would have to be done. By the 2020s the ruling order, with its corpse of a state, found it impossible to battle this ancient egregore, made powerful with rage.*

Perpetua stopped. 'How do you say that word? The *egre* one?'

Aoife shrugged a shoulder. 'I would say egre*gore*, but I don't think it matters. I know what you mean.'

Perpetua didn't want to go on reading. She had read quite a lot already. One of the springs in the old sofa she was sitting on was digging into the back of her leg. She decided to ask a question. 'Are egregores evil then? A *dark cloud over the land* sounds pretty evil to me.'

Aoife thought for a minute. 'No, an egregore in itself is completely amoral. It takes its character from the collective emotions and thoughts of those who give it life.'

Perpetua nodded. She didn't want to get back to reading the chapter, but she didn't know what else to add. It was all very strange. Suddenly, she had an idea for a question.

'Can you see an egregore?'

Aoife's face broke into a broad smile. 'No, but you can feel it. It's like an energy between people.'

'But I thought you said that you can see spiritual energy?' Perpetua remembered Aoife once telling her that sometimes she could see spirits around certain people. She had described them as dark birds fluttering near the person's face. *Or was it moths?*

'No, no, that's quite different. Although it does have to be said, individual spirits can end up being attracted to the energy of the egregore, especially to the people who are the strongest vectors between heaven and earth, such as military leaders. I can guarantee you that Commander Caldwell will shine like a beacon of fire through the cold grey mists of the spirit world. He will be surrounded by the ghosts of our ancestors. Not least the spirits of the men who died in the recent fighting. They will be looking to guide and protect him.'

Perpetua nodded. She remembered being told the story of the Battle of St Albans when she was a child. English nationalist forces, finding themselves routed in the High Street of St Albans town centre and facing an enemy closing in on them. were stunned to hear the bell of the medieval clock tower ring out and archers appear in the blown-out windows of the tower. Expertly aimed arrows rained down on shocked enemy soldiers, giving the English time to retreat. Nobody had known anything about who these archers were, which led to rumours that they were the thousand-year-old ancestors of the Englishmen now fighting to take back their land. Nothing was ever heard of their capture. At the time, Perpetua had assumed this to be another of those truculent but heartening bedtime stories told to sleepy English children who would one day be expected to take up arms themselves. Now she wasn't so sure.

'Does that mean the story about the Battle of St Albans is actually true?'

Aoife pondered the question. 'Honestly? I have to say that I don't know. I'm not ruling out that the spirits played a part in the battle, but I'm doubtful that they appeared as archers and fired arrows at the enemy. What happened was probably so strange that people imagined that part later, to make human sense of what they witnessed. The spirit world can warp space and time as well as matter, and can attack human beings on a deep emotional and energetic level. They don't need to fire human weapons.' She laughed at the idea of it, but then her face became thoughtful. 'You know how we were talking about egregores? Well **the town of St Albans has a very powerful egregore, because it is the site of the oldest Christian shrine in Britain, to the martyr-saint Alban. People made pilgrimages to that site for almost two thousand years and each pilgrim added his own spiritual energy to the egregore.**' Aoife went silent for a moment to think about that fact, before she snapped back into reality. 'Go onto the next page, the bit underlined is quite good.'

Perpetua obliged.

> *Mene, Mene, Tekel, Upharsin! You have been judged, O King, and you have been found wanting. The writing is on the wall, and yet you refuse to take heed of the sons of Japheth who cry out God's warning. Your black heart, filled with your sins against God and his people, weighs like lead on Archangel Michael's judgement plate. The evil unleashed* **by the six hundred and fifty prophets of Baal and the eight hundred prophets of Asherah has full reign of this land,** *and now God himself, through his Chosen, will restore righteous order. The common people serve God and call on the Father, but the sons of kings are serpents and sons of blood and death.* **And to our trumpet blare of justice, Jericho's worm-**

eaten walls will come tumbling.

Aoife brought her gnarled hands gently together in delight. 'Is it wonderful? Swanson sums up perfectly where we are right now in the struggle, yet he didn't even live to see it. It's my favourite part of the book.'

Perpetua nodded and said a few words of agreement. She had heard that bit before at the church. It was used quite a lot in sermons, and people seemed to like it. But she didn't see what Aoife or anyone else found so exciting about it. She looked back towards the page to find her place to resume reading but Aoife spoke again.

'Perpetua, the final battle will soon be upon us. I know that people have been saying that for years, but I can feel it. The time is nigh. There is something very, very dark happening in the English territories right now. I cannot be sure what it is, but it feels like it is something akin to the Final Judgement, like the first angel pouring out his vial on the land. People are getting very ill. Very ill. I don't know if this illness comes from nature, as a divine punishment, or if it is Man's work. We will soon find out.'

Aoife raised her eyebrows and began to speak slowly and with emphasis, making it clear to Perpetua that she was reciting something. '*For there is nothing covered, that shall not be revealed;*

neither hid, that shall not be known. I sense that very soon our lives will become unrecognisable.'

Perpetua nodded uncomfortably. She hoped that this wouldn't interfere with her wedding, which was only a week away. She heard the sounds of children playing outside. They were oblivious to worry, and talk like this. She envied them.

Aoife saw Perpetua's face, and appeared to read her mind. 'It will also soon be your wedding.' She was silent for a moment. 'You know how you were asking if egregores were evil? Well, the cult of the Virgin is a powerful egregore for good, as on the astral plane it has been the store of the power of maternal love for over 1,500 years. And understand this: the love of a mother is the most powerful love there is. It is selfless and self-sacrificing. Unconditional. It is for this reason that demons react most strongly to Mary's name being invoked during an exorcism, even more than the name of Jesus, because the Virgin symbolises this vast loving egregore.'

Aoife held up her Albionic rosary beads. 'Devotional activity feeds the egregore and binds you to it. You should be praying to the Virgin, because she is the symbol of the protective egregore of motherhood.'

Perpetua shifted on the uncomfortable couch. Aoife laughed and fixed on the fidgeting girl with her pale blue eyes. The intensity of the old woman's stare combined with the insistent *tick-tock* of the clock was too much for the teenage girl, who found herself looking away and rubbing the back of her leg.

'You think I don't know? I knew as soon as you came through the door! Don't worry, I won't tell.' She smiled and tapped her nose. She seemed to enjoy the conspiracy of silence, Perpetua thought.

Perpetua cursed herself for not considering that, if she came to visit Aoife, the old woman would work out her secret before Perpetua herself wanted it to be known. She looked down at the floor in frustration at her own lack of foresight.

'Don't worry. It is good news, even if you're not married yet. A baby is a clean thing.'

Perpetua wondered at the strangeness of the expression, but said nothing. She was lucky if she understood half of what Aoife talked about. But she still liked coming here. She liked when Aoife talked about the past and made vague predictions about the future. Aoife was the only old person Perpetua knew who did this. All of the other adults lived firmly in the present, as they had to, because even just meeting the material needs of daily life was a battle. If people were to start thinking about the past and the future, on top of the horrors of the present, they would probably go mad, Perpetua thought. They wouldn't find the energy to get out of bed in the morning.

A burst of distant gunfire echoed into the living room. Aoife paid it no heed and began to give her advice.

'It would be wise for you to get a set of rosary beads, or an amulet of the Virgin, on which to focus your thoughts. It will in turn embody the energies of the egregore. Egregores are vitalised through rituals and sacred objects. That's why we've got so many in the Albionic Church. Rituals are important because they concentrate energy into a specific time and place, which allows spiritual energy to manifest on the material plane, and every time that a ritual is repeated, that spiritual energy engrains itself deeper into our reality. Imagine the constant wash of the ocean, the waves crashing again and again against a vast cliff face, slowly but surely melting the limestone. The uniformity of the ritual strengthens the link with everyone else who has ever practiced that same ritual, regardless of where they are in space and time. And it strengthens the spirits who need rituals to honour them.'

Aoife sighed, and sat back in her chair. She had talked a lot, and now her joints were aching. If she had a real open fire by her chair her life would be so much more pleasant. But she could only dream of such luxury.

Perpetua's lerter sounded. It was Felicity asking her where she was. Perpetua took the opportunity to excuse herself from Aoife, who looked tired. But before she went she had one final question for the old woman.

'Can Felicity come and visit you at some point? She says that she has had some dreams she would like to talk to you about.'

Aoife still had her eyes closed. 'Yes, yes, that's not a problem. But it would probably be best after your wedding.' Aoife's eyes opened to look at Perpetua with a mischievous twinkle. 'I have to say that I am looking forward to the Eve Meal, Perpetua. I expect that it will be the highlight of my year.'

Perpetua made some non-committal noises by way of agreement and then said goodbye to the old woman lying back in the chair. She made her own way out of the house.

CHAPTER 32

Helena Caldwell lived in a studiedly nondescript house in the quiet town of Heswall, watched over by an equally nondescript secret service chosen specially for the task by her son. If he was honest with himself, David was not protecting her from a potential SAU attack – she was much too far westward for that – but from elements within his own people. As a way of extending their power into perpetuity, the old government regime had seen fit to nurture the disgruntled dregs of English society whose very disordered, anti-social existence ensured that a cohesive civic body could never form to rise up against the ruling elite. This criminally inclined underclass had become dependent on the state for its subsistence, and did not take kindly to the imposition of a martial order which, taking theological vindication in the second Paulinian letter to the Thessalonians, made clear that those who refused to work would find themselves starving, and which rewarded crimes against the common weal with summary execution.

From the Land All the Good Things Come

At the beginning of the Rivers of Blood decade, as civic order broke down, many of those killed by the English forces were members of this underclass, and while not all of this group were irredeemable, many reduced to this abject state by generations of government policy rather than genetic disposition, there were still some elements of English society that were extremely resentful of the current order, which followed to the letter the God-sanctioned determination of David's biblical namesake to *early destroy all the wicked of the land*. Particularly dangerous were the surviving relatives of the organised crime gangs which had battled with the vigilantes of the early EF for control of the lawless and marginalised territories of England which became the EF's first base areas. David would not put it past any one of these people to take vengeance for a perceived slight of decades before, and for this reason his mother enjoyed more personal security than he did himself, although she herself was blissfully unaware of it.

Helena Caldwell was now almost eighty years old, physically decrepit but with her mind and soul intact. She spoke with a will and intelligence which ensured that David still saw her as younger than she actually was. Perhaps this was because he didn't want to see how old his mother had become, given that she had been his moral anchor through all of his struggles. Women had come and gone in his life as each in turn had asked too much of a leader, but not one of them had understood him like his own mother did.

She sat now in her big wicker rocking chair, knitting a tiny child's jacket in blue wool, as one of her cockatiels sat on the left arm of the chair and tried to pick up the wool snaking from the knitting needles with his beak. She looked over at her son, who had lain his great form out on the huge couch. It occurred to Helena that this house, in which he had installed her just over ten years ago, was the closest thing that he had to a home. She continued rocking in her chair. She knew better than to ask him direct questions. He would speak in his own time.

Eventually he did speak.

'Operation Azrael is taking effect. The hospitals are full to overflowing.'

Helena nodded, and kept rocking her chair, which gave a little familiar rhythmic creak back and forward. She knew about Operation Azrael, and she had agreed with her son that it was the right thing to do.

David continued, 'The thing is, people are going to start dying, and at some point we are going to have to address the rumours. The people are going to have to know. The question is, when to tell them, and how.'

Helena continued rocking in her chair, gently wresting the wool from Georgie's beak. She spoke with a flat voice. 'I don't think that there can be a right time to tell people. The die has been cast. People are going to die regardless of what happens.' The chair continued to rock as Helena pondered the matter further. 'I think that you should wait until the situation cannot be denied. Because otherwise all that you will do is engender a general panic in the population. And people who know that they are going to die can do extreme things.'

David made a grunting noise in agreement. 'I don't expect that the families of the dead will understand. I've done this to *save* English lives overall. It will make the final offensive so much easier. The sacrifice of a few could save hundreds of thousands of English lives.'

Helena interjected. 'Yes, but you've got to remember that most people don't look at the big picture. They only see their own pain. They don't care about saving the life or even thousands of lives of people they don't know. Most people don't reason their way through life - they live through their emotions. And a leader must acknowledge that if he is to retain his position.'

David pondered his mother's words. She was correct, as always. He struggled to understand the world as ordinary people saw it. Since his teenage years he had seen the world in predatory terms, with the instincts of a wolf, who understood that most of his people were sheep who needed to be protected from the other wolves. The thing was, to protect his people in the long term it meant having to make a sacrifice of a small number of them. How could he get them to understand that? As he had grown up he had been stunned by the number of his countrymen who cared about stupid things like designer kitchens and new cars, when for decades their borders had been lying wide open like a drugged twelve-year-old English sex slave on a dirty mattress. To David it was as insane as a vain woman obsessing over which colour of lipstick to wear for a party while blood gushed from an open wound in her abdomen.

The click-clack of the knitting needles resumed. 'How long until people start dying?'

David swiveled his feet from the arm of the couch and sat up. 'I think it will start to happen in the next couple of weeks. I was advised that first there is up to two months of flu-like symptoms, then the hemorrhaging begins. At that point, people are dead within a couple of days, if not the same day.' He took a deep breath. 'At that point it will be impossible to deny what is going on. Especially because it will be the SAU who will be most affected, and we need to let the people know that. So that they know why this is happening.'

Helena nodded slowly, and sighed. She put down her knitting and even the sound of rocking of the chair stopped as she stilled herself to think.

'In the long term... in the *long* long term... the English will get over this. We've got over worse. And history will judge you as a brave man who was capable of making the most difficult decision a man can make. Most leaders are not capable of making such difficult decisions. They are not real men, and their people perish.' Helena looked directly into her son's remaining eye, his mutilation a permanent reminder of the viciousness of the enemy that they were facing, the same enemy that had made her a widow. She continued.

'The most difficult part will be the initial stages of shock, as people will not have expected this turn of events. Shock affects different people in different ways. Most people can handle any kind of atrocity being done to them, if it is done gradually enough. The key thing is not to alter a person's perception of normality. This, however, is unavoidably going to be a jolt to the system. So when they find out the truth they are going to be shocked, and in that shock they are going to feel that the EF has betrayed them. That *you* have betrayed them. It's going to be a very dangerous time for you.'

David nodded, his head bowed. For a moment, despite his outward manliness, Helena saw him as a lost little boy.

He composed himself and looked up at his mother. 'It's possible that Paris could fall to the Russians in the next six months. And that would change everything for the Old Families. They will become desperate and will look to end things before we do. We have to strike first.'

The old woman nodded her agreement as she looked at her son. His face looked so haggard at that moment that it occurred to her that he could be her brother rather than her son, who so long ago had been a tiny baby in her arms. She got up and sat beside him.

'What you have done is a terrible thing, but it was the only option to ensure our people's survival. Power politics doesn't care about right or wrong, it just cares about winning, and our enemies thought that they had won when they left us with a Gordian knot that they knew we would be unable to unpick. They assumed that this would ensure their power forever.' She paused, and smiled proudly at her son. 'They did not count on someone deciding just to cut through the knot.'

David grimaced, and Helena stroked her son's face tenderly. She could not imagine the burden that he was having to bear in his own quiet moments.

'You have done the right thing. And history will judge you accordingly.'

'Maybe, but that will be long after I am dead. In the meantime, how will I handle things when I am alive? The chaos that this could cause could spark a mass rebellion, and destroy EF authority. If we get anarchy, or we have to fire on our own people, all of this will have been for nothing. We need to maintain morale and discipline for the final push against the SAU.'

The smile faded from Helena's face. She suddenly saw how this would play out, and what her son had planned. To her horror, she heard her son's voice enunciate her own thoughts.

'A leader always takes responsibility for the actions of his force. And I was the one who ultimately decided to go ahead with this strategy. If we engineer it so that I take all responsibility for Azrael, and I manage to convince the people that the regional leaders did not know all the facts, there is a chance that the wrath of the people can be concentrated onto me, so that the rest of the high command, and the EF as a whole, will be spared.'

Helena spoke in a barely audible voice. 'They will kill you.'

'Yes, I know. But what is one more death when so many are going to die? I can't see myself as in any way special. And if through my death it means that order and trust is maintained and leadership transfers to the right man, then surely this is the wisest move.'

It was Helena who bowed her head now. By her own cold, implacable logic she knew that her son was right. But that did not stop her feeling the desperation of realising that she was running out of time.

David sensed his mother shrink and wither on the couch next to him as they both contemplated the spectre of his imminent death. He was her life force, her reason for living. It was because of him that she had shelves full of military biographies and war histories, as she had tried to understand herself as the mother of a *great man*, whose job was to know as best she could how great men thought, and the superhuman pressures placed upon them.

She knew that her son would not shrink from scapegoating himself if it meant overall victory for his people, and there was nothing she could say, or should say, to stop him.

They sat together in silence for a minute as they each contemplated the upcoming end of the road. Helena refused to show any emotion which would upset her son. She got up and looked down at him in a bid to take charge of the situation. 'Would you like to stay for tea? I could make us a chicken stew... I've got some cooked chicken pieces in the fridge right now that you could eat. You must be hungry.'

She used the excuse of going and getting food as a way to escape into the kitchen. With that temporary wall between her and David, that beautiful big son of hers who was soon to die, she could have a few moments to herself to cry out silently to God before getting back into her son's presence, her beautiful boy who would soon no longer be with her and whose company she did not want to miss another second of.

CHAPTER 33

Valerie Ellacombe wore her years well, Alan Wansbrough thought. From what Jack had told him, she must be at least 66 years old, but the bones of her face, forming a perfectly balanced harmony of sweeping arches and hollows, provided cathedral-strength foundations for her classic Gallic features, her high cheekbones and sharp jawline far outweighing the wrinkles around her eyes and mouth as an indicator of age. She moved her trim body with a natural elegance and composure that betrayed, even after half a lifetime in Merseyside, her Parisian origins. A sleek bob of caramel-coloured hair, greying with dignity at the temples, was swept off her face in a way that happened to showcase her high, broad forehead and aquiline nose, giving her a somewhat noble air rather out of place in St. Helens. As she ushered her guests into the kitchen, Dr. Wansbrough spent a few seconds imagining that he had fallen into a timeslip in which Valerie Ellacombe was a minor aristocrat or courtesan in the Sun King's Versailles Palace, ushering in guests to a literary salon. She was of a vanishing stock. *Maybe now a vanished stock*, thought Dr. Wansbrough sadly.

But the kitchen table they were being led to was far from a banqueting table, and the chairs were of the most functional design. 'I am so glad you answered my call. I wasn't sure what Jack would have told you.'

'Not at all, Mrs. Ellacombe. What he told me was very intriguing. The pleasure is all mine.'

The woman shook her head in vague embarrassment and rose to her feet as her guests sat down. 'Please, call me Valerie. I will get us all a drink.'

In other circumstances, Dr. Wansbrough, given his natural inclinations towards formality, would have resisted using her first name in view of Mrs. Ellacombe's age and civil status. But she had such a youthful continental air that it felt impolite to insist on form. Dr. Wansbrough's mind flitted briefly to her deceased husband.

'Here we go!' Valerie placed a glass teapot with an infuser in the middle of the table and went to the cupboard for some glasses. 'It's mugwort tea. I had it brewing for your arrival.' She poured the tea out into the glasses as the doctor and the boy watched in silence, waiting for her to sit down. Dr. Wansbrough glanced at the folder crammed with paper lying on the table. He assumed that this would be to do with what she wanted to tell him.

'When Jack told me how excited you had been when you found the Enid Blyton books, something stirred in me. I realised that you are a man who cares about preserving the truth of the past. And it got me to thinking about what happened in France. I realised that the things I had been keeping for my daughter would be better off with you. I think that you will understand them more, and keep them safe.'

Valerie pulled the heavy folder towards her. 'As you can probably tell from my accent, yes, I am French.' She smiled at Alban, who at this point had still said nothing. 'The Parisian accent is very strong. It can fade a little over time, but it never completely dissolves.'

Dr. Wansbrough nodded dumbly. He wanted to say that she had a charming voice, but he was frightened of coming over as obsequious to a woman he had only just met. He erred on the side of caution and said nothing, but was simultaneously annoyed at his own lack of social graces when he missed the moment to respond and Valerie resumed her explanation.

'I wanted to tell you about some things that happened in Paris before I came here. I cannot tell you everything. I am not a historian, and as things were happening I was like so many others, not paying very close attention. But some of the things that happened were so crazy that I decided to keep little bits and pieces. I don't know why.' She pulled the folder towards her and began looking through it.

Dr. Wansbrough felt he should say something encouraging but he couldn't think of anything to say. So he simply said that he understood.

She continued. 'I don't know how much you know about what happened in France before the war. So many things had been happening on a small scale that it almost became normal to the French. I was a young woman and it just seemed like part of life. I think the first time I started paying attention was when the *Charlie Hebdo* attack happened.'

Valerie passed a double newspaper page to Dr. Wansbrough. 'Jack told me that you speak French. This is a full report on the attack. Islamic gunmen broke into the office of the magazine *Charlie Hebdo* and shot over a dozen of the staff. The magazine was the mouthpiece of some ridiculous *soixante-huitards* who refused to listen when they were told that France had changed since their student rebellion, and they couldn't mock Mohammed the way they had mocked Jesus.' Valerie waved her hand dismissively in a very Latin way, the energy of her suppressed urge to speak French being transmuted to her arms. 'I have no sympathy for those *nihilistes*... it was their very deconstruction and ridicule of France which led, in its final conclusion, to their own deaths. That is not what interested me. What interested me was the official reaction to the incident.'

She passed a second newspaper page to Dr. Wansbrough. Alban leaned in to him to take a look.

'There was a huge parade, and all the Western political leaders defended what they said was the cause of free speech. Lots of people said *Je suis Charlie*, even though they didn't know what the magazine was about or what it had said. And yet... we didn't have free speech in Europe. Far from it. The people who had protested Islamic immigration into Europe, the people who, if they had been listened to in the first place, would have ensured we didn't have blood in the streets, were denounced for 'hate speech' and racism. They lost their jobs and social positions for expressing their opinions. So to say *Je suis Charlie* was just sheer hypocrisy. And of course, *Charlie Hebdo* found it funny to mock Muslims and Christians, but it never dared to touch the Jews.'

She passed some photographs over to Dr.

Wansbrough. One showed some young people waving around an inflatable pencil and the gay liberation flag beside a fountain. Another showed a skinny young man holding a placard of a hand gripping a pencil which dripped blood. 'I took these photographs on the day of the gathering. The young were carrying banners that said stuff like "Where is Charlie? I am here!" "Liberté" and "The pen is mightier than the sword" to get media attention, but the fact was, that there were soldiers surrounding the rally, making the rally possible, and they knew it. This wasn't bravery, this was signalling for the cameras. The idiots talking about freedom of expression were always very careful to keep with the crowd, and close to the soldiers. But the politicians saw the power of inflatable pencils to sway the mob to their side, and clearly, it stuck with them.'

Valerie took a sip of her tea, and Alban took the opportunity to try his. He wasn't sure if he liked it, but he sipped it anyway out of nervousness.

'The next thing that I kept souvenirs of – I'm not sure if *souvenirs* is the right word – was the attack on the Bataclan. It happened the same year as Charlie Hebdo. 2015. It was part of a series of attacks on Paris during the same night. Some suicide bombers had blown themselves up outside the Stade de France where the president was watching a football game between the nations. France and Germany I think it was. *Monsieur Le President* was quickly removed from the scene, but the game played on. *Rien ne s'arrête pour le spectacle!'*

Valerie looked towards Alban and smiled, then was suddenly aware that the polite, quiet little boy would be completely lost by the conversation. She looked at Dr. Wansbrough. 'Are you okay with me talking about these things with him here? I'm going to be talking about some very horrible stuff.'

Dr. Wansbrough laughed. 'Oh don't worry, Alban's fine. He wouldn't be with me if he wasn't mature for his age. It's good for him to know about what went on. And they get a lot of it in their history lessons at school.'

On hearing this, Valerie threw her head back and laughed. Dr. Wansbrough imagined her in her heyday. She must have entranced the men around her. 'History lessons at school! When this stuff feels like yesterday to me! Should it really be called history when there are still people alive who were there?' She laughed again, and Dr. Wansbrough smiled and nodded in agreement.

'The Bataclan was a theatre. That night they were holding a rock concert. A small group of heavily armed terrorists gained access to the building, and proceeded to rip through the crowd with Kalashnikov bullets. It was a... an *abbatoir*. The dancefloor ran thick with blood, bodies were piled up everywhere. There were rumours that the terrorists had been given access to the building by the Algerian security team who were employed by the theatre. I don't know if this is true, but the killing was definitely based on race. The killers were Maghrebis and were targeting Europeans, and let their own kind go wherever they could. Hundreds were injured and killed that night. Hundreds. The death toll rose much higher in later weeks, as the injured, often trapped under corpses or playing dead, died in hospital. These men were all armed with automatic weapons and grenades, while the people inside were unarmed. They tortured and mutilated people. They gouged out eyes of their victims. They cut off the victims' private parts and stuffed them down their throats. The state gave them three hours to have this fun.'

'What? Three hours? What do you mean?' Dr. Wansbrough didn't understand.

'The state hesitated for three hours before intervening. Various bureaucratic arms of the state were apparently arguing over who had jurisdiction over the event. It's France, so they were probably having a philosophical discussion whether they should even intervene.

Qu'est-ce que c'est le terrorisme? Qu'est-ce que c'est la sécurité?' She rolled over the French vowels with exaggerated gravity and her hands gestured wildly about her head as she mocked her countrymen. She shook her head grimly. 'Meanwhile, people were being slaughtered inside like chickens as the security forces did nothing.' She passed over a photograph to Dr. Wansbrough.

'It is a photograph of the dancefloor after most of the bodies were cleared. But there are still some bodies and bits of bodies lying there, and you can still see the blood patterns where they dragged the bodies across the floor. I printed this off the Internet so that even if they starting taking websites down I would still have it as evidence, in my hand. It turned out to be a good move, as this is unpixelated version, which was quickly removed from the mainstream websites. Even the pixelated version of this photograph was very quickly deleted from social media platforms before it had a chance to spread.'

'Fucking hell.' It was Dr. Wansbrough's voice. Alban started. He had never heard Dr. Wansbrough swear before. He got a glimpse of the photo before Dr. Wansbrough turned it away from him. 'You don't need to see this, lad,' he said, in a low voice.

'I don't understand,' said Alban. 'Was France already at war? I thought the war didn't start until 2028.'

Valerie refilled the boy's glass, and poured some more for herself. Dr. Wansbrough hadn't touched his. 'Yes, it was. But not officially. The government wanted to pretend to the people that all was well in order to keep their power. So that meant psychological control.'

She passed two stapled documents to Dr. Wansbrough and Alban.

'After the Bataclan carnage, they lit up the Eiffel Tower in the *Tricolore*, and the narratives of the mainstream media and social media were strictly controlled.'

Dr. Wansbrough looked down at the document he had been given. It was headed #prayforbataclan and underneath appeared to be various short comments.

'What is this?'

After the attacks of that night, because there were several different attacks, two slogans started rising on Internet social media, mainly Twitter and that other one… what was it called?' Valerie clicked her fingers, trying to jog her memory.

'Facebook?' asked Dr. Wansbrough.

'Yes, Facebook. They spread like wildfire, I believe, because they were being promoted by the French government. They were *Pray for Bataclan* and *Pray for Paris*. There were others, like *Nous Sommes Unis* and *I Stand With My Country*, but the ones asking people to pray were the main ones. Alban, you have the pages I printed out for the hashtag Pray for Paris. People were changing their self-portraits on social media to be tinted with the French national colours, and other governments were lighting up their official buildings with the Red, White and Blue. People were commenting about how sorry they were that it had happened.

Alban was confused. 'What difference would that make?'

Valerie laughed at the young boy's facial expression. 'You are exactly right. It served to feed individual vanity, and the need for social validation and in doing so it calmed the autonomic nervous system of the nation. People left teddy bears holding Tricolore love hearts on the pavements, along with flowers and tealights. People hugged each other in crowds, and they poured out their sympathy on social media. When they were all together, in vigils protected by the police, they all made declarations that they weren't frightened of the terrorists, that the Islamists would not win out over 'Love', that the French people would stand defiant, and yet when someone let off firecrackers in the Place de la Republique, these same defiant people stampeded over each other in their desperation to escape the place, and the shrines of teddies and tealights were trampled in the panic. They scattered like rats at the first sign of danger. *Nous n'avons pas peur?* My arse!

Dr. Wansbrough laughed loudly at the evidence of Valerie's subsequent assimilation into the culture of Merseyside, and then shook his head in disbelief at what she was saying. He looked down at the stapled document in front of him. It was a print out of some of the Twitter reaction to the *prayforbataclan* hashtag. He read through the comments.

> *R.I.P. Parisian Angels... Pray for Kindness!!!*
>
> *OMG!!!!!!! 100 morts au Bataclan!!!*
>
> *United together we will be stronger.*
>
> *Apprends à écouter le Silence, et tu verras qu'il est Musique*
>
> *We are with the people of France.*

Emojis of crying faces and hands in prayer were popular. The emojis were often repeated several times in the same comment, as if to make it clear to the reader that the sender truly felt the emotion. Graphics of the French flag overlaying crying eyes. Dr. Wansbrough turned to the second page of the document.

As you can imagine, there were thousands of comments – I could only print out the first few pages. But as you'll see the comments get very samey, very quickly. It's the same with your one, Alban, which was what I printed out for *Pray for Paris.*

Alban looked down his list of comments, which seemed to be just as trite and indulgent as the doctor's list.

'What's that supposed to be?' The boy pointed at a geometric image which clearly meant something, but he wasn't sure what.

Valerie got up and went to his side, and chuckled to herself. 'Well spotted. It is a representation of the Eiffel Tower, which was still standing at that time, placed in a circle so that it looks like a peace symbol. It is saying that what we need to do is seek peace in France.'

Alban was now completely confused. 'I thought you told me that hundreds of French people had been tortured and killed by Islamic terrorists. I don't understand anything at all.'

Valerie laughed a little and put a reassuring

hand on the boy's shoulder. 'That's because you have normal human instincts and you are full of good sense. That wasn't the case fifty years ago.'

The elderly French woman returned to her seat. 'The terrorist attacks after that followed the same model – individuals signaling their solidarity over social media, candles being lit, teddy bears. The mainstream media always focused on the stories of the brave survivors, especially where there was a romantic story involved. The dead were quickly forgotten, because they don't exactly inspire a message of hope. They are dead, and their deaths should, in a healthy society, cry out for vengeance. But our society was very sick, and people forgot quickly and got back to their own life of self-regard and consumerism. Even the truck attack in Nice six months later, which had a death and injury toll of several hundred, didn't change the mindset of the French. No number of children's corpses strewn across the promenade could cleave them from the government narrative of 'Love' and 'Peace' and 'Tolerance'. *Pray for Paris* soon became *Pray for Nice*, and other countries' elites soon copied the strategy. *Pray for London*, *Pray for Berlin* … the list goes on and on.

'Yes,' said Dr. Wansbrough. There was a *Pray for Stockholm*, *Pray for Barcelona*, *Pray for Manches-*

ter. I remember it – just.'

'And did any of this praying actually work?' asked Alban.

Valerie smiled at the boy in his blond doubtfulness. She liked him, and was glad that boys like him were the future of England. 'Of course it didn't. The irony is, the people retweeting this nonsense were the least likely people to pray. They were thoroughly atheistic. They would never hold to a religion which had any form of absolute moral standard. Value judgements are not inclusive. They were as *nihiliste* as the *Charlie Hebdo* cartoonists.'

Dr. Wansbrough felt the need to intervene. 'It wasn't just the French. I have a photograph of a little Swedish girl whose body was broken into pieces under the wheels of a terrorist's lorry driven into a crowd of Stockholm shoppers. The blood and offal from her body parts had barely been sluiced into the gutter before stiletto heels were crossing the road to get back into the department store, yards from where she was killed. Make the gesture of lighting a candle, maybe take a sad selfie, but not so sad that you don't look pretty in the photo, then it's business as usual.'

'Especially if there is a sale on!' Valerie chipped in humorously.

Dr. Wansbrough felt himself falling in love with her.

'And don't forget the pop concert, put on to reinforce the values of Love, Tolerance and Globalism. They became de rigueur as a way of "bringing the people together"'.

Now Dr. Wansbrough was sure that he had fallen in love with this beautiful widow. He decided to ask her directly. 'So why hadn't you left Paris already by this stage? Surely it was dangerous for you?'

She sighed, and poured the last of the tea into her and Alban's glass. Dr. Wansbrough had barely touched his. 'People say things like "Why don't you just leave?" But it's never that straightforward. My life was in Paris. I was working on a PhD, and I had a boyfriend. And there was the question of where to run to. The rest of Western Europe wasn't much better. And the French government had deliberately resettled migrants into every provincial corner of France, meaning that *la belle vie* no longer existed. Everywhere was *enriched*. And there was always the hope that in 2017 the election would deliver us Le Pen. She wasn't perfect, but she would be a step in the right direction. Instead, we got… *this*.

Valerie reached into her folder and brought

out a couple of photos.

'*Messieurs, je vous presente, Le Président de la Cinquième République!*' She slid the photographs across the table straight towards Alban, and watched in amusement for his reaction.

The boy's dismayed expression did not disappoint. 'Who is *THAT*?' He looked at the photographs of a fresh-faced, well-dressed man getting up close to semi-naked black youths. One photograph showed the man between two other men. The man on the left was a young African exposing his underpants and sticking his finger up aggressively to the camera, while the other African to his right was in a vest and a bandana. He had tattoos and was giving some kind of secret sign or irreverent gesture, Alban wasn't sure which.

'That was the Rothschilds man whom the French people had charged with keeping them safe and sound into another century.'

Dr. Wansbrough snorted. He saw Alban looking at the pictures of the president and his mother-wife in the palace, surrounded by flamboyant black homosexuals. He was sure that Alban wouldn't understand the sexual signifiers of the animal collars, the hot-pants and the fishnet tops that these men wore. Such things would be as mysterious to an English boy of 2060 as an Ethiopian stretched lip or a Chinese bound foot. And he was grateful to God that He had made such a return to innocence possible.

Alban looked up in anxiety at Dr. Wansbrough. He didn't understand what was going on at all. He pointed to the T-shirt that a black man was wearing in one of the photographs that had a message on it. 'What does that say?' He wondered that it might give him a clue to understanding the Europe of before the war.

Dr. Wansbrough peered at the photograph. 'It says *Fils d'imigrés, noir et pédé.* He paused. That's French for… "the pendulum is still, the moment before it swings back"'.

Valerie laughed uproariously. Dr. Wansbrough felt a warmth in his body and a joy to be alive that he had not felt since he was a teenager. He wanted to be in Valerie's company for longer than just this one occasion.

'Ah,' said Valerie, still laughing. 'You are too hard on *Manu*. Compared with what came after, he was like De Gaulle.'

Dr. Wansbrough smiled when he thought about Donatien Dupré, France's first openly homosexual leader but the last of a long sorry line of banker-presidents that would eventually oversee France's collapse. The doctor realised how much he would love to spend an evening with Valerie, just one-on-one, talking about France and French history. And life in general. She was a sophisticated, intelligent woman with life experience. And she was very attractive.

'That video of Dupré. You know the one. The one that became notorious... Was it actually real? Or was it an urban myth?'

Valerie's eyes sparkled mischievously at his question. He suddenly saw her as a young woman. 'Oh it was real, alright. It's what gave him his nickname of *Dupré le Depravé*. And for a French politician to earn the nickname of *depravé*, well, he had to be pretty bad.'

Dr. Wansbrough smiled at her joke. 'Well, it was par for the course in those days. Just as our countries did not have walls, our people did not have self-control.'

Valerie was just about to pass over a photograph of a giant sculpture of an anal dilator installed symbolically in front of the Ministry of Justice, a 24-metre high celebration of France's rule by sodomites and international banking elites, when she was interrupted by the sound of the front door opening. Her face suddenly acquired a seriousness and she hurried to put the papers back in the folder. 'It's best if the grandchildren don't see this. I can't believe I have more things to show you and we've run out of time. I haven't even got started on the *gilets jaunes* or Notre Dame. Would you like just to take the folder with you?'

Dr. Wansbrough took the opportunity to make his move. 'No, no, I'd like you to keep it for now. Because I'd like you to go through what else you have in the folder with me. To explain the importance of what is there. You bring the events to life.'

They exchanged glances. Both were old enough to know what the other was thinking.

'Why don't I lert you later on today and we can arrange something?' Valerie said quickly, rising to her feet but still smiling, as her youngest grandchild rushed into the kitchen and hugged her legs, followed by Valerie's daughter, the child's tired mother. Valerie could see from the look on her daughter's exhausted face that she would not appreciate strangers in the house at that moment. Dr. Wansbrough caught the sudden flash of anxiety in Valerie's expression and ushered Alban out of his seat.

'Come on, lad, it's best we get going. We'll meet Valerie again soon.'

'Thank you for meeting us, Mrs. Ellacombe.'

'Not at all, young man. The pleasure was all mine.' Valerie showed the man and boy smoothly to the door and said a few quiet words to Dr. Wansbrough before waving them both goodbye as they made their way up the garden path.

When the door finally closed Alban took his opportunity to give his view, relieved to no longer be the politely silent child listening in on the adult conversation.

'I like Valerie. She's really nice.'

'Yes, she is,' said the doctor thoughtfully. 'A very nice woman indeed.'

CHAPTER 34

There was another power cut, and the living room fell suddenly into gloom. The lard lamp on the table gave only the tiniest sliver of light as it ran out of fuel, and Morgenna didn't want to attempt the messy job of refilling it in the dark.

'Never fear,' she said, 'I've got plenty of candles in the kitchen'. It was standard for the mains supply to cut out momentarily, and usually people just sat through the outage and waited patiently for service to be resumed. But this was the third one tonight, and it looked like there was a problem. And with CeeCee sitting there, it was interrupting their conversation.

'Give me two minutes', said Morgenna in the hazy half-light of evening, 'and I'll have this sorted.'

She fumbled her way into the kitchen and made her way towards the middle drawer of the dresser, where she kept her stack of emergency candles, for just these situations. Such was her preparedness that she wasn't far off the mark in her prediction that it would take her two minutes to get the candles lit, fitted into candle holders, and brought back through to the living room. Seb came downstairs and started making excited whooping noises when he saw the candlelight. There was something about the thrill of a naked flame and ten-year-old boys that would never change, Morgenna thought to herself.

Seb, in his excitement to mark the occasion, started singing *The Human Candles of Rinkeby*, which had become a bit of a jocular if macabre tradition among the English when candles were lit during power cuts. It had been written at some point during the 2020s, in response to what later became known as *The Great Swedish Energy Crisis of 2022*, when a massive infrastructure failure saw the country suffer nationwide blackouts during a particularly harsh Scandinavian winter. What happened during that time served as a salutary lesson for all of the other multicultural nations of Northern Europe.

> *The New Swedes set the cars ablaze*
>
> *To keep their thin blood warm*

Morgenna cut him short mid-verse. 'Seb, that's enough. We've got guests.' She knew that CeeCee, of a more sensitive nature, would not appreciate the ending of the song. As far as she was aware the 'human candles' legend was actually true, because she remembered, or thought she remembered, as a child seeing a newspaper clipping at her Uncle Frank's house. She couldn't forget the headline. *From Superpower of Hearts to The Heart of Darkness*, set over a double-page spread. And among the grizzly photographs etched into her brain was one of a baby's arm poking out of a brazier. That particular picture had given her nightmares for weeks, and even now it chilled her to the bone just thinking about it. Maybe because she was pregnant she was feeling more sensitive herself.

Seb made a symbolic protestation but knew not to push his mother. It was no fun being in a house with just women, and he wished his father was back home.

Morgenna tried to steer the atmosphere back to a more adult tone, in a voice that made it clear to Seb that he was welcome to stay in the room if he were seen and not heard. She turned to CeeCee. 'So, anyway, you were going to tell me something about Margaret Ramsey?'

'Yes. I was just going to say that she is another one who has been taken away. So many people are being taken away now that it's starting to get frightening.'

There was the sound of a mousetrap going off in the kitchen, but both women carried on their conversation as if they had heard nothing.

'And the official line is that this is just the flu? If it is, why are they taking people away?'

'They say it's because it is so contagious,' CeeCee replied. 'They say that they don't want it making further inroads into the general population. Which makes sense I suppose.'

'Hmm,' said Morgenna, unconvinced. That explanation made sense on the surface, but it was still all a bit weird. Normally when there were epidemics people weren't taken to a central location but were told to keep indoors, and other family members were also relegated to house quarantine, even if they themselves didn't have symptoms. In such instances the EF arranged for supplies to be dropped off at the houses affected. *Why the change in policy?*

CeeCee continued. 'And the thing about this flu is, it has been going on for weeks now. And people aren't getting back home. That's not normal for the flu. Normally it just lasts for a week or so. And I've heard that people are getting nosebleeds. Since when was that a symptom of the flu?'

Morgenna nodded slowly as she took in this information. 'Maybe it's a new type of flu. There are new strains of diseases popping up all the time. It would be nice to really get some decent information about this though. It's like nobody knows anything, and I'm sick of listening to the Haresfinch rumour mill to try to work out what's going on. The latest one to go round is that it is only dark-haired people who are affected by this flu.'

CeeCee sat there thoughtfully in the gloom. The candlelight emanating from the low coffee table exaggerated her features quite harshly, giving her an unfortunate and unjustified hag-like appearance.

'You know, there might be something in that. I can't think of anyone who has been taken away who's blonde. Or red-haired for that matter. So you're definitely safe, Morgenna!'

CeeCee tried to make light of things by making a little joke of it. But Morgenna couldn't laugh. *She* might have red hair, but Seb was dark, like his father. She would sooner get the flu herself than have another of her boys taken from her. She instinctively put her hand on her belly. Though maybe she should hope that that particular rumour was true, in her state.

'Does anybody know what happens if a pregnant woman gets this illness?'

'The only thing I know is that Juliana Morgan got taken away, and, as we all know, she's pregnant.' CeeCee gave Morgenna a knowing look that was lost in the gloom. 'But I don't know what has happened since she got taken away.'

Morgenna rolled her eyes at the name of Juliana Morgan. 'That gold ring in a pig's snout? If I were her, I'd be quite glad to be taken away. I wouldn't be able to step outside my front door if I had been cabbaged like that. Who knows, she might see this as a blessing in disguise!'

'Oh that's a bit harsh. But maybe you're right. I know that I would probably die with the mortification. Who needs stones when you've got rotten vegetables?' CeeCee cringed as she thought back to the very public humiliation of Juliana for charges of adultery. The EF pursued a policy of social shaming for women who misbehaved, as they found it a more effective way to keep women in line than any corporal punishment. And the women subjected to the *cabbaging*, as it came to be called, had the additional humiliation of not being able to move to a new EF jurisdiction to start afresh, as both the EF and the Albionic Church refused them the official papers which would grant them such a move. Strangers were not accepted into new areas without an official reference from both the EF and the Church, which left women like Juliana Morgan forced to live their life under the same scornful eyes of the women who had 'cabbaged' them. Such fallen women could redeem themselves, but it would take years of abnegation and good works. The English had long memories.

Another loud snap in the kitchen told the women that a second trap had closed its tiny metal jaw on its prey. Such sounds were common as the day turned to night, and Morgenna chose to ignore the noise when she replied to CeeCee.

'Yes, I wouldn't like to be her. And if she's got this flu thing, it looks like God is punishing her twice.'

CeeCee nodded, but Morgenna could barely see her silhouette in the growing darkness. At the height of Midsummer there was no curfew bell, or it would have tolled over two hours ago. The solstice sun had almost set. A sure sign that CeeCee should be heading home.

'It's getting late. I'd better go. Thanks for the tea.' CeeCee struggled to move her matronly frame off the soft cushions.

'It was great seeing you, as always. But I'll be seeing you again in a couple of days, won't I?'

There was a silence, as CeeCee wondered what Morgenna was referring to. She wondered if

Morgenna was talking about the St John's Day service at the church. Then she remembered.

'Perpetua's wedding. Yes, of course, I wouldn't miss that for the world. She's going to be a very beautiful bride. A real English rose. You are going to cry when you see her in her wedding dress, so be prepared for that. I don't think there will be a single dry eye in the house.'

CHAPTER 35

Summoned to their usual wasteland spot after an enigmatic lert, the boys crowded around him in a buzz of anticipation. Seeing that everyone who was going to arrive was now beside him, Chad pulled out a large thin book from inside his jacket.

'Check THIS out!'

The boy edged themselves around to either side of his body, two on each side, to be able to look at this new object the right way up. It appeared to be a bright, colourful chapbook, soft and strangely shiny. Two of the gang were absent. Andrew was still up at his uncle's farm, and Jimmy had been taken to hospital, along with his mum. Both of the boys would be sorry to be missing this, had they known about it.

Chad opened up the commentary. 'This is what they thought was beautiful in 2024.'

He pointed to the morbidly obese woman on the front of the magazine. The boys stared at the picture in amazement.

'How can somebody get that fat?' Thomas asked.

Ambrose answered. 'My gran said it was quite common in England around that time. She says that lots of people were fat. Even the young girls.'

'But it looks disgusting though. Like she's been poisoned or something. And those horrible black marks all over her body.' Sam pointed to her arms, neck and legs. 'What's that?'

Seb answered him. 'Those are tattoos. You still see them on some of the very old people. They were very popular back before the war.'

Sam peered closer at the magazine. 'But I don't understand. This woman is very ugly. Why is she acting like she is beautiful?'

He looked at the rest of the boys for an answer but only Thomas met his gaze, and he shrugged. The rest were too interested in this forbidden artefact of the past. Andrew dramatically opened the middle pages wide and watched as his friends jumped back in fright. He laughed.

'Oh my God!'

The boys gathered back in towards Chad after their momentary shock, but looked at the magazine cautiously. The words on the page said *Acid Survivor Beauty Tips: Be Bold and Beautiful This Summer*. Once the initial horror wore off, the boys were transfixed at the figure whose face looked like melted wax that had cooled. One of its eyes was cloudy.

'Is that a monster?'

'No, I think it's a woman. Why would a monster be in a bikini?'

Sam knew he could be an authority here. 'My dad says that acid attacks were common in the English cities before the war. So they tried to make acid faces desirable. Acid models were used quite a lot. I don't know if it really worked though.'

Thomas shivered. 'All I see is the greatest horror.'

Chad laughed. 'If you think that that is bad, wait till you see this!'

He kept the magazine closed so that the other boys couldn't see inside, and searched for page 17. Once he had found the number in the top corner, he opened the magazine dramatically.

'What about *this* for beautiful women?'

The boys inched cautiously forward, frightened at what Chad had planned to assail their eyes with next. At first glance, it wasn't as frightening as the woman who had artfully tried to affix false eyelashes to her destroyed face, but the horror of this next feature was more insidious. On the surface, it looked like it was three women in lacy underwear, but on closer inspection, it was clear that there was something very wrong with these women.

'Keep looking', said Chad, clearly enjoying himself. He had poured over this document from cover to cover after discovering it at the bottom of an old cabinet in his grandmother's house, and knew the secret behind this photoshoot.

'Those women look weird. It's something about their bones. I don't know.' Seb was looking hard at these models. Something was definitely off about them.

'There is something about them that looks fake, or dead somehow. Let me guess, are they corpses?' Seb knew that he was being silly asking if they could be corpses, because the models had their eyes open and they were smiling. But they still seemed dead somehow. Maybe they were reanimated corpses or something.

'Well...' said Chad, enjoying the suspense of the moment, '...they look weird, because these women... are actually men!'

'No....'

The boys peered in closer in amazement. Thomas spoke. 'But they have boobs. And the one on the right has a woman's hips. Look at her... his bum. That's a woman's bum!'

Chad nodded. 'Keep looking. The breasts are fake. The bum is fake. These men injected silicone and fat into their bodies to give them a woman's curves.'

There was a short silence as the boys tried to understand what Chad was saying.

It was Thomas who broke the silence. 'But why would they want to do that?' He doubted what Chad was saying. He looked again at the knickers that the women were wearing. 'No, they can't be men. There are no... bits.'

The boys laughed at the word 'bits'.

'Yeah,' said Chad, savouring what he was about to say next. 'But that's because they've cut their bits off.' He made a scissors motion with his fingers as the other boys gazed at him open-mouthed in amazement.

'No... fucking... WAY!'

The boys peered back at the pictures, now armed with this new knowledge. These women didn't look like men, but they didn't look like women either. There was something wrong about the jaws, or the shoulders, or the hands, or the hips, or... something. Something was missing. But it was creepy and freaky and strange. And yet they were modelling women's underwear. For women to buy. Or would it be other men who would be wearing this underwear?

Sam finally weighed in with his judgement. 'This is Satanic. Seb, you were right - these men *are* corpses. They are possessed by demons. Their souls have gone.' He was only ten but he knew quite a bit about demonic possession from his Uncle Hugh, who was a priest of the Albionic Church. He looked at Seb. He hoped that by backing up Seb's comment it could help mend their friendship.

Sebastian nodded. 'Yeah, there is something dead in their eyes. Maybe that's what comes from opening yourself up to another man... like a woman.' He shuddered. He didn't want to think about what he had heard the sodomites did.

Sam spoke again. 'Yes, my uncle says that sodomy is a gateway for demonic possession. If you do not take care to protect your strength as a man the demons will steal it from you and turn you into a woman, to mock God's creation. First spiritually, then... like *this*.' He pointed back to the magazine, but Chad had already moved on to another page. A young woman with lip piercings was exposing her shaved tattooed vulva to the camera and telling the magazine how proud she was to have been spit-roasted by strangers on live television, and that her mum was also very proud of her for getting so famous. The other boys were silently absorbing of this information, trying to understand it. It was like it had come from another planet.

Sam's eyes opened wide as he looked at the picture of the girl holding herself open for the viewer to gawp at. 'This is openly promoting the worship of one of the Baals. Baal-Peor I think it is.' He suddenly wondered if he should ask his uncle about becoming a priest. The demons he had been told so much about were clearly real. Suddenly an image of his late grandfather Lenny came into his head, sitting in his armchair, one Sunday afternoon a few weeks before he died.

'The last time I ever saw my granddad, he said to me: "It wasn't enough for them just to destroy us. They had to degrade us as well."' Sam felt suddenly very sad, thinking about his grandfather, and looking at the girl's dead eyes. The girl herself would probably be long dead by now. 'Now I know what he meant. Come on, Seb, let's build a fire.'

The others boys continued to be engrossed in the magazine, like ancient prophets studying the entrails of a sacrifice, as Sam and Seb got a small fire going by the back of the clearing, an endeavour greatly aided by the hot and dry day. With a hint of his father's martial authority in his voice, Sam shouted over to Chad.

'Whenever you're ready, Chadwick!'

Chad looked reluctant for a moment, then walked towards the boys. He had seen all he needed to see anyway. The fire was all it was fit for.

CHAPTER 36

In a house on Crocketts Walk, three miles from the impromptu wasteland bonfire burning the last of England's gutter press, Mrs. Valerie Ellacombe trailed her long, slender fingers along the spines of the books in Dr. Wansbrough's bookcase.

'You have a lot of books...' She checked herself. '...for England in 2060.'

Valerie's decision to qualify her statement made Dr. Wansbrough laugh out loud. *So she had noticed as well!*

'Yes, we're not exactly a bookish culture these days. If we ever were, really. But maybe that's a good thing. Maybe we needed to get away from the abstract and the life of the mind, and back to the land and to the flesh we live in.' He paused. He immediately regretted saying the word 'flesh'. The cultural backlash had seen Freud's ideas thrown onto the pyre of history, but Alan Wansbrough maintained that Freud had been right about some things. He was more nervous than he cared to admit about Valerie being in his home. A woman had not set foot over his threshold for more than ten years, and Valerie's very presence, her female energy, transformed the space. It was like every corner of the room became different once she had glanced on it. Dr. Wansbrough felt very exposed, especially without the self-contained, curious spirit of young Alban nearby to ask questions and diffuse the tension. The boy had been given the chance to visit his family, and Wansbrough was now starting to question the wisdom of that decision.

Valerie smiled. 'Ah yes, the life of the mind! I see here that you have *Lady Chatterley's Lover.* You clearly have a taste for banned books.' She looked from the bookshelf to the man, who stood there, slightly flustered, but smiling.

'Yes. If memory serves the obscenity trial was exactly 100 years ago this year. Although believe it or not, I think that the most dangerous aspect of this book is not the sex scenes, but the descriptions of the English woodlands.'

Valerie began to laugh, then stopped when she realised that the doctor was being serious. Her face took on a delighted intrigue. 'Explain that one to me.'

Dr. Wansbrough took a deep breath. He had never put this idea into words before. 'To me, the main thesis of the book was that when the English lose their natural connection to the land they... they lose their natural sensuality and then their urge to procreate. They become denatured and broken. The most subversive element of the book is, for me, not the sex scenes but the huge vocabulary Lawrence uses to describe the English woodlands, words for flora and fauna which most people no longer used. Seriously. An English boy or girl before the Rebellion couldn't tell a curlew from a lapwing – they saw and said, a 'bird'. They did not know a beech from an ash from a larch, and simply saw a 'tree'. They did not truly *see* or experience their land, not as it truly is. And when someone does not understand the natural world, or their place within it, they do not understand themselves as an organic part of the land. From there, the natural role of a man and a woman withers on the vine, and babies are no longer born. For a modern government which pushed the native people into the cities in order for them to survive, that was a very dangerous truth.' He paused, and started to get flustered. 'I must sound like some kind of crazy hippie.'

Valerie put her hand on his arm. 'No, no, I think that you are on to something. The government wanted it that way because people without roots are much easier to control. Everyone knew that the native French people felt a part of French landscape and French history in a way that the non-natives never could. But the government said that it was not a problem, as long as the people identified as "French". But then, what does "French" mean if it doesn't mean being part of the land or the history of the land?'

Dr. Wansbrough nodded. 'Yes, that's why the EF schools take the kids on nature walks from a young age. Because it is essential that they feel the soil under their feet. England can no longer be an abstract. We are physical beings, and this is physical land.' He cringed again and imagined Freud grinning through his cigar smoke. But it was true.

Valerie made her way from the bookshelf and went to sit at the table. Dr. Wansbrough took his cue.

'Would you a drink? I've got pretty much everything.'

Valerie smiled, and decided to be playful. 'Would you happen to have a bottle of Sauternes in the cellar? It's been forty years since I've tasted it.'

Dr. Wansbrough laughed. 'Now French wine really *would* be something, wouldn't it? I'm afraid it's the produce of these isles only.'

Valerie gave a wry smile. 'I know, don't worry. You know, sometimes I wonder if I'll every taste French wine again, or another Camembert… Sometimes I dream of being back home in France and everything being good again. Not that it was ever truly good in my youth. Even in my childhood the idea of France had already become just that – an idea.'

Dr. Wansbrough nodded grimly. 'I know it's not the same, but what about a nice glass of English cider?'

'Yes, ok, why not? Sorry to sound a bit down. I suppose all of the things happening recently, Gareth's dying, having to clear the house, and then the memories stirred up by the attic being cleared. It really gets you to start thinking about your life. Gareth was like you, he understood what was going on. I remember how he came by those Enid Blyton books. We were at a car boot sale in Birkenhead when he spied them. He bought them just to have them. Just to keep them safe in the attic. I had forgotten they were even there.'

'Was Gareth an antique hunter? Is that where the Gallé came from?'

Valerie laughed. 'No, his interest was only in old books. That vase that belonged to my aunt. She was a Professor of Natural Sciences at the

University of Liverpool. It's thanks to her that I managed to get out of France. I had somewhere to go. I'm ashamed to say that I had forgotten that the vase was there – Gareth and I put it up in attic when the children were small, to prevent it getting broken. Then with events... you know.'

'Oh, I know, only too well.' Dr. Wansbrough thought back to the chaos of 2030s England. Yes, it would be easy to forget about an old vase in an attic, as beautiful as it was.

Dr. Wansbrough brought the glasses of cider to the table, along with a plate of cut fruit. It wasn't much, but as a long-term bachelor he did not have a clue about cooking, much less entertaining women at home. He hoped that Valerie would see that behind his gesture lay good intentions. He sat down. The folder lay on the table.

The Frenchwoman pulled the folder towards her and opened it.

'OK, so, where were we? Oh yes, we had been talking about Dupré's film, *le porno presidentiel*. Yes, I can attest that the video was real. A solid half hour of a middle-aged man inserting a variety of household objects into his rectum, waggling his tongue in his mouth and murmuring obscene sweet nothings into the camera.'

Valerie's looked at Dr. Wansbrough, who had taken off his glasses and was pinching the bridge of his nose. She laughed. 'No, seriously, it's true. The absent muse of this home-made porno was a Morrocan rent-boy who immediately leaked the phone footage, and became a bit of a minor celebrity as a result. I watched just enough of the video to verify that the rumours were true. I saw the neck of a wine bottle, a toothbrush and the handle of a toilet brush disappear up...' Valerie shuddered, and closed her eyes momentarily at the memory of it, still vivid after forty years. 'Like most people, I only watched it because I refused to believe that such rumours could be true. But I think most people were like me and switched off by the time it came to the toilet brush.' She paused and looked at Wansbrough with a wry face. 'Even we French have our limits.'

There was a silence, in which Dr. Wansbrough found himself at an uncharacteristic loss for words after what had just been said. Valerie picked up the glass of cider and took a sip. 'Do you want to know what *really* takes the *palme*? That even despite that video, which as you can imagine spread like wildfire before it was purged from the Internet... even despite that video, Dupré held on to his throne. He had just put the capstone on the rebuild of the Notre Dame cathedral, or should I say, as per the wishes of its corporate sponsors, the Bet Shalom Ecumenical Centre for LGBTQ Pride. And his PR team managed a fantastic campaign which targeted his critics as intolerant Christian homophobes. If anything, he came out of it stronger than ever with the Whites under forty.'

Valerie reached into her folder and pulled out a grainy photograph. It took Dr. Wansbrough a minute to work out what he was looking at, then he shuddered as it dawned on him what it was. Valerie laughed. 'What is seen cannot be unseen. I took a screenshot for posterity. As awful as it is.'

Dr. Wansbrough nodded. 'Yes, and I'm glad you did. This is important testimony of the darkest days.'

'Well the darkest day for Dupré was still to dawn, with the Louvre gas attack in 2026. Just over two thousand dead, several hundred injured. It was a very sophisticated attack, one thought impossible with the top level of security that the Louvre enjoyed, but it was later found that many of the corpses of the security team were wearing two sets of underwear.' Valerie stopped and gave a knowing look to Dr. Wansbrough, who nodded wearily. 'At this stage, the question of the state's relationship to the terrorists became the burning question. People started to ask if the French government were not just criminally negligent in protecting the populace, but if they were actively *complicit* with the Islamists and *permitting* these attacks. If the so-called Islamists were not actually part of the government machine. When the First Minister proclaimed: "La France va devoir vivre avec le terrorisme" it provoked great anger. Mass social unrest beckoned. And then *this* happened...'

Valerie took out a series of photographs and slid them towards Dr. Wansbrough in a neat line. He looked at them all in turn. 'I printed these out from my phone, because, you know, technology becomes obsolete, or else things get lost or confiscated.'

Dr. Wansbrough nodded to acknowledge what she had said as fixed his attention on the photographs. A huge inflatable floated in the sky above a big crowd of people. He tried to work out the size of the inflatable, but it was difficult to get a sense of its proportion. Even so, it looked as if it was a hundred metres high. The details of the blimp were quite blurry due to the lack of focus of the camera, but it looked like it was a representation of a human figure.

'What is it?'

'Have you ever read *Le Petit Prince*?'

Dr. Wansbrough thought hard. That title rang a bell in his mind.

Valerie clarified further. 'It's a children's book by Antoine de Saint-Exupèry.'

On hearing this, Dr. Wansbrough nodded. 'Yes, I think I have. I think we got it in French class at school.' He smiled. 'But that was a long time ago.' He looked at the photographs again, and found that he could make out the blond quiff of the Little Prince on the inflatable figure. 'There appears to be something written on the inside his long coat.'

Valerie turned around the photograph that Dr. Wansbrough was looking at and peered at the large white letters written into the red lining of the Little Prince's green coat. 'Yes, it says *On ne voit bien qu'avec le cœur* – one only sees properly with the heart. It comes from the book. Suddenly, the angry crowd who had gathered the Place de la Bastille were overcome with emotion at the Little Prince appearing overhead with his simple message of love, and social media went wild. It was a propaganda masterstroke.'

Dr. Wansbrough was doubtful. 'Really?'

'Yes, really. Despite all that had happened, people still wanted to believe that liberal democracy in a multiracial state could work, and this icon from their childhood, Le Petit Prince, told them that it was ok to keep believing. *On ne voit bien qu'avec le cœur* became the buzzphrase everywhere. It was on placards, T-shirts, TV stations, Twitter, Facebook. Everywhere. People were high on the idea that this little blond boy, with his innocence but an immense capacity for love, would help France find its way out of the morass of hate into which it recently become embroiled.'

Dr. Wansbrough frowned. 'That sounds insane.'

Valerie grimaced and laughed at the same time, then took a long drink of her cider. 'That's because it is. It was a collective psychosis. People went around upbraiding critics of the regime with quotations from *Le Petit Prince*, such as *on ne voit bien qu'avec le cœur* and *l'essential est invisible pour les yeux*. The idea was that *liberté*, *egalité* and *fraternité*, the lynchpins of the modern liberal multicultural state, couldn't be seen, but that they were more important that the material world in which people actually lived and drew breath. People were told not to trust their eyes and ears, because of the idea that the material world was subservient to the one of noble emotions, in which the human spirit would transcend the human animal. As people started to say *mais les yeux sont aveugles, il faut chercher avec le cœur*, they were told to ignore the burning cars, the homeless and the rubbish in the streets, that what was beautiful about Paris was the treasure of its hidden ideals. People were saying of the France of 2026: *Ce qui fait sa beauté est invisible.* Because according to this doctrine, what makes the desert beautiful is the idea that there is a well hidden somewhere within its vastness.

'Bloody hell,' said Dr. Wansbrough. 'These people sound suicidal.'

'Indeed,' said Valerie, 'but it was an idea that seriously caught on. It gripped the populace. I think because they wanted to believe that everything they had grown up with wasn't wrong, and the alternative was just so disturbing and violent that they didn't want to face it. As the original energy of the Little Prince meme started to fade, intellectuals began to provide an exegesis of *Le Petit Prince*, like it was some sacred text of France that, if only it could be interpreted correctly, promised to lead them out of the darkness that otherwise lay ahead. From these interpretations came the idea that the prince's rose was a symbol of France's multicultural liberal democracy.'

'I'm sorry,' said Dr. Wansbrough. 'What was the rose again? It has been so long since I read the book.'

'The rose was the delicate flower that the prince loved, and which he protected from the elements and predators. He had spent a lot of time on his rose, caring for it, and this too began to be used in the propaganda. I've got an article and a list of some of the most-used quotations here.'

Valerie drew out some stapled sheets of paper from out of the folder.

'Very powerful was the idea that Little Prince was responsible for his rose, having spent so much time caring for it. The quotation *Je suis responsable de cette fleur* and its variants within the book, soon became *Je suis responsable de cette France*, the new slogan and battlecry across the media. The prince's faithfulness to the flower caught people's hearts and was much used by Leftist journalists.'

Valerie passed a print-out of an online article to the stunned man sitting opposite. It was written by someone called Claude Askolovitch. Dr. Wansbrough read the headline. *Il faut bien protéger la lampe de la France democratique: un coup de vent peut l'éteindre.* 'The headline comes from the book, I take it?'

'Yes, well, paraphrased. By this point the exegesis had got quite esoteric. The idea in the book was that the prince's faithfulness to the rose shone from him like the flame from a lamp. From there it was easy for our journalists to make the leap that liberal democracy was the light in the darkness. Look here...'

Valerie pointed to a section that she herself had highlighted. 'This is where he talks about "the democracy of France" being "a fragile treasure, of which there is nothing more fragile on Earth". That too comes from the book. The mainstream pundits were using the idea that the problems of multiculturalism were just teething troubles on the way to the dawn of a new equal, enlightened France, and that the disgruntled legacy population represented the Darkness, the reactionaries who had to be defeated, on the way to the Light. That might help you understand the last line, which is also adapted from the book.'

Dr. Wansbrough looked down at the last line. *'Et, marchant ainsi, nous découvrirons le puits au lever du jour.'*

'Walking like this, we will discover the well at the break of day?'

'Yeeep.' Valerie made a face at the ridiculousness of the sentence. 'By this point, the journalist class were competing to outdo each other in esoteric references, but there was a limit to how much clever wordplay could re-imagine the reality outside their offices and coffee shops. On the streets, ordinary people were continuing to get beaten, robbed, raped, stabbed, run over and blown to pieces as bit by bit the whole of Paris was turned into a giant *zone urbaine sensible*, and no amount of pavement widening was going to change that.' Valerie snorted contemptuously as she remembered the changes made to urban planning in the 2020s. 'As a result, people were starting to accept their fate, and were using their imminent mortality as way to signal friendship on social media, using the words of *Le Petit Prince* himself: *C'est bien d'avoir eu un ami, même si l'on va mourir.*'

Dr. Wansbrough muttered something under his breath, and Valerie continued. 'At that point, I knew that I had to get out of France. I had moved to a Jewish commuter town on the outskirts of Paris in 2022 because I reasoned that if mass violence came, state resources would go into protecting the Jewish neighbourhoods before the others. But by 2026 I realised that this was too risky a bet to keep making. I gave up my job at the university and moved to Liverpool.'

She sighed, and took another drink of her cider. 'It was hard at first. My English wasn't very good, and I was working in a bar. But then

I met Gareth, and everything changed. He says that it was love at first sight.'

I bet it was, thought Dr. Wansbrough.

Valerie scooped up all of the papers, ordered them, then put them back in the folder. 'So yes, here you go.' She slid the folder towards Dr. Wansbrough. 'One to keep safe on your bookshelf. I hope that my explanations helped you to make sense of the material I collected.'

Dr. Wansbrough came to himself. 'Oh definitely, it does. Certainly, your explanation of *Le Petit Prince* was something I had not properly understood before. I had no idea that it had been so powerful.'

Valerie nodded. 'Well-loved children's characters have more power in society than people realise. Because we come to love these characters just as we are forming our own view of the world and we come to trust them. Even though they aren't real, the emotions that we have for them are. It takes us back to an earlier state of mind, and that is very powerful for the propagandists. Do you know the author Astrid Lundgren… Pippi Longstocking?'

Dr. Wansbrough laughed. 'Know her? I use her books as primers to teach Swedish for my Arabo-Swedish classes. Her books are just down from D. H. Lawrence on the bookshelf.

Valerie got up and went to the bookshelf and pulled out one of the books. *Pippi Långstrump i Söderhavet.* 'Oh wow! You've got the original editions. And some of the Emil series as well. These are very rare nowadays.'

Dr. Wansbrough nodded. 'The originals began to be destroyed in the 2010s because they were deemed too dangerous for children. They were labelled *gender-determinative*, *heteronormative* and *racist*, if I recall correctly. State broadcasters also recast Pippi as a homeless Roma in Rinkeby around this time and broadcast the bowdlerised versions of the books over the radio in Arabic. At that point Arabic and Swedish had not yet begun to merge linguistically, at least not that I know of.'

Valerie put the book back in the bookshelf. 'I stopped listening to the news coming out of Sweden around 2022, when the blackouts were happening. It was all too grim. I know that that's rich to say with me being French. But I found it so depressing. I remember being told how in 2025 Pippi Longstocking was being used in schools and government adverts to teach young Swedish girls how to masturbate and use sex toys.' She shook her head. 'What is it the Bible says? *To the pure, all things are pure, but to the defiled, nothing is pure.*'

Dr. Wansbrough took off his glasses and placed

them on the table. He rubbed his face and groaned, as if in pain. 'The sheer... utter... fucking... EVIL of these people! That's what it is. Evil. There is no other word for it. They do not fucking stop until everything beautiful, good and innocent is destroyed. I wasn't brought up with religion but those fucking demons brought me back to God. Because when you hear about stuff like kindergarten teachers putting little boys in dresses and teaching them to desire other little boys, you know that Hell is fucking real.' He sighed, and cursed inwardly that alcohol no longer worked as a balm to numb the horror. Nothing worked. There was no escape. 'Sorry for swearing like that.'

Valerie dismissed his concern with a friendly shake of the head. 'Oh don't worry, I feel exactly the same. We all need an outlet for these feelings. The young don't understand how bad it all was. And I'm glad they don't, in a way.'

'Yes,' said Dr. Wansbrough. 'But at the same time, we have to let them know what these people are capable of. Or we risk it happening yet again. We must never let our guard down. Yet throughout history, we keep doing just that. We let people move the boundary stones, and the devil creeps into our home.'

From the Land All the Good Things Come

Valerie inhaled sharply and looked squarely at Dr. Wansbrough, or Alan, as he had shyly asked to be called. He had a worn face, but it was rugged in a manly way, and his keen blue eyes still shone brightly. She liked being around him, being here.

'I'd better get back,' she said. 'The family will be wondering where I am. But it would be nice to come back, just to pop by. I feel that we have so much to talk about.'

'Yes,' said Dr. Wansbrough. 'I'd really like that. And Alban would like to see you too. He enjoyed meeting you on our last visit.'

Valerie picked up her handbag, and started making her way to the door. 'I'm glad about that. He's a lovely boy. So we'll definitely meet again at some point then, Alan?

'Yes, definitely.' He flushed, much to his embarrassment. It had been a long time since anyone had called him by the intimacy of his first name. He was always just plain Wansbrough, or Dr. Wansbrough to those who wished to accord him respect.

Dr. Wansbrough's heart almost leapt from his chest as Valerie leant forward and gave him a kiss on each cheek goodbye. She smiled. '*C'est bon de pouvoir faire les choses à la française.*'

He only managed to catch his breath again when the front door finally closed between them. A faint smell of her perfume still lingered in the hallway.

CHAPTER 37

After the stress of the preparations for the Wedding Eve Meal, although the meal itself had gone well (if not without a great deal of hidden help from her mother), Perpetua had found it incredibly difficult to reconcile sleep when she eventually went to bed around midnight. The situation was not helped by a little voice telling her that it was pointless trying to sleep for what were now only a few hours, because it was already the day of her wedding. She did, however, fall asleep from sheer exhaustion around 4 a.m., and slept soundly before she was woken up by her mother three hours later.

Her insomnia had been caused by an analysis of the events of a few hours previously. Aoife had been very complimentary on the Eve Loaf, and assured her that the bread was the most important element of the meal. 'A good bread makes for a good marriage,' the old woman had intoned. There had not been a great deal of commentary on the other elements of the meal, and the latter realisation of this fact had set Perpetua to worrying during the wee small hours. *Had Aoife only been so complimentary about the Loaf because there was so little to say about the other courses? Was this a bad omen for the rest of her life?* She didn't want to wake her mother up with these concerns, so she lay in bed and let the dark thoughts take on megalithic dimensions in the darkness.

But the concerns that had seemed so overwhelming in the night-time vanished in the dazzle of the Midsummer morning. Even with little sleep it was very difficult for a sixteen-year-old bride to look anything but young and fresh, and she soon got into the excitement of her bridal toilette, aided by her bridesmaid Felicity, who arrived to the house at ten o'clock.

Meanwhile, CeeCee had installed herself in the Houghton's kitchen, and had picked sprigs of meadowsweet and St. John's wort from Candice's herb garden. CeeCee grew these plants to make teas, but with the flowers CeeCee could also weave a diadem of white and yellow blossom, perfect for this summer wedding.

She had just finished making the floral tiara when Perpetua came downstairs wearing her wedding dress, and CeeCee motioned her to the table.

'Here, try this on!'

Perpetua stood before the older woman, still in her misshapen woollen jumper, as she carefully fitted the diadem to Perpetua's head. She picked up another sprig of St John's wort, and added it into a gap in the design.

'There!'

Just as CeeCee stood back to survey her work, Candice came into the kitchen. Her daughter in her full wedding finery, turned to look at her. Candice gave a cry of anguished happiness and began weeping.

'You are so beautiful!'

Perpetua felt sympathetic tears rise up in her own eyes at this show of emotion. 'Mum, stop! I'll start crying myself, and I've just finished my make-up!'

She went over to take her mother's hands and calm her down. Candice started to laugh a bit at her own silliness, as Perpetua wiped away her mother's tears delicately with her painted fingernails.

Candice stood back from her daughter to look properly at her dress. 'CeeCee, this is wonderful. I can't imagine how this dress could be any more perfect.'

She spoke from the heart. The dress fitted her

daughter's slim form perfectly. It was a white satin, with an embroidered detail on the bodice of oak foliage. Candice noticed to her delight that the acorns had been picked out with gold thread. In the middle of this foliage was the red cross of the Albionic Church.

CeeCee beamed broadly at Candice's reaction, her wide face going redder than usual. 'Yes, I do have to say that I am particularly proud of this dress.'

Candice looked at the humble woman before her, who was soft and round and warm, like a ripe pear. She felt close to tears again.

'Thank you for everything, Clare. You have no idea how happy you have made me.'

CeeCee looked bashfully at the floor. She felt awkward being the centre of attention, but she felt a flush of joy at her friend's words. A bible verse came into her head: *pleasant words are as a honeycomb, sweet to the soul, and health to the bones.* 'It was no trouble at all, you know that. Well, I'd better get ready myself. You wouldn't want to see me at the church in this old thing, would you?' She gestured to her old jumper in a bid to lighten the mood. 'I'll see both of you at the church ceremony. Be careful with your diadem, Perpetua. It's very delicate.'

Candice looked at her daughter, and felt the

From the Land All the Good Things Come

tears stinging her eyes again. Her little girl would soon be a mother, and would have her own home. Matt had already secured them married accommodation from the EF. Candice couldn't believe that her little girl would soon be leaving her to be a mother herself.

Perpetua stroked her mother's arm. She could tell what her mother was thinking but thought it best not to annunciate her mother's emotions, lest this intensify them. She decided that it would be better to distract her mother with thoughts of the groom.

'I just hope that Matt is looking presentable. You know how much he hates *occasions*.'

'Oh, don't you worry about that. Deborah will make sure he is ship-shape. And anyway, I'll let you into a little secret… nobody's looks at the groom. It is the bride's day.'

Candice looked at her daughter, suddenly serious. She pronounced the Albionic bridal blessing:

> *May you have so many children*
>
> *That they shine in God's sunlight*
>
> *Like a thousand ears of corn*

Then she made the sign of the cross on Perpetua's forehead.

There was the sound of children's footsteps running down the stairs, followed by much slower, heavier footsteps. Modesta the flower-girl came running into the room. Look at my nails, mummy, Felicity has given me pink nails!'

Felicity smiled shyly.

'You've made a lovely job of her hair, Felicity.' Mrs. Houghton spoke sincerely as she looked at the young girl's curls, artfully interwoven with small ornamental grips that looked like flower buds.

'Thank you, Mrs. Houghton.'

The poesies of the girls were sitting in vases of water, waiting to be picked up.

'Have you got the throwing-salt?' Perpetua suddenly asked, in an anxious voice.

Mrs. Houghton intervened. 'Oh don't worry about that, Perpetua. The guests always bring plenty of throwing-salt. But I've got some here just in case that wasn't to happen. Which would be the first time in English history!'

There was a pause. The girls all looked around. Everything was pretty much organised. Now they were just waiting on Perpetua's father to come back from the church with the car.

Perpetua checked her make-up in the mirror again.

'I know it's supposed to be tradition for the bride to arrive at the church after the groom, but I want to us to leave as soon as Dad gets back. I don't mind being early at the church. In fact, I *want* to be early. I know it might sound weird but I don't want to leave anything to chance, and if we are at the church, nothing can go wrong. Can we go early, Mum?'

Candice looked at her daughter. She knew that Perpetua could get anxious about things and it made no difference if they went into the church a bit earlier. All of her friends would already be there, and it would be a chance to socialise. Albionic weddings were not formal affairs, and everyone knew everyone else. Many of the church elders would have already brought cakes and nice breads, and would be organising the drinks. A wedding was a community celebration.

'Yes, if you want to go early, we can. It's not a problem.'

Modesta went over to the poesies, picked hers up out of the vase, and pointed out the roses to Felicity.

'Did you know, Felicity, that every flower has its own nature. Just like every plant and animal. Did you know that?'

Felicity smiled, and decided to pretend not to know the school lesson. She was about to answer in the negative to let the child tell her more when Candice, distracted by a noise outside, interrupted.

'Perpetua, that's your father back home. You're right. We might as well leave now. Come on, let's get ready to go.'

Perpetua went to get the poesies and took one last look around the kitchen. This would be the last time she would see her family home as a single woman. Her new life of wife and mother was about to start.

CHAPTER 38

Now that it was approaching early evening, the bright Midsummer sun of the morning and afternoon had started to retreat behind clouds, and the sky was turning grey. A petulant wind dared to blow through the trees around the medieval gravestones of St Oswald's Church of Winwick, a restlessness in the weather which suited Caldwell, who felt just as unsettled in his own mood. His nervous loitering in the graveyard owed itself to the anticipated arrival of the Church of Christ in Albion's Father of Fathers to this tiny Domesday village, the location chosen in a bid to avoid unwelcome attention from civilians. He wanted things to unfold his way, and he wanted his final communion with God to be free of all earthly considerations.

The priest at St Oswald's, an elderly, discreet man, had arranged for the church to be empty in order to permit a private summit between the Supreme Commander and the Great Hierophant, the latter making a long and difficult journey from the flatlands of Norfolk to the other side of EF territory for the event. It was a significant expedition, because it required the Norwich-based patriarch to first have to cross the Wash into the dangerously exposed territory of vestigial Lincolnshire, always keeping east, and from there to cross the Humber, the natural line of jurisdiction between the Northeast and Southeast Divisions. From Northumbria, he then had travel west across the dangerously exposed Yorkshire Moors into the Yorkshire Dales, then down around the relative safety of the Lancashire coast. Not a few EF men had needed to be involved in all of the stages required for this pilgrimage, but none of them understood its true nature. They would simply have surmised that there was to be a meeting between the leaders of the church and the military, the twin arms of the state, and nothing more than that. The Father of Fathers was well within in his rights to tour the country, as unsafe as travelling was, and indeed many of the English who had the privilege to attend to him during his journey, whether driving for him, cooking his food or turning down his bed, were grateful to God for giving them the rare lifetime opportunity to be in Aldhelm's presence, a presence which was rarely experienced outside of his remote Norfolk See.

The arduous and lengthy trip to visit Caldwell in the Northwest would not be wasted. Once his assignment with the Leader was over, it was arranged with the regional Northwest command that the Hierarch would be taken to Warrington, for a surprise visit to the town. As one of the EF's so-called 'lymph-node cities', one of the key transit points between EF regional territories, Warrington was the focus of many savage SAU attacks, and as a consequence morale was particularly low there. An unannounced visit from The Great Patriarch, who was much loved by the people for his wise and learned homilies, would be a huge boost for the beleaguered population. The English outside of the Southeast could only know of Aldhelm through his published writings, homilies and encyclicals which were printed as pamphlets and which were read and re-read by a laity who enjoyed the poetry and simple truths of his measured prose. Aldhelm, conscious of the priestly role of preacher, wrote for his words to be read aloud, because he understood the power of the spoken word and the energy which built up during communal reading sessions in homes, churches and factories. The English community of 2060 was an ethnos which took its knowledge only from people that it vetted and trusted. Books no longer had the unalloyed authority of previous centuries by mere dint of the author's ideas having been typeset, printed and bound. The West had learned its lesson in that regard, and now trusted the man, rather than the form. However, when both of these elements came together in the same individual, it was a joy. For this reason, Aldhelm was a precious treasure to the English, and was loved in all five territories. His visit to the Northwest would be precisely what we needed in light of what was to be revealed.

A humble man, born Robert Brunham in the farming plains of Haveringland, Aldhelm had no time for the trappings of status that came with being the Great Patriarch. He had his robes for official occasions, but most of the time he could be found in a simple Albionic monk's habit of brown wool with the red cross of the EF stitched front and back. It was clear to everyone that he was not of this world, and that his only concern was the souls of his people. His faith in God meant that he had no fear of death or injury, and such was the spiritual force around his person that even the coarsest and most battle-hardy soldiers fell as silent as awed children in his presence, his superiority ipso facto precluding the need for an official protocol regarding treatment of his person. People kneeled out of instinct.

He stood now before Caldwell. They were

both equal in authority, if in different terrains, but Caldwell immediately kneeled before Aldhelm.

'Rise, my son.'

Like Caldwell, Aldhelm believed that speech was overrated and that people talked too much, viewing prolixity as a reliable indicator of spiritual darkness. With the understanding that the kingdom of God was not in word but in power, he measured each of his utterances carefully. This parsimony of self-expression, combined with Caldwell's natural reticence, augured a meeting of few words and many silences.

Caldwell rose to his feet, and looked Aldhelm in the eyes, man to man. He glanced behind the old man to the small group who stood twenty yards behind them, the security escort who had brought Aldhelm to this ancient village church.

The military leader then spoke in a low voice. 'Can we go, just the two of us, to a place to talk?' He gestured to his open-top jeep that was parked a few yards away.

Aldhelm looked again at Caldwell and nodded.

Caldwell looked past Aldhelm's left shoulder and shouted to the waiting men. 'We're going for a short journey. Don't follow us. We're not going far.' He added that last bit because he knew that the soldiers would be concerned. Winwick was the last village before the borderlands, and as such was not the safest territory.

Aldhelm followed Caldwell to the vehicle. Both got in without saying a word. Caldwell did not look back to the church but knew that the soldiers watching behind him would be concerned that the Supreme Leader had turned up Golborne Road, a main road out of the village that led to the edge of EF territory.

Within the space of a minute of being waved through the checkpoint, the landscape of houses had turned into disused fields, overgrown with wildflowers. Still not a word was said between the two men as the hedges and flowers flew past them on the hill-free plains which stretched as far as the horizon and the wind blustered against their faces. The sky had gone even darker in some places, with angry rain-filled clouds alternating with shards of white sunlight. Now a few ruins of houses could be seen on either side of the road, which was getting increasingly bumpy and potholed. It was clear that no one lived there. Another half mile or so, and the landscape would be dotted with solitary enemy heads impaled on poles, which after a generation in the open air were reduced to skulls picked clean by the carrion birds. Aldhelm wondered briefly if Caldwell really was planning to drive into SAU territory.

But just as he had that thought, the jeep slowed and mounted the narrow pavement that lined the road, then parked up. Caldwell had parked the jeep very close to the hedge that bordered the field. The holy man saw the soldier begin to exit the vehicle, and made to open his own door.

'Wait, Father, let me help you out.'

Caldwell got out of the jeep and scrambled to the other side. But Aldhelm had already eased his barely sandalled feet onto the pavement and stood now on the deserted road, looking around at the bushes and occasional tree being blasted by winds which could reach their full ferocious potential in the vast emptiness of the open flatlands. He wondered what he was being brought to.

'If you follow me, Father, we can get into the field through here.'

With great difficulty, the old man followed Caldwell up the short embankment and crouched to get his body between the gap in the trees made wider by Caldwell's hulking frame, and the general was now putting out his arms to hold and steady the priest through the undergrowth. Caldwell noticed that one of the trees had a Christian cross carved into it. Carving crosses into tree trunks had been particularly popular in the 2030s as a way of marking territory, particularly away from the built-up areas. It was also a way of signalling that countryside belonged to the natives. But over the years these tree crosses had come to take on a deeper spiritual significance for the faith. Caldwell felt heartened to see one here, at this moment.

'Are you through ok, Father?'

'Yes, I am now.'

Caldwell waited until he was sure that Aldhelm had a sure footing and had caught his breath, and then guided him through the long wild grasses, up towards a tall thicket a few yards away. Something tickled at the back of the old priest's mind just as Caldwell arrived at an opening in the thicket that led into a grove of tall grass strewn with low-lying shrubbery. The soldier pointed to a series of stone steps that led down to a dark stonework opening, its square shape almost obscured by the fronds of overgrown ferns.

'This is St Oswald's Well, Father.'

Aldhelm nodded slowly in a vague sort of recognition, and remembered what the Venerable

Bede had said about St. Oswald, the Christian warrior king who had died at this very spot fighting the infidel of Mercia. In life, Oswald was renowned for sanctifying his people with the love of Christ and for practicing that love towards the needy. In death, many miracles were attributed to him.

Aldhelm spoke. 'What troubles you, my son?'

Caldwell looked down towards the dark mouth of the well. 'Father, my time on Earth is coming to an end. And this is due to actions that I myself have committed. I know that. I would like you to housel me with this water, at this place, to prepare me for what is to come. I want to be made ready for death.'

The old man looked steadily into Caldwell's remaining eye, which stared fixedly back into his. He knew that this leader had resigned himself to his fate, and did not want to discuss his actions in the world.

'I can commend your soul to God through the highest authority of the Albionic Church, but it means nothing without you repenting your sins and asking God's forgiveness for your deeds. Do you truly repent your sins?'

'I truly feel sorry for my actions leading to innocent people suffering and dying.' Caldwell said.

Aldhelm was sharp enough to note that Caldwell had chosen a reformulation for his answer. He repeated. 'Do you truly repent your sins?'

'I do not like what I have done here on Earth, and yet if I had my life to live again, I would do it the same. Because I had no choice in what was to be done, if it meant my people were to survive. I have committed evil, but only to prevent greater evil.'

Aldhelm looked up at the leader of men, who towered over him. 'It is written: *God shall bring every work into judgment, with every secret thing, whether it be good, or whether it be evil.* And I cannot know what God's judgment on you will be. But I as a man understand the situation you have been placed in, nay born into. I understand that at many times you will have been forced to choose the lesser of two evils, because there was no virtuous path left to take.'

Caldwell looked at the kindly face of the old man, and felt a weight lift from his heart. That the Father of Fathers understood him lifted the burden that he had been carrying alone.

'Yes. I decided to bear the stigma, to take this stain on my soul into eternity, so that future generations could have the luxury of a virtuous path.'

The old man placed a hand on Caldwell's arm as much for balance as for assurance, and with Caldwell following, walked slowly down the steps of the well, crouching laboriously to reach the healing water. He cupped his hands into the shallow bracken pool and instructed Caldwell to kneel before him so that he could pour the water over his head. As he did so he recited some vocative formulations in Latin, English and Anglo-Saxon.

Caldwell felt the intensity of the holy water pouring onto his head as if it were burning into his scalp. The reality of what he had done hit him now more than ever, even more than when he had heard the *slurp* of the bodies of the newly dead as they hit the pile of older corpses and slithered down the lifeless mass of limbs and heads. Everyone had blood on their hands, but as the leader of the English Front, his were caked in gore.

When Aldhelm finished the standard ritual, he saw the crown of the head bowed before him and realised that for this man to find peace, he would need to hear a performative utterance whose sounds reverberating in the air through time would release him from the bondage of his own conscience. The priest therefore continued: 'With this blessed water, I commend your soul to God, and ask him with this water to wash the sin from your soul. May the angels and the saints watch over you and protect you, and guide you to making the best choices as a child of Christ.'

Caldwell sighed hard, as if a demon were leaving his body. He lifted up his head and looked at the old holy man, and nodded silent thanks. He made his way back up the wet stone steps, with Great Patriarch steadying himself on his arm to ensure that he did not slip on his way back up to the safety of the grass.

The wind, which had been playing like a mischievous spirit child in the expanse of the flat fields all around, was now starting to whip the shrubbery around the well and the hedgerows by the roadside. The horizon was far away on all sides, allowing for a dense swathe of sky with its darkening clouds to bear down on the two men. Caldwell could tell that a storm was brewing, and that it was prudent to leave now before it began its overtures. He turned back towards the holy man, and realised that he was praying silently beside the well.

Caldwell waited until the Father of Fathers had finished his prayer, then led him out of the field, through the foliage, and back to the car, to return him safely to the bosom of his worried retinue.

CHAPTER 39

At the church, Perpetua was surrounded by a sea of smiles, but still there was something wrong. The smiles did not reach the eyes of their bearers, and the eyes themselves had a glassiness about them, as if people were humouring her. Even if the words they said sounded positive and encouraging, there was something strange in the air. Perpetua looked around for reassurance and finding none, went to the side-room to check her reflection in the church's full-length mirror. No, it wasn't the dress, many people had expressed their admiration of it. And her hair and make-up were perfect. Perpetua paused, and looked around her. Was it just her imagination? Was she being paranoid? And people *did* seem to be smiling. It just felt that there was something wrong, and Felicity wasn't any help.

She racked her brains for an answer. Maybe it was last week's hospital bombing that was still on people's minds. Fourteen had been killed and forty injured. Just because it was her special day she could hardly ask people to put all of their cares to one side. And there was this flu thing. Lots of families had a relative or two taken away to quarantine. That must be a worry. She took a deep breath, checked the reflection of herself smiling, and got ready for Matt's arrival and the ceremony to come.

※ ※ ※

The ceremony itself had been quiet and solemn, the congregation subdued. *Which wasn't all bad*, Perpetua reasoned. A lifetime commitment *was* a solemn thing. But now, at the evening celebration, the subdued mood that she had sensed earlier could not be denied. People should be dancing and laughing, and while they came up to her with their best wishes and to compliment her on her dress or on her youthful radiance, it felt as routine as it was sincere. And it wasn't as if there were a lack of music, or of food and drink. Rather, it was as if people were holding back. Even Matt seemed distant. She caught him looking off into the middle-distance with a serious look on his face.

'Matt, what's going on?'

Perpetua eyes bore into his with the intensity of a jealous wife, her gaze scrutinising every inch of his face for the smallest sign of a lie. She thought for a split-second that she saw a flash of fear cross Matt's face. It made her heart race. *Fear? What did he have to be frightened of?*

Matt's eyes looked around Perpetua as if to check if anyone could hear her question. 'Not here, Perpetua.'

Now Perpetua was properly frightened. Her mind immediately went to the thoughts of Matt no longer loving her, of him regretting the wedding. But that couldn't be it. Everyone seemed to have the same kind of hidden worry that Matt had. Something was going on.

Matt caught the look on her face and stooped to kiss her on the lips. He stroked her face and whispered in her right ear 'Come over here.' He beckoned to a dark corner of the function hall, that hadn't yet been filled with courting teenagers seeking privacy. No-one would hear them over the music.

Matt kept in close to Perpetua, and eased his mouth down to her ear. He was well aware that the official penalty for rumour-mongering, a crime which served only the enemy's interests, was immediate death. 'It's not to do with you, Perpetua. It's nothing to do with *us*.' He pulled back from her to look her in the eyes, so that she could see that he was being sincere. 'It's something else.'

He paused. He wasn't sure how to continue.

'What is it?' Perpetua was now worried. 'Come on, tell me.'

Matt went back to stroking her hair, so that anyone looking at them would assume that the newlyweds were exchanging the sweet-nothings of their wedding day. He already regretted saying as much as he had, but he knew that he was trapped now. Once Perpetua got a bee in her bonnet about something, she would not let it go. He looked around the room and caught Candice's eye. Her worried look told him that she knew as well. Everybody knew. Matt understood that if he didn't tell Perpetua now, she would just go to her mother, and it would be Candice who would be put in this awkward position.

He struggled to hear the sound of his own voice over the loud Northumbrian pipes carrying the melody which filled the room with a raucous jig, so he kept his mouth close to Perpetua's ear.

'There's a rumour going round. Only at this stage, it's not really a rumour. One of the EF soldiers on special duty disobeyed the direct order of silence to tell the people that the hospital quarantine is a lie. There is no quarantine – these people were being taken away to die and are being buried in mass graves, in secret. This "flu" is a death sentence, and the EF commanders are trying to keep this from us.'

Perpetua stood in silence, open-mouthed. Matt kept stroking her hair to maintain the pretence of a romantic interlude.

Perpetua's mind raced. 'Are you sure? I mean, this guy could be lying.'

Matt shook his head. 'He's not lying. He apparently showed photographs of the mass graves to people before he was caught and the evidence was destroyed. The fact that he was killed so quickly points to him telling the truth. And so far, the EF high command has said nothing. They will have to though. It's soon going to get to the stage that everyone will know. And they will have to prove that this is not true. It looks like they can't.'

Perpetua's head was reeling. Suddenly the music became too loud and was making her nauseous. She wanted fresh air.

'But why hide it? I don't get it. Why not give the bodies back to the families to bury properly?'

Matt looked around again. 'It's... well... they say that the final stage of the illness is a massive bleeding out. Blood pours from the nose, the mouth... everywhere. It's not flu, Perpetua, and they have been telling us all this time that it *is* flu. *Something* is going on. Something strange, maybe even evil. I don't know. But it's best not to talk any more about it.' He smiled at her, a loving smile, and kissed her again. 'If anything, this should make us grateful that we are still here, and that this day was able to happen.'

Suddenly, Perpetua remembered something that Aoife prophesied about her wedding day. *You will get your wedding, but it will not be how you expect.* Or it was words to that effect. Well, that was certainly right. The guests were all here, the ceremony had gone without a hitch, the music, food and drink were all plentiful and perfect, and yet. And yet. This could be a wake. People were smiling and making the right noises, but it was mechanical. *There is no joy here*, Perpetua thought. People were going through the motions, not just out of respect for the newlyweds and their families, but because of the fear that to talk about these things openly could result in being disciplined by the EF for rumour-mongering. Perpetua looked around at the guests. *They were smiling out of fear...*

Everyone knew someone who had been sent to the quarantine hospitals. Some people had loved ones who had been sent away. Perpetua saw a few people sitting at tables who looked downright miserable. Now they would be wondering if their friends and relatives were actually dead, their corpses lying under a pile of others in the ground like worthless landfill. Maybe their loved ones were dying right now, alone and frightened. Of those sitting forlornly, Perpetua recognised Mr. Jackson and two of the Davies sisters among them, but could not make eye contact. They were all looking down at their drinks, or at each other.

Perpetua's thoughts were interrupted by the sight of her neighbour Mrs. Broadhurst coming up to the couple.

'Perpetua, my love, it has been a lovely day, but I'd better be getting home now.' She looked at Matt, then back at Perpetua. 'I hope the two of you have a wonderful marriage.'

Perpetua was going to protest that it was only 8 p.m., but there didn't seem much point. There was no happiness in this party. The music jarred and no-one seemed in the mood. As the drink flowed things would only get morose, rather than celebratory. It was clear that this wedding had been a wash-out, even if CeeCee had made the most beautiful dress in the Northwest and everyone had complimented her on it.

Matt saw his bride looking downcast and kissed her tenderly on the forehead.

'It's maybe not how you imagined, but we got through it. We're married now, that's the important thing. Nothing else matters except that.'

Perpetua nodded, saying nothing. She felt like she was going to cry. So many hopes had been placed on this day, and it had been all for nothing. She saw CeeCee over by the trestle tables laden with food and suddenly felt the urge to go and talk to her.

'Matt, I'm just going to talk to CeeCee, I won't be long.'

Matt watched as his bride made her way self-consciously across the near-empty dancefloor toward the woman who had spent hours embroidering every golden acorn, and fussing over the various shades of green of the oak leaves of her bridal gown. A dress which so much love had gone into, and yet seemed out of place right now, on this day. He watched as the two women fell into conversation, and then older woman put her arms around the younger woman's slender shoulders, and the younger woman cried.

CHAPTER 40

Sam poked his little brother lightly in the ribs. 'You're as stupid as the Swedebird'. The little boy laughed and giggled and rolled around on the bed, waited for the onslaught of his brother's tickles.

'Swedebird, swedebird, SWEDEBIRD!' Sam pounced on five-year-old Ignatius and tickled his belly. Sam always ended the fable about the Swedebird with tickles, which was why Iggy requested the Swedebird story so often. The Swedebird was a bird who was clever with tools, who was smart enough to use twigs as levers and who dropped shellfish onto rocks to break their shells, but who was so silly that he made his nest in the road because he did not fear the approach of men or snakes. The Swedebird was a staple of EI moralistic teaching, which taught children the importance of situational awareness, and that sometimes, clever people were not clever in the most important things. The choice of name for the bird had been a way for the English to recover some of their self-image, in the face of the black legend swirling around Europe which told of how the English had allowed foreign men to gang-rape and murder their little girls before putting their bodies in kebab meat to sell back to the girls' oblivious kith and kin.

Iggy squealed in delight as Sam pretend to be the tickly snake sliding against his legs, and an impatient voice came back from the other bedroom. 'For God's sake can you two be quiet in there?'

Sam and Iggy looked at each other and went quiet. Their dad was always annoyed at things these days. In the silence Sam could hear his father talking to his mother, and his heart thumped in his chest as he realised that they were talking about the *dreaded lurgy*, and that they didn't realise that he could overhear some of their conversation.

Sam turned back to Iggy. He looked at the little boy with wide open eyes and raised eyebrows of intrigue, and slowly put a finger to his lips. The little boy smiled in delight thinking that this was a new part of the game, and he stayed silent, waiting to see what Sam was going to do next. But Sam did nothing except strain to hear his parents' conversation. He soon realised that he could hear his father better than his mother, whose high voice didn't travel as well through the wall.

> ...no, Wales is shutting its borders to refugees, but it wouldn't matter anyway, the virus is borne in the air as well as the soil, it's impossible to keep it limited to one place...

> ...there's no quarantine line, there's nowhere to run...

> ...Who is there to care about us? There's no longer a world conscience. Nobody can hear us outside of these borders...

> ...No, they can't. Scotland will shoot on sight any trespassers in their borderlands. They don't give a fuck. It's as barbarous as ever, they live like beasts. People are better taking their chances here than starving to death or getting raped and eaten...

> ... the new chieftain Donaldson is a fucking madman...

> ...the place into a famine-striken congo, but he's stopped invasions from the south...

Sam then heard the sound of his mother's voice, but he couldn't make out the words of what she was saying.

Then he heard his father's voice again, and heard his father laugh.

> *...the Irish are just the fucking Irish – they can't be trusted. There is too much water under the bridge for us not to expect a trap... they're a treacherous people and always have been... we should be more afraid of their wile than their war...*

Then Sam heard a mumbling between the two of them, and managed to picked out the phrase *the whiter they are, the slower the death.* He looked back at his little brother, who was now imitating him by putting his own finger over his mouth.

> *...people are dropping like flies and it's only going to get worse...*

> *...not even a thousand years to come will purify him of this guilt...*

> *...they are going to make an official announcement tomorrow. I want you to stay in the house under all circumstances, do you hear me?...*

> *...no, I don't know, but I can't see how this situation will not end without violence. So I want you to stay in the house with the boys until I say otherwise...*

At that point Sam heard his father's heavy footsteps thudding towards his bedroom and in a panic he quickly grabbed Iggy and started tickling him. The little boy responded by giggling as if there had been no pause in their play, just in time for Sam's father to open the door.

'You two were very quiet.' William scrutinised his eldest son as if he had spied sedition in a military underling. Sam went red and tried to look like a stupid child of ten who didn't understand his father's suspicions.

'We were just playing the Swedebird.'

William looked at his son again. His son's face told him that he had been eavesdropping.

'Just to let you know,' said William, 'if I find out that you have repeated anything, ANYTHING, I have said outside of this house you will wish that you had never been born. Do you understand?'

Sam nodded. His father was very tense, and Sam didn't want to risk him getting angry by speaking.

Little Ignatius was no longer laughing. William hated to see the little boy upset so mussed his hair and told him softly. 'It's ok, son. There's nothing to worry about.'

Then he turned back to Sam. 'I'm serious, lad. People who gossip are getting shot. I'm telling you this for your own good. You need to watch what you are saying to your little friends and be careful not to repeat anything that you've been told. By anybody. We haven't seen children being shot yet but it's only a matter of time. I don't want you being the first.'

Sam nodded again. 'Yes, Dad.'

A squall of rain spattered noisily against the window. William looked at his son with the seriousness of a soldier talking man-to-man. 'Things are going to get bad over the next few weeks, son. Very bad. Maybe they'll never get better. You need to be as smart as possible, and trust no-one except me and your mum.' He paused for a moment, then repeated the motto known to all EF children as he made his way out of the bedroom, but said it with the gravitas of imparting a great wisdom:

'Don't be the Swedebird.'

CHAPTER 41

At five months of pregnancy Felicity's breasts were growing ever more swollen and tender, and her nipples were starting to darken and puff outwards. She looked down at her bare chest. Blue veins were starting to show through her translucent pale skin, and the baby bump jutted impudently between her full tits. Morgenna had told her that the quickening would be any time now. She was just waiting for that magical first kick.

As she put on her bra she suddenly imagined Edwin breathing a lustful comment on her neck about her bigger breasts, cupping their weight in his hands and marvelling at how his seed had made her body blossom and ripen from its once gamine and twig-like state. In the silence of the bedroom that they had once shared, knowing that she would never feel his caress again and never hear his voice of approval or his laughter, Felicity felt a chasm of grief opened up before her that threatened to drag her into the centre of the earth. Her legs suddenly weak, she sat back on the bed. There was no point in crying. She was too sad to cry. But it pained her to see the change in her body, so aromatic and sexy and grounded now that it carried this new life, and not have the man who gave her this gift by her side.

She recalled this scene now as she sat on Aoife's living-room couch, when Aoife had told her about a great blackness around the young girl as she had come into the room.

'I can see that you are still struggling to re-enter time, after it was so cruelly snatched away from you.'

Felicity didn't understand what the old woman meant. Surely she was just as much in time when she was with Aoife, sitting on her couch, right at that moment. But she was too shy to ask the old woman to explain herself, especially if the explanation ended up making even less sense than the first statement. Felicity was scared of looking stupid and annoying people, so she usually didn't ask for an explanation to things, but rather hoped that she would be able to work things out herself. Sometimes she couldn't though, and needed help, like now. She decided to get to the point of her visit, lest Aoife take her off in another direction.

'I have been having dreams, so many dreams

that I don't understand. And Edwin is in them.'

Aoife looked at the young woman with her red top on, and was happy to see that her advice was still remembered.

'Well, we all dream, dear. And it is natural that Edwin would appear in your dreams, he is a martyr now.' Unbeknown to the young girl, Aoife was subtly teasing her into defending why she had come to visit, and Felicity did not disappointment.

'Yes, I get that, but these are not ordinary dreams. They are so vivid. It's like I'm being given a message. But I don't quite understand what it is.'

Aoife nodded. 'Go on.'

'I keep dreaming that I am a refugee along with dozens of women and children. I think it is because the women are pregnant, I'm not sure. And I'm not sure if Edwin is telling me that I will soon be sent somewhere else, or that I need to escape this place myself.'

'And where do you go, in these refugee dreams?'

Felicity sat back on the couch's worn cushions, and distractedly tucked strands of dark hair behind her ears.

'I had a dream where I was on a refugee ship that was trying to dock in America, and Morgenna and Perpetua were with me. But the port authorities were refusing to let the ship come into the harbour. I woke up before anything happened, but I remember that there was a feeling of despair and panic. It was a definitely a nightmare.'

Aoife interrupted. 'Are they all nightmares?'

'Yes. They are now.' Felicity looked straight into the old woman's eyes and a sudden chill passed over the old woman.

'Go on.'

'In another dream, we had managed somehow to sneak our way into the middle of Wales, I don't know how, but it was like we somehow managed to get past the checkpoints. I kept hearing this voice. But then we got caught and were driven back up to the Northwest by EF soldiers. And the man who had driven us there was shot by the roadside.' She shivered. 'Are these dreams telling me that I have to get away from here? Is something going to happen to me?'

Aoife sat silently for a few moments with her chin resting on her hand. Finally, she spoke.

'One runs towards one's fate all the more

surely by seeking to escape it. I believe that these dreams are warning you of an imminent danger. But this is not a danger that you will be able to run from, hence the reason that your attempts at escape are shown to be futile.' The old woman rocked back and forward slightly while trying to gather her thoughts. 'There is going to be great upheaval in this land. I have the foreboding of many evils, and you, my dear, are a very vulnerable target for this evil.'

Aoife straightened up in her armchair, and took her arm off the armrest to gesture towards the tall dark cabinet behind the couch where Felicity was sitting.

'There is a cupboard at the bottom of that cabinet. Have a look in it, and you'll find a metal hand bell. Bring it out and give it to me.'

Felicity obediently got up from the couch and went behind it. She realised that she would have to kneel to be able to see what was in the bottom cupboard, and there was very little light to see what she was looking at. It appeared to be just a few pewter mugs on a shelf, some envelopes, and a few children's toys.

After a few minutes, to let Aoife know what the problem was, Felicity called out.

'I can't find it!'

'Oh, it's there. It's a silvery colour. Quite heavy.'

Having rummaged through the entire cupboard, Felicity's eyes went back to what had first looked like a metal cheese grater. Looking at it again, she realised that it couldn't be a cheese grater, because the metal was solid and smooth. As she lifted it up, a sweet note rang out. She turned it upside down to look in its dark oblong mouth. Yes, there was a metal clapper inside. This was the bell that Aoife was talking about.

'I've found it!'. She closed the double doors of the cupboard with a click and scrambled to her feet with a teenager's litheness made clumsy by the state of pregnancy.

In the light of the living room, she was able to look at the bell more closely. It was quite crudely made, a flattened quadrangle of dull metal with edges that were not quite straight. The handle at the top was a sturdy loop of metal attached lengthwise to each end of the bell's body.

'It's not at all like I expected,' Felicity said as she passed the bell to the old woman.

'That's because it is very old,' the old woman said. 'Very old indeed. I imagine that the American collectors would love to get their hands something as old as this.' She looked again at the bell in the light. 'It might well date from over a thousand years ago, from the days of the Celtic saints. Or it might be quite recent, maybe just be a few hundred years old.'

Felicity eyes grew wide. 'Even if it's only a few hundred years old, you could definitely sell it for a lot of money.'

Aoife's mouth curled into a sneer. 'And have it end up with some stranger in America? Never! Felicity, you need to understand. Place matters. It *matters*, Felicity. Zion was a real holy hill, with a latitude and a longitude, before it was swallowed up by the sea. We have roots in this soil. Water is the natural divider of tribes, which is why our ancestors had a fear of crossing water. The spirits do not like crossing water either.' She ran her gnarled fingers along the rim of the bell's mouth. 'If this bell were to end up in America, I can guarantee that it would lose all of its power and meaning. It would pass from the present into history. It would cease to be in time.'

Felicity frowned again. *There she was with that time thing again. It didn't make any sense.*

She watched the old woman hold up the bell and swing it gently, and close her eyes as a warm, golden note reverberated around the room for almost a minute before melting in the air around them. For such a small nondescript bell it chimed very richly, like a royal bell.

'This is a sacred Bangu bell, Felicity. It is infused with the Holy Spirit and centuries of the prayers of the priest and the parishioners, who used it to heal the sick, uncover perfidy, and drive away evil. It is a powerful weapon against the forces of darkness. The vibrations of this little Welsh bell can clean the air of malevolent spirits and call out to the saints to watch over us...' Aoife paused '...if we have faith.'

Felicity nodded. She had been told at school that the churches rang the ave, curfew and dusk bells every day, not just to mark the hour in the ears and hearts of the English people and momentarily bring them together with the soothing sound, but as a declarative reminder that the Albionic Christian faith ruled over the land where the bells shed their holy charm. The SAU, understanding this defiant symbolism, had removed the bells from the great cathedrals within their territory and hung them upside down as giant lamps in their mosques, as a way of mocking the English and their Christian faith. Other church bells were melted down for weaponry. To the SAU, silence meant submission. Felicity remembered what Father Oldfield had told the class at school. 'When the land is taken back, the first thing we will do is reclaim and reconsecrate the bells.'

Aoife sounded the bell again. 'Every ring of this bell is a declaration of God's power. Evil spirits do not like metal.'

Felicity nodded and thought of something to say. 'Is that why the Albionic Church ring their bells during thunderstorms?'

'To a certain extent. But it is more as a plea to the faithful to turn their minds to God at a dangerous time. Evil spirits can only do damage with God's permission.' Through her wry smile, Aoife scrutinised the young girl sitting opposite her. Her body burgeoned with cellular energy and new life, and it was attracting the wrong kind of attention.

'Felicity, my love, you might not understand it now, but being corporeal is a gift. To eat and love and even to feel pain and grief are all gifts. Gifts that we take for granted. You have no idea how the young blood in your veins is envied by hungry ghosts who yearn to be embodied in this realm, so that they can experience time. It might feel painful now, but trust me, when this is over you will want to come back and experience the bittersweet intensity of being in time again.' She held out the bell to Felicity.

'Take it.'

Felicity reached forward and took the bell from Aoife with both hands.

'I want you to take this bell home, and use it to protect yourself. Ring it in every corner of every room, every morning and evening, and it will drive away evil. See it like a mini beating of the bounds. And whenever you feel yourself having a sad or an angry thought, ring the bell and focus on God. Recite the Albionic prayer if you need help to do this. Or any one of the Psalms.'

Felicity hesitated. 'Are you sure I can take this? It must be so valuable.'

Aoife grunted a little laugh to herself. 'Oh it is, my girl, more valuable than you could know. But it's purpose on Earth is to be of use. And as the hereditary keeper, I am allowed to lend it out to people in need, but they must swear to give it back to me. I will need it before I die.'

'Oh don't worry, I can give you my word on that,' said Felicity, still clutching the bell.

Aoife smiled widely, like she had just found something very funny and Felicity again felt confused. 'Well, you've sworn on the Bangu now, so you're committed. And another thing – it's important, very important, that the polluted hands of vile scoffers do not get to touch this bell. It is so powerful that it could actually harm one of them to touch it. Of course, Morgenna is fine to use it, she is a woman of faith. And take good care of it. Do not let it touch the ground.'

Felicity nodded. She felt full of questions, but she didn't know where to start.

'Do I need to do anything else?'

'Only that you must do the ritual every day. It is not enough to just think about it. It is important that you don't just live in your head, you must live in your body. If you are to really live in this physical world, as you need to, you must *act*.' Aoife looked down at the young girl's belly. 'A woman thinks with her heart and with her womb, not with her brain, and it is a mistake for her to try to reason like a man. Her job is to intuit, and she does this through the body. And in order to be fully present in the world, to truly be *in* her body, she must *move*. So raise your body's energies. Sing, spin around for no reason. Enjoy *being* in the world. You have no idea how much your being is envied by the silent watchers.'

Felicity nodded, and felt herself stretch involuntarily when thinking of her body. She thought back to her nightmares. She wasn't fully convinced that Edwin wasn't telling her that she needed to escape this place.

'And this will definitely work to protect me?'

Aoife smiled, 'It will always work, until the moment someone expresses doubt.' Felicity watched as the old woman smiled broadly again, as if laughing at some private joke. 'I am being serious, Felicity. Without faith, these rituals mean nothing. The bell will not lend you its power. With faith, nothing can touch you.'

Felicity nodded.

'I'm very grateful to you for your help, Mrs. Osborne.' Then she suddenly remembered something from her dream the night before.

'My dream last night was very different. I'm frightened to say it. It's like saying it sort of gives it a power to come true.'

Aoife narrowed her eyes to look better at the young girl again. The same chill from before came over her.

'Oh don't worry about that, Felicity, tell me.'

Felicity looked down at the bell, as if hoping it would give her strength. She suddenly had the thought to let it chime before she spoke.

'I dreamt that they were attacking our beautiful dear Supreme Commander, like they wanted to kill him. Only the people who were attacking him weren't our enemies, they were EF soldiers. And then there was this message that came loud and clear to me. It said – Felicity struggled to remember the words – "A dozen brazen trumpets will soon sound forth… the Lord's reckoning for the man… for the man who fought to save the blue diamonds."'

Felicity looked at Aoife open-mouthed after she spoke, as if in shock at all that she had remembered the whole of the mysterious message. Then she realised that there was something strange about the silence.

'The clock has stopped!'

Aoife stopped to listen for a few seconds then smiled. 'Yes, you're right. Don't worry, it just needs wound up again. I'll get one of the children to do it later with the curfew bell.' She looked at Felicity's face.

'Don't think anything of it. Mechanical clocks wind down all the time. Not everything is a sign, you know. But just out of interest, what time does the clock say?'

Felicity looked at the clock's stilled hands. 'Just before three o'clock.'

Aoife said nothing.

❋ ❋ ❋

On her way back home, with the Bangu bell in a yellow satin bag that had seen its best days long before its bearer was born, Felicity felt buoyant and cheered, like a weight had been lifted from her body. She became mindful of Aoife's advice to move, and started to skip with difficulty along the pavement. But skipping made her breasts jiggle, and that was sore, so she started sing instead. A song from school came into her head, no doubt from all the talk about bells.

> *The Bells and Chimes of Motherland,*
> *Of England green and old,*
> *That out from grey and ivied tower*
> *A thousand years have toll'd;*
> *How heavenly sweet their music is*
> *As breaks the hallow'd day,*
> *And calleth, with a Seraph's voice,*
> *A nation up to pray!*

The first verse was the one that everybody knew. Like most people, she couldn't remember the next one. But it didn't matter. She was now coming into a street with people and if she started singing again people might think that she was mad.

CHAPTER 42

They had to pass by the rubble on the way to the market square. Thankfully, only part of the hospital had been hit, but not all of the building had been evacuated in time, and there had been casualties as well as building damage.

'What's that in the tree?' Alban asked, pointing to the pieces of rags that were hanging from branches of the trees flanking the ruins, like some kind of pagan votive offering to the grove spirits.

Dr. Wansbrough squinted at the trees through his glasses and took a few moments to think. 'Some of the body parts were thrown up into the trees with the force of the bomb blast. Those must be pieces of the corpse clothing that got caught in the branches.' He paused, and looked around. 'I heard that some of the babies, being so light, were thrown on that wall over there. Look at the bloodstains.' Dr. Wansbrough pointed at a thick stone wall opposite the bombed-out shell of the maternity unit. 'They couldn't have survived long.'

The breath left Alban's body when he saw the dark patches on the stonework. He had witnessed a bomb blast before, when he was very young, and his memory of it was patchy. Of the explosion itself, he remembered the falling masonry, the panic and the screaming. But of the time after the blast, he could only remember the smallest details – the stray dogs that had come to lap up the blood in the street; the old woman sitting on a heap of bricks, singing to herself. In this instance, he had arrived too late to see any of the action; the bodies had been cleared days ago and it was strangely peaceful. It was hard to imagine the corpses of women with their children in this deserted early morning filled with birdsong emanating from the votive-offering trees.

'Who would be sick enough to bomb a maternity hospital?' Alban asked. He wasn't expecting an answer, because it was just a comment he made for something to say. But Dr. Wansbrough answered his rhetorical question.

'Oh, you would be surprised. The English were not above such tactics in the Second World War. What is justified in the arena of warfare becomes a very malleable concept in some leaders' hands.'

Alban shook his head. 'I hate seeing so much destruction. I don't think I go a day without seeing a building in ruins.'

'Yes, but at least you can see those ruins,' said Dr. Wansbrough. 'It was worse when I was a boy, and I was living among pristine buildings, but the ideological ruins of my nation. Ideological ruins are more insidious than the ruins of cities, because unlike the physical ruins they are not seen and travellers do not shake their head when passing by the debris. But they are far more deadly to the people, and much more difficult to rebuild. You should celebrate that the English Front has rebuilt us spiritually, even if we still have so much of our physical landscape in pieces. They rekindled a flame in those ideological ruins that was smouldering and almost extinguished.'

The doctor turned back towards the direction they had been heading, to signal that they resume their journey. 'Come on, I don't want us to be late. I want you to see something.'

After ten more minutes of brisk walking under a blue sky, past the factories, houses and the smell of broth in the air from the big volunteer kitchen, the man and the boy reached the market square. There must have been about fifty stalls, with a few blankets laid out in spaces where the vendors could not afford, or perhaps did not need, a stall.

Dr. Wansbrough stood at the edge of the market square and beamed proudly. 'Tell me, Alban, what do you see?'

Alban noticed that the doctor had stopped short of entering the market. He did not know why his master had stopped like this, outside of where things were happening, but the boy dutifully stayed by his side and looked straight ahead. All of the stalls were set. The butchers had hung up their joints; the farmer's wife had spread her butter upon a white cloth, onions and apples stood tempting on the pavement side. A few stalls displayed prominent badges of the guilds to which their owners proudly belonged.

Alban wondered why the doctor was asking him that question. He always knew that there was a trick in it. *Wait a minute – where were the customers?*

'Nobody seems to be trading,' said Alban, and he looked up at the old man for confirmation. Dr. Wansbrough did not look back at the young boy's expectant face as he tried to keep a serious countenance, but Alban noticed that the corners of the old man's mouth were beginning to twitch.

'Look over there.' Dr. Wansbrough pointed leftwards to a big wooden board staked into the ground, onto which was nailed a sign of hand-painted letters. Above the sign hung a large brass bell with a rope trailing down from its clapper. The sign read:

> THE FOLLOWING ARE SUBJECT TO HEAVY PENALTY:
>
> FORESTALLING
> BADGERING
> REGRATING
> ENGROSSING
>
> BY ORDER OF THE ENGLISH FRONT

'See that bell?' said Dr. Wansbrough. 'That's the market bell. It regulates trade. Not an atom can be bought or sold until that bell is sounded. It is unlawful even to handle a goose before the allotted time.'

Alban's face crinkled up in bemusement. 'But why?'

'Because it's forestalling. It's getting an unfair advantage over other people. Some people live further away from the market than others. It's to ensure that everyone gets a chance to buy goods at a fair price.'

Alban nodded. He thought he understood. 'But then surely the person who bought the thing first could just resell it to the person who arrived later?'

'No,' said Dr. Wansbrough, that would be regrating, and would lead to the regrater taking a profit for doing nothing but being wily enough to get here early. In the same way, wholesale buying also needs to be licenced for specific purposes, or you get engrossing, which leads to a vital commodity needed by the community being controlled for commercial ends. This is wrong – the economy is to serve the people, not the other way around. If you do not regulate with vigilance, what you get are exploitative middle-men, speculators and monopolies. From there it is a few short years to oligarchy and tyranny, and we, the masses, having to endure our own labour being sold back to us with an interest charge in order just to eat. No, Alban. It might have taken us over two hundred years to relearn the wisdom of our ancestors, but we English have gone back to the days of the market bell, and we've spilt enough blood to make sure that it stays that way.'

Just as he said that the large hairy hand of the chief market inspector grabbed the rope beneath the bell and struck the clapper heartily. The big brass bell rang out in the bright sun of the morning.

'You may begin trading!'

Alban watched as people who had been standing on the edge of the market with their empty shopping baskets moved forward to the stalls. Dr. Wansbrough still did not move forward, and Alban realised that he was still watching the scene. The older man pointed to a man in a grey uniform. 'Do you know who that is?'

Alban shook his head.

'He's a finance expert for the EF. Our economy is carefully planned to sure that everyone earns the just fruits of their labour. The experts watch over markets and other areas of economic activity. They watch prices, and if prices go up or down, they find out if this is due to fluctuations in supply or demand, or if there needs to be more or less currency in circulation. It's a very carefully calibrated process, Alban, involving quality checks, weights and measures, designed to keep the price of bread and milk the same for the next 500 years. And most importantly, speculators are shot. Nothing keeps the prices as stable as the threat of death to those who would dare to speculate in commodities or currency. And farmers can choose to pay their taxes to the EF directly in essential produce, so that avoids middlemen.'

Alban went wide-eyed for a moment. He couldn't imagine a man getting shot over the price of a loaf of bread.

'What you've got to understand, Alban, is that gold is fictional wealth. A nation's only true wealth is the quality of its people. It is their labour that make or break the fortune of a nation, because money is nothing but credit on the labour of the nation. And a nation's greatest single asset is her great men. For it is the great men who express a nation's soul.'

Alban pondered that comment, and thought of the Supreme Leader. He was definitely a great man.

Dr. Wansbrough continued. 'The EF encourages private initiative, and protects private property, but not to the extent that its accumulation impacts on others. For God said through Isaiah 'Woe to you who add house to house and join field to field till no space is left and you live alone in the land'. This was a divine injunction against capitalistic monopolies. And He also cast his divine judgement upon those elders of Judah who used their wealth and power to distort the economy and further benefit themselves.'

Dr. Wansbrough cleared his throat, and much to Alban's delight, began to speak in a deep sententious voice.

> *It is you who have ruined my vineyard;*
> *the plunder from the poor is in your houses.*
> *What do you mean by crushing my people*
> *and grinding the faces of the poor?*

Alban imagined the voice of God as being quite similar to Dr. Wansbrough's booming baritone impression of him. But the doctor returned to his normal voice to be himself.

'This is the reason why the EF has banned opaque financial structures, and joint-stock companies are now under EF control. Co-operatives and guilds are the preferred form of trading structure, and even these are carefully monitored to ensure that they do not grow in unchecked power and become cartels. Ultimately, as no-one would be able to trade without the military protection the army affords them, so ultimately it is the English Front who decides the economic policy of the people, because it ensures the people's very existence. As a wise man once said, the sword must stand before the plough, and an army before the economy.'

Alban nodded. 'So you're saying that it's the people who control the violence who get to decide the trade?'

Dr. Wansbrough smiled broadly. 'Of course. And the English Front is honest about that transaction. All economic and political systems are backstopped by violence, and anyone who imagines that the human world can be any other way is an idiot. Back in the previous centuries, people honestly thought that it was possible to create a perfect economic system that could run independently of the strengths or the beliefs of the humans within it. That is a nonsense. There is no 'neutral' system that can be proofed against the society in which it is embedded, just as it is impossible to build a perpetual motion machine which never gathers friction. Human beings, with their weaknesses and their vices, are the entropic force which impedes an ideal system. The Nuremberg trials proved that. All systems ultimately rely on the character of the men who uphold them.'

'What do you mean, "the Nuremberg trials"?'

Dr. Wansbrough paused as he weighed up what to say and what not to say; he did not want to go off on another of his tangents. He decided to go around the topic.

'Part of the way that the beast maintained its power throughout the 20th and early 21st century was through its pretence of universality. It cleverly spread the idea that its own totalising episteme, including its own system of ethics, was neutral, natural, the only possible worldview any rational person could hold, as if somehow it stood outside of ideology or interested parties. It was a very clever move, and a highly successful one in the main. It shaped the collective mentality of the West.

But there were times where the mask of benevolence slipped, and the beast behind it could be glimpsed. The Nuremberg trials exposed as a sham the idea that Western jurisprudence could be neutral in its administration of justice. It was the most blatant display that justice was dependant on the whim of those who ruled over us, and that human rights, or lack of human rights, are not enforced by abstract nouns on pieces of paper, but by very real violence. And as the decades went on and the dark forces became ever hungrier for control, these faultline events became more and more common.'

Dr. Wansbrough looked at the boy's face, which still showed puzzlement, and he realised that his explanation hadn't helped. He needed to remember how young Alban was, despite his precocity.

'I think that we should leave the Nuremberg trials for another day. It's a big subject, and I wanted to use today to tell you about the rationale behind the various tokens of the currency system. It's a good chance now that I've got this dinner to make.'

'Are you sure... are you sure you want me to be there tonight?'

Alban liked Mrs. Ellacombe but he didn't want to be in the way of the adults, especially if Dr.

Wansbrough wanted to be on his own with the lady. He knew that Dr. Wansbrough would like her to be a girlfriend, and even if Alban was silent throughout, he was sure that his presence was not going to help.

'Don't be silly, of course I want you there!'

'Sir, you don't have to be polite...'

'Don't worry, Alban, I will let you know whenever you are going play the gooseberry. Come on.'

'What's "playing the gooseberry"?'

Dr. Wansbrough laughed loudly at the consternation on Alban's face as he ignored his question and led the boy into the market, as it became thronged with the housewives who up until that point had been milling around the market periphery and in the side streets waiting for the bell to ring. Alban struggled to keep up with the old man through the narrow passageway of bodies as he made his way to the far end of the market.

'Our first stop is to buy a shopping basket,' said Dr. Wansbrough. 'That's something I always forget to bring.'

Alban did his best to cast sideways glances at the stalls falling behind him as he struggled to keep up with the doctor, who kept a brisk stride in front. With the narrowness of the walkways and the burgeoning crowd it was impossible to walk two-abreast, and it made sense for the doctor's large frame to be the ship's prow cutting through the sea of people, allowing the smaller Alban to scamper forward in his wake. But the boy had to keep close to the doctor's body as it advanced, for the waves of shoppers soon closed back in on the space, buffeting Alban from side to side as they did so. Alban did not yet have a man's presence that could plough through the female bodies were confidence. It was difficult for the boy to see the stalls from this position, but at least he could hear the voices.

One man was shouting rhythmically, like he was lulling the crowd into a hypnotic trance.

'...candles, lamp oils, soap... candles, lamp oils, soap...'

The deep voice was so powerful that no other seller could compete against it close by. It was only when they got near to the other, quieter, end of the market that a woman seller's voice came into earshot: 'Two eggs a pound. Fresh today. Two eggs a pound.'

'We'll be buying eggs,' said Dr. Wansbrough. 'But first, a shopper'.

There was a stall near the corner of the market which sold baskets and bags for shopping. Some were made of wicker, others of raffia or jute. All were made to last. Dr. Wansbrough looked at the prices.

'Now these are paid for in blue coinage,' said the doctor. 'Why is that, Alban?'

'Because they are non-essential items,' said Alban, remembering what he had been taught in school.

The stallholder, a middle-aged woman with tired but friendly eyes, butted in jokingly. 'Non-essential? You try carrying your weekly shop home in your hands!' But she smiled and nodded in the doctor's direction. 'You're right though. Nobody will die from lack of a good carrying bag, more's the pity!'

Dr. Wansbrough asked to see a large blue shopper made of some kind of raffia-type material, and was pleased by the sturdiness of the handles and the width of its reinforced base. He smiled at the boy. 'You'll be carrying this one, Alban.'

He gave twenty blue pounds to the woman, who tried to give him three pounds back, but he asked her to keep it. The woman looked into Wansbrough's eyes and nodded, saying nothing, her professional garrulousness lost for a moment.

When they moved away from the stall, Alban asked Dr. Wansbrough why he had not taken his change.

The answer came back with a quiet stillness in his voice that Alban had come to associate with the doctor's more mystical moments. 'Because it was worth twenty pounds, and I knew that,' said the doctor. 'Therefore it was un-Christian to not give the woman what the item was worth.'

'But she was only asking for seventeen pounds,' said Alban.

'Yes, but that is because she is not in a strong enough financial position to ask for its value. And as a Christian, I am not going to exploit that. Come on. There's a lot of food we need to buy for tonight. And I want to get some fragrant lamp oil. Fragrant lamp oil – red or blue pounds?'

Alban thought for a moment. 'Blue... no, red... no, blue.'

The doctor smiled. 'What made you say red?'

'Because... because people use oil for light. And light is a necessity. Isn't it?'

The doctor grinned broadly. 'You can see how this dual exchange system can get complicated, eh? No, fragranced lamp oil is blue. But only because it is fragranced. Such details were created to ensure that the economy could expand beyond the basic sustenance-level rationing system of the red pounds. It's a way of allowing more luxury items, but without allowing money made from these to interfere in the essentials market.'

They had stopped at the cheese stall. Dr. Wansbrough consulted his list, and looked back at the cheeses on display. He couldn't get Valerie a Camembert, but he wanted to get her something luxurious enough to show that the English could rival the French in the finest blue cheeses.

Pointing to one of the artisan blue cheeses on the back shelf of the stall, Dr. Wansbrough asked: 'Red pound or blue pound?'

The smell around the stall was pungent, and reminded Alban of his big brother's laundry basket. That couldn't be an essential item – no child with a nose in his head would eat that. And if a child wouldn't eat it, such a food surely wouldn't be essential.

'I think,' said Alban, 'that this particular cheese is paid for with blue pounds.'

'And I should hope so!' said the man behind the stall in a humorously curt tone.

Dr. Wansbrough slapped the boy heartily on the back, pleased with his interior reasoning, whatever it had been.

'Correct, my boy. And would you like some tonight?'

'Not for me, thanks.' Alban was careful not to make eye contact with the cheesemonger, lest he cause offence. The smell coming from the cheese-stall was rank and he would be glad to get away from it, but he didn't want his eyes to betray his thoughts.

As Dr. Wansbrough was paying for the cheese Alban took the chance to look around the market. The stall beside the cheese stall sold jams and preserves, then there was a vegetable stall and a stall selling cured hams and pork products. After that point, the bodies of meandering and peering housewives prevented Alban from seeing any further. But he liked being in the hubbub of people, looking at the produce, taking in the colours and the noises and the smells under the bright sun that beat down almost directly above them now that it was at its highest point for both the day and the year. It made a change from the bookwork of the day-to-day, which was nothing but the decoding of one set of symbols into another. These people knew nothing of that world, and would care less about it. Theirs was the meat-and-drink of life, not the ideas.

'You seem to be in a bit of a daydream, sonny Jim. Come on.'

The doctor moved to the next stall with Alban in tow, and laughed when he saw a row of cloth-hatted glass jars of green jam, near the front of the display. 'I think,' said the doctor, 'in light of our earlier conversation, that we should buy this. It seems fitting, somehow.' He held up the jar of gooseberry jam just long enough for Alban to read the label. 'Not that you'll be playing a gooseberry at all tonight. Your company will be most welcome.'

CHAPTER 43

'And how is my littlest swineherd?'

Andrew came in to the main house from the barn to find his father sitting at the kitchen table with Uncle Bob. Nobody had said anything about his father's arrival and his unexpected appearance at the table caused a feeling of fear to grip Andrew's stomach. A fear not completely unjustified given Kevin's regular role as the official bearer of bad tidings. 'Is every ok?'

Kevin looked at his young son's worried face and flashed a reassuring smile. 'Yes, son, everything's fine.' He looked down at Andrew's feet. 'Dirty boots!' Andrew looked at his wellingtons, and quickly stepped back onto the other side of the door, hoping that Uncle Bob hadn't noticed. Uncle Bob, however, was much too taken up with the presence of his brother in the farmhouse, and the news he brought.

'Yes, that's what I heard as well. It was a combination of skyscanner failure and the watch-boy getting ill suddenly. I mean, what are the chances?'

'Yes, I know, I know. They're now talking about putting two watchboys at every watchpoint. Hopefully that will be enough. The drones don't get through often, but when they do it can be catastrophic.'

'But you're ok for next Saturday though?'

'I certainly am. It'll be fun. Who doesn't like a hog-hunt?'

Uncle Bob turned to look at Andrew after he said this. Then added, to the boy's excitement: 'Do you think our little tantony pig is too young to hunt wild boar in the woods?'

Kevin looked at his son's expectant face with a father's love and pride, but Andrew sensed a little bit of pity in there too, and a few seconds later the boy's suspicions were confirmed when he heard his father say 'no, Bob I don't think so'. He then turned to the crestfallen child. 'I'm sorry, son, but you're just a bit too young. Maybe after your twelving. Boar-hunting can be dangerous, and to be honest I'm personally not too keen on having any lad younger than fifteen with me. Ten is certainly too young.'

Andrew tried to hide his disappointment and smiled weakly at his father. But he was getting really tired of being a child.

Boar-hunting had become incredibly popular with the English Front in the 2050s. Wild boar had been known to dwell in many of the woods of England after their reintroduction at the end of the 20th century, but their numbers were given a boost during the Struggle when, due to a combination of amateur animal husbandry and deliberate sabotage, a large number of domesticated pigs escaped from rural gardens, wastelands, and farms, and returned to their feral woodland roots. As the years went on, large roving herds of hybridised wild pigs could be found feasting on the mast of the forest, every year becoming more hairy and tusky as contact with their wild boar cousins became inevitable. They made the English wild woodlands a place to be feared for the ethnic SAU, who had an inexplicable terror of the earthy boar and its dark, chthonic nature.

The English, on the other hand, recovered their ancient Germanic delight for the feral boar, and saw great symbolism in its uncovering of the earth's hidden bounty with its continual rootling and snuffling. The nocturnal adventure that was the Boar Hunt became a rite-of-passage for a young man, and proved a safer way for the EF to train a young man in trailing, stalking, and killing than anything they could learn on the field. The joy of killing brought men together, as they learned to work as one in catching and tying the hog. One of the hunters would then be chosen go through the masculinising ritual of slitting the animal's throat, his hand gripping his knife, his muscles tight with tension, defying the deafening ungodly screams echoing through the trees, begging for mercy. No, thought Kevin, Andrew was far too young for such an ordeal, even as only a spectator. Without the protective surge of teenage testosterone girding the loins and viscera, what exhilarates the man can traumatise the boy.

Then came the celebratory carrying of the hog out of the depths of the dark forest, watching not to twist an ankle tripping over brambles, or over the roots of the trees around which the boars went digging. A massive celebration was then held in which the body was toasted, before being taken for evisceration. This was what Kevin was asking now – if Bob would be able to hold this raucous after-hunt party, should the hunters be successful. It was not sufficient just to kill, there needed to be a suitable social recognition of the killing, in which the boy's achievements were recognised by his peers and superiors, and all of the hunters felt part of the group.

'Of course,' Bob said, when Kevin asked him

if he would host the after-hunt. 'You'll never catch me saying no to a piss-up. And if we get a boar, I can put it in the curing shed.'

Kevin nodded, and looked thoughtful for a moment.

'I would say, Bob, that you should think about building up a stock of cured hams for the coming months. I can't say too much right now, but I think it's safe to say that the supply lines are going to be such in the next few months that transporting live animals and fresh meat is going to be difficult. I think it would be a good idea to have a lot of meat prepared – cured and smoked – for easy transport and storage.'

'Are you trying to tell me something, Kev?'

'Bob, I can't right now, but the chances are that when I come up with the Wolves next weekend the news will already be out. I think...'

Kevin shot a glance over at his son, who was standing innocently by the kitchen sink.

'Andrew, can you go outside for a minute. It's nothing personal, but me and your Uncle Bob have got to have a quick chat. I'll call you back in when we're finished.'

'Okay,' Andrew replied obediently. He opened the back door, stepped outside and closed the door behind him. He walked down to the bottom of the three stone steps which led up to the back entrance and sat on the bottom step in his stocking soles, waiting to be called in. Feeling suddenly quite exposed, the young boy surveyed the landscape, and imagined the points at which intruders might try to enter the grounds of the farm. Uncle Bob had set trip wire and security lights around the perimeter of the farm, and an alarm would sound in the farmstead if the lights were tripped. As the English Front held the castle doctrine sacrosanct, not only did Uncle Bob have the right to kill any intruders, but he was also permitted, after a private agreement made with a local official in 2055, to feed any unidentifiable bodies to the pigs. Such intrusions were very rare occurrences, however, and Andrew had never been on the farm when an intruder struck. But the thought of it made him excited and frightened at the same time. He pretended to lift an imaginary shotgun to his right shoulder and aimed it towards the barn door. *Bang!* He threw himself backwards to mimic the recoil of the firearm, as it fired towards two ghostly thieves trying to sneak out of the barn towards the tractor shed. But pretending to shoot a gun wasn't much fun. He would have to wait until his twelving, when he took the Oath and his Life Duty was made official, before Uncle Bob would let him even touch one of his shotguns. And because he wasn't twelve yet, he was sent outside to sit on the step when the men were talking.

It was very frustrating having to wait to grow up.

CHAPTER 44

Sunlight filtered through the tissue-paper sea of CeeCee's Ark window and hit the surface of the meeting table as patches of bright blue light. It was the Saturday meeting of the Haresfinch branch of the English Mothers' League and Morgenna was sitting at the top of the table with her agenda. But the truth was, as much as she needed to run through the items, no-one was focussed, least of all her.

A few hours ago, an announcement had been made by the Deputy Commander of the Five Divisions, Harry Talbot. The Supreme Leader, the Commander-in-Chief, the man who had led the English people back from the brink of oblivion after the genocidal horrors of the 2030s and 2040s, the man who had put the spirit back in the people to fight on after the destruction of the only world that they had ever known, and who had played a great part in creating this new society, David Caldwell, the saviour of his beloved English people, was being hunted for a war crime against those same English people.

All of the women sat around stunned. Mrs. Langley had been silently sobbing on and off into a handkerchief, an action which was making Morgenna herself feel tearful. It was the shock more than anything. Only four of the women had come to the meeting, probably out of that same impulse for duty and routine, but it was only as they sat here that the real impact of the announcement hit them.

Morgenna wondered if it was worth bringing up the home visits planned for Thursday when Mrs. Smith spoke.

'It just doesn't seem like something that our leader would do. Biological weapons are so… well… *sneaky*. Caldwell is a fighter – he meets his enemies head on. I can't imagine him doing something that would endanger his own people. Do you think that this is a slander for some kind of… you know… army coup? Like someone wants to topple him, so they're putting this fake charge against him? I know that it must sound like a conspiracy theory, but I just can't get my head around this announcement. It's too… weird.'

There was a silence as everyone thought about what Mrs. Smith had said. Mrs. Turville decided to play devil's advocate, even though she wasn't herself convinced of the argument she was putting forward. 'Well they say that he is on the run, and that there is a bounty on his head. A guilty man wouldn't run, he would face the music. Wouldn't he?'

Mrs. Smith shot back. 'Yes, and that's out of character as well. Can you imagine David Caldwell, *the* David Caldwell, *running* from anything? Something's very strange about this. I know you people always say I overthink things, but something's off with this story.'

Morgenna knew at that point that it was pointless to try to carry on with the meeting's agenda as she had planned it, and that they might as well talk about what was on everyone's minds. Especially because some of the families that the League was most concerned with were now themselves among the victims of the virus. This supposed 'biological plot'. The theory itself made sense, but like Mrs. Smith, Morgenna struggled to believe that David Caldwell, or the English Front, would be capable of such a thing. It was all so utterly horrifying and unbelievable.

Father Jones came up to the group, and Morgenna suddenly felt relieved by his presence. His calmness, his rationality, his maleness, even the red cross on his priest's cassock, reassured her. This was somehow a mistake, and it would all be sorted out.

'Isn't it terrible what has happened?' said Father Jones in a faint voice, and at that point Morgenna knew that he was in as much shock and confusion as the women were themselves.

'Yes,' said Morgenna. 'I can't believe it. I would declare this meeting ended but for the fact that I'm glad to be in church right now with you all at this time.' She looked around at her friends and a sense of gratitude came flooding into her, as they sat in this holy place, with the coloured light from CeeCee's window streaming onto them all. Sebastian was on a camping weekend with the Young Pups, John was on duty, and Felicity was at an embroidery class, where CeeCee was doing her best to resurrect the body of Opus Anglicanum. If it hadn't been for this meeting she might have been on her own in the house, with nothing but her own thoughts rattling inside her head and the ghost of her eldest son. She put a hand instinctively on her womb. It might feel like an illusion, but she felt stronger when she was around other people. It was like together, there was a chance of survival. Things felt less likely to go wrong when they were together in church.

Mrs. Benjamin had been sitting quietly and had said very little. It was unlike her to be so quiet. But Morgenna suspected that she knew why. The reason that Caldwell was being hunted for his life was because the plague he had unleashed on the land was said to be race-specific, and it targeted non-Europeans. Hardly anyone behind the lines of English Front territory was a hundred percent non-European, not in 2060, but there was a significant minority of mixed-race people, even if by only a tiny amount. No-one knew what this bio-weapon meant for them. For pure-blooded Asians and Africans the virus was fatal. But for someone like Mrs. Benjamin? Looking at her, it was difficult to ascertain she was even technically mixed race. And who was to say to what extent her Caribbean great-grandfather's genes had been passed down to her? This virus was like a horrendous Russian Roulette among the people. This is why to the original rumours that the virus had a racial profile had been held in doubt, because people could point to cases in which one person had taken ill while their brother or sister was unaffected.

Morgenna sensed that asking Leticia Benjamin if she was ok was redundant. It was clear from her face that she wasn't. She looked like she was going to be sick, and Morgenna couldn't blame her. So Morgenna decided to ask the group if they would like another cup of tea. Hearing the murmurs of consent around the table she got up and went to the pantry. No sooner had she boiled the kettle than she heard

From the Land All the Good Things Come

a shout coming from the main hall.

Rushing back through, she saw that everyone had left the seats and were kneeling on the wooden flooring behind the table. To her horror she saw that Mrs. Benjamin was lying on the floor, convulsing, and there was blood pouring out of her nose and mouth. There was blood everywhere. Morgenna pushed through the women and put her hand on Mrs. Benjamin's chest. Her heart was beating faintly and frantically like a dying bird. She was slipping away.

Morgenna began slapping Mrs. Benjamin's face, as if to try to wake up her from a faint, and dispensed with formalities. 'Leticia, can you hear me? Leticia, don't worry, you're going to be fine, but you need to wake up. Work with me, Leticia. Come on now, wake up!'

Morgenna decided to take a no-nonsense approach to this situation as the other women fell back and let her take control. She was going to will Leticia into the staying with them, and would scold her spirit for any attempt to leave. There would be no suggestion made that Leticia Benjamin was in any serious trouble. To vocalise such fears was to bring the Angel of Death closer.

At this point the other women became silent in order to let Morgenna do her work. Father Jones was frantically muttering a prayer over

Leticia's body. But Leticia's face was swollen and blue and she had lost consciousness. It was clear that she was dying. Father Jones got up from the scene and ran to find the ostiary. 'Toll the passing bell, quickly!'.

Leticia's heart had stopped now. Morgenna was frantically compressing Leticia's chest, trying to get her heart beating again, when she heard the slow melancholic toll of the passing bell. At first a wave of anger went through her when she heard the bell, as it was like an official admission that they had ceded the battle for this woman's life to the Angel. On the other hand, she knew that the passing bell was a symbolic beseeching of all those in the surrounding parish who heard it to think of and to pray for the person *in extremis*. And those prayers would help to guide Leticia's spirit into Heaven, and not have her languish, confused, on an earthbound plain.

Strangely, in the passing on one moment, Morgenna knew that the life had gone from Leticia Benjamin's body, and that all efforts to revive her from that point on were not just futile but also vaguely disrespectful. She looked around for Father Jones but could not see him. She looked at the other women who were too stunned to even cry. Slowly, Morgenna shut the dead woman's eyes and marked an unction cross on her forehead with her right forefinger, and as she did so realised that to her horror she realised that her forefinger was covered in Leticia's blood, because her finger had marked out a red cross.

She sat back, stunned, as Father Jones came running back up with the Holy Chrism, and jolted back momentarily when he saw that not only was Mrs. Benjamin dead, but she had a blood cross on her forehead. He knelt in front of her body and began muttering some kind of liturgy, tracing the blood cross with his own finger anointed with the holy oil, then crossed Mrs. Benjamin's arms over her chest and anointed her hands with the same oil.

Morgenna shut her eyes tightly as the tears started to come. She did not want to look at anybody, and she did not want to deal with anyone else's emotions. After a few minutes she got up and walked to the toilet, oblivious to the enquiring voices asking behind her.

When she got into the toilet she locked the door and burst into loud incoherent animal howls of anguish. The tears flowed until her eyes hurt and she became choked up and she struggled to breathe. The grief for her eldest son, so long suppressed, finally came tumbling out as she grieved for the sweet soul of Leticia Benjamin, her passing now lamented by the new sound of a death knell reverberating through the church's stone walls. To her distress and derangement was compounded the horrified shock that this plague covering the land was deliberately perpetrated by Man, not an act of God. And not just any man, but their very leader! A treachery which was not only destroying the lives of many good and innocent people but threatened the very existence of the English Front. Finally, with what was left of her will to live, a will that she felt slipping away with her sanity, Morgenna grieved for the terrifying future that faced her unborn child.

and as she did so realised that to her horror she realised that her forefinger was covered in Leticia's blood, because her finger had marked out a red cross.

She sat back, stunned, as Father Jones came running back up with the Holy Chrism, and jolted back momentarily when he saw that not only was Mrs. Benjamin dead, but she had a blood cross on her forehead. He knelt in front of her body and began muttering some kind of liturgy, tracing the blood cross with his own finger anointed with the holy oil, then crossed Mrs. Benjamin's arms over her chest and anointed her hands with the same oil.

Morgenna shut her eyes tightly as the tears started to come. She did not want to look at anybody, and she did not want to deal with anyone else's emotions. After a few minutes she got up and walked to the toilet, oblivious to the enquiring voices asking behind her.

When she got into the toilet she locked the door and burst into loud incoherent animal howls of anguish. The tears flowed until her eyes hurt and she became choked up and she struggled to breathe. The grief for her eldest son, so long suppressed, finally came tumbling out as she grieved for the sweet soul of Leticia Benjamin, her passing now lamented by the new sound of a death knell reverberating through the church's stone walls. To her distress and derangement was compounded the horrified shock that this plague covering the land was deliberately perpetrated by Man, not an act of God. And not just any man, but their very leader! A treachery which was not only destroying the lives of many good and innocent people but threatened the very existence of the English Front. Finally, with what was left of her will to live, a will that she felt slipping away with her sanity, Morgenna grieved for the terrifying future that faced her unborn child.

CHAPTER 45

In his bid to please the woman he was falling in love with, Dr. Wansbrough had found himself preparing a veritable feast, and as he laid out the dishes on the cork table mats, the mats in turn protecting the linen cloth that had been placed on the kitchen table for the occasion, his initial fear of falling short in the eyes of a beautiful woman now replaced with a fear of having overdone things. He looked at Alban, whose eyes were bulging out of his head in astonishment and excitement. The boy had never seen so much fine food laid out before.

'Do you think I've prepared too much?'

Alban shook his head as he surveyed the table with an attempt at adult authority. 'No, not at all. She'll love this.'

The doctor looked at Alban's skinny growing frame and laughed heartily. 'I think,' said the doctor, 'that your reply is what is known as *projection*'.

The boy looked at his teacher quizzically.

Dr. Wansbrough explained. 'I get the feeling that your reply came directly from your stomach, not your brain.'

The boy grinned. Some things could not be denied.

'Well, at least I don't have to worry about any of the food going to waste,' said Dr. Wansbrough, as he lit the candles in the middle of the table.

'Do you want me to bring out the lard lamps?' asked Alban. 'They give better light than candles.'

Dr. Wansbrough laughed. 'No, it's not about the light. We're in the middle of summer. The candles are more a gesture, a nod to civilised ways. I don't think a lard lamp as a centrepiece would have quite the same effect.'

Alban accepted this answer without question, but he didn't see what was so funny about putting a lard lamp in the middle of the table. Lots of families did that, including his own.

For the main meal, the doctor had decided on fried fish and boiled new potatoes with a fresh side salad. He decided against a soup starter, not least because it would be the kind of thing he would be likely to spill if nervous. In its stead, he decided to put some small *hors d'oeuvres* in the middle of the table that Valerie could sample while she was waiting for her main course, and for while they were chatting. He imagined that there would be a lot of animated conversation, and he did not want any sense of ceremony to inhibit his guest unnecessarily. He would be embarrassed by appearing too formal, and he wanted Valerie to be relaxed, like this was her home.

So in addition to the large salad bowl for the main meal, in the middle of the table Dr. Wansbrough had also placed a shallow basket full of freshly sliced bread, a butter dish, a tray on which half an hour had been spent coiling thin slices of dark-smoked ham artfully into roses, another tray of tomato halves cut into jagged stars lay on a bed of basil leaves, a tray of sliced hard-boiled eggs, a bowl of pickles, a bowl of dried apricots, a plate of small sausages, a pâté in a stoneware terrine, a goat's cheese slivered with the utmost care, and finally, the *pièce de resistance*, a small dish of olives, a tinned delicacy which the doctor had managed to procure at great effort and expense from a trader who regularly received supplies from the Southwest EF. The Southwest Division, with its Atlantic peninsular geography, enjoyed the strongest trade in Mediterranean goods of any of the divisions, having revived Dumnonia's ancient Atlantic trading route with their Celtic cousins in Galicia. This cousinhood extended to direct descendancy, if one considered the ancient Britons who escaped Saxon persecution to form the settlements which came to be known as *Britonia*. Not that this shared ancestry made the olives any cheaper on their arrival to British shores, Dr. Wansbrough reflected to himself. Still, he was grateful for small mercies as he was sure that Valerie's reaction to the olives would far outweigh their cost.

France's situation was now far too chaotic to receive any meaningful level of imports. Up until a few years ago the Southwest Division had maintained a trading arrangement with Brittany, but the best intentions of the exporters could not compensate for the reality that the Breton farmers were now even more beleaguered than their counterparts over the channel, especially now that supply lines throughout France had been shattered. The French themselves were struggling to survive, and despite geographical proximity to England, news of events had been difficult to obtain. But Wansbrough knew that everyone in France would be alarmed by Germany and the Low Countries now being in Russian hands. It was only a matter of time before France was in turn conquered by Orlov's forces.

Wansbrough knew that it was what Valerie

would be thinking about right now. Stories had begun to trickle out, from Danish fishermen who had washed up on the Norfolk coast, that life under an Orlov overlordship was particularly unpleasant for the native vassals. Order had been restored to their countries indeed, but at great cost. The Russians might end the war in France, thus granting the French people a chance at long-term survival, but the vassal tribes of Europe would not thrive under the slave economy instituted by the Third Rome. Dr. Wansbrough wondered how long it would take the Great Bear to swipe Paris from the moment it set its heavy black paws on French soil. Would it be as long as six weeks? Would the civil war help or hinder Russian designs? He had watched how the Orlovs had allowed Europe to tear herself apart over decades before acting. Clearly, if they wished it, the autarkic Russians could bomb France into the Stone Age, then skip into Paris like a children's tea party. But as they had shown with other countries of Europe, that was not their style. They aimed to preserve as much of the existing infrastructure as possible so that France could still retain its value as a source of indentured labour and natural resources. And turning the country into a wasteland, devoid of native industry and talent, would not be a productive move for the new colonists.

The doorbell sounded. Dr. Wansbrough's heart leapt momentarily.

'Will I get it?' Alban asked.

'No, let me,' said Dr. Wansbrough. He took off the apron protecting his good shirt and trousers, and went to answer the door, cursing himself for having the nerves of a fifteen-year-old boy on his first date.

✣ ✣ ✣

In the event, much to Dr. Wansbrough's relief, the conversation did not steer towards Europe. Perhaps because the issue was already so much on Valerie's mind that she wanted a break from it, Wansbrough thought. After all, what more could be said? At this stage, everything was conjecture, some of it reaching the point of absurdity. All they could do now was sit and wait for the events of hundreds of miles away to unfold.

Dr. Wansbrough's theory about Valerie's light choice of conversation was correct. To Valerie, the endless talk about the current situation in Europe only served to remind her of her own powerlessness, and the powerlessness of those who speculated and gossiped on the topic to give themselves the illusion of authority. For at least one night, she wanted to stop thinking about the war, and to remember what life was like before the political climate lay heavy over everyone like a plume of volcanic ash blotting out the sun. Tonight, she would do her best to recreate the convivial conversations that men and women used to have, before politics and war distorted and coloured every human perception. And to this end, Valerie had decided that she would ask Dr. Wansbrough about his life. But as she understood that asking such a private and self-contained man about his personal life would be nothing short of torturous for him, so she knew that she would need to be subtle in her questioning.

As she sat down at the table with a glass of elderberry wine, after complimenting him on both the quality and the presentation of the smoked ham roses, and going into nostalgic raptures at the long-denied taste of an olive, Valerie asked Dr. Wansbrough how he came to know Arabic.

The answer, for a man unaccustomed to talking about himself, was a simple one.

'The army.'

Realising quickly that such a short answer risked looking curt, he kept talking, but the shortness of his sentences betrayed his awkwardness at talking about himself. 'The Royal

Signal Corps. Twelve years. I was an engineer by training, but I picked up Pashtun in Afghanistan and the army realised my linguistic talents. I was put on the Arabist programme, and from there Army Intelligence.'

Valerie's eyes went wide and she looked at Alban, whom she could tell was also learning this information for the first time. She thought of the orderliness and cleanliness of this bachelor's home, and his army background made sense. His bearing was also very straight, and it would explain his natural tendency towards a formal and disciplined life.

'That's very impressive,' said Valerie. She thought quickly as she buttered a slice of bread, and took some more ham. The food was a useful way to disguise her probing. 'I suppose then... I suppose you were too much of a career man to have a family life?'

Dr. Wansbrough looked at young Alban, who was tentatively trying to pick up some pieces of boiled egg with the tongs. The boy had been reminded sharply before Valerie's visit to always use the tongs when reaching for food during her visit. *Don't have her thinking we're barbarians, lad.* Dr. Wansbrough was glad that Alban was here with his endearing clumsiness to diffuse the tension he felt inside.

'No, it wasn't that. The British Army of the 21st century was no place for British nationalism, and I was dishonourably discharged for political reasons. There were events that happened that led to me being put in prison. Things got very difficult for me after that.' At a loss for how to continue, Dr. Wansbrough got up to go to the oven, where the fish and potatoes were being kept warm. 'I think it's time for our main course.'

Alban's mind was spinning. He didn't know any of this stuff. Of course, he would never have felt it his place to ask, but he always assumed that Dr. Wansbrough had always been a scholar and a teacher. He had no idea that he had once been a soldier. Alban remembered the doctor once telling him, 'happy indeed is he who is able to know the causes of things' as an explanation of his life's work, an aphorism which had given Alban the distinct impression that the doctor's had only ever been dedicated to the pursuit of wisdom. This impression of his mentor had been strengthened by Wansbrough's assertion that the scholar was a martyr to 'the constant anxiety to know more', a never-ending quest for illumination which wearied the body but which made the soul precious to God. Now Alban was learning that Dr. Wansbrough had once been a soldier in the British Army.

Dr. Wansbrough set the plates at the table and sat down, but what he said next had his audience more interested in what he had to say than the food in front of them.

'They threw me in prison, on a charge of *suspicion of preparing acts of terrorism*.' The old man made a scornful face. 'Of course, it was total nonsense, but you have to understand what the mood was like then. The British Establishment was on tenterhooks. It was right before the uprising, and they were terrified of dissension within the ranks. Quite correctly, too, as it turned out. I was thrown into Whitemoor prison.' Dr. Wansbrough laughed faintly to himself, oblivious to the growing apprehension in the faces in front of him. 'They knew what they were doing. There was nothing white about Whitemoor. They had signed my death sentence.'

The fish was going cold on Alban and Valerie's plates as they sat, open-mouthed in disbelief, listening to Dr. Wansbrough tell his story.

'I had just received a prison visit from my lawyer, but instead of returning me to my cell, for some undisclosed reason the guards put me in a strange holding cell. There were four Somalians in there waiting for me. Clearly it was a set up. As soon as the key turned in the lock they laid into me, punching, kicking, then stamping when my body hit the ground, which was probably within a minute, though it seemed much longer. I remember frantically trying to call out the *Bismallah* in a bid to get them to stop stamping on my stomach and testicles, but I think I lost consciousness before I even reached *Raheem*.' At this point, Dr. Wansbrough looked at Alban in a pointed and vaguely amused way, and Valerie realised that there must be some kind of inside joke for Arabic speakers. But she didn't want to interrupt his flow by asking him something that wasn't really of importance.

'It goes without saying that I don't remember anything after that, except that I came round ten days later in intensive care. I had three broken ribs, a broken arm, and a ruptured… lower abdomen, for which I needed further surgery. Once I was sufficiently recovered from the surgery I was returned to prison, and spent two months in solitary confinement, before I was finally released on appeal. I should never have been in there in the first place.' Dr. Wansbrough suddenly noticed the effect that his words had had on Valerie, and urged her to try her fish.

But Valerie just sat there stunned. 'It must have been awful for you. Solitary confinement… for two months? They say that people can start going mad after a week in solitary.'

'It wasn't pleasant. But the worst part was that the other inmates made clear to me with taunts through the walls that if I ate the prison food brought to my cell I was risking my life. And I had to keep my window closed at all times, lest the guards think I was mounting a dirty protest. I survived on a tin of tuna and a piece of fruit a day. I think if I hadn't been released on appeal I would have starved to death before anything else.'

Valerie shook her head. She didn't want to ask if he had had a woman on the outside to keep him sane because it sounded like he hadn't. 'How did you get through such an ordeal? I mean, from being around you now, you would never know how much you have suffered.'

Dr. Wansbrough smiled and gestured gently to Valerie to eat. As she cut into her fish he thought about her question for a minute, about that time in that small, stinking cell when so many people would have gone under. When many people *did* go under. When they listened to the voices, of demons within or without, exhorting them to kill themselves, to stop fighting. What *had* kept him going?

Dr. Wansbrough thoughtfully chewed over a chunk of boiled potato before he finally spoke.

'The thing is, I would be lying there, in that

cell, day after day, still sore from my injuries. And I would imagine a beautiful pile of gold, shining with the radiance of the sun, in the corner of my cell. And I would think that the Truth is like that gold. They could do what they wanted to me, to my body, to my life, but that beautiful gold would still be there, visible in my mind's eye, shining outside of space and time, eternal, untouchable to those who wished, who still wish, to destroy all that is good and beautiful and true. Maybe it was the raised endorphins, because they didn't give me painkillers, or maybe because my body had gone into starvation mode, but I found myself having a mystical experience when they threw me into solitary. And it is a way of seeing the world which has never left me ever since.'

The doctor and Valerie exchanged glances and in her eyes he saw a new gentleness and understanding, and something else that he hadn't seen before. He smiled shyly and looked towards Alban, who was absorbed in finishing his food. A twelve-year-old boy can only remain shocked for so long, thought Dr. Wansbrough, before his raging metabolism brings him back to reality.

Dr. Wansbrough topped up both Valerie and Alban's glasses before refilling his own, and felt Valerie's eyes still upon him. She spoke, with that soft cooing in her voice normally only heard in teenage girls.

'Your level of learning is astounding. You know so much more than ordinary people... and yet you serve them. I know you've got your classes with the boys, but you've also got your community classes for adults. You've become a living legend among the people.'

At that point Alban, always happy to see his master praised for his vast erudition, joined in.

'Yes, you are so correct, Mrs. Ellacombe. My teacher knows so much about everything, I don't think I will ever get close to knowing as much as he does, even if I live to be a hundred.'

Dr. Wansbrough took the opportunity to convert his acute embarrassment into a gentle chiding of his protégé.

'Alban, I've told you before, it's not how much you know that's important, it's the lens that you view that knowledge through. And right now, I am fitting you with the correct lens. I am teaching you *how* to think, how to challenge the preconceptions on which knowledge is founded. Because without this, you could 'know' all of the information in the world, and yet it would be useless to your quest for wisdom.'

Suddenly aware that he had not acknowledged the compliment of his dinner guest he continued wryly, 'And I thank you for your kind remarks, Mrs. Ellacombe, but I'm old enough to remember the so-called academics who were thrown out of windows, so maybe it's for the best that I don't regard myself as an intellectual.'

Valerie returned his lively smile, and took another sip of her elderberry wine. She wished that Gareth were still alive to be here to enjoy this conversation, and yet for the first time in months she did not feel incomplete without her husband by her side. She looked down at her plate. She knew that she had to at least finish the fish to show her appreciation of the efforts that Alan had made for her, but it was proving difficult with a stomach already full of butterflies.

A silence fell over the table. Valerie continued with her meal and Dr. Wansbrough wondered if he could steer the conversation to lighter topics. He wondered if he should regret telling Valerie so much about the suffering in his life. It had certainly cast a serious tone over the table when he had wanted this evening to be one of laughter. He was on the verge of asking Valerie about her family when Alban, placing his knife and fork gently over the empty plate, casually decided to ask:

'Sir, could you tell us about the Nuremberg

trials? I'm sure Mrs. Ellacombe would be interested too.'

Dr. Wansbrough sighed and was just about to launch into an exasperated *now isn't the time, Alban* when his utterance was stopped dead in its tracks by Valerie laughing out loud. It was a hearty laugh, a cathartic laugh, its energy taken from the inner tensions caused by the horrors of France and England now released on hearing Alban's question, the absurd culmination of this most untypical dinner-party conversation.

Dr. Wansbrough smiled broadly at Valerie's laughter, and suddenly understood why she was laughing. He affected a mock formality.

'Do you remember a time long ago, Mrs. Ellacombe, when it was considered improper to discuss the Nuremberg trials over dinner?'

Valerie wiped away a tear of laughter with her hand. 'Or to bring up Hitler before pudding?'

Alban looked at them both with confusion. He didn't know why they were laughing. But he assumed it was best to be quiet and let them keep talking. He was glad to see the doctor and Mrs. Ellacombe getting on so well. Dr. Wansbrough spoke again.

'Oh yes, Mrs. Ellacombe. I can remember such a time. And it feels such a long time ago now.'

Valerie's laughter had subsided, although her smile broadened again on seeing the consternation of the boy at the table. She heard Dr. Wansbrough mention something about pudding and as he got up to get the final course she turned to Alban and addressed the boy's question herself.

'The Nuremberg trials. All you need to know is that is that they were nothing but a costume party for Negro kings.'

Dr. Wansbrough ears pricked up in recognition of the words and he turned around to face the woman and the boy at the table. 'Yes, a masquerade of Negroes in starched collars.' He beamed at Valerie, who smiled back at him knowingly. He knew at that point that he was in love.

Alban looked at both Dr. Wansbrough and Valerie in turn, and realised that they were sharing a joke which they were not about to let him in on. So he focussed his eyes on the pudding instead. A bread-and-butter pudding with summer fruits. Dr. Wansbrough had even put single cream on the table. Alban had never eaten this well in his life.

Dr. Wansbrough laid the pudding bowls before the woman and the boy, and then sat down himself. As the summer light of the evening faded into a warm lilac, the flame of the candles seemed to burn brighter. This evening had cost Dr. Wansbrough a fortune, but it had been worth it. He was savouring every moment. Just as life had its worst of times, as he himself had been forced to remember tonight, so it also had its best of times.

He looked into Valerie's eyes again, the intensity of the candlelight adding a new intimacy between them.

'It's funny, but the Albionic preachers are always telling us about how England needed to be forced into humility to rediscover God's grace. That we needed to feel the poverty, the destruction and the continual threat of annihilation to appreciate who we are and what we have been given. And despite everything, it's at times like this that it really does feel like God has renewed his covenant with us, and his presence is finally with us again. England *is* our Promised Land.'

CHAPTER 46

Saturday, July 17, 2060, was the day that Sebastian Weston went from being a boy to being a man.

He had been walking with Chad and Sam to the wasteland. They were the first of the gang to arrive there that morning. But they might be the only ones to arrive. The gang wasn't the same as it used to be. Andrew was always up at his uncle's farm in Tarleton. Even before his twelving he had been given his Life Duty, and it was like he now moved in different circles, in the adult world.

Jimmy was dead.

Ambrose's mum had become very protective of her family since the Announcement. Not that they had anything to worry about – the Mayberry family had been of solid Anglo-Saxon blood for at least forty generations, the kind of people that were immune to Caldwell's plague. But even with that knowledge, it was clear that Ambrose's mum did not want her boys outside more than they had to be. So the rest of the boys had not seen Ambrose for weeks.

Thomas had given a non-committal response to meeting up, so there was hope that he might still arrive in an hour, but it was unlikely.

Since the Announcement three weeks before, everything was different. The boys had even noticed it among themselves and had commented on it. It was like time had stopped, and they were waiting for something. They couldn't have fun in the same way anymore. If they were honest with themselves, they had only come to the wasteland out of tradition rather than anything else. Because it was the place that held the shared happy memories that bound them together.

But that day the memory that would be forged between them would prove to the undoing of what was left of their little gang and their wasteland playground.

It was only a few seconds after the boys walked around the back of the bombed-out shells of houses on Helston Avenue, and into the wasteland, that Sam saw the black mound lying on the ground about thirty yards away, beside the broken tree. He put his arms out protectively across the chests of the other two boys on either side of him to stop them moving forward as they talked.

'What is *that*?'

They stopped, as if paralysed. They knew the drill for suspect packages on the ground. But it did not look like a bomb. It was too lumpy and uneven for that.

They knew that they shouldn't approach the mound any more than they already had, but they couldn't help themselves. Saying nothing, they moved away from each other so that they could take slow steps towards to the object from different angles, their collective silence a tacit compact of disobedience that could later be denied as long as no words were uttered between them. They knew that they should not be doing this, that they should go looking for an adult. But this had never happened before. This was exciting.

Suddenly, on the left of the group, Seb broke the silence. 'That's a woman's leg!'

The boys stopped, and peered closer.

He was right!

It was a woman's naked leg, barefoot, sticking out of the black cloth. Now the boys walked faster towards the mound, and soon they were by its side. They stopped short as they realised what they were looking at.

It was a young English woman, in black Islamic dress, and she appeared to be dead. The bottom of the chador had ridden upwards and exposed one of her slim bare legs, which was covered in cuts and deep bruises.

The boys all looked at each other, and each was met with a face of fear and confusion.

They looked back at the body. The woman's nose had been cut off, but it was clearly an old wound, because it was surrounded by thick white scars and there was no blood. The dark holes of the nasal cavity were all exposed, like a skull, making her look very ugly. But the rest of her face was very beautiful. Her eyes, staring upwards at the heavens, were glassy and dead, but the irises reflected the vivid cornflower blue of the summer sky.

Seb spoke first. 'Fucking hell. We'd better run and get help.'

But Sam put a hand on Seb's shoulder, as if to take command of the situation. 'Before we do, we'd better check that she is dead.'

Sam bent down and unfastened the woman's hijab so that he could look for any head injuries. Blonde hair came tumbling out from under the black material. Something made him jump back, like he had touched a live electric wire, and for a few seconds he stared stupefied at Seb and Chad, who were too frightened to touch the body. He breathed deeply a couple of times to calm himself and then lifted up the woman's hair to show his friends what had frightened him, and took satisfaction from seeing that they too jumped back in fright.

The woman's ears had been crudely hacked off and the remaining cartilage had healed very badly. Seb instinctively drew back in horror when he realised what he was looking at, but after the initial shock Chad leaned forward to inspect the scarred ear-holes.

'My gran told me that during the 2020s dogs tied up outside shops in Blackburn and Oldham would get their ears sliced off. It was a way of showing who controlled the territory.'

He watched as Sam gently put the tips of his fingers against the woman's newly bared neck, just under her chin, and stayed in that position for about a minute, staring off into the middle distance. He turned to the boys, with the air of authority he had hoped he had gathered in the meantime, and pronounced that she was indeed dead.

Sebastian stood back and surveyed the scene. He then looked towards the empty flat miles of the borderlands which divided the English Front from the SAU. He surmised that she must have crossed all of that dangerous territory under the cover of night, in her bare feet, somehow escaping her SAU captors, then dodging the landmines of the borderlands and the EF border guards. He found it all hard to believe, but at the same time the soles of her feet were cut and filthy. He glanced at her hands, not wanting to touch them. They too were bloody and dirty, like she had fallen on the ground as she made her way to this spot. The loose black sacking of the Islamic garb that covered her whole body was also covered in mud around the knees and arms. Yes, she had walked here. He looked out over the expanse between the territories. At some point she would have walked through the Heads.

'She must have been terrified,' he said. A heavy wave of sadness washed over him. He wanted to cry.

Chad asked Sam to check to see if she had a dog tag under her clothes. Since 2050, every man, woman and child in EF territory wore a small fire-proof dog tag around their neck that it was forbidden to remove.

Sam looked up at Chad. 'Look at what she's got on! Look at her ears and her nose! Do you think she'd be wearing an EF dog-tag?'

Chad shrugged with a child's imperturbability. 'It was just a thought', he said.

Sam decided to take control of the situation. 'I'm going to get help. Seb, can you stay here and watch over the body, just in case anybody comes? Chad, do you want to come with me, or stay with Seb?'

Chad looked at Sam and then looked back at Seb and the dead woman. He imagined all the drama of the adults reacting to the tale, and then following the soldiers as they rushed to the wasteland. 'I'll come with you, Sam.'

Sam looked back towards Seb. 'You don't mind staying here, do you? Obviously, don't touch the body. We won't be long.'

Seb nodded his consent blankly. The sorrow that had come from thinking about this young English woman and all that she had suffered had paralysed him. He thought about how terrified she must have been in her last moments, and what she must have been thinking when she collapsed in this wasteland. Maybe she saw the outlines of the Helston Avenue houses and feeling that she was safe, found that the last of her strength deserted her. Finally home.

By the time he lifted his head up from these thoughts, Sam and Chad were nowhere to be seen. He was now alone with the body. He looked down at the exposed leg, and suddenly felt a sense of impropriety. This English woman would be given respect, finally, if only in death. He was rocking the body slightly to pull the crumpled-up cotton skirt out from underneath her torso so that he could cover her leg properly when he heard a heavy sigh.

She was still alive.

He jumped back in shock then approached the woman's face. He noticed some faint colour in her cheeks and what he thought was faint breathing. He put the back of his hand up to her nose, and he was sure he felt some heat. In a panic and not sure what to do, he started to jostle her body gently and began hitting her face to bring her round.

'You're safe, you can wake up now! Come on, wake up!'

Now frantic, Seb slapped at the woman's cheeks with hands that seemed to have lost all of their strength and feeling. There was the tiniest movement in her eyes towards him. She could definitely hear him. Seb's heart leapt as he thought he saw her blink.

'Come on! You're home now. Time to wake up! Don't go to sleep on me!'

There was still a thread of life holding her in this world, Seb thought, she was just unconscious, so he started pressing her chest, trying to shock her into coming back. He didn't know what he was doing, and he started praying to Jesus to help him save this woman from her final ordeal. She didn't deserve to die like this, not when she had finally reached the safety of her people.

Seb looked at her face again, searching for signs of life. But her beautiful blue eyes had returned to staring glassily ahead.

Suddenly he felt himself being thrown backwards, as a large pair of hands hooked under his armpits and lifted him forcefully away from the body.

'What the fuck do you think you're doing? There could be a bomb under there! For fuck's sake, get out of the way!'

Seb watched helplessly as the men took over, palpating the woman and cutting away her garments. She was thin and completely naked under the black sacking, and her abdomen and thighs were covered in bruises and burn marks. He watched as the men opened her mouth to peer inside and saw that her front teeth had been knocked out. They then moved down her body and one of them turned and shouted to someone behind him. 'Get that fucking kid out of here!' The body of an EF soldier who he didn't know suddenly blocked his view of the woman and pulled him away from the scene.

'But she's still alive! I saw her blink! Please, try to save her!'

Seb was crying now, but out of frustration more than anything else. One of the EF soldiers had shunted him to the very edge of the wasteland, and here he stood, helplessly, seeing nothing but the soldiers crowded around the body. Finally, the soldier who had torn the women's clothing down the middle stood up, and wiped the sweat off the brow with the back of his hand. He was a short, heavy-set man in middle age. He looked over directly at Seb and their eyes met. The previous irritation in his face had softened to the same sadness that had overcome the boy.

It seemed to take an eternity for the soldier to reach Seb, who was standing at the edge of Helston Avenue, where the broken tarmac turned to clay earth and rubble. But Seb was too frightened by his previous chastening to meet the man halfway, so he stood rooted to the spot like an idiot and let the man make the journey to him. But the soldier didn't seem to mind. Once he reached a couple of yards from Seb he began speaking as he approached him.

'She didn't make it, son, but she wouldn't have. She had... internal injuries. She wasn't going to survive.'

At this point Seb felt his bottom lip tremble and he was worried about breaking down in tears in front of this tough, grown-up man. But it seemed too much to contain himself.

'But… but… if she was so hurt, why did she risk coming all this way?' He stammered trying to get out the words.

The soldier turned away from Seb and scanned the wasteland of burnt tree stumps, briars and thorns.

'Maybe because she could,' said the soldier '… and that in itself is significant. Maybe she wanted the dignity of dying with her own people.'

He turned back towards the boy, his tone now more conspiratorial. 'And if she *could* come all this way, that means that things are not good in SAU territory right now.' He gave the boy a pointed look, as if talking man to man, not to a ten-year-old boy with red and puffy eyes. *This lad will need to grow up fast for what's coming. He'd better have cried the last of his tears.*

'If their slaves are able to escape, things are not good for the SAU at all.'

CHAPTER 47

It had been three weeks since the announcement of Caldwell's betrayal of the people had been broadcast across EF territory and the deposed leader was declared officially on the run from justice. A bounty had been placed on his head by the EF, usefully putting a distance between the disgraced man and his erstwhile commanders, and stirring up the people to hunt even harder for the bad man. Thus was Caldwell on the run, not only from the uniformed soldier, but from the civilian bounty hunter.

What the people did not know was that this was a deliberate ploy, a psychological operation instigated by the EF high command and Caldwell himself, to concentrate the anger of the people onto the head of one man. Moreover, the high command knew that the longer this man remained uncaptured, the more the people would focus all of their anger and sorrow at recent events onto him. It was a successful tactic; mob hysteria and carefully seeded EF misinformation had filtered back such eyewitness reports as Caldwell being spotted leaving a pub in Penzance, Caldwell flitting among the crowds of a fish market in Rhyl and Caldwell hiding from deer hunters behind the trees of a forest in Northumberland. On the same day, individuals all over the country could be found swearing on their Bibles that they had personally caught a glimpse of *The Great Betrayer*. Caldwell was everywhere and nowhere, and not a single man who was roused by the popular call to *throw the sinner overboard* did not dream of what he would do with the bounty reward if he were the one to catch him. Of course, for most it was a distant fantasy, not least because one of the stipulations of the bounty payment was that David Caldwell was to be taken alive. His once-loved portraits now defaced, except in those cases where someone had argued that it were perhaps more sensible to preserve the likeness of a fugitive still on the run, Caldwell had been judged in the court of public opinion, and the fate of the man who had led his people faithfully for over twenty years came to be crystallised in the Bible verse which was heard from the mouth of every self-righteous English man, woman and child:

> *Bloodshed pollutes the land, and atonement cannot be made for the land on which blood*

> *has been shed, except by the blood of the one who shed it.*

The reality was however, that the new EF leader Harry Talbot, anointed for succession in a secret ceremony by Caldwell himself, knew the secret hideout of his friend and mentor perfectly well, and was protecting him until it could be judged that the public hysteria for a scapegoat was at its peak and the resulting catharsis at its most invigorating for the Final Push. That time was soon to be upon them.

Now Caldwell was yomping across open fields, the pink rays of the dying summer sun intensifying the gold of the wheatsheaves that served to hide him from any passers-by on the nearby country roads. The whole area was deserted; the only figure he had come across was a statue of St Denise the Grieving Mother nestled in a roadside shrine an hour back on his journey. Caldwell had felt compelled to stop to honour the sadness of the little shrine and think for a moment of his own grieving mother. Now another woman would be receiving him for this final night, and he wondered if, like this statue, she would have sorrow in her eyes.

Half an hour later he spied the dark outline of her house on the outskirts of the village. He could not see the back door for the large leafy oak and the high hedge which formed the boundary of the back garden, but he knew that she would be there, waiting for him, excited, watching at the window.

He climbed over a side fence into the back garden. He saw the door open as he stepped into the long grass.

As he entered the house he looked into her eyes. The look that those green eyes returned back at him was the most immediate and pure form of female seduction, challenging him to a duel of desire. Pulling him outside of time, that look had a power over him which was more ancient than words. Words were man-made, unnecessary. Words would destroy the animal strength of the connection between them. That she dared to look at him with such a sensual intense gaze, knowing what he was going to do to her, and could maintain it without experiencing the vertigo he was starting to feel himself, made him extremely hard.

He began kissing her, slipping her blue silk dressing gown off her shoulders so that he could enjoy her standing there naked in front of him, then he picked her up and carried her to the bedroom.

He took his T-shirt off so that she could revel in his chest, as broad and hard as a warrior's shield, but he kept the rest of his clothes on as he ravished her, his heavy wide body engulfing her small frame and forcing her thighs to open flat against his heavy girth. Suddenly aware that he still had his boots on, he felt compelled to say the first words to her since he stepped into her home.

'You do know that you are giving yourself to a dead man?'

She nodded almost imperceptibly, and breathless, she whispered in a voice torn between defiance and resignation.

'We are all dead in time.'

He forced himself into her and she cried out.

He bore into her body with the primal forces of hunger and love, losing himself in her flesh, savouring this moment in time when he could finally be out of time with the woman he loved, when all of a sudden Diana felt his body go still, as if startled by something. Seeing her face turn from pleasure to confusion, he lifted up one of his arms from the bed and put a finger to his lips to bid her silence. That sound again, outside.

He got up from her body, leaving her feeling suddenly cold and defenceless, and went to the side of the bedroom window. He peered down at the back garden.

'Fuck!'

He exited out of the room in a few strides, his chest still bare, then she heard him creep rapidly down the stairs. Frightened, she got up and went to the side of the window to where her lover had stood moments before and looked down.

To her horror she saw an unknown man by the tree in the garden scrambling to his feet, a large broken tree branch lying on the ground by his side, torn leaves from his fall scattered in the grass. In shock, she realised that he must have been hiding in the thick canopy of the oak tree. Watching the house. Lying in wait.

She drew her head back from the window as she saw him looking up, and wanted to rush to cover her naked body. But now she heard the back door bang open and in an instant she saw the broad back of her lover, the soul of her life, facing this stranger. David, the man for whom she would happily sacrifice the rest of her time on Earth to have a single minute more with him, was striding towards this man with the arrogance of a handsome god. The interloper, a dark-haired, scraggly looking man in his 30s, had pulled a huge hunting knife from her belt. Diana felt a wave of terror wash over her and felt herself outside of her naked body, as if time were standing still, and she was watching a scene which had already taken place.

Now the stranger was stepping backwards under the canopy of the oak tree, confused at Caldwell's apparently lack of concern for the knife that he was brandishing as Caldwell rushed forward. The stranger, now on the defensive, tripped over one of the tree roots protruding from the ground, and fell backwards. Caldwell wasted no time, and slashed at the man's right arm, in a bid to get him to drop the weapon. The man however, struck back, and managed to slash Caldwell's shoulder. Caldwell used the time the stranger took slashing at him to stab him in the chest. The man staggered backwards, his body being stopped from careering further away from his assailant by the tree trunk behind him. Diana could no longer see the stranger's face for the dense foliage of the oak leaves. Then the man slumped down against the length of the tree, and as did so his pain-racked face came back into view through the dappled shade cast by an uncaring, dying sun. A moment later the man was obscured to her again, but this time by Caldwell's frame, and she watched mesmerised as her lover kicked the knife out of his opponent's hand and proceeded to stab him three times in the chest. She watched as her man stood back and looked around the garden, obviously scanning for other assailants. She would have seen him look up at the window but her naked flanks were already bolting down the stairs towards the back door.

Caldwell was already back in the house by the time she made it downstairs. He looked stressed and was perturbed by her nakedness.

'Christ, cover yourself up!'

She wanted to go to him but embarrassed, she scrabbled for the pile of blue silk lying sluttishly on the floor. By the time she had tied the dressing gown shut he was already at the sink, washing the blood off his hands and knife, and splashing water on his wound. He was cursing under his breath.

'Do you have a first-aid kit?'

She thought frantically, and opened a cupboard. There was a bandage in it, a few plasters, some cloths, and a bottle of disinfecting alcohol. She put the alcohol onto the cloth and started to dab the wound at the top of his arm. It wasn't a very deep wound, but it was drawing a lot of blood, and if it got infected it could kill him. Seeing his blood running like this inflamed her strangely, knowing that the wound had come from killing another man. She felt even more aroused than she had in the bedroom. Now more than ever, she wanted his seed inside her. But watching him now, as he took the cloth from her and started to treat his own wound, she knew that his head had returned to mundane matters. The spell of the sanctuary was broken. His final private space, to love and to be himself, had been desecrated by outsiders.

She tried to take her mind from her own sorrow, the knowledge that this was the last chance to take his essence, the most perfect reminder of him, inside her, and moment by moment that chance was slipping away. She looked at his beautiful injured body, his furrowed brow, and noted for the first time, as he asked her to knot the bandage wrapped around his left shoulder, that grey hair had started to make an appearance around his temples.

She watched helplessly as he began typing out a message on his lerter, then started speaking to her as he typed.

'I need to go. That man... People know where I am. It's not safe for me to be found here.' He sent his message and looked up from his device. 'It's not safe for *you* for me to be found here.'

He kissed her forehead. Diana found herself starting to cry. At the shittiness of her life. At how it had all gone wrong. At how even this final night had gone wrong. At how these were the final moments that she would ever spend with him, and how her own life was over when he walked out of the door to his death. Moments she was trying to savour but which slipped away from her as soon she tried to concentrate on them. She buried herself in his body, in his manly smell, a smell that she would soon never be able to recall. He reciprocated by putting his arms around her, but the sexual moment had passed. The air around her swirled and swam in her ears as if they had both survived a shipwreck, and she was clinging to him for ballast in an invisible stormy sea. She clung to him wordlessly, for a what might have been a minute or an hour, but it was a time that she wanted to stand still forever.

His lerter sounded, and it startled her. David held out his arm behind her body and read the message as he kept her nestled into his chest.

'They are outside now.'

He held her body back from him to look at her directly in the eyes. He already had the look of a condemned man, a dead man walking, whose spirit had already begun the process of leaving his body.

'I'll see you on the other side. Diana. I'll be waiting for you.'

There was a knock at the front door.

'Another van will be coming around later to pick up the body. Let them in, just let them do their job.'

He kissed her again, then picked up his jacket and made his way towards the front door. She followed him dumbly like a dog, but she was screaming inside. He lifted her crestfallen face with a finger under her chin so that he could look intently into her eyes for a final time.

'I'm sorry.'

Diana's eyes no longer radiated seduction, but the misery of a woman condemned to keep living when she knew that her life was over.

CHAPTER 48

It was the feast day of Jeremiah, and Brother Dunstan was giving a special Tuesday sermon on the message of the prophet to mark the occasion. Given the nature of the sermon, it was decreed that there would be a separate storytime in the church for the under-twelves, as the brother wanted to tell some fundamental truths about why God had taken vengeance on his people, truths that were not suitable for young ears.

Candice sat on one of the front-row chairs on the left-hand side of the aisle, angled so that the rows formed an almost semi-circle around the altar. She wasn't sure how many people would turn up. This was an extraordinary meeting, and recent events had left people shaken and in little mind to hear the words of the doom-laden Jeremiah. She nodded a greeting to Mrs. Glover, who had taken a seat in the opposite aisle. Other people filed in – the Smith boys, Katie Murray, old Mrs. Farrow... Candice's eyes wandered from the people taking their seats to the shrine of Saint Margery Kempe at the side of the pulpit. Kempe, as the mother of fourteen children, had been canonised by the Albionic Church, who saw in her the perfect avatar for a female rejection of materialism which simultaneously rejected the gnostic abjuration of sexual reproduction. She was the Albionic symbol of how even the most imperfect of women could seek piety and humility with the sole adornment of her own good deeds, while fulfilling the Pauline injunction of childbirth for female salvation.

Kempe had become, as the years went on, the saint to whom English women prayed when they were having problems conceiving or bringing their babies to term. Testament to this fact was that haphazardly attached to the latticework around Margery Kempe's figurine there were dozens of what first appeared to be tiny love-hearts, made of tin. It was only when one looked closer that one realised that these votive offerings were in fact representations of tiny wombs.

Candice watched as a woman in a woolly beanie now approached Margery Kempe's shrine, and stood before it, her head bowed. When the woman turned around Candice was shocked to see that the pale, drawn face under the woolly hat was that of Morgenna Weston, who looked like she was suffering some kind

From the Land All the Good Things Come

of illness. The two women locked eyes, one set of eyes radiating shock and concern, the other existential fear.

'Morgenna, please, come sit next to me.'

Even the way Morgenna moved was different, thought Candice. She was now moving like an old woman. Normally she was such a strong presence, and she would be flitting around, talking to people. Here, hunched over and hiding her trademark russet hair under a woollen hat, it was like she did not want to be recognised.

Morgenna sat down on Candice's left, to be on the margins of the group, away from prying eyes. Candice intuited that Morgenna did not want to talk, so waited for Morgenna to speak. Finally, Morgenna, still wearing her hat and her coat, spoke, as if to herself.

'If Margery Kempe were alive today, she could have won a Platinum Mother's Cross. And I couldn't even earn a bronze cross.'

Candice made a small consolatory smile, and looked at Morgenna, whose gaze was locked on the rosary beads she carried in her pale, thin hands. 'God blesses us with the children he decides. The matter was out of your hands. You might not have had many children, but you have been a great blessing to the wider community of mothers and children with all that you have done for them.'

Morgenna smiled faintly at the praise, still unwilling to make eye contact with Candice.

Brother Dunstan began his sermon. Morgenna's words rolled around in Candice's mind. *Where I couldn't even earn a bronze cross.* Something in the finality of the word *couldn't* bothered Candice. She realised now beyond doubt that Morgenna had lost her baby. Suddenly feeling her cheeks flush as her suspicion became knowledge, Candice was oblivious to the brother's words as he spoke of the God's message to the people. She wanted to talk to Morgenna so badly, but Morgenna was now staring intently at the man in the pulpit, as every word he brought her about His divine grand providential plan for the universe would somehow release her from this misery and sense of failure. Candice started to zone back into Brother Dunstan's sermon. He was drawing parallels to the behaviour of the English before the war, and how dark foreign elements in London had drawn the people into whoring after false gods and carrying out great sins, in turn provoking God's ire.

> *Were they ashamed when they had committed abomination? nay, they were not at all ashamed, neither could they blush: there-*

> *fore they shall fall among them that fall: at the time that I visit them they shall be cast down, saith the Lord.*

Candice recalled her life as a child. That was correct. Sin was not only not condemned or hidden in the England of before the war, but it was openly celebrated. Anyone who called out the evildoer was cast down and locked up by the government. Brother Dunstan then told the congregation that, just as in the days of Jeremiah, it was the fate of the English, who had strayed from God's light, to be smited by an invading army.

> *I am bringing a distant nation against you*
> *an ancient and enduring nation,*
> *a people whose language you do not know,*
> *whose speech you do not understand.*
> *Their quivers are like an open grave;*
> *all of them are mighty warriors.*
> *They will devour your harvests and food,*
> *devour your sons and daughters;*
> *they will devour your flocks and herds,*
> *devour your vines and fig trees.*
> *With the sword they will destroy*
> *the fortified cities in which you trust.*

Candice thought of the greatest English cities, London, Birmingham and Manchester, as well as countless market towns, now under occupation by a coalition of foreign ethnic groups.

Yes, the English were indeed being divinely punished for their sins against God, even if their own Satanic state had taught them as children that the sins of whoredom, sodomy and infanticide were virtues. The Satanic sacrament of 'holy' matrimony between sodomites cried out to heaven for vengeance, as did the state-sponsored mutilation and sterilisation of innocent children, an act so diabolical that even the Bible could not imagine such a thing coming come to pass. The prophets had warned against such Satanic inversions.

> *Woe to those who call evil good*
> *and good evil,*
> *who put darkness for light*
> *and light for darkness,*
> *who put bitter for sweet*
> *and sweet for bitter.*

And yet these sins were preached as the highest virtues by the ideologues, the men and women who were *wise in their own eyes and clever in their own sight*. A few of them did actually believe the soul-destroying lies that they peddled; most were bought for a price at Quarantania. But just as souls are destroyed so are nations, and the English people would wither on the vine within three generations of this false doctrine.

> *...as tongues of fire lick up straw*

*and as dry grass sinks down in the flames,
so their roots will decay
and their flowers blow away like dust.*

But it was the dark secrets revealed in the 2020s that shook the foundations of the nation. By allowing this conquering army to take root in its homeland, God had exacted revenge upon a people who, if they did not commit the sins themselves, had been indifferent to others committing them. Had not God himself said in Leviticus that anyone sacrificing children to Moloch was to be stoned to death by the community? How far the English people had fallen in their apathy to the greatest of crimes! Candice tuned back into the sermon as she saw Brother Dunstan turning back to the Bible to recite God's word.

> *Listen! I am going to bring a disaster on this place that will make the ears of everyone who hears of it tingle. For they have forsaken me and made this a place of foreign gods; they have burned incense in it to gods that neither they nor their ancestors nor the kings of Judah ever knew, and they have filled this place with the blood of the innocent. They have built the high places of Baal to burn their children in the fire as offerings to Baal—something I did not command or mention, nor did it enter my mind. So beware, the days are coming, declares the Lord,*

when people will no longer call this place Topheth or the Valley of Ben Hinnom, but the Valley of Slaughter.

In this place I will ruin the plans of Judah and Jerusalem. I will make them fall by the sword before their enemies, at the hands of those who want to kill them, and I will give their carcasses as food to the birds and the wild animals. I will devastate this city and make it an object of horror and scorn; all who pass by will be appalled and will scoff because of all its wounds. I will make them eat the flesh of their sons and daughters, and they will eat one another's flesh because their enemies will press the siege so hard against them to destroy them.

Candice felt Morgenna shake slightly in the seat beside her, and she wondered if the woman should really be here in such a vulnerable state. But Candice found herself shuddering when she remembered the bloated bodies floating in the Mersey, the charred corpses piled up like refuse in the streets after the jet-fuel and phosphorus bombs, the hellish firestorm that trapped children in the boiling tarmac and reduced their bodies to pitifully small black logs. Then there were the men crucified for show by enemy forces. Others were brutally sodomised then castrated, their standard cultural practice with enemy prisoners. But this retribution didn't feel divine, it felt diabolic. England had indeed been smashed beyond repair like the potter's jar.

> *They will bury the dead in Topheth until there is no more room.*

Topheth or Toxteth? She cringed again as she remembered how it was decided in 2039, after so much slaughter, that the bodies of the enemy dead would be processed to be used as agricultural fertiliser. The tons of human bone meal in the ground led to the macabre ballad, *The Bumper Crop of Carrots of 2042*, being regularly sung in public houses for years afterwards. Black humour was the only way that some people could deal with the horror, Candice thought.

Her mind went to thoughts of her daughter Perpetua, who was now living twenty miles away in army married quarters, twenty miles which were like an ocean between them in the current circumstances. Candice wondered about her eldest child several times every hour, worrying about how she was. It was a sore loss not to see her beautiful girl every day, especially with her pregnancy, but at least she was alive, Candice reasoned. Not everyone was lucky enough to have their children alive and with them.

Realising that she had lost the thread to the preacher's argument with her own mental wanderings, her focus on his figure relaxed, and her gaze came to rest on the all-too-familiar triptych that formed the altarpiece. On the left panel, the painting of a heavily pregnant woman, smiling up to heaven with her hands on her large bump. The middle panel, the widest panel, featured a priest celebrating the Albionic Mass. The painted figure of the priest faced towards the right panel, which was of a criminal hanging from the gallows with the angel who had executed him by his side, a reminder that the law was not, as some had said before the war, a social construct. No, the law was divine, mandated by God, and He had told the people that if they did not kill the source of evil, that he would desert them. For had not God said: *I will not be with you anymore unless you destroy whatever among you is devoted to destruction*? The dirty blood, the criminal blood, had to spilled in order to spare the good blood, not least because so much of this good clean blood was now being spilled in the war effort. The finest and fittest were perishing by the thousand, and the EF had a divinely mandated duty to exterminate the vermin behind the lines. Not least as a counterbalance to the deaths of the good men, to prevent a dangerous situation of disorder. The death penalty for vandalism, mugging and, as Candice had suffered herself, opportunistic theft (all of her vegetables being dug up from their vegetable patch one fateful blackout in 2057) might have seemed excessive before the war, but not now, when social liabilities could not be tolerated. *He who commits a crime against the community is worthy only of death.* A man needed to know that his wife and children were safe when he was fighting for his people, and it was imperative that the EF stamped its earthly authority. Without confidence in the justice system, in which the *salus populi* was the whole of the law, there could be no order or happiness in this besieged nation of half-starved people. The law, the will of the most just reason, was the single most important thing in EF territory. *If the Anglo-Saxon can get justice, he can put up with any hardship*, Candice thought.

She broke from her reverie on law and order to find that Brother Dunstan was in the middle of a discussion of Babylon, which he was comparing to London and its huge global banking power.

> *Babylon was a golden cup in the Lord's hand,*
> *making all the earth drunken;*
> *the nations drank of her wine,*

and so the nations went mad.

Those last words tickled at the back of mind, distracting her from what the preacher said next, and she took to wondering why. Then she realised it was because it reminded her of something that another prophet had once said, namely, that those whom the Gods seek to destroy, they first make mad. But she didn't know which prophet it had been. She would need to ask Brother Dunstan after the sermon.

But as with all great prophets, the message then turned to one of redemption. Yes, God would raze the crops and rip open the bellies of pregnant women with enemy swords, but for those who turned their faces back to Him having learned their lesson, he would restore them to their former glory. Here Brother Dunstan took the congregation from the pit of despair about their current predicament to the all-important assurance that their return to piety would ensure that God would once against favour the English, as God himself had said.

> *But all who devour you will be devoured;*
> *all your enemies will go into exile.*
> *Those who plunder you will be plundered;*
> *all who make spoil of you I will despoil.*
> *But I will restore you to health*
> *and heal your wounds,*

*I will restore the fortunes of Jacob's tents
and have compassion on his dwellings;
the city will be rebuilt on her ruins,
and the palace will stand in its proper place.
From them will come songs of thanksgiving
and the sound of rejoicing.
I will add to their numbers,
and they will not be decreased;
I will bring them honour,
and they will not be disdained.
Their children will be as in days of old,
and their community will be established before me;
I will punish all who oppress them.
Their leader will be one of their own;
their ruler will arise from among them.
I will bring him near and he will come close to me—
for who is he who will devote himself
to be close to me?*

Candice noticed how a few people bristled and bowed heads rose attentively on hearing the last lines about the leader, and she realised that people were hoping that the priest would make reference to Caldwell and the current situation. For had Caldwell not been one of their own who had risen from among them? What could this religious brother say about Caldwell's actions, when so many of the congregation had lost loved ones? The air in the room had become heavy with anticipation, and Brother Dunstan seemed to notice this. He talked about the importance of a leader being close to God in all that he did, and then nervously turned the sermon towards the shamed commander.

'What David Caldwell did, well, we are still struggling to comprehend it in all of its ramifications. The Albionic Church, rather than condemn this great leader outright, has sought to understand his actions, because he has always served his people to the utmost, dedicating his life to our continued survival.'

He coughed nervously. Candice noticed the flush in the young man's cheeks, the last vestiges of adolescence. *He must be twenty-two at most*, Candice thought.

'I think we can agree that, in order to preserve a civilisation, the type of men who created it must also be preserved. Civilizations are not destroyed by war but because they lose the stamina inherent in a pure bloodline. Anything in this world that is not of sound racial stock is a useless husk which will be blown away in the wind.' Brother Dunstan paused, and took a deep breath. He understood both the dangerousness and the import of what he was saying. 'I know that this will upset some of you my saying this, because as individuals many people of other races and mixed-races are worthy people but this is not about the value of the individual, but the value of the group. And it is only as a group that we survive. Every event in world history is an expression of the racial instinct for self-preservation, and so the nation has to be homogeneous and strong, and not fear defeating the other.'

He coughed again and took a drink of water. It was the height of summer, and the crowded room was getting hot. One of the men at the back of the hall shouted 'HITLER!'. It was unclear if this interjection was an accusation, an endorsement, or a simple echo from the collective unconscious. The priest maintained his composure.

'This isn't about that man called Hitler. This is about an eternal, divine Truth, understood the world over. The Indian sacred book the Bhagavad Gita was written before Christ's birth, and it too made clear how a lack of religion in a family leads to the corruption of women, and from the corruption of women comes the mixing of the castes or races, the prohibited interweaving of linen and wool. What follows is the loss of ancestral memory, and from this loss of memory, the loss of understanding about who the people are. From there it is a short descent into hell. No-one can deny that what happened to England came from us abandoning our relationship with God, and no-one who lived during the reign of Elizabeth can deny that our women were seduced, inebriated and corrupted to the marrow, laughing as they lifted their skirts over their own faces, devoid of shame. And our men, the withered figs who...' he stopped himself, trying to think of a suitable euphemism '...turned themselves into parodies of women in the most demonic of ways. We defiled the land. Is it any wonder then that the land tried to vomit us out?'

Some of the older members of the congregation looked down at the floor.

'This chaos came about from our land being opened up to alien opportunists, whose aim was to destroy our nation by turning this land into nothing but an economic area, no different from any other economic area on Earth. Economic areas that could then be merged into one global order. And as we know, globalisation is Satanic. For it is written: *From one man He made all the nations, that they should inhabit the whole earth; and He marked out their appointed times in history and the boundaries of their lands.* God wanted us as separate nations, and God allotted to us, the English people, the land of England. He also gave us our appointed time in history and by the grace of God that time is not over yet!'

many people of other races and mixed-races are worthy people but this is not about the value of the individual, but the value of the group. And it is only as a group that we survive. Every event in world history is an expression of the racial instinct for self-preservation, and so the nation has to be homogeneous and strong, and not fear defeating the other.'

He coughed again and took a drink of water. It was the height of summer, and the crowded room was getting hot. One of the men at the back of the hall shouted 'HITLER!'. It was unclear if this interjection was an accusation, an endorsement, or a simple echo from the collective unconscious. The priest maintained his composure.

'This isn't about that man called Hitler. This is about an eternal, divine Truth, understood the world over. The Indian sacred book the Bhagavad Gita was written before Christ's birth, and it too made clear how a lack of religion in a family leads to the corruption of women, and from the corruption of women comes the mixing of the castes or races, the prohibited interweaving of linen and wool. What follows is the loss of ancestral memory, and from this loss of memory, the loss of understanding about who the people are. From there is a short descent into hell. No-one can deny that what happened to England came from us abandoning our relationship with God, and no-one who lived during the reign of Elizabeth can deny that our women were seduced, inebriated and corrupted to the marrow, laughing as they lifted their skirts over their own faces, devoid of shame. And our men, the withered figs who...' he stopped himself, trying to think of a suitable euphemism '...turned themselves into parodies of women in the most demonic of ways. We defiled the land. Is it any wonder then that the land tried to vomit us out?'

Some of the older members of the congregation looked down at the floor.

'This chaos came about from our land being opened up to alien opportunists, whose aim was to destroy our nation by turning this land into nothing but an economic area, no different from any other economic area on Earth. Economic areas that could then be merged into one global order. And as we know, globalisation is Satanic. For it is written: *From one man He made all the nations, that they should inhabit the whole earth; and He marked out their appointed times in history and the boundaries of their lands.* God wanted us as separate nations, and God allotted to us, the English people, the land of England. He also gave us our appointed time in history and by the grace of God that time is not over yet!'

Looking at some of the unmoved faces in front of him, the young priest started to get flustered. He could feel that he wasn't winning the crowd. 'I am not asking you to condone what Commander Caldwell has done, but rather to understand it. This world is so fallen, that sometimes to 'do good' in it, one needs the courage to destroy, rather than construct. He understood that his act would greatly devastate our enemies, which would save thousands of English lives in the long run. If not all English lives. None of us wants to see our sons killed trying to retake Birmingham, or our daughters captured as sex slaves because we have run out of men to protect them. People are calling for Caldwell's head, and the EF has pronounced a death sentence upon him, but as Christians we also need to see the big picture, to understand his motivations. We owe him that.'

A man Candice recognised as a fishmonger at Haresfinch market spoke up. He looked disgruntled. 'What you failed to mention during your sermon, Brother, was the identity of the man who rescued the prophet Jeremiah from certain death.' The man looked straight at Brother Dunstan, demanding a response.

Brother Dunstan looked vaguely embarrassed for a moment. 'Yes, Ebedmelech was a Kushite, that's to say an Ethiopian. He was also a eunuch. A fact that is overlooked by many. Outsiders were permitted, but their numbers were controlled, because it was understood that ethnic groups are dynamic breeding populations that can soon become *barbs in your eyes and thorns in your sides*. If anything, Ebedmelech's presence proved that some outsiders are good people, but nevertheless *this is our land.*'

The emphasis that the priest made on those final words made clear that he was stating the Church's final position on Caldwell's actions, and that, regardless of whatever unctuous attempts at conciliation were attempted towards aggrieved parties, the Church would perform the final rites upon the controversial prisoner and allow his bones to be buried in consecrated ground. Candice wondered if Caldwell's name might even be inscribed in the catalogue of the saints within a generation.

❋ ❋ ❋

Little Modesta sat cross-legged on the floor, listening to Mrs. Blakelock tell the story of the bad gardener. It was a story that she had heard before, so she wasn't really listening to the first part. She instead focussed her attention on the mural of the red squirrel on the wall to the side of Mrs. Blakelock. She had never seen a red squirrel in real life, and was told that they were very rare. The squirrel was holding out a hazelnut towards her, as if it was trying to give her a gift, and underneath the squirrel someone had painted the words '*It lasteth, and ever shall: for God loveth it. And so hath all thing being by the love of God.*' She wasn't quite sure what that meant, but Modesta liked the squirrel. He had shiny black eyes that seemed to be looking at her whenever she looked at him. She turned back her attention to Mrs. Blakelock's voice.

> *...and as the weeds began to grow among the sweetpeas and the peonies, so they began to choke out the little flowers' access to living space and sunlight. Soon the delicate flowers, planted neatly in lines by the good gardener, thirsted for water, as the nettles and the bindweed, linked by their deep solid roots under the soil, pushed the shallow roots of the little flowers out of the way. As the weeds spread and grew taller, the flowers that belonged in the garden, those that had been planted by the good gardener, started to wither and die, and their coloured petals, now curled and brown, were feasted on by an invading ant army. The power of the weeds grew and grew, and they pushed up the garden's paving stones, making it diffi-*

> *cult to walk in the garden. Then the Japanese knotweed, the strongest and most destructive tare of them all, worked its way into the garden via its deep and extended root system, hidden underground, and sprang up in a corner of the garden. The gardener saw it growing there, but he left it, because it was only a little shrub, and it looked quite pretty in the sunlight. It added diversity to the garden, he thought. He did not want to pull it up from the roots and throw it in the fire, which is what the good gardener had told him to do. It would make him feel bad.*

Mrs. Blakelock stopped for a moment and closed the big book she was reciting from, holding the place open with her finger. 'Did he do the right thing, children?'

The children, in unison, chorused: 'Noooooo!'

She smiled in satisfaction, re-opened the book, and continued with the story.

> *So the Japanese knotweed grew quickly, reaching taller than a man and pushing its roots so deep into the soil that now no gardener could possibly dig far enough to pull the roots completely out. Its tall dense forest of bamboo canes, hard and sharp, and the profusion of its big leaves blocking out the sun from the little plants underneath shoved out the other plants, even the other*

weeds, and soon it was in complete control of the garden. Nothing else was able to grow or thrive. The whole garden was one whole ugly bush of Japanese knotweed, silent and foreboding, with no bird song and no butterflies. The roots of the knotweed blocked the drains of the fountain, and cracked the pipes underneath, and soon the water stopped flowing, and the fountain dried up and became dirty. The pretty petals of the forget-me-nots and the roses had long since disintegrated into the ground. But the bad gardener looked out of his window and shrugged. 'I am letting nature take its course,' he said. But then the walls of his house started to wobble, and he realised that his house was crumbling around him. The Japanese knotweed had been tunnelling its deep network of roots under his house, and was undermining the very foundations, exploiting every weakness in the structure, putting pressure on every crack and mortar joint in its search for more moisture. And so, after many years of neglecting his garden, the bad gardener found that the knotweed had blocked the house's water pipe, cracked the sewage system, broken the electricity cables and had even started to grow through the floorboards of the hallway. In the end, the bad gardener's house fell down. All because he did not follow the good gardener's advice and pull up the weeds from his garden and throw them on the bonfire when they first appeared.

The children stayed silent as the story ended. Modesta wondered if little Hulda had fallen asleep. Mrs. Blakelock had a very calming voice and it was hot in the room. Modesta had some questions for Mrs. Blakelock.

'Miss, are tares the same thing as weeds?'

Mrs. Blakelock thought for a moment. 'Yes, yes they are.'

Modesta paused in the light of this new information. 'But doesn't it say in the Bible that we shouldn't pull up the tares, that God will do it during his harvest? Because we might pull up the wheat by accident?'

Mrs. Blakelock smiled broadly. A bright child was truly a gift from God. She knew that Modesta's question did not come from impertinence, or a desire to undermine authority, but from reflection on what she had been taught. Modesta had probably been told this story by an older family member with a King James Bible.

'This is correct, my little mustard seed. There will always be tares that can wrap themselves around the wheat, and tares that imitate wheat, and they can escape that good gardener's eye. And these particularly evil tares, only God will judge. But for the others, what is required from the gardener is discernment. D – I – S – C – E – R – N – M – E – N - T. This means being clever enough to spot the good from the evil, the genuine from the imposter, and knowing how to act on that knowledge. Without discernment, everything is judged as good, and this allows evil to flourish.'

Modesta nodded to show that she had understood. That was a new word for her. *Discernment.* She liked that word. It was another word for being wise. She would need to tell her mummy the new word when Church was over.

The younger children were starting to rouse from their semi-slumber and some were getting fidgety. Mrs. Blakelock decided that storytime was over and that they should play a game. She had another half an hour to keep these children occupied until the adult sermon was finished.

CHAPTER 49

'Ma'am, if you come this way...'

The soldier gestured towards a small fishing boat moored on the edge of the quay. Old and battered by the years of tides, its white paint had chipped from parts of the hull. Another soldier was waiting on the boat, and when they approached he held out his hands so that that the old woman could steady herself as she climbed in to the swaying craft. Seeing the old woman's hesitation as her other hand clutched the heavy wool shawl around her head, and realising the potential dangerousness of a fall, the soldier leaned forward to hold her steady under her armpits and found himself lifting her gently into the boat. She was as light as a feather.

The journey across the river was a short one. The old woman sat on an upturned plastic bucket, clutching at the shawl which almost covered her face, her head down, seemingly oblivious to the wind and rain which assailed the little boat and made it rock on the choppy waters. Only once did the skipper, who watched her out of concern for her wellbeing, see her look up at the vast grey sky looming over the river, but the old woman seemed to be looking through the clouds, not at them.

An unsteady alighting onto the stone steps of Liverpool dock, and the old woman breathed deeply and lifted her head so that her rheumy blue eyes could take in the reality of what was happening. 'If you would like to walk with us, ma'am. We would take a vehicle, but the crowds are a problem, and it would probably bring unwanted attention. It is best to go on foot, via the side-streets, so that we can get to the main square unnoticed.

The little woman nodded, and blindly followed the men through Liverpool's city centre. The streets were indeed crowded with people milling about, and there was a distinct tension in the air, like an electricity, a prelude to anger, maybe violence. Violence could rip through a unsettled crowd easily, and yet people still milled around, as if wanting to be part of whatever was to come.

As they turned down into Mathew Street, the old woman, with her head down, saw that they were approaching what appeared to be a man leaning against a wall, in front of a broken cellar window. As she lifted her head to get a better look, she got a momentary shock to see that the man had been decapitated. Her body suddenly short of oxygen, she stopped for a moment, the sudden fright getting the better of her. The soldiers by her side saw the vandalised statue and realised that this was what had caused her to stop short. They waited patiently by her side, finding nothing that they could say that would not make the situation worse. It took the old woman a full minute for the pain in her chest to subside.

As they approached Richmond Square the crowds got denser. It was clear that it was going to be very difficult to get into Williamson Square itself. The taller of the two soldiers radioed his superior, and gave his location. A squad of soldiers would meet them at the end of the street to guide them safely through the packed bodies to the far end of the square, where the act was to take place.

Helena's old heart thumped hard against her ribcage as they reached the opening to the square and she saw the distant scaffold erected high over the crowd. Now encircled by soldiers who formed a tall phalanx around her, she moved under the aegis of these strapping young men, her son's men, towards the barrier behind which stood the EF dignitaries from all five divisions, who had travelled from every corner of the land to be able swear testimony to the event. A few representatives from the North American Confederation were also present, and were setting up recording equipment. A military brass band waited patiently in the right-hand corner.

Just as the group started to slip through the narrow barrier in single file, a woman in the crowd recognised Helena. A shout went out. 'Even the devil has a mother!'. Someone spat at Helena, and it hit her shawl. The soldiers accompanying her pushed the crowd back and rushed Helena through the gap in the barrier, behind the line of armed soldiers protecting the dignitaries.

'Are you ok?' one of the younger soldiers asked awkwardly. The old woman nodded numbly in silence.

They brought her up to the side of the scaffold to a small improvised hut. They opened the door to the hut and gestured for her to enter. Away from prying eyes, her son was resting his bulk awkwardly on a low stool, looking at the floor. He looked up on the door opening and was immediately troubled to see his mother in front of him.

'Mum, you shouldn't be here. I don't want you to see this.'

She rushed to her son's body, and put her arms

around his head and shoulders, letting his head rest on her bosom.

'Don't be silly. I was there for you right at the beginning of your life, and I will be there for the end. Some things you cannot control, David.'

Her almost stern tone at asserting her maternal authority made him smile weakly through the sadness, and he did not push the point further. He knew that his efforts to contain this tragedy to himself were in vain.

The brass band started up. The opening bars to *England Awakens* could be heard on the cold wind blowing through the cracks in the hut's wooden panelling. The noise level from the crowd could be heard rising. It was clear that the spectacle was about to start.

Helena held her son tighter to her. 'Will they be giving a speech before the event?'

'No, I don't think so,' he replied. 'The action speaks for itself.'

After a moment, he continued. 'Anyway, I don't think anyone could find the words to justify what they are about to do. My men are as unhappy about this as I am. But they know that this is the only way, if we don't want our people to tear themselves apart.'

The music stopped. A soldier came to the hut. Helena stood paralysed as her son pulled out of her embrace and stood up. He was suddenly distant from her. Like he was already halfway between life and death, not quite on the same plane as the living.

He mumbled as he left her. 'Mum, I'm sorry for letting you down. But I got it sorted.'

No, no, no! Unable to speak with no air in her lungs, Helena tried to shake her head to tell him that he had nothing to be sorry for. She suddenly realised that his whole life had been a way of making up for that day when he did nothing when they humiliated her. *But what could he have done? He had only been a boy!*

Helena watched in horror as he walked slowly up the steps of the scaffold and on to the platform. The hangman was wearing a mask.

The noise of the crowd was now at fever pitch. Some of the crowd were crying, others were jeering. The situation threatened to turn very difficult, and the EF wanted it over with quickly. Realising that Caldwell's voice would be drowned out by hecklers, one of the American soldiers stationed a few feet from the scaffold with recording equipment, handed Caldwell up a microphone. Caldwell realised grimly when he saw the man's Holomaker that his own corpse, swaying in the rainy breeze, would soon be reproduced in seven dimensions for future generations of American schoolchildren.

A macabre vision accosted Caldwell's mind, and left him struggling to remember what he had prepared in his head by way of a speech. He realised that he had forgotten how he was going to begin. But he knew that he had to say something. Time was overtaking him. He said what came into his head.

'Before I die, at the hands of the English Front, I, as your former leader, David Peter Caldwell, wish to explain why I released a bioweapon upon English soil, a weapon which I knew would do great damage to our enemies, but which would also damage our own side.' He paused. His mind had gone blank. In the subdued murmurings of the crowd, which had largely gone silent to hear him speak, a woman shouted *YOU ARE A MONSTER.* Rather than daunt him, however, this charge roused Caldwell to his own apologia, and he continued as if directly answering the woman and all those who thought like her.

'The reality of survival isn't about right and wrong, or good guys and bad guys – the game of nations is about winning, and this is about fucking surviving to see another century. Even for the pain that I am causing now, I cannot regret what I have done, because I have done it to ensure that the English exist as a people in a thousand years. This land is now deadly to Arabs and Turks and Africans. There will be no caliphate here. The Russians, if they want to take Britain, will need to use their Rus to do so. Because the Mongol hoards which took Europe will perish on this contaminated soil. The Chinese also have this land closed off to them for a millennium.'

Caldwell paused, and he realised that the crowd had gone suddenly quiet, filled with curiosity about what he would say next.

'When a limb is gangrenous, one must cut where the tissue is healthy to ensure that the disease is removed. I have had to cut through healthy tissue, which has killed good people, and it pains me. But I did it to ensure that the body of England survives. And history will judge me on that basis.'

He bent down to place the microphone on the wooden floor of the scaffold. Oblivious to the crowd, the man once known as the Supreme Leader nodded to the executioner, who hesitatingly put the canvas hood over the great man's head. On that sign, the band began to play *Elegy to England's Fallen*. At the mournful sound of the French horns some of the women near the front started crying. Some of the men in the crowd also started getting upset, an upset that was a hair's breath away from violence. The EF knew that they needed to wrap this show up quickly before a riot broke out.

The hangman put the noose over Caldwell's head, and took a few seconds to adjust it. Then he stood back from the trapdoor. There was a pause of three heartbeats, and the executioner pulled the lever down.

Those who had come to see their bloodlust sated were disappointed. Caldwell's body jerked for a few seconds before going still. The EF were careful to avoid sadistic punishment when dispatching criminals, as needless torture was seen as both the domain of cowardice and a portal for summoning demons. Certainly, the promise of cruelty seemed to draw out the worst elements of the English population, whom the EF wanted to see chastened but not enflamed by these public displays of executive power. Theologically, the condemned were considered to be suffering souls who were to be released from their suffering with a level of mercy, as one Albionic theologian had decreed in 2047, 'that Longinus himself would be proud of'. Longinus would certainly have been proud of the care that had been taken to ensure that fellow-soldier Caldwell's death was as swift and as painless as possible. Now the former Commander-in-Chief's lifeless body swung gently under the grey sky, a silent exclamation mark marking an anticlimactic event in which revenge had been fruitless and people now felt cheated of their hard-won pride in their recent history, their beloved shepherd who had made this history possible, and their very identity under his leadership.

The crowd started to get restless and people began jostling each other. It was not long before the jostling turned into shoving, and a few punches were thrown. Someone shouted 'Caldwell, tool of the Yanks!'. Then a gun went off. The EF gave the crowd orders to disperse, and a panic set in, with people fighting to get away from the front of the crowd. A stampede ensued, and several dozen people were injured. In the chaos, three men tried to rush the barriers, despite the armed soldiers behind the barriers training their guns on the crowd, and all three were killed by one of the EF snipers stationed on top of one of the buildings overlooking the square.

Eventually, the EF cleared the square of public onlookers, and posted soldiers at every entrance to prevent people wandering back. Only the dignitaries behind the barriers were left, and the Americans had stopped filming. It appeared that they had received some important news as they were suddenly deep in discussion. It was left to the executioner, three EF soldiers and the priests to cut down Caldwell's body, and put it in a body bag for transport. Caldwell's mother followed two of the priests up the steps of the scaffold as they prepared to cut down the body and enact the Albionic rites over it.

'We will need to take great care of this body, Mrs. Caldwell. Relics of your son will become very precious. His consciousness will stay close to his people, and the people will know that. May I have your permission to take a lock of his hair for our parish monstrance?'

Helena nodded robotically, indifferent to what she was agreeing to, her eyes sore with tears. Instinctively, she moved towards her son as his body began to be lifted up by the EF priests. But she saw that the priests were having difficulty with the body, which appeared to weigh almost as much as a horse, judging by their number of men that were needed and the way that these were struggling. Noticing the scene, a large EF soldier, almost a foot taller than she was, decided to block the old woman's view with his chest. 'It's best you don't see that, Ma'am. We'll let the priests handle this. Please come with me.'

Something in the man's tone told Helena that

From the Land All the Good Things Come

she would not be permitted to see her son's body. Perhaps the man knew that had she looked at the dead face of her son, a life more precious than her own, it would be like looking at her own dead face, and she might not last the night. As it was, her life was now a countdown to seeing him again. She had a flashback being in a car and seeing a multitude of desperate arms behind barriers, packed together and moving in unison like the tentacles of a sea anemone washed by the tide, stretching their sinews to their limits in a bid to have the fingertips brush against their beloved leader. A person whose touch the sick believed could heal them.

That voice again, this time more insistent, but also more caring.

'Come on, come with me.'

The Americans were fully packed up now and ready to go. The rain was starting to get heavier, and everyone was starting to move. Helena was led out of the square with the rest of the EF dignitaries and their protective retinue. She tried to get one final look behind her, but she all she could see were the priests hovering and kneeling around the precious commodity of her son's body, their busy black cassocks blocking the length of him but for a narrow gap at the level of his chest, where she noticed that the buttons appeared to have popped in his shirt, exposing his bare flesh to the sky.

CHAPTER 50

'Just *look* into those eyes. A lot of dogs are quite stupid. But this one...', Dr. Wansbrough tickled underneath the dog's chin as the animal watched him with bright inquisitiveness, '...*this* is a dog of agonizing intelligence. I wouldn't be surprised if he could read your mind, Alban.'

Alban looked at the young Alsatian and wondered if that was true. Big dogs like Mister Fox were quite unusual in the town. People preferred cats or small terriers as pets. Not only was it easier to feed a smaller animal, but cats and terriers were the best option for dealing with the massive vermin problem. Rats and mice played among the rubble and broken brickwork of St Helens like they owned the place, and they were a major problem for the English. Mr. Duckworth's terrier was such a top ratter that people paid good money for her pups. So it was quite unusual to be in the company of a German Shepherd, and Alban was quite excited about it. Mister Fox's need for a walk also meant a welcome break from the study of the vocative voice in Arabo-Swedish, an element of the language which was proving particularly difficult for Alban to master. It was good to be out in the open air during the day, and good to have another heartbeat in the house that belonged to a fun, cheerful spirit. Even if he *was* as agonisingly intelligent as Dr. Wansbrough said he was, Mister Fox, now bounding after a ball that Dr. Wansbrough had thrown into a patch of grass, didn't know that Paris had fallen to the Russians, and even if he did, Alban reasoned, he would be unlikely to care. *Maybe it's such indifference that is the sign of true intelligence*, thought the boy.

'You're very quiet,' said Dr. Wansbrough, as the two of them walked over the grass through the park. Mister Fox came bounding back to Dr. Wansbrough with the ball in his mouth.

'I'm just thinking about everything that has happened. You know, the Russians taking France. Commander Caldwell…'

'Yes, I know what you mean. Even though everyone fully expected France to fall, even though it was inevitable, it's still a shock when it happens. The Russians have been gathering countries like birds' eggs.'

Dr. Wansbrough paused, as if trying to remember something. Then he recited to the empty grassland around them.

> *As one reaches into a nest,*
> *so my hand reached for the wealth of the nations;*
> *as people gather abandoned eggs,*
> *so I gathered all the countries;*
> *not one flapped a wing,*
> *or opened its mouth to chirp.*

Alban was quiet for a moment as thought about what Dr. Wansbrough just said. He didn't want to ask where it came from in case he was supposed to know. Maybe it was from that Kipling book that Dr. Wansbrough had told him to read. So he decided to ask a question.

'Do you think England will open its mouth to chirp?'

Dr. Wansbrough said nothing for a few moments, but swung his arm back to throw the ball as hard as he could in direction of the trees. Mister Fox began bounding in the predicted path of the ball before the man had even released it from his hands.

'I don't know. Talbot is now the man in charge of this heap of ruins. And he is a good pick, not only for his character, but because he was born in Kent, which helps to quell the unrest in the Southeast Division, which had been starting to challenge the rule from the Northwest. The physical distance and poor communications between the various EF regions have just served to exacerbate the cultural, dare I say ethnic, differences that already existed between the groups. The tensions between North and South, and East and West, have been going on for over a millennium and it takes a very strong man, a very ruthless man, to keep the English united and not fighting like ferrets in a sack. And when you add in the Welsh element, well, it's a total nightmare.' He sighed, and took the ball from the dog's mouth. He made a gesture to throw the ball again but the dog wasn't fooled.

'There are going to be boots on the ground, but whether these boots come from the Great Plains or the Great Steppes remains to be seen. Maybe both will arrive on this soil at the same time. But whoever comes here to conquer, it will be a very vulnerable time for the English.'

'But are the Americans going to conquer us? Surely they are our brothers? The good guys...'

Dr. Wansbrough threw the ball suddenly without giving Mister Fox any warning gesture. The dog shot off after the ball and Dr. Wansbrough smiled tersely and renewed his leisurely amble through the grass.

'That is simplistic thinking. Whether it is

the Americans or the Russians who ultimately wrest this land from the legacy government, it will still be an occupation regardless of the language spoken or the racial similarities. Just because someone is an enemy of our enemy doesn't make them our friend. And that is why Caldwell had to go. Not just because of the bio-weapon, but because people were suspicious that he had been manipulated for a greater American agenda.'

'Do you believe that?'

'I don't know. I mean, no, I don't think it's the case. But I can't *know* that. And while there is room for doubt, his position as leader was untenable. It's what the people would always demand, eventually. A leader must be beyond divine reproach... because the fortune of the king is the fortune of the land. You can call it superstitious, but it's what the English people believe. But even if he *was* being manipulated by the Americans, who have used these weapons to great effect in their own territory, people are innocent if they think that we would ever be allowed to live in the world as an insular people, sovereign of ourselves.'

Alban took a minute to digest this information as the dog jumped around Dr. Wansbrough's legs, waiting for him to throw the ball again. He was a young dog, only three years old, but the extra energy and excitement was likely due to being shut indoors for the past few days with his owner, who was nursing a broken foot.

'So when Commander Caldwell said "*the thousand years of the alien blood are over, now a new thousand years will rise*", what did he mean by that?' Alban felt the need to call Commander Caldwell by his official title, even though the man was dead and had been officially declared an enemy of the people. Somehow, it still felt wrong to disrespect him, as if his spirit would hear him and be hurt by it.

Dr. Wansbrough made a strange face. 'When did he say that?'

'On the gallows.'

'Who told you that?'

Alban paused for a moment. Who *had* told him that? He racked his brains trying to remember. He visualised where the conversation took place, the classroom, yesterday lunchtime. 'It was Lawrence, I think.' Yes, he was sure it was Larry, because Larry was trusted to have good information.

Dr. Wansbrough tone remained skeptical. 'Well, I'm not sure Caldwell actually said that. We have to be careful of anything that ends up being attributed to him now that he is dead,

From the Land All the Good Things Come

as certain things will be difficult to verify. I get the feeling that in the next few years a lot of such attributions are going to be made by interested parties looking to push an agenda, and I wouldn't be surprised if the process is starting already. What was the phrase again?'

'The thousand years of alien blood are over. Now a new thousand years will rise.'

Dr. Wansbrough looked thoughtful. 'Hmm. I'm not saying that it's true, but the thousand years of alien blood could be referring to the Norman conquest and their aristocrats controlling the land. To these people, the native Anglo-Saxons were just farm animals, a source of revenue, no different to the leaseholder Pakistanis or Nigerians who displaced them. The House of Lords did nothing to stop the many laws which were designed to facilitate the entry of alien peoples, when by doing so they could have strangled this treacherous plot at birth. Their indifference to the fate of the English people suggests to me that they saw the increase in peasant population as being in their own interest, as more people fighting for a place to live means higher land values and higher ground rents. It's all about the coin with these people, and it always was, even before they took strange wives.' He stopped to think for a moment, then called out dramatically to the empty winds:

Men groan from out of the city,
and the soul of the wounded crieth out:
yet God layeth not folly to them.

As he finished talking Dr. Wansbrough swung his whole body round and launched the ball towards the trees. Mister Fox, ecstatic, bounded after it. Within sixty seconds he was back, feeding the ball back into the man's hands with his mouth. Dr. Wansbrough juggled the ball lightly from one hand to another, trying not to get dog-spit on his hands, and Mister Fox jumped up in excitement as the old man lurched exaggeratedly to the left and right in a bid to bamboozle him. 'We've got to tire this animal out before we take him back to Billy. Do you want to throw for a bit?' Dr. Wansbrough handed Alban the ball, and suddenly Mister Fox transferred his full attention to the boy who, feeling suddenly overwhelmed by the big dog barking and jumping up against him, threw the ball a bit too quickly for it to be effective.

'What about "*a new thousand years will rise*"? What do you think he meant by that? Lawrence says that it refers to the decolonisation of England.' Barely had Alban finished speaking than the dog was back with the ball in his mouth, and was using his muzzle to try to push the ball into the boy's hand so that he would throw again. *Yes, he was a very intelligent dog.*

Dr. Wansbrough thought for a moment and shook his head. 'If this statement is true, and that's an *if*, there is no reason to think that the 'thousand years' Caldwell speaks of necessarily refers to the plague vial he poured onto the land. People have called this a war of decolonization, but make no mistake, Alban, this is a civil war. The SAU, believe it or not, are incidental enemies – the prime mover of this conflict lies elsewhere. You are too young to know what England was like before the war, but our standard of living and our culture is vastly reduced from what it used to be. Part of that is, of course, because the war smashed the infrastructure and collapsed an economy that was recklessly specialised and dependent on imports from abroad. But another reason that people don't like to admit is that a great deal of expertise and intellectual capital was lost when most of the middle class opted for the wrong side in the culture war, and then stayed with that choice when the war got hot. Perhaps when the uprising came they felt trapped by the choices they'd made, by the identities they had given themselves, and preferred to sit on their sacks of coins as fellow travellers, and ride it out until order and tranquility eventually returned. Their children and grandchildren are now paying the price for that cowardice and venality, as they sit behind the lines in Islamic strongholds in which kinship and blood is everything. The virus will have had no effect on these people, and they are more dangerous than any Islamist fighter, because their contempt for English Front values runs back centuries. It is a personal rancour. The kind of hatred that only brothers can feel. *These* are the people that need to be defeated, Alban. What will happen in the next thousand years is anyone's guess. We cannot even predict what will happen in the next month. The silence right now is unnatural. There are secret plans afoot, and they are being made by behind closed doors.' Dr. Wansbrough went quiet for a few moments, and then laughed to himself. 'Or maybe I've got that completely wrong, and Caldwell was referring to the Book of Revelation. You know, Satan, the ancient serpent, being bound for a thousand years so that he could no longer deceive the nations...? I have to admit, I'm not too sure. I'd have to think about that one.'

Alban went quiet as he tried to absorb everything that Dr. Wansbrough had said. The boys had been saying the same, that the final fight would still be difficult because of the English contingent on the other side. He remembered his History class. So many of the remaining English of London and the other big cities had not heeded Garrick's legendary call of *come out of her, my people!* because it would mean having to abandon wealth and status, or because they had already hitched their religious wagon to what they had perceived as the *strong horse*. There had been a window of time to cross the lines, but that was long before Alban was born. Now the fates were sealed.

He became aware as they walked along that Mister Fox had not returned with the ball. Dr. Wansbrough seemed to have exactly the same thought at the same time.

'Where *is* that dog?'

Dr. Wansbrough looked around. There was a large patch of brambles over by the trees to their right, but that was a hundred yards away. He looked around for signs of other people before shouting, feeling vaguely self-conscious for having to shout the dog's silly name. But there was no-one else within sight.

'MISTER FOX!' He then whistled to try to get the dog's attention.

Nothing.

Then there was the sound of a dog barking, and Alban realised that it was coming from the direction of the trees. 'He's over there.'

Dr. Wansbrough called to him, but the dog

wouldn't come.

'I think he must have found something.'

They walked over to where the dog was intently shaking something in the undergrowth, so intently that he seemed oblivious to the approach of the man and the boy who crept up behind him.

'Jesus Christ!'

There was alarm in Dr. Wansbrough's voice. Alban immediately felt frightened, because he had never heard his mentor blaspheme like that. As the boy leaned forward to get a better look at what the dog was pulling at, he heard a tone of angry authority that he had never heard from Dr. Wansbrough before, and it startled him into drawing back. It also clearly scared the dog, who shot out of the bushes so cowed that he whimpered.

'Don't look at it, Alban. Come on, let's get out of here.'

When Dr. Wansbrough bent to pick up the ball which lay forgotten on the ground, Alban stole the chance to defy his master and take a quick look back at the object in the shrubbery that had so engrossed the dog. His heart started racing when he thought he saw what looked like a human jawbone. He whipped his head around quickly and focused ahead of him. A good way to pretend that he hadn't seen anything would be by trying to return to the previous conversation. Alban got the feeling that he had seen something that he shouldn't have, and that Dr. Wansbrough would get angry with him if he found out.

'So,' Alban said, trying not very successfully to keep his voice steady, 'what is the worst-case scenario? That people talk about Commander Caldwell as David the Martyr or as David the Monster?'

Dr. Wansbrough appeared preoccupied and was throwing the ball in the direction of the way home, but doing so without really noticing the dog. He answered sullenly, in a tone which did not invite further questioning. 'The worst-case scenario? The worst-case scenario would be that there are no longer any English people to remember David Caldwell, let alone talk about him.'

CHAPTER 51

If she put her ear close to the passenger window and listened for it, Aoife could hear the toll of dusk bell through the raucous grumble of the van's engine. It was the signal that the territory was now in blackout, and that all light, even reflection of light, had to be covered. Breaking the blackout carried a heavy penalty; Aoife knew that at the sound of the bells mothers who had not already closed the heavy regulation curtains would be doing so now. At this point in summer, with sundown so late, the children would already be in bed, the mothers would be closing the curtains themselves, having enjoyed the last rays of light of the long summer days. The bells would ring for another quarter of an hour, but by that point Aoife and her military driver would be out of the built-up area. She fancied that the sound of the bell was already growing fainter.

The van was only on the road at this hour because it had official permission, though the true nature of the operation was restricted to a handful of people at the highest level. Ironically, were they to be told the truth of the mission, most people would assume that what they were hearing was an outlandish yarn spun to hide the real truth. Such was the condition of England in 2060.

In a way, it *was* a military operation, but one which operated at a subtle level beyond most people's understanding of war. *And perhaps it was better that way*, Aoife thought. When English society first fell apart and the people were cast adrift on a violent sea of meaninglessness, it had been a time of preachers and cult leaders, misfits with resentments, utopian visionaries, charismatic neurotics and psychotics who presented themselves as messianic driftwood to cling to; like the mad dogs they were they had to be shot for their own safety and that of others. The metaphysics for the masses had been settled with much blood, and it was too dangerous to the social order for people to understand that there was a veil that could be lifted.

The journey towards the site would probably take about an hour. Maybe longer if there were delays at the checkpoints. Back when Aoife was young it would have been a much shorter journey, but the motorway, which now led into enemy territory, had been sabotaged beyond use and most of the remaining roads were in very poor condition. Every pothole and bomb crater jolted Aoife's old bones through the cushion that one of the soldiers had thoughtfully placed there to bolster the vehicle's raddled upholstery. The van's suspension had also seen better days, which was to be expected with a road system like this and the van's advanced age. New machines were a rarity in EF territory, and as a consequence mechanics were expected to work miracles with ancient and ill-matched parts.

Up until this point, both Aoife and the driver had remained silent during the journey. Aoife liked this silence. She was preparing herself for what was to come. Clouds shifted in the sky and the fields around the road lit up as a large full moon came into view and threw its silver light onto the road ahead. The driver spoke.

'Look at how light it is! Fucking hell, I almost don't need the headlights on!'

It was true. It was an exceptionally bright night.

'It's a supermoon,' Aoife said. She could have told the driver that the date of this meeting was fixed exactly for the reason, but she decided that it was better not to. It might lead to more questions.

Aoife herself had not fixed the date of this mis-

From the Land All the Good Things Come

sion. She was not an astrologer. But she knew that the connection between the worlds was at its strongest when the moon was closest to the earth, and its magnetic force pulled at the water within the ocean's basins and within living bodies, amplifying the emotions and the senses. She wondered if the Great Conjunction between Saturn and Jupiter still had any of its energy left. It had happened a few months ago, but the Great Chronocrators moved very slowly, particularly Saturn, the Crystalliser, so there might still be some power in the aspect. Aoife wasn't sure. She closed her eyes and imagined Jupiter, the Great Benefic, juddering mechanically into position in front of the Great Malefic, and as it did so, ringing out like a titanic planetary bell across the solar system, its reverberations penetrating every atom on Earth and signalling a global change. *A new age.*

Aoife remembered the priest from Somerset coming to her home to talk to her about it at the beginning of the year. It was a big deal to the upper echelons of the Albionic Church, who predicted that it would spell the end of the political era, and that if that were the case, Caldwell's life might be in danger. Aoife pondered if Caldwell had somehow known his fate. Certainly, as his meeting with Hansen had been timed to coincide with the Great Conjunction, he would probably have known of the prophesy, though she imagined he would have given it little credence.

Her eyes were open now. She surveyed the vast plains which stretched to the horizon on either side of the country road. The terrain was so flat and deserted in the ghostly light that, but for the occasional shrub or tree, they could be on the moon itself. Moonlight was beautiful, Aoife reasoned, but it was also deceptive. You could not trust your senses to be faithful to you in the light of the moon which, like a beautiful woman, promised to reveal things unseen during the day, if only you came closer. But it was deception. Night-time was the time that God handed over to the devil to let him seduce or destroy, depending on his mood. Sometimes he chose to do both. There was a reason that the Albionic Church advised the people to be asleep before midnight.

Only the sentries should be awake during the witching hour, young children were told.

The landscape turned into village now, and the van whizzed through a few silent roads with sleeping houses at either side, before the familiar farmland plains returned. A few minutes more, and they would reach two of the vigilant sentries of the mother's refrain, whose checkpoint would mark the official end of EF territory. The fields just beyond it were still Eng-

From the Land All the Good Things Come

lish-held, but the EF were much less keen to try to defend them, so they were not, as a rule, inhabited. Aoife remembered something from years ago about severed heads being placed on spikes as a ghoulish warning to those who would think to invade from the east. It was so long ago she wasn't sure if it were true or she had just dreamt it, but she shivered all the same at the thought of decomposed heads, shorn of their bodies, hanging in the light of the moon.

The van slowed up, the driver said a few words, and the van was waved on. Their visit was expected, and they were making good time.

Aoife heart raced a little as they drove past the checkpoint. She knew that it wouldn't be long before they arrived at the meeting place, and she was starting to feel nervous. She was calmed by what she perceived to be a rise in the supernatural energy from the fields as the old van rattled its way along the road.

A few careful minutes driving down Hermitage Green Lane, made dark by tall trees on either side of the road, and soon they were pulling into the old farmstead. Three vehicles were already parked up in front of the farmhouse, and there was a soldier posted outside the door of the barn. They were waiting for her.

The driver pulled up and parked the van. As he got out and walked around the front of the van to get to the passenger door, Aoife noticed how young he looked, maybe only in his twenties. She took a deep breath. The atmosphere was oppressive but intoxicating. There was a tightening in her solar plexus.

The young soldier said nothing when he held out his hands to allow Aoife to steady herself as she got out of the vehicle, as if out of discretion.

'Please, come this way, ma'am.' He led her to the front door of the barn, and nodded to the soldier on duty.

Inside the barn, dark but for the light of half a dozen lard lamps on a table, stood two women waiting for Aoife to arrive. Aoife counted a total of seven soldiers, including Aoife's driver and the guard at the door. She knew both of the women well; Monica and Mary were well-known figures in institutional divination, and they returned her nod and smile. Energy had to be focused and mundane social niceties detracted from that. Four of the soldiers went outside to guard and patrol, leaving Colonel Piper, who stood awkwardly at the farthest side of the barn, close to the window, and two young privates who guarded the barn's en-

From the Land All the Good Things Come

trance.

All three of the women felt themselves overwhelmed by the powerful lure of the spirits who sought to submerge them into the past. The forces of time weighed heavily upon this place and prickled their skin. It was difficult to stay in the present. They all stood in their own minds, cut off from the others, for several minutes.

Then Mary spoke.

'There was a great battle here. A decisive battle. It ended a war. Over a thousand men died in this place.'

Aoife and Monica nodded slowly.

Mary spoke again. 'It was a civil war. Very bloody. I think it was the English Civil War.'

Aoife looked up at Mary in surprise. 'I too see a battle here, which ended a war. I see the death of a king. But it was long before Cromwell. About a thousand years before Cromwell. I see... it was very bloody too, a king was cut into pieces, no prisoners were taken. Men were left to die in the fields all around here. This building is in the middle of where they died.' Her face went stiff, as in inspired by another force. 'The plains all around were white with their bones.'

Monica spoke with her characteristically soft, sweet voice. She was the youngest of the three women, blonde-haired and shy. 'You are both right. I think that there were two battles here. And there is sacred water near here, which keeps the spirits of the dead earthbound. This earth draws violence to it, to resolve it.'

The three women linked hands with each other to form a small circle and bowed their heads.

The soldiers glanced at each other awkwardly. They didn't know if they should leave but they were frightened of making a noise and disturbing what the women were doing. And they wanted to see what was going to happen, if anything.

The women began with the Albionic Prayer, followed by Swanson's *Declaration of the English, Living and Dead.*

> *...we, the foot-slogging peasant-soldiers deserted by our king and our knights, will ascend from the earth...*

> *...we, the good, the disrespected, will rise from our graves to avenge those who grind our living seed into the dust...*

The *Declaration* went on for several minutes, then Mary intoned something in a foreign language under her breath. After that, there was silence. The women stood with their eyes closed, continuing to hold hands. The silence went on for so long that the two young privates started to make questioning faces at each other in the gloom. All of the men were thinking the same thing. Should one of them say something? Was it over? Nothing was happening.

Just as the colonel, as the most senior-ranked man in the room, decided to intervene, Mary's reedy voice echoed through the barn.

> *The hand of the Lord was upon me, and he brought me out by the Spirit of the Lord and set me in the middle of a valley; it was full of bones. He led me back and forth among them, and I saw a great many bones on the floor of the valley, bones that were very dry. He asked me, 'Son of man, can these bones live?'*
>
> *I said, 'Sovereign Lord, you alone know.'*
>
> *Then he said to me, 'Prophesy to these bones and say to them, "Dry bones, hear the word of the Lord! This is what the Sovereign Lord says to these bones: I will make breath enter you, and you will come to life. I will attach tendons to you and make flesh come upon you and cover you with skin; I will put breath in you, and you will come*

> *to life. Then you will know that I am the Lord."'*
>
> *So I prophesied as I was commanded. And as I was prophesying, there was a noise, a rattling sound, and the bones came together, bone to bone. I looked, and tendons and flesh appeared on them and skin covered them, but there was no breath in them.*
>
> *Then he said to me, 'Prophesy to the breath; prophesy, son of man, and say to it, "This is what the Sovereign Lord says: Come, breath, from the four winds and breathe into these slain, that they may live."' So I prophesied as he commanded me, and breath entered them; they came to life and stood up on their feet—a vast army.*

There was a pause, then the three women chanted loudly in unison:

> *I will make breath enter you, and you will come to life!*
>
> *I will attach tendons to you and make flesh come upon you and cover you with skin!*
>
> *I will put breath in you, and you will come to life!*
>
> *Come, breath, from the four winds and breathe into these slain, that they may live!*
>
> *Amen.*

It was quiet all around as the women raised their heads and opened their eyes. Colonel Piper suddenly felt very stupid to find himself in this situation. The Irish had allowed the Americans to use Ireland as a staging post for their invasion, and the Americans were mobilised and ready. Three warships had been spotted off the Lancashire coast. They would be setting foot on English soil at any moment, to end this stalemate once and for all. And what was he, Colonel Arthur Piper, doing? He was in a disused barn in the middle of nowhere summoning spirits with three women. He needed to put an end to this nonsense now.

Aoife seemed to sense the lack of perfect faith radiating from the back of the barn where the colonel was standing. She looked at him and spoke with little regard for their difference in social status.

'It is done. Look out of the window.'

The air of authority radiating from this little old woman disorientated the colonel for a moment and he did as he was told, shifting the makeshift curtain of sacking cloth to peer out of the window behind him.

He jumped back in shock.

A vast army of ghostly soldiers, made grey by

the moonlight, stood silently in the field behind the barn, their lines of heads stretching back as far as the colonel's eyes could see to the horizon. There must have been tens of thousands of them. Piper saw some khakis and helmets that looked like they came from the World Wars of the previous century.

Aoife did her best to contain her sense of triumph at his stunned reaction. *He of little faith!*

'These are our dead, Colonel, many killed unjustly, victims of lies and betrayal. Sacrificial lambs in a sick, demonic game. But the earth will disclose the blood shed on it, and will conceal its slain no longer. They, the armies of the bodiless, will join us in the final fight to return this land to us, their descendants.'

Colonel Piper stood pale and open-mouthed. He had the demeanour of a lost child. The other two soldiers had rushed to the window to see what their commander had seen. But all they saw were empty fields bathed in moonlight.

'I don't see anything.'

'Neither do I.'

A violent bang against the barn walls shook the young soldiers out of their disappointment and confusion, but it was not enough to jolt the colonel out of his shock. Before the young soldiers could find the source of the noise, it came again, and this time they raised their guns and aimed them at the barn door.

'Don't worry,' said Aoife, 'it's just the spirits.'

As if to prove her correct, a third knocking came, this time from the wooden beams in the roof. Aoife looked towards Mary and Monica, who were picking up the lard lamps.

'It's probably best that we go now, before the knocking gets worse. The mission has been successful. The spirits of our dead have been raised, and they will fight with us.'

She smiled in a maternal way at Colonel Piper, who appeared to have lost forty years' worth of hard-won self-assurance in the space of a few minutes. Shadows danced impishly about the barn and cast themselves on the colonel as the lard lamps being carried towards the barn door swung on their handles, but for the first time in his life Arthur Piper seemed oblivious to his surroundings.

Aoife went over to the colonel and put a reassuring hand on his back. Only with the shock of human touch did he seem to realise where he was.

'Come on, we need to get going.'

CHAPTER 52

CeeCee was worried as soon as she saw the young boy on her doorstep. It took her just over a second to recognise him as Morgenna's son.

'Seb, what's wrong?'

The expression on the young boy's face and his very presence on her doorstep told her that something bad had happened to Morgenna.

'It's... it's my mum. She's not getting out of bed, and...'

Sebastian felt embarrassed about ending the sentence, which was that he hoped Miss McAllister would be able to help. He felt so powerless. As a child, he couldn't tell his mum to do anything, and seeing her the way she was frightened him. He didn't know what to say or do to make her better. Seeing her like that made him feel like the helpless little boy he was. His mum might be angry with him for fetching CeeCee, but he didn't know what else to do. He didn't want to lert his father, as he

From the Land All the Good Things Come

was on operations, and it could lead to a massive fight, of which he would be the cause.

CeeCee didn't need any further explanation. The fact that this boy had come all the way to her home told her all that she needed to know. 'Don't worry, Seb. I'm coming now.'

She grabbed her shawl from the sofa and wrapped it around her. The shirts soaking in the bottom of the dye tank were good for at least another couple of hours.

On the way to Morgenna's house, walking with Seb, she asked, 'So what is the matter with your mum?'. CeeCee had a good idea of course, but she wanted to know what the boy understood of it.

'Well, you know that she... lost the baby...'

CeeCee nodded as they kept walking. 'Yes, I've seen your mum since then. She was down, but she was getting by. What changed?'

'I don't know. She went to Church last night, and when she came home she went straight to bed without saying anything. I had to lock up, which I have never had to do. Then she didn't get up with the ave bell, and the only time she has never got up with the bell was the scarlet fever epidemic. But she was sick then. Most of the time she is up before the bell. Mum never stays in bed.'

'Is she sick now?'

Seb shook his head. 'I don't think so. Not in her body anyway. I went into her room this morning and she was turned away from me and she told me to go away. I don't know what's wrong...' His voice trailed off, like he didn't want to finish the thought.

CeeCee wondered why the boy hadn't mentioned Felicity, but realised that now wasn't the time for interrogations. The answer would become clear to her in due course. It was her job now to take the reins of the situation and put energy and hope back into the young boy, who had been through a lot himself. 'Well, you did the right thing in coming for me. We'll find out what's wrong with your mum, and we'll put her right.'

Seb liked CeeCee and he was glad that his mum had her as a friend. She was cheerful and full of good sense, and was one of those people who could rescue others.

When Seb opened the door in Hawes Avenue it felt strange. The house was cold and silent. It frightened him when it was like this. He liked the house to be as it should be during the day, with people doing their routine activities. He liked things to be as he recognised them.

CeeCee put a finger to her lips and walked up the stairs towards Morgenna's bedroom. Normally she wouldn't dream of walking upstairs without an invitation from her friend, but these were not normal times. She knocked twice on the bedroom door and stepped inside.

Morgenna's body was turned away from the door, and she did not stir to acknowledge the people in the doorway. She was on her left side and a merciless daylight had broken through a narrow gap in the curtains, illuminating her contour in the bed. With the sharp contrast of light and dark, the blanket draping over her right hip made her body look like a small mountain range to Seb's eyes.

'Morgenna, it's CeeCee. I'm walking towards your bed and I'm going to sit on your bed and you can't stop me.'

The body in the bed did not move, but it was breathing and awake. Still it did not speak.

CeeCee went and sat on the bed, and then looked up at Seb, who had stayed in the doorway.

'Seb, could you do me a big, big favour, and go downstairs and make a cup of tea for your mother and me. That would be very helpful.'

Her tone was friendly but with an assertive edge that told Seb that she was taking charge now, and that he had to do as he was told. On one hand, he was annoyed, because he was curious to see what she would do to get his mother up. On the other hand, he was relieved that there was now an adult dealing with the problem, and he could go back to being a child.

Knowing what ten-year-old boys were like, CeeCee waited for that final heavy thud on the ground as Seb jumped past the last stair on the staircase before she addressed her friend.

'If you think that you are going to turn your face to the wall at the age of forty, Morgenna Weston, you've got another thing coming.'

CeeCee's tone was of the usual bustling brightness, but there was something new in there as well. A hardness or immovability that Morgenna had never heard before. Not that Morgenna cared. She kept corpse-still in bed, hoping that CeeCee would go away.

CeeCee seemed to read her friend's mind. 'Just so you know. I'm not going to go away.' As she sat there she surveyed the room, and noticed to her satisfaction that her embroidered wedding gift to the Westons was hanging on the bedroom wall.

There shall no evil befall thee, neither shall any plague come nigh thy dwelling.

It was a verse she knew well, having written it in her finest hand for countless mezzie scrolls.

But Morgenna remained motionless, staring at the blue paint on the wall. It had been a long time since the wall had been painted and parts where the paint had flaked off were like the map of an imaginary archipelago. She tried to imagine herself on a faraway island now. Walking along a deserted beach, the waves lapping on the shores of white sands, the grains as fine and clean as sugar.... England was nothing but war and poverty and death. Every day more struggle, more horror. She couldn't take it anymore. She wanted God to release her from her constant suffering.

CeeCee tried another tack. 'What happened at Church last night? Something happened, didn't it?'

There was an involuntarily shift in the bed. Morgenna gave no reply nor even looked towards CeeCee to acknowledge the question, but CeeCee realised that she was on the right track. Something had happened to put Morgenna in this state of mind.

'Did someone say something to you? Was Judith Broadhurst shouting her mouth off again?'

Another shift in the bed. After a minute Morgenna spoke, but her eyes remained fixed to the wall.

'No, it wasn't that. Nothing like that.'

CeeCee's smiled to herself. Finally she had made contact.

'What happened?' Then she had a thought. If it hadn't been anything caused by a person, maybe something demonic had struck her down.

Taking her time to ask the question, and watching for her friend's reaction, CeeCee asked, 'Do I need to get a priest?'

But there was no reaction to suggest that something evil had entered her person. The bed lay still and Morgenna was unresponsive. CeeCee stayed sitting on the edge of the bed, and said nothing. She thought she heard the faint sound of a bell chime in the air and someone moving around in an adjacent room.

Morgenna, perhaps realising that her friend was never going to go away, that her wish to lie alone in misery had been thwarted by a stronger, more energetic will, finally spoke with the tone of the defeated.

'Last night, at Church, I touched the statue of the Great Mother holding baby Jesus in her arms. I took the baby's foot in my hand, ever so gently. And the foot became real flesh and blood in my hands. A real baby's foot, CeeCee. I don't know how long it lasted, maybe it was a few seconds, maybe a minute, it's hard to know, because it felt like time had stopped, but it did happen. I thought that God had given me a miracle.'

CeeCee leant forward towards the window to try to get her friend to look at her. But Morgenna kept her face firmly towards the wall.

'But surely that's a wonderful thing! You have been given a sign that the age of miracles has not passed, that we are still in God's light! So many people have said that we live in the time in which the love has grown cold, but I never believed that. You should be celebrating.'

Morgenna turned her body even further into the bed and away from CeeCee. CeeCee pondered on why her friend would have this reaction. *A baby's foot in her hand.* Suddenly CeeCee was overcome by such a wave of sorrow that she understood why her friend, who was normally out guiding other women through the heartaches of life, had taken to her bed. She said nothing.

After a few minutes of silence punctuated only by the gentle bell chime, Morgenna spoke. 'Remember what Jesus said to his disciples? "Heal the sick, cleanse the lepers, raise the dead, cast out devils"? Now *those* are miracles – healing the sick, raising the dead. If God had wanted to grant me a miracle, he could have saved my daughter, and let her live. But what happened last night felt like He was mocking me. He has the power over life and death, and yet chooses death for my children. Far from being in God's light, it actually feels like I am in Hell.'

CeeCee bent forward and rubbed a hand up and down the blanket covering Morgenna's body. 'No, you are not in Hell. Far from it. We are living in a giant miracle right now. We just don't realise it because we are so familiar with it. The creation of heaven, the revolution of the planets, the germination of every seed of grain, the recurrent breath in our own bodies, we despise these miracles in favour of what we see as rare, like raising the dead, or turning porcelain into flesh. But in the greater scheme of God's government of the universe these novelties are nothing but signs and wonders.'

Morgenna didn't stir at CeeCee's best attempt at philosophy, which sounded so impressive because it had been lifted in large part from her favourite Aldhelm encyclical. But seeing that this did not work, CeeCee was at a loss for what else to say. She had never experienced motherhood, let alone lost a child, and Morgenna had known loss at both extremes. She had suffered the martyrdom of her eldest child, her beautiful, vigorous son on the cusp of manhood, and then she had suffered the horror of holding the pearl of her youngest child in her bloodied hands, the exquisite, perfect pearl which despite its tinyness contained all the love of its mother's heart. The pearl of a time that would no longer be. CeeCee wondered if she too would be as paralysed as Morgenna, were she to have suffered the same agonies. She decided to be honest, and her words, her own words this time, came out slowly.

'Morgenna, as you know, I have never been a mother. I can never *know* the pain you are going through. But I do know what it is like to feel that God has abandoned you, and that everything is meaningless.'

For the first time since CeeCee came into the room, Morgenna turned to look at her friend. She had never heard CeeCee talk like that before. CeeCee only ever talked positively, and would never admit to ever having doubted God, or giving up hope. She never talked about herself, but only about how she could help others.

Morgenna suddenly saw another CeeCee from the one that everyone, including Morgenna herself, thought they knew. The CeeCee whose life had been defined by a great tragedy. The CeeCee who as a young woman had been madly in love with a young electrician who was killed while working on a project in his shed, a tragedy which had caused her such grief that she placed her engagement ring in his coffin with him, telling the other mourners matter-of-factly that there would be no-one else. The CeeCee who never spoke of the loss again after that day, and who dedicated her life to others. Morgenna suddenly realised how much hidden sorrow her friend must have gone through as she watched her friends get married around her, and have their children, and be part of families. And yet CeeCee had nothing but smiles and encouragement and love and support for everyone. She never once spoke of her own pain when giving succour to others in distress. Morgenna felt a surge of new respect for the woman now sitting on her bed.

'How do you do it, Clare?'

CeeCee felt awkward on hearing Morgenna's question and feeling Morgenna's eyes on her. She didn't like talking about herself, but she realised that here it was unavoidable. It was what Morgenna needed.

'I just think of the EF motto *I serve* and I always remember what the Church says, that when people chase their own happiness, they fall from Heaven straight to Hell. I try to focus on other peoples' needs as much as possible, and always have lots of projects on the go, to keep me busy. I think if you sit still, you go under. The secret of life is to keep moving, even if you don't want to move. If you want to keep strong, Morgenna, have some shirts steeping in the dye tank and a Sabbath bannock in the oven.' CeeCee's humorous matronly tone had returned, and the moment of fragility had passed.

The bedroom door pushed open tentatively, as Seb came in balancing the mugs and the teapot on a tray.

'I'm not sure if this will be any good. I had to throw out the first pot.' He looked up from the tray to see his mother sitting up in bed, pale-faced and with messy hair. He thought it best to not to say anything, and went to put the tray down on the bedside table, but hesitated on seeing that his mother's copy of *The English, God's Chosen*, was in the way. Noticing his hesitation, CeeCee looked towards the table and swooped forward to pick up the book so that the boy could set the tray down.

'Don't get tea on the Divine Revelations,' she

said, only half-joking. Morgenna touched the boy's hair as he put the tray down to let him know that he wasn't in trouble for the highly irregular situation of calling CeeCee to the house.

CeeCee opened the book and started flicking through the pages, and noticed that like her, Morgenna had made marks in the margins around her favourite passages. Some people could quote Swanson chapter and verse, but she wasn't one them. Certain lines of course, but then everyone knew the most popular lines.

She read one of the marked biblical verses aloud.

> *And though a tenth remains in the land,*
> *it will again be laid waste.*
> *But as the terebinth and oak*
> *leave stumps when they are cut down,*
> *so the holy seed will be the stump in the land.*

CeeCee inhaled sharply at the perfectness of the verse. 'They are trying to kill the seed. But as long as a remnant remain, no matter how small, we will survive. We will be the Holy Seed. It might not be you or me, Morgenna, but we will live on in our people. Did you know that half of the population of England died during the Black Death? We recovered from that, and we will recover from this.'

Morgenna took a sip from the mug Seb had handed to her. 'I think the Black Death was a walk in the park compared to what we're going through now.' She started laughing at the absurdity of it all, but it was a hollow laugh, of a woman who was exhausted and had nothing left in reserve.

The gentle chiming sound was heard again.

'What *is* that noise?' CeeCee asked.

'It's Felicity's bell,' Morgenna answered. 'She rings it as she reads the Bible, which appears to be all the time. She's got it into her head that she has the gift of prophesy. I think that she might be starting to lose her mind, but I'm not one to talk. I think we're all losing our minds in this house.'

Morgenna made a face as she took another sip of dandelion tea.

'And a lack of decent tea doesn't help.'

✽ ✽ ✽

Felicity tolled the little bell by her side and it responded with its familiar warm chime.

She did not think that reading the Psalms brought her closer to God. She did not understand them. Some of them sounded dark, like something closer to Satan than to God. Earlier she had read Psalm 137, and it had contained the lines.

> *Daughter Babylon, doomed to destruction, happy is the one who repays you according to what you have done to us.*
> *Happy is the one who seizes your infants and dashes them against the rocks.*

On reading that she had instinctively put her hand over her swollen belly and closed the book. She didn't understand how these could be the words of Holy God. And if she didn't understand the meaning of the words, how could the words protect her? This thought plunged Felicity into an even deeper depression, and she didn't open the bedroom door when she heard Seb's timid knock.

She needed the consolation of the Bible now more than ever. The night before, she had had another of her apocalyptic dreams. Aoife had told her that her spirit of prophesy might be a sign of the last days, when it was written that the Holy Ghost would pour the gift of second sight onto everyone, young and old, male and female.

Her dream of the night before, from which she had awoken with her heart pounding, left her certain that she had been told vital details of the Eschaton, and as such she had a duty to tell the Albionic priests about her dream.

She had been floating weightlessly through a great hall of what appeared to be an ancient palace. Every inch of the vaulted ceiling was covered with oil paintings and framed with ornate golden curlicues and cherubs, and these were reflected onto the polished marble floor below. But what really defined the hall was the glass. It was everywhere: as the mirrors under the archways along the length of the hall, the glass beading and pendants of the chandeliers, the magical fruits in the hands of the silver statues, and atop plinths of marble and gold. The sea of delicate glassware refracted the candlelight into a thousand tiny rainbow colours. Felicity had never seen anything so beautiful in her whole life.

Then a voice sounded in Felicity's head. The voice said:

> *For you, this city within a city*
>
> *By your sorceries were all the nations deceived*
>
> *You killed your own brother*
>
> *And turned his city into blazing pitch as the angel of goodness looked on*
>
> *But your lies and crimes will collapse under*

their own weight

Faster than the seventh temple of Mammon

And the Truth will triumph in a new dawn.

As she heard the voice, bolts of lightning came from nowhere and smashed the mirrors of the walls into tiny shards, and exploded the fragile glass into what looked like a million droplets of water. Then the flames rose from the fire of the lightning and it became so hot that the glass and the stone and the precious metals, all of the elements of the great hall, began to melt in the heat and become nothing.

It was at this point that she awoke, and felt that she had dreamt something important. She wanted to speak to Aoife about it. She remembered Aoife telling her, when Felicity asked the old woman about the Day of Judgement, that the present heavens and earth were reserved for fire, just as water had been the destroyer of the previous evil world. Felicity was sure that her dream was a sign that the Day of Judgment would soon be upon them.

But Felicity knew that when she told Aoife this the old woman would laugh at the idea that time could be intuited from a prophesy.

'*With the Lord a day is like a thousand years, and a thousand years are like a day,*' Aoife had told her one day when she had asked about it. 'Time has no meaning for God. He is outside of time. It makes the job of understanding events, for us who live within time, and human time at that, very difficult indeed. *He has set eternity in the human heart, yet no one can fathom what God has done from beginning to end.*'

Aoife had told Felicity that she had to be careful not to assume that what she saw in visions had any relevance to her own lifespan. Her own life was shorter than the blink of a gnat's eye in cosmic time. 'It is why we must never get impatient for things to happen,' Aoife had said. 'God works on a different timescale to us. We are lucky if we see justice within our own lifetime. But God will always ensure that justice is done, even if we do not live to see it.'

Remembering Aoife's words now, Felicity wondered what the point of it all was. She heard the sound of laughter in the next room, and strained to make out who was with Morgenna. She decided that it was CeeCee, but she opted to stay in her room. She wasn't feeling sociable, and the older women always made her feel young and stupid, even if they didn't mean to. Felicity rang her little bell again. It gave her comfort to hear the chime reverberating through the air and then gently dying into silence. It marked the passing of a moment, at a time when she wanted to savour every moment before the day when she would be forced to confront the agony and mortal danger of childbirth. But these days the moments seemed to slip from her grasp at lighting speed, and she felt herself being carried helplessly on the rushing torrent of time towards her fate.

CHAPTER 53

Valerie looked around at the shelves of books and grinned broadly. 'I *knew* that you would have a plan. This is wonderful.'

Alan smiled back at her, sharing in her joy, oblivious to the bare brick humility of their surroundings. 'We have to take the little victories where we can. It goes without saying that this is top secret.' He made a face to imply discretion, and Valerie nodded immediately.

'Oh, of course. I will say a word to no-one. Not that my family would find it of much interest anyway. They would not understand the importance of a library.' She stopped herself from adding *but Gareth would have*. It would not be right to bring up the memory of her dead husband so soon into the relationship, lest Alan come to think of Gareth as a rival for her heart.

Valerie wandered around the shelves. 'Are there any books in French?'

'*Mais bien sûr*,' Alan replied. He pointed to the shelving in the far right-hand corner. 'The bottom two rows. I've put the foreign language books separately given that so few English people speak a second language nowadays.'

Valerie's turned from the books to look at Alan with amusement when he said this. 'Wasn't that always the case though? I think the English have always been, shall we say, *uniquely insular* in that regard. They seem to take pride in knowing no other tongue. Although *you*, my man, are quite the exception to the rule.' She went up to him and slipped an arm under his, and gave his torso a quick squeeze before returning to the bookshelves. It was the spontaneity and openness of her affection that delighted Alan. He didn't know if it was because she was so feminine that her emotional expression had such a child-like innocence, or if it was her Frenchness that made her less inhibited than most of the other people he knew. Maybe it was a combination of the two. Whatever it was, it was utterly intoxicating. He never wanted to leave her side.

He decided to tell her his idea.

'You know, I've been thinking of something that I would like to do. I think it would be a good idea. But I would need you to help me.'

'Tell me,' said Valerie, enthused at the thought of being an essential part of one of his plans.

Alan took a deep breath. 'Well, you know the documents you gave me, the ones from France?'

'Yes?'

'Well, it makes sense that such documents should be kept safe here, in the library along with all the other historical records. But then I thought, those documents alone don't tell anyone the story of what happened in France in the first half of the 21st century. Without an explanation like the one you gave me, they will be meaningless to the future generations who will come to inherit this library. So that's why I think it would be a good idea if you... if I... if together we write the testimony of your life. To accompany the documents. I mean, I will do the writing. You can just talk to me and we can put it together. But I do think that there should be a written record of your experiences in France and England. Your own perspective.'

Alan looked at a surprised Valerie as he got his breath back after the tumble of words. His voice took on a more sombre tone. 'Especially because we don't know what information will ever come out of France in the coming decades. It would be good to have a first-hand, reliable testimony for the official record. Don't you think?'

Valerie's eyes wandered over the bookshelves as she considered what Alan had said. She didn't like to think about the long-term future, especially the future of France. But he was right. It was exactly because things were so bleak that the truth needed to be set down in writing. As Alan had pointed out, what was considered recent experience for her generation was taught as history to the youngsters, and it would soon be ancient history when her generation was permanently silenced by time. A written record would help to stop that silence, to prevent the erasure of her voice.

'Life seems so real, until it is not,' she said finally. 'You are right of course. But I have no experience in writing books, so I'm afraid that you will have to do it for me. If I try to write a testament of my life it will come out all jumbled and no-one will want to read it.'

Alan smiled. He had predicted that this is what she would say, and he was well prepared for the task. 'Don't worry, I can be the ghostwriter. I'll just ask you questions and write things down based on what you say. Then I'll put it all together on my own.' He paused. 'Just one other thing…'

'What?' Valerie asked, a smile now playing about her lips. She had the feeling that there was a trick somewhere in this other thing.

'I think, because this is the story of your life, that there should be a picture of the author, so that future readers can know what you look like.' Alan paused to give the proposition to follow more impact. 'So I would like to paint your portrait for the book.'

Valerie threw her head back and laughed. She laughed for many reasons. She laughed at this old man and his imagination. She laughed at the thought of this old man who was so in love with an old woman that he wanted to stare at her face for hours to paint a portrait of her. She laughed at the thought that future readers would even want to see the face of an old woman, whose bloom had long since faded. And finally she laughed at the fact that if one wanted a pictorial record of a loved one in 2060s England, one had to draw a likeness of them.

Alan looked vaguely disconcerted by her reaction. 'Well, you know, I'm more of a draftsman than a true artist, but at least the final result would be very accurate, if a bit... *flat*.'

To his consternation, this just amused Valerie all the more. But as a man, he could not begin to understand. What woman of a certain age wants a careful draftsman intent on accuracy to paint her portrait for the world?

He wondered if she was laughing because taking a photograph would be much simpler, and the best way of capturing her likeness. But she knew as well as he did that photography was not only illegal but might still be condemned by future generations, if it was still believed that the photograph stole something of the subject's soul. And Alan would never risk Valerie being condemned by future readers for allowing her photograph to be taken in 2060.

'We cannot know what future attitudes will be. But there is the strong possibility that the Albionic position on photography will still be in place. The propaganda has been extremely successful with the young and I can't see attitudes changing any time soon. I wouldn't want people to judge you for letting yourself be photographed.'

Valerie nodded. She understood. The children had been easy to persuade, but the adults had taken more work. Of those who laughed at the new religious doctrine, they were ordered to stab through the photograph of a relative's face with a knife. Their resultant hesitation was all the priests needed to prove that a person's essence was captured in the reflected light of a photograph. Hence the reticence to destroy photographs of loved ones. It was social control at its crudest, but a necessary evil to make people paranoid about cameras and recording devices, so that even after the government's mass surveillance system had been dismantled, all of what came to be known as 'soul-capture technology' continued to be shunned by the people.

The older generation, those of Alan and Valerie's age, had not been taken in at all, but supported the doctrine because they understood its expediency for greater goals. Alan knew without even asking Valerie that she thought the basis for the photograph taboo was nonsense.

'So, will you sit for me?' Alan's voice was playful now.

Valerie's laughter had faded, and her face took on a mantle of seriousness. 'Yes, I will. And I will give you my story. At least, I will give you my story as it pertains to the story of France. I'm not vain enough to believe that the people of the future will want to read about my marriage and children. But they might be interested in an honest witness' account of what led up to the war.'

Alan thought that Valerie glowed like a candle when set against the dirty brick walls of this old cellar that still smelt vaguely of engine oil. He leant down towards her and gave her a kiss.

'Thank you.'

Slightly overwhelmed by his sudden physical expressiveness and the proximity of his body to hers, Valerie pulled back for a moment, and turned towards the bookshelves.

'It really is an excellent idea to have this library. Do you think you will ever add extra categories to the books already here?'

'What do you mean?'

'I mean books that aren't big serious tomes like these, but they still tell truths of a different sort.'

Alan was puzzled. 'I don't follow.'

'Well… you might laugh at me for saying this, but maybe there should be a part of the secret library for fiction. I know that you say that fiction isn't true, that it isn't *truth*, but they are still our stories.'

'You mean like have a shelf of this Cat B-classified English Front library dedicated to Enid Blyton?' It was Alan's turn to smile now.

Valerie playfully pushed him on the arm when she saw that his smile was about to break out into laughter. 'I'm serious! A big part of the oppression of our people was that we were not allowed to tell our own stories. But myths and stories are just as important as real history when it comes to telling our children who they are.'

Alan's smile went from one of playfulness to one of admiration and his eyes gleamed. 'You are absolutely right.' He looked thoughtfully at the books for a moment. 'We were not allowed to have our heroes. It didn't matter if they had once been real, or were only fictional. They were banned or distorted just the same. And the English people without heroes is like the fig tree without fruit, and withers just as quickly. The ancient Anglo-Saxon tradition *centres* on the warrior hero, for God's sake – the ideals of the English people cease to exist without him. And those who sought to destroy us knew that. To add insult to injury, on the few occasions when our heroes were acknowledged in the culture, they were deliberately portrayed by people who weren't us.' The old man grimaced for a moment, as if in pain. He put a hand to his side.

'Do you remember the reports of the massive book burnings in Birmingham during the winter of 2033? Or maybe it was 2034, I don't remember now. It was the year we had that really bad winter, the one where there was something like five feet of snow and the roads became impassable. Well, the entire inventory of Birmingham University Library was taken out of the building by the cartload and burnt. Hundreds of thousands of books and manuscripts destroyed in massive bonfires. Not for political reasons, you understand, just so that people could keep warm. The fuel-looting spread to the university libraries of Leeds and Sheffield as well. They were vast repositories of learning, but why not? It's not like the books in the libraries had any relevance to the people burning them. It's not as if it was *their* culture or history. Why should the new population care? When you vanquish a people, you don't just genocide them, you obliterate their written record.'

Valerie looked towards him with a face full of sadness.

'Like they never existed.'

Seeing him look troubled, she went over to the good man whose bulk belied his thoughtful nature, and nestled into his chest in a bid to comfort him. Alan Wansbrough was a big man, and Valerie stood at least six inches shorter than him, despite not being a short woman herself. She felt a reassuring large hand, like a bear's paw, come around to encircle her shoulder. She felt safe for that moment, in that cellar. Moments like this were all she had now, she reasoned. But even so, she felt blessed. A meeting between two beings who completed one another, who were made for one another, bordered already, in Valerie's mind, upon a miracle. And when she met Gareth back in 2027, just a few months before the upheaval of the Rebellion, she had thanked God for having granted her that unlikeliest of chance meetings, a meeting which had led to the happiest of marriages. Never could she have imagined that lightning could strike her twice, and for the miracle to repeat itself. She had resigned herself to widowhood, but being grateful for having had such a loving man for the time she did. Some women did not even get to have that. And now she had found love again, in the winter of her years. Valerie wondered what she had done to merit such good fortune.

'I wonder if we'll see the end of this.' She spoke into Alan's chest and her voice sounded into his body.

'What was that?'

Valerie moved her head so that Alan could hear her more clearly. 'I wonder if we will see the end of this. If we will still be... here when this *impasse* ends.'

Alan stroked her hair as he spoke. 'If I'm being honest, I don't think so. None of the adults who were part of the Exodus were ever allowed to see the Promised Land. They were doomed to wander for forty years as a punishment. And I do think that we are being punished.'

'But why? We didn't do anything. I mean, not us, not our generation.'

Alan continued to stroke her hair as he thought about her question. Her hair was strong and straight, a shiny chestnut brown with only the occasional grey hair. He loved its sweet cinnamon smell and to feel it smooth under his big, rough hands.

'Maybe not our generation, at least directly. But haven't you heard the proverb *the fathers have eaten sour grapes, and the children's teeth are set on edge?* Aren't the sins of the fathers visited upon the children, and the children's children, until the third and fourth generations? We are the third generation, and we are working out God's punishment for our grandparents breaking the covenant.'

Puzzled by his words, Valerie peeled herself away of Alan's body to be able to look at him in her response. 'The covenant? What do you mean?'

He answered her with his customary calm. 'The covenant of civilisation. Society is a covenant between the living, the dead, and those who are yet to be born. And the Generation of 68 broke that covenant when they sold their children's birthright for a mess of pottage.'

Valerie gently returned her head to resting on his chest, so that she could take a minute to make sense of what he had said. *A mess of pottage?* Alan resumed his stroking of her hair. But as much as she thought about it, she still didn't understand. She pulled away from him momentarily to ask what had been troubling her.

'For a plate of soup?'

'Effectively, yes. Or *stew*, as we say in English. Because whoever gives up their children's land and future for the promise of free love, weed and consumerism is as stupid as Esau giving up his birthright for a hot meal.'

Valerie thought for a moment. 'Don't forget the incredible range of restaurants!'

Alan laughed at Valerie's reference to the bitter joke told during the 2020s, a joke that wore ever more thin with each new terrorist atrocity. 'I often wonder what it must have been like to be part of that generation. How easy it seemed for them to just go with the flow, to give up their land so magnanimously, so that they could show themselves to be *cool* and *modern* by their lack of concern with status or possessions. Or the future. It must have felt like being under a deep analgesic, and having your arms and legs cut from your body as your mind floated in the ether. Only the morphine in this case was easy finance and rock and roll. They must have felt so light and free, unencumbered by the duties of every generation before them to be the custodians of the land and of Western tradition for those yet unborn. Just floating free, out of time and space. Do what thy wilt *did* become the whole of the law and every man did what was right in his own eyes. But as we know, the Satanic doctrine always ends in death, even if down to Hell the trip is smooth.'

'It was certainly smooth for that generation, with their final salary pensions. They were insulated up until the end.' Valerie grimaced as she remembered her grandmother's extended cruise around the Caribbean during the *gilets jaunes* protests. Marianne Beaulieu hadn't wanted to know the news. Her only concerns had been the values of the stock market and Paris property.

'Well the ways of death might not have affected those who bore the torch for them, but the reaper most certainly came for the grandchildren and great-grandchildren of the generation who moved the boundary stones. Sometimes, while those children were still in the womb.' Alan paused, and curled his lip as he stared beyond Valerie to the dirty brick walls of the cellar that his library was reduced to. 'Because who could have imagined that the boundary stones had been put in their place for a reason?'

Valerie shuddered at the thought of the millions of dead babies, the silent victims of the sexual revolution. She returned to leaning her head against Alan's broad chest. When she nestled into him like this she felt warm and safe, like she didn't need to think or worry. He did her thinking for her, with his superior male mind. Like Gareth, he understood the world in a way she couldn't begin to fathom. There was a silence as she let him continue to stroke her hair, and she felt him bend slightly to kiss the crown of her head. The silence continued, which was a sign that Alan was thinking. Valerie wondered if he ever stopped thinking. Finally, he spoke in a lighter tone, like he was toying with an idea in his head.

'You know, they almost took it from us.'

Valerie waited for him to explain his comment, but there was a silence as he continued to run his hand gently over her head.

'What?' she asked.

His voice reverberated through his body as he answered her. 'The ladder to reach God.'

Valerie wasn't quite sure what he meant, but she didn't trouble herself to ask further. She wanted some respite from the hauntings of the past and the fears for the future. Right now, she was enjoying this moment with the man she loved, here in his arms, and she wanted to concentrate on nothing else but the sensation of him stroking her hair. She pressed her ear against this wonderful man's breast and let her head fill with the reassuring sound of the rhythm of his heart, a *thump, thump, thump* which masked the distant rumbling in the ground.

Printed in Great Britain
by Amazon